SETTING THE TRAP

"The problem is that we don't have a single hint as to who the killer might be," Hyte summarized, handing his report to his commander, Phil Mason.

"Have you given any further thought to the possibility that they're terrorist reprisals?"

"Yes. And it doesn't add up. Terrorists don't use crossbows; they use machine pistols and bombs."

"If not, terrorists, then who?" Mason asked.

"One of three possibles—a passenger who's gone a little nuts, a psycho, or a relative of one of the original victims."

"All right," Mason said, nodding ponderously. "You have conditional authorization to extend the preliminary investigation."

Hyte sighed. A task force had to be headed by someone of the rank of captain or above. "I want this one and I don't care what you have to do to get it for me!"

He nodded. "I'll think of something. How many more people will you need?"

Hyte exhaled slowly. Phil Mason had given him his task force. "One for now. And I'd like to keep this close for a little longer."

"You'll handle this exactly the way I tell you. If you want this case, you'll play by my rules!"

Hyte knew he had no choice. "I'll play."

THE
HYTE
MANEUVER
DAVID MILTON

PINNACLE BOOKS
WINDSOR PUBLISHING CORP.

PINNACLE BOOKS

are published by

Windsor Publishing Corp.
475 Park Avenue South
New York, NY 10016

Third printing: March, 1990

Printed in the United States of America

To Bonnie M.,
for all the usual reasons
and so many, many more.

Acknowledgments

Without the willing help of the following people, this novel could never have been written, and to these people go my deepest personal thanks and appreciation: Detective Sergeant Joseph Clabby, NYPD retired; Dr. Melvin Swartz, Professor of Clinical Psychology; Bruce McLane, Frank Knowles, Dennis Crosby, and Mike Villare, retired NYPD Officers; from the R. Bruce McLane Security Agency, Susan Collins; Mark Breithaup, Investigator, Rockland County Medical Examiner's Office, and a special acknowledgment to a man on the Job, at One Police Plaza, who wishes to remain anonymous.

One

It was a clear night, dark and moonless. Humidity gave the hot night air a fetid taste. But those who had lived their lives in this ancient land were used to the corrupting tang of the ocean mixing with the dry desert breeze.

At Tangier's barely modern airport, the air was further debased by burned oil and airplane fuel. The darkness girdling the airport was broken by the occasional lights of planes taking off or landing; the sounds of their engines contrasting to the stillness of the Moorish landscape.

Beneath this tarnished Arabian night sky, a lone security guard walked his rounds of the Trans Air maintenance buildings and hangars. The last Trans Air flight of the day had been serviced two hours before and was now sitting on the runway, its engines building power in preparation for takeoff. Trans Air Flight 88 was one of three planes that would leave Tangier between now and midnight.

The guard liked this last half of his four-to-twelve shift. The quiet hours suited his disposition. The guard, his tan uniform darkened in ink blot splotches of sweat, reached the white concrete and steel supply-maintenance building just as the engines of the 727 screamed out their fury. Turning, he watched the plane rise into the sky.

Flight 88 was airborne. The guard looked at his watch. On schedule.

9

He stepped inside the maintenance building. A minimum of light was used at this late hour, just enough to illuminate the gray cement walkways. The air was stuffy, laden with the scent of spilled disinfectant.

Footsteps emanated from the center of the long building; three workers moved out of the shadows and came toward him. The guard stopped. When the workers reached him, they nodded in passing. The guard waited patiently for the three to exit and close the door behind them. Then he punched in the time on his handset and continued toward the back of the building.

The guard took his job seriously, for he enjoyed the benefits that came with it. Work was not easy to find in Tangier, where dozens of men with hungry families waited to step into another's shoes. Pay did not matter, work did. The guard was smart enough to do his job properly.

Still, he was human enough to allow himself a little latitude. His shift was the least observed, his sector not considered a terrorist priority. Indeed, there had not been any terrorist trouble at the airport in months—not that he didn't sympathize with the Palestinians who had lost their homeland and had to strike out in order to regain it. At least they weren't as religiously fanatic as others.

The guard shuddered. He had lost a younger brother in Iran and was well acquainted with the stifling oppression of Moslem religious rule.

The guard reached six small and independent storerooms, twenty feet from the rear of the building. He checked the first five methodically, making sure each door was locked.

At the sixth, he unlocked the door and stepped inside. He put the Detex clock recorder on a waist-high shelf. According to the device, it was eleven forty-five.

He reached behind a pile of towels on the fourth shelf and fished around for a few seconds. A momentary panic rose, ebbing quickly when his fingers touched the cool glass of a bottle. The guard had followed this same routine for the past five years. In three areas of his sector patrol, similar bottles of liquor were secreted. He needed those occasional drinks to get him through the nights.

He took a drink, swallowed greedily, and took another before capping the bottle and putting it away. While the alcohol was warming him, he took out an unfiltered oval cigarette, loosely packed with dark Turkish tobacco, and lighted it with a stainless steel Zippo. The lighter had been a gift to his father during World War II.

The high flame, dancing about the cigarette's tip, gave a ghostly illumination to the small room. From the corner of his eye, he sensed something not right in the shadows; that elusive something did not register on his senses until he'd snapped the lighter shut and taken in a lungful of smoke.

It came as an afterthought, the impression of a jumbled form in the counter of the storeroom. Reaching out, he flicked on the overhead light.

The guard focused on the corner. At first he thought it was a discarded tarp. Yet there was something about the haphazardly placed canvas that puzzled him. Soon the reason came. There should be no tarps in this room. And the dark stain? Oil?

A painful memory surfaced. He had gone to Teheran to find his brother. Instead of his brother's animated and jovial face, he had found rows upon rows of shapeless forms covered by white canvas. Dark and random stains marred their uniformity; stains just like those on the tarp he was looking at the corner of the storeroom.

Oil glowed black. This was blood.

The guard pulled the tarp back. Bile rose in his throat at the sight he had exposed. Two dead men lay naked in a bath of their own blood. He knew them both.

Their heads hung at impossible angles. Their necks were slit almost all the way through, transforming the skin between their shoulders and chins into gaping, red-rimmed mouths. Painted in blood on their foreheads was a single word, in Arabic: *Adulterer*.

The guard's stomach convulsed. A thin rivulet of liquor and stomach fluid disgorged from between his pinched lips and struck the cement floor with a flat, wet sound.

* * *

11

Captain William Haller's hands manipulated the controls, much the way a man lovingly caresses the familiar curves of his woman. Haller's breathing was slow and regular, betraying none of his inner tension. His blue eyes scanned the instruments with a practiced glance, noting not what was right but seeking anything that might be wrong.

"Altitude," Richard Flaxman, copilot of Trans Air 88, said to the pilot.

Haller exhaled. For him, the takeoff was always the tensest part of the flight. "Control, this is Trans Air 88, leveling off to thirty-five thousand feet."

From forty miles behind Flight 88, came the surprisingly American voice of the Tangier air traffic controller. "Roger, Flight 88. Closest approaching traffic, Pan American Flight Charlie three-six, bearing two-one-seven, five miles east at twenty-four thousand feet. Have a nice trip 88. And good luck, Bill, I'll miss you. Air Traffic Control Tangier, out."

The voice belonged to expatriate Toby Mathers. Once considered the hottest jet fighter ace in Vietnam, Toby was now a legless senior air traffic controller for Tangier International Airport.

"Roger that, Control. We thank you. Trans Air 88 out," Haller said, easing his tense grip on the controls.

Haller's hair was cropped short and fit his weathered face well. He was that rarity among commercial pilots: a captain who insisted upon and received the respect of his crew, in much the same way as a military man.

"How's it feel?" the copilot asked as he studied Haller from the corner of his eyes.

Haller scratched his jaw with the back of his thumb. "I don't know yet."

"I think I'd either be extremely happy, or so damned depressed I'd have to be carried on board," Flaxman said.

Haller didn't want to think about it, but he had no choice. This was his last flight. When he touched down at Kennedy, it would be all over.

At fifty-five, with twenty-two years on the record sheets of Trans Air, Haller was retiring from active flight duty to take over the vice-presidency of Allied Air Freight, the world's number three air freight carrier. A public relations coup, he thought bitterly. He was a trustworthy and experienced face to sell to the corporate men who made the shipping carrier decisions.

"It's a good move, Bill," Wyman Van Pelt, Chairman of Allied Charter had said when Haller signed the contract that gave him an annual income of two hundred and fifty thousand dollars. "Your name will give people confidence in Allied. And," he'd added with a smile, "it will also make you quite wealthy."

The son of a bitch, Haller thought, knowing how cleverly his brother-in-law, Van Pelt, and Haller's wife had maneuvered him into leaving the airline before he had planned.

"Be right back," said Flaxman, breaking into Haller's reverie.

Haller nodded. His eyes flicked to the windshield, watching the reflection of the copilot as Flaxman made his way to the engineering panel. He heard the low sounds of Flaxman and the flight engineer speaking. A moment later, Flaxman laughed, slapped the engineer on the shoulder, and went out the rear of the cabin.

The door closed, leaving Haller alone in the subdued illumination of the cockpit, listening to the chatter emanating from his headset. The sights and sounds mingled together in a smothering reminder that this was his last flight.

He swallowed past the thickness in his throat, unable to stop wishing that this flight would not end. Not tonight. Not ever.

Later, Captain William Haller would remember this wish.

Two

In the first-class galley, flight attendant Elaine Samson was setting up the drink cart of champagne for the first-class passengers. Behind her was senior flight attendant Joan Bidding. Bidding was crammed into the recesses of the narrow stainless steel flying kitchen, checking over the list of first-class passengers. There were eleven—the entire flight was only forty percent full.

"Two major VIPs," she said, tucking a stray strand of hair into place.

"How major?" Elaine asked.

"J. Milton Prestone, former senator from New Mexico. The other is Cristobal Helenez. He brought his wife along."

Elaine nodded. "I had him on a flight from Paris two months ago. Nice enough. We have time for a quick smoke?"

Joan looked at her watch. "Sure."

Elaine took out a Salem and lighted it. She leaned against the tray wall. Although not tired, Elaine's insides ached, somewhat pleasurably, somewhat painfully. "God, why do I punish myself with copilots?"

"Flaxman?"

"He can't just enjoy it, he's got to go for the Trans Air duration and frequency record. Jesus."

"That's the price you have to pay. Are you coming to Haller's farewell party?" Joan asked.

14

"I promised Flaxman I'd go with him. It's really too bad, you know. I like crewing on Haller's flights."

Joan smiled, showing the perfect teeth that had been part of the prerequisites when she had applied to the airlines, eighteen years before. She had made the minimum five-foot-six-inch height by two inches. Her weight, at age thirty-six, was the same one hundred and twenty-three pounds she had weighed when she'd first started with Trans Air.

"How long have you known him?" Elaine asked.

"It seems like all my life. My first flight was on his plane."

"Does it feel strange?" Elaine asked.

"No. It makes me think about getting through the next two years and retiring."

"And do what?"

"Stay home with the kids. Enjoy them and Ron for a change."

"And be bored out of your mind," Elaine said just as a call bell went off. "Time to get to work."

"Not bored," Joan Bidding said. "Content, happy, but not bored."

The first-class cabin of Trans Air Flight 88 was partially darkened. The late-night snack had been served two hours before. Now most of the passengers were either reading or sleeping.

The attendants had removed the food trays, served the second cups of coffee, and poured the after dinner liqueurs.

Bill Haller stepped into the first-class cabin. A half hour or so after reaching the midway point in the flight, he had left his copilot in charge of the plane. His practiced gaze flicked over the seven rows in first class. A twinge of memory carried him back to the time when first-class seats dominated the aircraft and the powerful men in business and politics occupied those seats. But that was before the days of corporate jets that could match the commercial airlines in size and speed.

Of the fourteen first-class seats, eleven were occupied.

15

Not bad, Haller thought. Earlier, when he had looked over the passenger list, he had recognized several names. Occupying seats 2C and 2D was a man he knew only by reputation—J. Milton Prestone. Just before flight time, Prestone's private pilot had called Haller and explained the situation that had put the former senator on Haller's flight— a blown engine oil seal.

In seats 4A and 4B, were Mr. and Mrs. Cristobal Helenez. He had been required to know who Helenez was—after all, the Portuguese financier owned a seven percent block of Trans Air.

Seats 6A and 6B had been assigned to Jonah and Anita Graham. But, as he glanced at them, he saw that only Mrs. Graham, whom he had never met, was there. The lavatory sign read OCCUPIED; that was where Graham must be.

Over the years, Haller had come to recognize the quiet and dignified businessman who was on no fewer than a half dozen of his Middle East flights each year. He had learned, on one of those flights, that Graham was the president of a specialty mail order house that catered to middle- and upper-income consumers.

Two weeks after speaking with Graham, the first of four annual issues of the Graham International catalogue had arrived at his home. Haller had been impressed by the products and had ordered several.

Haller walked through the cabin to the coach section. Looking down the aisle, he experienced a sharpening of the melancholy that had been dogging him since takeoff. He suddenly thought that making his final tour had been a mistake. He should have stayed in the cockpit.

On his left, he saw a little girl, sitting alone in a window seat. Turning, he motioned to a stewardess. "Is she flying alone?"

The stewardess nodded. "Her name is Lea D'Anjine. She's going to New York to meet her new parents."

"Adoption?"

"She's from one of the mission orphanages."

Haller looked at the little girl and, despite himself, gave way to another memory of the past, when children were routinely brought into the cockpit. But that had changed with the advent of the airplane hijacker. It was another of those things Haller missed—seeing the children stare with awe at the instrument panels, and at the pilots.

Haller couldn't take the little girl into the cockpit, but he could do something for her. "Bring her into first class," he told the stewardess. "Let her enjoy the rest of the flight. I'll tell Joan to give her the royal treatment."

In the first-class lavatory, Jonah Graham flushed the toilet, and washed and dried his hands. Then he unlocked the lavatory door and stepped out.

Another first-class passenger, bearded, of medium height and swarthy Middle Eastern features, stepped back to allow Jonah passage. With the brief but polite nod and smile of two men who will never see each other again, they continued on their way.

Jonah did not stare at the well-known face of Senator J. Milton Prestone, who occupied two first-class seats. Nor did he intend to eavesdrop when he passed the couple in seats 4A and 4B.

Graham recognized Cristobal Helenez from an article in *Newsweek*. The man was deep in conversation with his wife. Their voices were subdued; their tone was strident.

They were having an argument. Jonah's thirty-five years of marriage was experience enough to sense that. Smiling, and pleased that the days of trying to pick a smooth path through the early and rocky stretches of marriage were long past, he returned to his seat and his wife.

"I'm glad to see you've relaxed a little," Anita Graham said, covering Jonah's hand with her own. The only jewelry she wore was the wedding band he had placed on her finger thirty-five years ago tomorrow. "It'll be nice to get home," she continued. After almost four decades of knowing this man, she was still in love with him. The heavy graying of his hair, the recession at his temples, the facial lines that grew increasingly more elaborate each year, did not bother her. She could still see the same handsomeness that had

17

attracted her from the beginning. He may be getting old, she thought, but he's aging well. His rough features were highlighted by what she called his Sinatra eyes—sharp, blue, and clear. His body was only five pounds heavier than it had been when she had fallen in love with him.

"Yes, it'll be nice to get home," Jonah agreed, thinking of their anniversary.

For an anniversary present, Jonah had bought her an XJ-series Jaguar—white on white. He could already envision her reaction. Anita did not like flashy cars or flashy clothes. She liked quiet quality. But this time he was determined to make her enjoy the opulent present. Jonah smiled to himself.

"Care to share the humor?"

"Eventually," he said and glanced about in the subdued light of the cabin.

The couple across from him, their legs and waists covered by an airline blanket, were snuggled together, oblivious to anyone else. The woman was startlingly beautiful, a model he guessed. The man was at least twenty years older than she. Was she his mistress?

J. Milton Prestone, tall, thin, angular, tugged impatiently on the lapel of his hand-tailored blue silk suit. A moment later the same hand fingered the full Windsor knot of the matching blue tie.

J. Milton Prestone was always impatient. He believed it was his right. It wasn't egotism that made him feel that way, it was simply the knowledge that he was an important man. Prestone turned to look at the other first-class passengers, and slid his index finger along the side of his, as the newspapers referred to it, "hawkish" nose.

It was nose that suited him well, for J. Milton Prestone, a former senator from New Mexico, was a hawk. He had voted for more arms increases than any other member of the Senate during his eighteen-year tenure. Then he had taken over the chairmanship of Lentronics and had guided the nation's largest weapons manufacturer to unparalleled profits.

"Hate these damned things," he muttered, meaning the commercial aircraft that was taking him home. But he had no choice. He could not afford to wait seven additional hours for repairs on his own plane. He was needed in the board room of the Lentronics New York offices by 10:00 A.M. At 3:00 P.M., he was due at the Pentagon for a meeting with the Joint Chiefs.

Prestone lifted his attaché case from the neighboring seat, which he had purchased along with his own. He opened the case and looked at the figures on the top sheet. Those figures were only part of the reason J. Milton Prestone never allowed anyone to sit next to him on a public airplane.

"Everything all right, Senator?" came a drawling voice from over his shoulder.

Prestone glanced up at the airplane's captain, resplendent in his gold braided black uniform. "Fine. Still on schedule?"

"Right on schedule, sir."

"Thank you," Prestone said in dismissal as he picked up the cellular phone he'd appropriated from the wall in the front of the first-class cabin.

He waited until the captain disappeared into the flight deck before attaching a small black mechanism to the mouthpiece and dialing a special number in Washington. The phone was answered on the second ring.

"This is Prestone," he said in a voice he believed would not carry far. As soon as he finished speaking, he pushed the only button on the scrambler attachment. A pinpoint red dot glowed in response.

He heard two clicks as the call was transferred and, when a familiar voice spoke, Prestone said, "The meeting is a go. All terms have been agreed to."

"So easily?"

"There were some concessions on my part," Prestone admitted.

"Such as?"

"I'll give you the details when we meet. You just authorize my other deal, understood?"

"The President isn't happy about this."

"You tell that ass backward conservative that's his problem. I gave him what he wanted, now he gives me what I want—full approval for the sale to the Israelis."

"Senator," the man in Washington began, but Prestone cut him off.

"Any further discussion on the matter will result in a complete disclosure to the press."

"That would be a mistake."

"Yes, the President's," Prestone said.

In seat 1D, in front of J. Milton Prestone, the same dark-skinned man who had passed Jonah Graham at the lavatory door, nodded to himself at the conversation he had overheard.

Shifting slightly, the man reached beneath his seat to finger the packages taped to its bottom—it was a gesture of reassurance.

Sonja Mofferty, her head resting on her husband's shoulder, readjusted her position so that her lips were touching his ear.

"Want to get laid?"

Startled, Jack Mofferty drew away and looked down at her. "Here?"

"It would be fun," she whispered. Beneath the blanket, her hand drifted along the inside of his thigh. She continued to let her fingers rise until she could feel the start of his erection. Her nail scratched lightly at its head.

"Stop," Mofferty laughed.

"Why?" she teased. When she had agreed to marry him, she had doubted that a man of his age would be able to satisfy her for any length of time. So far he had surprised her.

And Sonja was glad. She had married Jack when her

20

career's quick and not so subtle downhill slide had begun. She had chosen Jack because, although he was not worldly, he was rich. She had been surprised, shocked actually, to find out just before they married, she had fallen in love with him.

Sonja smiled. Never had she imagined loving a Jack Mofferty—short, balding, potbellied, and sweet, too, although he did his best to hide it.

"You really want to?" Mofferty asked, cutting into her thoughts.

She lifted her hand and caressed his cheek. She liked the way the stubble of his beard felt on her palm. "We'll see."

"What about the attendants?"

"They're used to it," Sonja said, hitching the blanket up over their waists.

When her fingers resumed their play, Jack did his best not to let his pleasure show. How did I get this lucky? he wondered. Although he knew that initially it had been his wealth that had enabled him to catch her, he had, not too long ago, discarded the belief that it was the money that kept them together. Mofferty was sure that it was love, no matter what his brother and sister-in-law had said.

Just because he was forty-eight, had a twenty-four-year-old son, and had fought his way out of Sheepshead Bay and into the foreign car business in Long Island, was no reason to think that someone as young and beautiful and famous as Sonja couldn't love him.

Without warning, Sonja's fingers tightened on him. Her head left his shoulder and slipped beneath the blanket. He was hard pressed to hold back a groan. His eyes closed, and his hips pushed upward. He did not see the stewardess walk by, pause for a fraction of a second, and then smile to herself as she continued on toward the flight deck.

Laughing to herself at the all too obvious under the blanket loveplay, Elaine Samson passed the first row of seats when she felt an eerie sensation of being stared at. She stopped to

21

look over her shoulder, her features set in a professional expression that said, did I forget anything?

Her eyes locked with those of the bearded man in seat 1D. He held her stare for just an instant longer, before lowering his gaze.

A shiver slithered down Elaine's back. Turning, she went to the galley, thinking how foolish it was for her to be so uneasy about a man's gaze. And then she put the incident out of her mind.

Three

Flight 88's initial descent was experienced by the passengers as a subtle shift in airspeed. For most, the change meant nothing. For others it was a signal to prepare.

In seat 1D of the first-class cabin, adrenaline was released into Rashid Mahamad's bloodstream, giving his nut brown skin a slight flush. The bearded man's senses grew acute. Sounds were magnified; odors became intense and easily identifiable; cigarette smoke, American; a whiff of perspiration, not unpleasant; coffee from the galley; a hint of wine.

Mohamad looked casually about. His left fist clenched and unclenched, loosening his muscles. All the first-class passengers were in their seats. In the front, the curtain between first class and the galley was drawn. A second curtain, between first class and coach was also closed. There was very little movement in the cabin. Behind Mohamad, J. Milton Prestone continued to make prolific notes. Mohamad listened to Prestone's pen scratching across paper.

In the last row, a silver-haired older woman wearing a gold-and-diamond Star of David was engaged in a discussion with the man next to her. Mohamad doubted if the woman would want to continue her dialogue in another half hour.

He shifted, drew the red blanket higher in his lap, and reached beneath his seat. Removing the taped-on package, he slipped it beneath the blanket.

He unwrapped the package without looking down. His

23

sure fingers needed no guide to put the clip into the Ingram MAC-10 machine pistol and make sure the safety was on.

Mohamad opened the attaché case on the seat next to him. He listened for footsteps, heard none, and placed the machine pistol in his case and snapped it closed.

Standing, Mohamad folded the blanket and put it on the seat he had just vacated. Then he placed the case on top of the blanket.

His attitude was that of a man in need of stretching after hours of sedentary confinement. But his eyes were never still—never as relaxed as his body appeared. Mohamad walked toward the rear of first class.

His glance fell on the little girl who had been brought into the first-class section. When he'd seen the stewardess settle her into a seat, he'd felt a momentary pang of anger. Fate never quite let things go the way one envisioned them.

When he passed seats 7A and 7B—occupied by the silver-haired Jewess and the young man she was talking to— Mohamad gave a barely perceptible nod. Then he slipped through the curtained partition into the coach section of the plane.

"Can I help you, sir?" asked a stewardess.

Mohamad turned, a smile on his lips. The girl was pretty. Café-au-lait skin with amber eyes. He smelled the perfume clinging to her skin. Was it her father who was black, or her mother?

"Just stretching my legs," he said in an Oxfordian accent. "It is all right, is it not?"

"Oh, certainly."

"Thank you," he said, absently massaging his left shoulder with his right hand.

The movement was casual but studied. The eye contact between him and the man in the first row was so fleeting that no one could have suspected a signal had been passed.

The man who had received Mohamad's signal rose and went to the lavatories in the middle of the plane. He carried a large rectangular attaché case. When he reached the lavatories, he found them all unoccupied. He bypassed the first three in favor of the last.

A second later, Mohamad walked to the rear of the plane. There, standing just behind the last seat, he took out a pack of John Player Specials, and lit one with a gold Dunhill.

He took several deep drags on the cigarette and then went to the last center-aisle seat and looked down at the man sitting there. "Do you mind?" he asked, making a motion toward the ashtray.

The man shook his head without replying, Mohamad stubbed out his cigarette. "Thank you."

The cigarette extinguished, the bearded man returned to his seat in first class. Behind him, the passenger whose ashtray had just been used rose and, taking a bulky attaché case from beneath the seat, went into one of the lavatories. Inside the locked compartment, he opened the attaché case and took out a hexagonal recess key. He unlocked the towel compartment, removed the remaining paper towels, unfastened the back of the polished aluminum cabinet, and removed three items. A short while later, the three metallic pieces had been fitted together to make an Uzi machine rifle.

Still working with meticulous care and speed, the man placed the Uzi diagonally into the attaché case and replaced the cabinet's back. He put the paper towels inside and locked the cabinet. Then he pulled down his pants and voided his bladder and bowels. He knew he might not have another chance for several hours—if ever.

Eight minutes later, he looked down the aisle toward the middle lavatories. Standing there was another man, holding the twin to his own attaché case. Although the distance was too great for either to see the other's eyes, their silent message was sent and received.

The seatbelt sign was turned on. Seconds later, Captain Haller's voice came over the plane's P.A. system.

"Ladies and gentlemen, we will begin our final approach to Kennedy Airport in fifteen minutes. It's a beautiful night in New York. Visibility is near perfect, as you will notice if you look out your windows. The temperature is a comfort-

25

able seventy-nine degrees Fahrenheit. Humidity is seventy-two percent.

"On behalf of myself, my crew, and Trans Air Airlines, we thank you for flying with us, and hope to see you all again."

Joan Bidding and Elaine Samson collected the last two glasses from the passengers and returned to the galley, closing the curtain behind them. They did not notice Rashid Mohamad stand and start after them, a red blanket thrown carelessly over his right arm.

Elaine dumped the two glasses into the tray. "God, this trip seems to be taking forever."

"Not really," Joan said, as a passenger appeared in the galley's opening. "Can I help you, sir?"

"Yes, actually, you may," he said, offering his blanket draped arm.

Elaine reached for the blanket. Her bored gaze met the man's sensuous and brooding eyes; the unease she'd experienced earlier returned. Without taking her eyes from his, she took the blanket. Behind her, Joan Bidding gasped.

The man moved quickly then. His left arm circled Elaine's neck. His right hand rose, cruelly pressing the barrel of the machine pistol into the soft skin beneath Elaine's chin. Her cry of panic and fear was cut short by the tightening of his arm about her neck.

"If either of you do anything—anything at all—everyone on the plane will die! Is that understood?"

It had happened so fast that all Joan could do was to stare at the weapon. Her stomach twisted violently. Her heart pounded trip-hammer fast; her breathing turned shallow. She stepped back against the galley wall and searched for a hidden button.

"Don't do that," the man said, his arm tightening on Elaine's neck. Elaine's eyes bulged. Her mouth opened.

Joan quickly brought her hands before her. "Stop! Please!"

The man loosened his hold on Elaine. "Excellent," he said.

"What do you want?" Joan asked.

"Right now we are waiting," Mohamad said. Shortly, another man appeared behind Mohamad, revealing another pistol. The two spoke in rapid Arabic.

"You will now call the pilot on the intercom. You will act normal," he told Joan. "You will tell the pilot that there is a problem with one of the passengers. A heart attack. You need help. Do not cause him to become alarmed."

This can't be happening, Joan thought. But Elaine's bloodless face confirmed that the terror that everyone believed happened only to others, was now happening to them.

The incessant pounding of Joan's heart slowed. After her initial moments of fear, numbness was setting in. She clenched her hands to stop her fingers from shaking and forced herself to function. In the second or two that it took to turn and reach for the intercom phone, a dozen things went through her mind. All the attendants had been schooled in hijack situations. But now she saw that her training was not good enough to make her risk her passengers' lives.

Joan didn't want to die. She didn't want her passengers to die either. From the moment the man had grabbed Elaine and looked into Joan's eyes, she instinctively knew that he could and would kill. It was fact; she had no doubts.

She turned back to the bearded man. "The captain is on approach. He won't leave the controls."

"It doesn't matter," Mohamad said, relaxing slightly. The woman's words told him that she would try nothing. She had passed her first test. She would live, for now. "Get the flight engineer."

Mohamad stared at her for a moment longer. His eyes betrayed no emotion. Indiscriminate killing was not what this mission called for. Some people would, of necessity, die; wholesale slaughter was unnecessary.

Joan saw something behind the dark orbs of his eyes. Her fear quickened while she dialed the flight deck. The flight engineer answered. Joan forced herself to speak in a normal voice. "Alan, we've got an emergency back here. A heart attack."

"You're sure?"

She ignored his question. "We need help."

"Excellent," Mohamad said when Joan hung up. He backed slowly out of the galley and handed Elaine efficiently over to his companion. "Do not do anything stupid."

Alan Reynolds replaced the intercom, stood, and went to Haller. "Better call for an ambulance, we've got a heart attack."

"Damn."

Reynolds went to the cockpit door. He started to open it when, unexpectedly, the door latch was ripped from his hand. Caught by surprise, the engineer was knocked off balance. His arms flailed outward, seeking a hold to stop his fall.

Rashid Mohamad burst through the door. The hijacker's right arm was raised. Reynolds' eyes widened when he recognized the black object in the man's hand. He stared in helpless astonishment as the machine pistol arced down. A flaring pain erupted in the engineer's head. Darkness came before he struck the deck.

The copilot turned at the commotion. He started to rise, but he was too late. The barrel of the pistol was pointed at his heart.

Then Joan Bidding and Elaine Samson were pushed into the cockpit and the cabin door was closed. "Down!" the second hijacker ordered the two women as Mohamad tore Haller's headset off and put the barrel of his weapon to the captain's temple.

"Do nothing foolish," Mohamad ordered. "This plane has been commandeered by the Palestinian Liberation Organization. You are a prisoner of war. You will do exactly as ordered. One mistake and your passengers die. Is that understood?"

Haller nodded. The pistol came away.

"Very good," Mohamad said, looking at the instrument panel. "Change course to two-seven-seven. Maintain a level altitude."

Haller stiffened. A vein pulsed on the side of his forehead.

His fingers tightened on the steering controls. "We're on approach. I can't do that."

"Do as you are instructed, Captain, and while you do, you may contact air control and appraise them of your situation."

Haller thought of refusing. Then, in the reflection on the windshield, he saw the look on Mohamad's face. It was a look he had often seen prior to combat missions—bright burning eyes set amid the hard facial tension of someone prepared for battle, and for death.

"My headset?"

Mohamad did not allow himself an outward smile of victory when he handed the communication gear to Haller.

Haller put it on. "Air Control, this is Trans Air Flight 88. We're changing course to two-seven-seven-degrees. Clear all traffic from flight path. We have been hijacked, repeat. Trans Air 88 has been hijacked. Tran—"

Mohamad took off Haller's headset, ending communication with air control. "Thank you, Captain. You made the correct decision. Now, before anything else is done, I want you to understand that we are soldiers fighting for a cause. We will do whatever is necessary to win. We do not wish to kill, but we will kill, believe that, Captain. We will kill if necessary. It will be your actions, and the actions of your crew, which determine whether your passengers live or die."

Haller met Mohamad's eyes. He considered the alternatives—the actions he had been trained to take and the risks that had to be judged acceptable or not. At present there were no viable risks. "No one will attempt anything."

"Again, a wise decision. Khamil," he called.

The second hijacker stepped around the fallen engineer and past the two flight attendants. At the copilot's seat, he withdrew a rubber-tipped hypodermic syringe from his jacket pocket.

"Thorazine," Mohamad said. "As I've told you, we do not seek unnecessary deaths. We have certain objectives to obtain. I will avoid killing if possible. If you do not fight us, you and your crew and your passengers will survive."

Flaxman looked over his shoulder at the needle. A cop-

29

pery taste flooded his mouth. He unbuttoned his cuff and rolled up his sleeve.

"The effects of the sedative will wear off in a few hours," Mohamad said, and Khamil plunged the hypodermic into Flaxman's arm.

Four

Lieutenant Raymond Hyte stood in the doorway. Light spilled over his shoulder and into the bedroom, silhouetting the sleeping child in the center of his bed. He smiled.

The light wasn't strong enough to see her features clearly, but he knew them as well as his own. They were a part of him; he had created her eleven years before. Her cheekbones were sharp and precise. She had blonde hair with a hint of strawberry. Her mouth was a shade too small for her teeth, but she would grow into the teeth in another year or two. Her nose was small—aquiline, Susan had called it. He hoped it would stay that way. It was important that she have Susan's nose, not his.

Important? He shook his head ruefully. She was healthy. She was smart. Her mind hadn't gotten ruined by the divorce. Those were the important things.

He partially closed the door, returned to the couch, and then lifted a Scotch and water from the cork coaster on the coffee table.

He sipped the drink, tasting wood. He always tasted wood when he drank Scotch. It wasn't a bad taste. It sufficed. Like his life.

He rolled the drink around his tongue, reminding himself that he was supposed to relax. But relaxing was hard when his last five weeks had been made up of twenty-hour-days in an effort to catch a killer who liked to cut up old women. He and his men had finally caught him just before he'd plunged a butcher knife into a seventy-five-year-old lady. Now, he'd taken four days off to be with Carrie before she went to summer camp. He wanted to savor the naïveté surrounding his eleven-year-old daughter.

The phone rang. Hyte put down the Scotch and picked it up. He was off duty for the next four days. He hoped it wouldn't be the Department.

"Hello," he said tentatively, half expecting it to be his ex-wife checking up on their daughter.

"Lou, Sergeant Vicoletti."

The use of the title, *Lou*—departmental shorthand for lieutenant—made the call official.

Hyte sighed. "Yes, Sergeant?"

"We've got a big one. Kennedy Airport. Trans Air Flight 88 from Tangier was taken over by hijackers fifteen minutes ago. The fucking plane is circling Manhattan. They've had to reroute all air traffic at Kennedy, LaGuardia, and Newark. It's a real disaster. Your team is notified."

With thumb and forefinger, Hyte rubbed at the inner corners of his eyes. He wanted to say that he was on a four-day leave. He didn't; instead, he asked, "What happened to Conklin?"

"He's in White Plains. His wife's delivering right now. Not enough time to get him back."

Hyte glanced over his shoulder to the bedroom where his daughter slept. "Who took the plane?"

"No one knows. There's been one communication from the pilot, alerting the airport of the hijacking and change of course. Radar is tracking them in a circle around Manhattan. I—"

"Have any demands been made yet?"

"No, sir," Vicoletti said. "And I've dispatched a blue and white to your place. The copter will pick you up at Sixty-second Street."

Hyte tensed. "No copter. I can drive there just as fast."

"We don't know where *there* is. And you won't get through by car. Port Authority closed traffic to all airports."

"I'll be ready," Hyte said and hung up.

He stood, turned, and found his daughter standing in the

doorway. The living room light highlighted the slim body beneath the pink nightgown. Her hair spilled over her shoulders. Her blue eyes were alert. "Daddy?"

"I have to go out tonight, sweetheart. It's an emergency."

"Is it dangerous?" she asked.

"Come here," Hyte said, opening his arms.

Carolyn Samantha Hyte came into his arms. He kissed the top of her head. "A plane was hijacked. Someone has to talk to the people who did it. That's my job."

"Is it dangerous?" she asked again, drawing back far enough to look him directly in the eyes.

"Sometimes it is."

"Be careful, please."

He smiled and hugged her tightly. "I will. For you. Now, let me call Mrs. O'Malley."

"I can go over there until you get back."

Hyte shook his head. "You go back to bed. Okay?"

Carrie nodded, rose onto the balls of her feet, and kissed Hyte's stubbled chin. "Okay."

When she was back in bed, Hyte dialed his neighbor. Helen O'Malley, a grandmother of seventy, had moved into the apartment next to Hyte's two years ago. It had been a godsend to the cop.

She arrived four minutes after his call. Her iron-gray hair was in curlers, an ankle-length peach velour robe was belted securely around her waist. Hyte thanked her, got his gun from the kitchen drawer, and raced downstairs. Moments later, he closed the door of a patrol car and was taken to the helicopter pad adjacent to the East River Drive.

The situation on Trans Air 88 was exactly the way the hijackers wanted it. Mohamad had instructed Haller to make an announcement that they would be circling the airport for a little while, and the landing would be slightly delayed.

Behind Haller, Elaine Samson sat on the floor, her arms hugging her knees. Joan Bidding held the unconscious engineer, stroking his head. "Khamil has tape," Mohamad said. "You will please secure his wrists and ankles."

Elaine glared up at him. "Why do you have to be so fucking polite?"

"Would you prefer I use force?"

"Do it, Elaine," Haller commanded.

The women bound the flight engineer's wrists and ankles and then laid him on the floor. "You tie her hands," Mohamad told Joan.

After Joan secured Elaine's wrists, she was sent back to the passenger cabins to tell the other flight attendants that they would be landing shortly. Under no circumstance was she to warn anyone. If she did, Mohamad explained, the captain would be shot.

Joan Bidding believed him.

Twelve minutes later, Haller told him that their fuel was running low. "We'll have to land soon."

Mohamad glanced at the fuel gauges. "We have at least forty-five minutes of circling at minimum air speed."

The man, if not a pilot, had done his homework, Haller knew. He exhaled in capitulation. "Mind if I smoke?"

"Yes. You will make no movements other than to fly the plane."

Haller looked at the man. "You can't get away with it."

"Get away with what, Captain? We've already hijacked your plane. We'll get what we've come for. And," he went on, his voice smooth and calm behind its British tones, "we hope to cause only a minimum amount of harm to your crew and passengers."

"You've already done more harm than that."

"That depends on how you view the situation. No one on this plane has died. Concentrate on your flying and contact the control tower, please."

Haller called in as Mohamad took Flaxman's headset and put it on. When the tower replied, it was Mohamad who spoke. "This is Rashid Mohamad. I have commandeered this airplane. To insure the safety of the passengers and crew, the following must be done. All flights landing or departing from Kennedy Airport are to cease. All air traffic is to be diverted to other airports. When that is accomplished, we will return to Kennedy and land. Have a fuel truck prepared.''

''Impossible!'' came the reply. ''The best we can do is close off one runway.''

Mohamad exhaled. It was a sound not unlike the leading edge of a storm. ''I am truly sorry to hear this. In that case, everyone on board this craft will die when I crash the plane into an apartment building on Fifth Avenue.''

Dead silence, filled by low static, followed Mohamad's words. Mohamad's smile told everyone on the flight deck that he was amused at the consternation within the control tower.

''Captain Haller, what's the fuel situation?''

Haller looked at Mohamad who nodded.

''Control, we have forty minutes left if we push it.''

''Hold on 88, we'll get back to you.''

''That would be a good idea,'' Mohamad said dryly.

Thirty seconds later the radio crackled. ''Flight 88, the airport will be shut down.''

Hyte looked down at the cars on the Belt Parkway. The helicopter was flying fast at an altitude of twelve hundred feet. A low groan caught in the back of his throat. He knew nothing about what was happening, except that the plane would be landing at Kennedy. Instead, he thought about how he had gotten involved in hostage negotiations.

His record had been part of the reason. Philip Mason was the other part. Captain Philip Mason had been his father's closest friend in the Department. Philip Mason was his mentor. Hyte held him responsible for his divorce. He knew he was being unreasonable. He couldn't help it. If he hadn't met the captain at the restaurant. . . .

No, if Susan hadn't wanted to try the restaurant that her friend had told her about, he wouldn't be a divorced police lieutenant flying in a helicopter to Kennedy Airport to talk to a lunatic who was holding millions of dollars of airplane and its passengers hostage.

If he hadn't majored in political science and minored in psychology at N.Y.U., and then gone to law school, he wouldn't be in the helicopter either. He had never consciously planned on joining the Department. He wanted to enter politics—his father had always pushed him in that direction. "You can do more by making laws than by enforcing them," he'd said.

But his father's advice had come too late to abrogate the influence of growing up in a police family. He had known the code since he had taken his first step. He had seen the highs of being on the job, and he'd lived with the lows.

And he had always been proud of his father. His father was important. What he did was important. Who he was, was important.

The chopper shuddered. Hyte watched the pilot make a minor correction and felt the flying machine steady. He looked down at the lighted buildings below.

His first flight in a copter had set the pattern for all the rest. A midnight phone call from Mason—Uncle Phil—had awakened him. Twenty minutes later he had been airborne over Manhattan, on the way to Staten Island.

Hyte's father had been shot by a sniper who wanted revenge on the precinct captain responsible for his arrest, he was told as he flew across New York Harbor. Captain Mason was waiting for him, but Raymond Hyte, Jr., was too late to say good-bye to his father, who had died minutes before the helicopter had landed.

Hyte always thought about his father when he had to fly in a copter. He couldn't help it, just as he'd been unable to heed his father's advice when, a year after graduating from law school and marrying Susan, he ended up facing his future in the form of Philip Mason and the Organized Crime Squad.

The helicopter pilot dropped his craft several hundred feet, drawing Hyte back to where he was—two hundred and fifty feet above the Belt Parkway. "Jesus," he muttered, stopping himself from further thought as the telltale flashing of runway strobe lights drew near.

The pilot set the helicopter down fifty feet from the con-

36

trol tower. Shielding his eyes from the particles of dust kicked up by the helicopter's blades, Hyte scuttled from beneath the whirling rotors. Two Port Authority cops were waiting at the outer fringes of the helicopter's windstorm. They led him directly to the air security ready room in the main control tower. Behind him, the copter rose back up into the darkness.

Inside the ready room, Hyte took a quick inventory. Three members of his hostage negotiation team were present. Blond-haired, blue-eyed Brian Atkins, detective second grade and the youngest of Hyte's squad, was perched on the edge of a desk. Atkins's value was as a marksman. He could hit the center of an ace of spades at a thousand feet with a high power rifle.

The second member of the team was Joseph Moran. He sat behind Atkins, talking into a phone. Moran was shrewd looking and tall, and had a bored look firmly settled on his obviously Irish face. Hyte hoped the look would stay there tonight.

Harvey Bennet, the third member of the team, approached. "Where's Sy?" Hyte asked the bald-headed and compact twenty-year veteran of the NYPD. Detective Sergeant Simon Cohen was the fourth member, the team's second in command, and Hyte's first partner when Hyte had been made a detective.

"Upstairs," Bennet said as a man in a gray double-breasted suit, white shirt, and a blue tie came toward them. He was Charles Koenig, the Port Authority's head of security for Kennedy Airport. Koenig was a dapper man of fifty-six, with lively and intelligent blue eyes. His thinning white hair was combed neatly into place. A line of pink scalp was exposed at the left hand parting.

Hyte and the security man had worked together several times in the past. "Charlie, what's the story?"

"Not good," Koenig said. "The plane is carrying ninety-one passengers and ten crew. No word if there's more than one hijacker. He's demanded we close down the entire airport."

Hyte paused at that. "Why?"

37

Koenig shrugged. "To see what he can get?"

Hyte scratched at a spot on his neck at the base of his hairline. "Possibly. What was the threat? They'll kill a passenger?"

"You're not going to like this, Ray," Koenig said in a low voice.

Hyte blew a thin stream of air from between pursed lips. "I already know that."

Koenig nodded. "If the airport isn't closed down and all personnel evacuated from the runways, he'll crash the plane into an apartment building on Fifth Avenue."

"That's ridiculous."

"But effective," Koenig replied.

Hyte had no argument for that. "Let's get upstairs. Anyone know who these people are?"

"There's an FBI agent on his way. He might know." When Hyte gazed curiously at Koenig, the man went on. "I, ah, delayed the call until you were dispatched."

Hyte understood Koenig's ploy. No one liked the way the federal people took over during a hijack situation. And the first authority on the scene usually took command. Hyte represented that authority.

"I need a list of all the passengers," he told Koenig. "Where did the flight originate?"

"Tangier."

The answer caught Hyte off guard. "Tangier? Why the hell did they wait until they crossed the ocean? That doesn't make any sense. They should have gone to one of the Middle East countries."

No one answered him.

"Upstairs," Hyte repeated. He led the group to the waiting elevator.

It would be nice, Hyte thought, if this situation followed theories he had been taught. It would also be a first.

Hyte thought about his teacher at the government counter-terrorist training center outside of D.C. The man had summed up what everyone knew but didn't want to say. "No two hijackings are alike, no matter how similar they are in appearance. When you're involved in a hijack-

38

ing, pray that it's a lunatic after money, and not a political idealist. A self-serving hijacking—one for monetary gain—can be handled with more ease than the politically motivated. You can deal with a true criminal; you can't with a terrorist. Just remember that the methods we've taught you are the best available. But don't accept them as gospel. Your mind is the best tool you have.''

But to use that tool, Hyte reminded himself, I have to know what kind of hijacking I'm dealing with.

The elevator stopped and the door hissed open, revealing a windowed room dominated by electronic tracking equipment. Sy Cohen was standing at a supervisor's desk, talking on the phone. Cohen's tense features were accented by short-cropped gray hair and narrowed eyes.

Hyte started toward him. The sergeant hung up and turned. When Cohen's eyes met his, Hyte's apprehension increased.

''Ray,'' Cohen said, cocking a thumb toward the phone. ''That was Tangier. They found two maintenance workers. Their throats were cut. At first they thought it was some sort of vendetta, but they got a call a half hour ago. The dead men were the ones who should have serviced Flight 88. The Tangier authorities have no doubt that it's terrorists who've hijacked the plane.''

''Shit!'' Hyte said. He had his answer. The hijacking was political.

Five

Mohamad picked up the intercom and held it to Joan Bidding's mouth. "You will ask for Dr. Schmidt to come into the first-class section. Make the announcement in a normal manner."

Joan's eyes flicked to Haller, who nodded. "Would Dr. Schmidt please come to the first-class section. Your medical assistance is required."

Mohamad knew that everyone in coach would watch a man carrying a large attaché case leave his seat and go forward. They would all wonder who was sick. No sense of danger would be raised. Because the success of his plan required having the third of his four men in first class, he had to make the first-class passengers aware of their situation—but only the first-class passengers, and under controlled circumstances.

"Captain, keep to the same flight pattern we have been following. Khamil, if the captain does anything except fly the plane, kill him."

Mohamad pushed Joan Bidding into the curtained-off area outside the flight deck. "You will go ahead of me. You will inform the first-class passengers that the plane has been taken over. They are to remain calm and in their seats."

Joan nodded, unable to rid herself of the knot in her stomach. Her initial numbness was receding.

Swallowing hard, she parted the curtain. At almost the same moment, a man stepped through the curtain separating first class from coach. Her first instinct was to warn him of the danger. Then her eyes fell on the weapon he was holding.

She thought of her husband and sons. "Ladies and gentlemen, may I have your attention." She moistened her lips. "P-please, do nothing. The plane has been hijacked. We . . . we will not be harmed if you remain calm."

Disbelief was the most prevalent expression. The redheaded man in seat 3B, Michael Barnes, started to rise. "Who the hell—"

Mohamad pointed the machine pistol at him. "Do not be stupid. All of you, look behind you."

Mesmerized, they turned as one. Standing in the aisle, his back to the curtain, was the man with the Uzi. His face was blank. The barrel of his weapon swept over the passengers.

"That attachment on the front of the Uzi is a silencer. The weapon will not be heard in the coach section. For your edification, Abdul is a fine marksman. He does not miss."

Mohamad paused. He smiled. "Your own lives and those of the other passengers will depend on your silence." A low whimpering came from his left. He looked down at Cristobal Helenez. "Tell your wife to be quiet."

Helenez drew his wife close, holding her face to his chest to quiet her. Mohamad looked at the other passengers. The overriding expression on each face was fear. Yet, on some, hostility grew. When his eyes settled on J. Milton Prestone, he saw open rage. That was expected. The little girl who had been brought to first class earlier was cowering against the window.

"Please stay seated. Do not unfasten your seatbelts. I would not want Abdul to have to kill anyone." Mohamad started to turn, drawing the still trembling Joan Bidding with him. His body was tense, his senses alert. From behind came the low snick of a seatbelt opening. The scratch of a shoe on carpet followed.

Mohamad spun. His gun hand arched out, the heavy metal pistol butt striking quickly and accurately. Ex-army colonel and former United States Senator J. Milton Prestone collapsed a foot from the terrorist.

Mohamad ignored the unconscious man. "Do not make the same mistake. The penalty will be even more severe. Look at that child!" he ordered, pointing the machine pistol at seven-year-old Lea D'Angine. "Her life is in your hands. She will die if you do anything other than what you are told."

Hyte had taken over airport control, which now handled all contact with Flight 88 on a restricted frequency. His team was spread out. Atkins and Moran manned telephones, Harvey Bennet leaned casually against the wall, awaiting his instructions. Detective Sergeant Simon Cohen stood next to the radio man, waiting for the plane to contact them.

"How much fuel do they have left?" Hyte asked, looking up from the passenger list.

"Twenty minutes," the operator answered immediately.

"Are all runways cleared?"

"The last plane just took off," Koenig said.

Hyte turned to see a tall man enter the control room and start toward him. "I'm Arnel. FBI." He wore the regulation three-piece suit. His face was classic government issue.

Hyte, aware of the conflicts created by the last joint operation between the Bureau and the Department, shook Arnel's hand.

"Ray Hyte, NYPD hostage negotiations. I believe we'll be handling things here. No problem with that?"

Hyte noted the agent's sardonic smile. "Seeing as you're first on the scene, I was told to offer whatever assistance I could. I'm also acting as liaison with Immigration and Naturalization. Their two senior officers are unavailable."

"Do you know who in the hell took that plane?"

"We believe it's a PLO operation, but we have no confirmation."

"Christ! What about the government counter-terrorist strike force?"

"They're on classified maneuvers, I don't know if they

can make it back in time. But we've got another problem," Arnel said.

"Which is?"

"Former Senator J. Milton Prestone is on board."

Hyte looked at the list in his hand. His eyes stopped at the name. He spun to the detective lolling against the wall. "No press!" he ordered. "And I don't give a damn who tries to countermand that."

"Too late," Atkins said. "There's already two news teams downstairs, and there's a whole bunch more on their way."

"Jesus, they're getting fast. Okay. Nothing is to be said to them yet, nothing." Hyte closed his eyes. *Concentrate,* he told himself, *go by the book.* "Let's get the plane down."

"Ray," Sy Cohen called, "the hijacker identified himself as Rashid Mohamad."

"Alias James Westerwood," Arnel said quickly. "He's famous. Graduate of Oxford, holds an engineering degree from Stanford. And a fanatic. In the last seven years, he's killed two hundred people. He's a member of a militant faction of the PLO that split from Arafat because they believe Arafat's too soft."

Hyte stared out the window, thinking about the agent's information. "If this Rashid Mohamad is so fucking smart, what the hell is he doing here? He has to know that we can't let him get away—not after the last few hijackings."

"I guess that's what we're going to find out," Arnel said.

Hyte turned to Sy Cohen. "You go with the fuel truck." When the sergeant left, Hyte nodded to the radio operator. "Get Mohamad," he said.

"Come in Trans Air Flight 88, this is Airport Control, over."

Haller turned to Mohamad. "We're down to fifteen minutes of fuel."

"You may respond," Mohamad said.

"Control this is Trans Air 88, over."

43

"Trans Air 88, you are cleared for landing. All runways are unoccupied."

Mohamad spoke before Haller got the chance. "If, when we land, I see any movement, people will die."

"The airport is closed. The runways are shut down," the radio operator reaffirmed.

Mohamad nodded to Haller. "Proceed with landing instructions."

"Shall I make the landing announcement now?" Haller asked.

"Very carefully, Captain," Mohamad said.

His voice steady, Haller began the announcement that the terrorist had rehearsed with him five minutes earlier.

"Ladies and gentlemen, this is Captain Haller again. We've just been cleared for landing. We're sorry for the delay. At this time, I would also like to ask for your further cooperation. One of our passengers has suffered what appear to be a heart attack. A doctor is with him now. An ambulance will meet the plane on the runway. Until the passenger has been taken off the plane, please remain in your seat with your seatbelt on. We will be moving the plane again. Thank you for your patience."

"Good," the terrorist said.

The 727 touched down eight minutes later.

In coach, the man who had used the lavatory earlier unfastened his seatbelt and stood. The passenger next to him glared.

He returned the look with a smile and went into the galley. The three stewardesses in their jumpseats told him to return to his seat.

Ignoring them, he opened his attaché case and withdrew the Uzi. He held a finger to his lips. It was warning enough.

When the plane came to a stop, far out on the runway, he stepped into the aisle. Overhead, the P.A. system came to life.

"Ladies and gentlemen, this is not the captain. Please remain calm. This plane is now in control of the Palestinian Liberation Organization. If you want to remain alive, do nothing. If you think this is a hoax, look around."

Seventy-seven passengers and five stewardesses found themselves staring at two men armed with machine guns. Several women screamed. They were silenced by their seat-mates. No one left his seat.

In first class, the passengers had already been moved into the first three rows. All except Lea D'Anjine, who had been placed in the fifth row, where Mohamad had belted her into the seat. Of all the passengers, only J. Milton Prestone was not conscious. His hands were tied, and he had been laid across the first two seats.

Khamil Fasil stood guard over them. His eyes were never still. He held the machine pistol at the ready.

"They're down and taxiing," the radio operator called out.

Hyte watched out the window. Arnel was next to him.

"The commissioner wants to know what's happening," called Junior Atkins, covering the mouthpiece of the phone with his hand.

"Tell him," Hyte snapped, annoyance thickening his voice. He wasn't ready to speak with the brass; he needed his mind free for what was ahead.

"Trans Air Flight 88. Proceed to runway Delta seven east. The fuel truck is waiting."

The terrorist's voice came over the central speaker. His words were precise, his diction flawless. "We will proceed to a spot I choose. You will send out the fuel truck. Only two men will be permitted. The truck will circle the plane at a distance of one hundred feet. The cab light must be on. The truck will stop one hundred feet in front of the plane. The men will get out, undress to show they are unarmed, and stay undressed. I will then call you to send them to refuel the plane."

Hyte watched the silver and red plane. It moved slowly, its flight lights blinking. It stopped in the intersection of the three runways directly in view of the tower.

"Send the truck," said the terrorist.

Hyte spoke into a walkie-talkie. He relayed the instructions to Sy Cohen, who was waiting in the truck.

Two minutes later the truck reached the plane, circled it, and stopped a hundred feet away. The two men got out, removed their coveralls, and stood in the truck's headlights wearing only shoes, socks, and underwear.

Moran chuckled. "Sy looks good in boxer shorts."

"Shut up," Hyte snapped. The detective did.

"Commence fueling," the terrorist ordered. His voice echoed tinnily through the speakers.

The radio operator started to speak. Hyte stopped him and took the microphone. It was time to set the tone for what would follow. "This is Lieutenant Hyte of the New York Police Department. Refueling will not, I repeat, will not take place unless you release the hostages."

"Fuel the plane or someone will die," Mohamad replied.

"Give us the hostages." Hyte's nerves tightened. He knew that this opening gambit was but the first in a series of strategic plays for leverage. He and the hijacker would jockey for position. Bluff and sternness before give and take was the methodology. He had to find out what the hijackers wanted. The demands would contain information he needed to learn how far he could push them. It was a dangerous but essential move. Everyone trained in hostage negotiations accepted the theory.

Mohamad spoke in a bored voice. "Until now, no one has been killed. You will begin refueling in one minute. If you delay, you will cause the first death. And then one passenger will die for each minute the fuel truck sits idle."

"That will mean your own death, too," Hyte said.

"We are prepared for that."

It was simply said. Hyte didn't like it. He glanced at Arnel, one eyebrow cocked. The Fed's expression confirmed the terrorist's statement. "You don't have to die," Hyte told the terrorist.

"Thirty seconds."

There was something wrong. The hijacker should be spouting his organizational dogma and making demands, not calmly ticking off the time. "Let's talk," Hyte suggested, his eyes on the second hand of his watch. His counter

46

was designed to make the man think he would get what he wanted, whatever it might be.

"We have been talking. But apparently you have not been listening. Listen carefully. . . . Now!"

A gunshot. Hyte flinched. He heard screams. *Bluff*, he told himself. That, too, was part of negotiations. When you could not see what was happening, anything that was said could be a lie.

"Watch!" Mohamad ordered.

Everyone in the control room stared out at the plane. The forward cabin door opened. A body was thrown out of the plane. Although no sound could reach the men in the control room, everyone was sure he heard the thud of the body when it struck the tarmac.

Swallowing quickly, Hyte closed his eyes. "Fuel the fucking plane."

Six

Shortly after the plane was fueled, a Trans Air executive arrived and introduced himself to Hyte as Mark Stubbin.

"The dead man was the flight engineer," Cohen told Hyte after the lieutenant and Stubbin had shook hands.

"His name was Alan Reynolds," Stubbin said. "He is— was—married. Had three children."

Hyte looked at Arnel. "What do you think about this Rashid Mohamad?"

"Only that he's one of their best. He's hard to find, even harder to catch. And he's a master strategist."

Frustration laced Hyte's thoughts. His sense of unease was growing. The hijacking of Flight 88 was not following any regular pattern. Although no two hijackings were ever truly alike, they usually had, by necessity, certain points of similarity. And, by this time, the hijacker should have made his demands and spouted his rhetoric. But he hadn't. Why?

Hyte had to penetrate the enigma that the hijacker had set before him; Rashid Mohamad was the center of the puzzle. "What the hell is he doing here? He's got to know that he's a dead man."

"We've never been able to understand the psychological makeup of a terrorist with any degree of accuracy," Arnel said. "The closest we can come is that a terrorist has already resigned himself to death. Look at that Egyptian foulup in Malta, or the Pakistani hijacking where they tried to take out everyone. Who knows what motivates someone to kill and then let themselves be killed?"

Hyte didn't want to think about either incident. Too many people besides terrorists had died. "Mr. Stubbin, what's the pilot like?"

The airline executive shrugged. "A good man. This was to be his last flight. He's retiring."

"No. His background. Does he have a cool head? Is he a strong man, physically? Mentally?"

"Haller's been with us for a long time. He's considered to be one of the best pilots in our fleet. He was a highly decorated jet pilot in the early sixties, in Southeast Asia."

Cool head, Hyte decided, but getting on in years. He pushed his mind into gear.

When he had accepted the offer to be trained as a hostage negotiator, it was to be separate from his duties as a precinct detective. He had seen too many people die or get hurt before their attacker could be stopped. His hostage work was, he could admit in the sanctity of his mind, his personal act of contrition to those who had died.

"Hyte?" came Mohamad's voice, interrupting his reverie.

Hyte went to the console. "Here."

"We have a list of requests."

"Requests?" Hyte echoed sarcastically, mentally ticking off his negotiation tactics list, now that Mohamad seemed ready to talk. The demands were always first, after the fuel. And, he had gained another piece of information. Mohamad had said we, not I.

"When our requests are met, we will release the passengers and crew. We, the revolutionary arm of the legal government of Palestine, ask for the following."

Cohen held a small tape recorder near the speaker.

"First, we must have the release of our five brothers now held by your government in Ossining Prison. Second, five million dollars in cash—one million dollars for each of our brothers—is to be delivered to the plane. Third, the United States must publicly acknowledge the existence of the Palestinian cause, the Palestine Liberation Organization, and must pursue an active dialogue with a PLO representative. Fourth, the government of the United States must grant our five brothers amnesty and give myself and my three comrades amnesty as well."

Hyte covered his microphone. "Four of them."

"Lastly, we want a live television feed from inside the plane. One camera will be permitted. Those five things are all we request."

Hyte's knuckles turned white on the edge of the desk. He thought of the dead flight engineer. "Your demands are unreasonable."

"Our *requests* are not only reasonable, but possible. Take for instance the five million dollars. How much money are your pro-Zionist airlines losing by the closing of this airport? I'm sure they would volunteer that money themselves. And, do you so easily forget the man already dead because of you? There will be more if you don't facilitate our requests."

"If you kill the crew, you don't fly out," Hyte reminded him.

The terrorist laughed. "We don't need the pilot. I am one."

Hyte looked at Arnel. "It's possible," the FBI man whispered.

"We'll need time," Hyte said.

"You have twenty minutes to make the arrangements. Once that has been done, we will discuss a time limit to discharge our requests. Until you have made the initial arrangements, do not contact us."

A click sounded on Mohamad's last word. Hyte turned to Arnel. "Can you make the arrangements for what they want?"

"No. Policy."

"Try anyway," Hyte said, holding Arnel's gaze for several seconds. "And while you're at it, find out how they got the plane." Hyte reached for the telephone, dreading the call he had to make.

He dialed the number. The phone rang four times before

50

it was answered. "Commissioner Rutledge, this is a Lieutenant Hyte . . ."

In the coach section of Flight 88, fear was the viscous bond linking the passengers together. The coach passengers and stewardesses had been herded into the rearmost section of the plane. Those who found no available seats were made to sit on the floor. There was one guard at the rear, a second in the front.

All doors, including the emergency exits, were lined with narrow strips of gray plastique, which the terrorists had removed from beneath their seats. Clear filament trip wires had been added. Earlier, the leader of the terrorists had made his announcement: The brave commandos of the PLO were neither insane nor criminals. As long as the passengers obeyed instructions, no harm would befall them.

No hijacker on Flight 88 acted like a madman. No political rhetoric was recited. No pointless threats were made, only simple instructions delivered in clear and precise tones.

One woman asked to go to the bathroom; the guard told her to use her pants. The passengers were warned that any overt movement would be met with death. No one else asked to use the bathroom. No one talked.

In the first-class cabin, Rashid Mohamad had just closed the last of the collected passports and tossed it on the floor. The unconscious copilot had been left in the cockpit. The stewardesses and the captain, their wrists bound, were on the floor in front of the first seats. Mohamad stood before them. To his left was Khamil.

The passengers and crew had been forced to watch the execution.

Mohamad surveyed his prisoners. "Our requests have been made. As soon as they are complied with, you will be released."

"And you will be dead," J. Milton Prestone snapped. The former senator had regained consciousness shortly after landing. He sat with his wrists taped together.

"Perhaps," Mohamad said conversationally. "But that

51

is not your concern. Staying alive is. Should any of you decide to become a hero, *all* of you will die. There will be no exceptions."

Mohamad's eyes swept across each face, pausing only at a certain few. His gaze lingered on Cristobal Helenez, and then on Prestone. The silver-haired woman who had been Khamil's seatmate, identified as Sylvia Mossberg by her passport, stared through glazed eyes. Mohamad wondered if her heart could take the strain.

"I will be going to the rear. No talking will be permitted while I am gone."

As he walked, he did not miss the way the gray-haired man, whose passport had disclosed him to be Jonah Graham, held his wife securely, meeting Mohamad's eyes calmly and without fear.

It always amazed Mohamad that it was never the ones who appeared brave who were.

Mohamad did not notice Graham touch a leather-covered cigarette case in his breast pocket as he entered the empty middle section of the plane. The terrorist paused to look out one window. The tower was in plain view. The runways leading toward it were deserted.

He was pleased. Everything was going as he had predicted. His demands had followed the rehearsed pattern, as would the negotiations that were to come. His mission would succeed, as long as the passengers did not become stupid. Sighing, Mohamad continued on to the coach section, where the smell of fear and sweat permeated the air like a foul perfume.

"I know that you are afraid right now," he said. "If by chance you aren't, I assure you, you have ample cause for fear. However, we are not the bloodthirsty people your newspapers can make us out to be, and we would prefer that no harm came to any of you."

A restless stir—like a ripple in a lake—followed his words. People looked hopefully at each other.

"No harm will be done to you," he repeated, "unless your government does not grant our requests—which are not unreasonable."

"They won't!" shouted a middle-aged man with coarse, bloated features. "They won't give in to terrorists!"

"That would be a pity," Mohamad said.

"You are not being rational," a young man said in accented English. The youth, perhaps twenty, was Middle Eastern, a student. "Your fight is with the government, not with us. Myself and the other passengers are ordinary people. We are not the rich capitalists who are against your return to Palestine. You have the rich ones up front."

"Your name?" Mohamad asked.

The young man paled. "Ba—Barum Kaliel."

"Lebanese?"

The young student sat straighter. "I am from Jordan."

Mohamad continued to stare at him. "Barum Kaliel, you are an ignorant boy who is trying to bargain his life for those up front."

A man in the first row shot out of his seat, reaching for the terrorist leader.

With what seemed like an absent movement, Mohamad chopped down with his machine pistol. He caught his attacker on the forehead. The man let out a grunt as he hit the floor.

Before the passengers could react, the guards' weapons were trained on them. Mohamad bent over his attacker. Blood washed across the man's forehead.

Mohamad took a roll of adhesive tape from his pocket. "You two," he said, pointing to the men who had been sitting on either side of his attacker, "bind his wrists and legs."

Mohamad watched until his attacker's wrists were securely fastened. "Pick him up. Put him inside," he ordered, motioning toward the vacant midsection of the plane.

He told one of his men to watch them, then looked back at the passengers. "What that man did was stupid," Mohamad said. "It will be the last time any movement will be permitted. To show you that we are not madmen, my attacker shall live." He paused. The only noise in the compartment was the sound of the plane's ventilation system.

When Mohamad judged his silence had made its point,

53

he smiled at the hostages. ''Because we do not wish to kill any of you, the next person who makes an overt move will have his Achilles tendons severed. He will never walk again.''

Seven

Hyte had activated a stopwatch when Mohamad had set the twenty-minute time limit. Eighteen minutes and forty seconds had gone by.

Although the control tower room was air conditioned, Hyte's shirt stuck to his back. A cold cup of coffee was in his right hand; he rubbed his tongue over his teeth, trying to wipe away the clinging acidic taste.

Hyte contemplated his next steps. "By the book," he muttered under his breath. And, going by the book was a multifaceted effort. First he had to make himself sound believable and sympathetic toward the hijacker. Then he would have to make Mohamad believe that although Hyte was a cop, he understood what the hijacker was going through. At the same time, he had to try and talk the man into giving up.

From the corner of his eye, he saw Special Agent Arnel hang up the phone. "No go," the Fed stated. "They won't release the terrorists."

Hyte had known that already but had asked Arnel to try hoping that the FBI man's influence might help. Using the five men as negotiating pawns could get him the hostages in return.

Hyte thought of his daughter, sleeping in his bed. At least she was safe. He thought of the people on Flight 88. There were no extended families on board, only duplicated names.

Duplicated names usually meant couples. There were no notations of children on board. He considered that a break.

"They're giving us no choice. We'll have to use the Department counter-terrorist team, or the government unit if they can make it in time." Hyte preferred the NYPD team.

"They're eight fucking hours away!" Arnel shouted. The outburst was the first time the man had shown any emotion. *"You* have to get the passengers out before your terrorist team goes in. Especially Prestone."

"I intend to do just that," Hyte said, his temper rising.

"Forty-five seconds, Ray," said Sy Cohen.

Hyte exhaled. "The money?" he asked Cohen.

"They said they'll be able to get it from the Federal Reserve Bank if necessary. They also said it can't leave the country."

Nodding, Hyte met Cohen's eyes. He knew the rules. If the hijackers took off without passengers, the plane would be intercepted and destroyed. That contingency had been arranged several years before with the Air Force. Terrorists knew about it. That was one reason why hijackings coming into American airports were so rare. And it was another part of the growing puzzle. This hijacking should never have happened here. But it had, so there must be a reason for it. And a damned good reason, Hyte thought, at least from the terrorists' viewpoint. What else was behind it, Hyte wondered, besides the obvious desire to free the five convicted terrorists and to get the money?

The radio came to life. "Lieutenant Hyte?"

Hyte went to the console. "Yes."

"Your answer?"

Hyte closed his eyes for a moment. He had to work on Mohamad. "Rashid, I give you my word that if you surrender now, you and your men will not be harmed. You will be taken into custody and allowed an attorney. You will be given a fair trial, a public forum, to explain why you believed you *had* to hijack the plane."

"Let me assure you, Lieutenant, the formalities of negotiation are pointless in our situation. I know every nuance and subtlety of what you are attempting. Let us dispense with them, because you will not wear me down. We follow a precise time schedule that will not be altered. The first death was a crew member. You have one minute left to save a passenger's life.''

Hyte studied his stopwatch. When twenty-nine seconds passed, he said, ''Your demands will be met.'' The next step in the negotiations was underway: Hyte had to make Mohamad believe he'd get everything he'd asked for.

''Excellent.''

''But it will take time. A bank must be opened. Five million dollars takes a while to count. The men in Ossining Prison will be flown here, the arrangements are being made.''

''That is only two of our requests,'' Mohamad reminded him.

''We're getting a camera crew ready.''

''And the announcements by your government?''

''They are under consideration,'' Hyte said. It was his second outright lie. The announcements the terrorists had demanded would never be made.

''You have three hours to comply with all our requests,'' the terrorist said.

Hyte thought rapidly. Now that a time limit had been set, he had to try to change it. Win one concession and the possibilities for further concessions were good. ''We need more time. It will take at least five hours to get your men out of prison.''

''It is a fifty-five-minute trip by helicopter.''

Shit! Hyte gritted his teeth. ''That's almost two hours. One to get there, and one to get back. We need time on the ground to load them, and time to get their release activated.''

''Time is what I've given you. Three hours, Lieutenant. And remember, we have one of your statesmen on board. He is a very important man, is he not?''

''Everyone on that plane is important,'' Hyte said, keeping his voice unemotional.

''That is a good thing for you to think. But untrue.''

"Not for me! I'll get back to you when we've made the arrangements with the television crew."

He shut off the mike and called his men to him. Charles Koenig, the head of Kennedy security, stood with Arnel just outside the semi-circle of policemen.

"Harvey, go down to the news people and brief them. Give them the usual routine, that we are negotiating and everything looks hopeful. Then find a reporter we're on good terms with and bring him to the ready room."

After Bennet left, Hyte turned to Junior Atkins. "Has the counter-terrorist team been alerted?"

Atkins nodded. "It's Captain Lacey's squad. They're waiting for the word."

"Get him on the horn." Hyte exhaled. Tom Lacey was the head of the counter-terrorist unit; his team was the best. He turned to the FBI man. "Will we get any help from your people?"

"I thought you didn't want our help. Isn't that why we were the last to be notified?"

"That was done on my authority," Charles Koenig said.

Hyte watched Arnel's gaze shift from Koenig to him. "We'll do the usual," the FBI man said. "We'll screen the passengers after they're released. I'm here strictly for backup and any orders from Washington."

Hyte nodded. Everyone would go through an intense security check to make sure that no terrorist got away by impersonating a passenger.

"Lou," Atkins called, "I've got Captain Lacey."

Taking the phone, Hyte gave the head of the counter-terrorist unit all the details. "I'll need five men dressed in federal prison uniforms to take the plane," he said.

"Four and myself," Thomas Lacey replied.

Hyte had expected that. "Have everyone ready. We'll have to time it close. I'll get back to you when I know more."

"The commissioner," Moran called, handing him the phone.

Hyte's earlier call to the commissioner had been to relay the hijacker's demands. Now Rutledge would want answers to the questions he hadn't been able to ask earlier. "Yes, sir?"

Commissioner Rutledge's voice was fierce. "What are the chances of getting the hostages off the plane?"

Hyte believed Rutledge was a good man. The PC had a nice relationship with the Department—something unusual for a civilian head of the NYPD without any police background.

"I don't know at this time," Hyte told him.

"That's not good enough."

"It's the best we can do. We've got three hours to try and get some of the passengers out."

"What about an extension?"

He wondered if the commissioner thought he was clairvoyant. "I don't know. Their leader says he's following a time schedule. We tried to stall on the prisoner release. He quoted helicopter flying time from Ossining to Kennedy."

"Jesus!"

"Commissioner, there's something really screwy about this one."

"All hijackings are screwy! I've put out a call to Chief McPheerson. He's at one of those damned fund raisers," the commissioner said. "But if you think it advisable, I can come out there."

That was the last thing Hyte wanted. "That's up to you, sir. We've got things under control, but if we have to take the plane, we'll need the go ahead from yourself or the mayor."

"It will be from the mayor. Jerome Rosenthal is on the way there. He'll make the right recommendation to the mayor. What do you think our chances are?"

"This one's hard to judge," Hyte said honestly.

"You don't think you can talk them out?"

Hyte thought back to the hijacker's calm, confident words. "I'm not sure. Nothing about this situation is following the book, and the leader appears to know what he's doing. He's a real pro."

"Do your best, and remember Senator Prestone's value. I'll inform the mayor of your diagnosis."

59

When Hyte hung up, Harvey Bennet was standing next to him. "Did you find a news team for us?" Hyte asked.

"We lucked out," Bennet said. "WTBC sent over Dan Carson and his crew. He's waiting for you downstairs."

"Lou, Chief McPheerson," Atkins called from across the room.

Picking up the phone, Hyte gave the recently appointed chief of department the same information he had given the commissioner. McPheerson told Hyte to do whatever was necessary to keep the hostages alive. "But don't let those terrorist bastards pull your strings!"

Hyte wanted to tell the chief that Mohamad was pulling everyone's strings. Instead, he hung up and turned to Sy Cohen. Cohen was Hyte's backup on long sieges. They worked well together—they had ever since they'd become partners, eleven years before, when they'd spent two and a half years working out of a Precinct Detective Unit. "Take the mike while I'm gone." He moved toward the door. "Arnel," he called over his shoulder. "I need to speak to you, privately."

Arnel stepped closer to Hyte. "What?"

"Outside," Hyte said. In the hall, he turned to Arnel, doing his best to keep his tone level. "I need your help."

"For?"

"The truth. What the hell's going on? These people don't hijack planes *into* America. I keep asking myself why. I'm also wondering how they knew a VIP was on the flight when, according to the Tangier authorities, Prestone didn't anticipate being on that plane until a half hour before flight time. Are you ready to tell me about it?"

Arnel hesitated for a second. "All right. I just got confirmation that Prestone's plane was sabotaged."

Hyte stared into the agent's hooded eyes, knowing that his next question was one he didn't really want an answer to. "Why is everyone so much more concerned about Prestone than the others? Granted, he's an ex-senator. But he's not *that* important."

He saw Arnel blink twice. "The State Department informed us that Prestone was in the Middle East conducting the first stages of a meeting between the PLO and Israel. If he's killed, whatever chance there is for a settlement may die with him.''

Things began to come together. The hijacking was centered around Prestone. "If we let Mohamad think he's getting everything, including the prisoners, what will he do?''

Arnel shrugged. "You had the same training as I did. We both know we can't let him get what he wants. And, even if he thinks he's winning, he'll take everyone out anyway. Mohamad's on a suicide mission. Personally, I think he wants to become a martyr.''

Hyte felt as though he were somewhere else, not in the hallway of the control tower. He worked through Arnel's reply until he found the error in the Fed's logic. "Does he? The rundown you gave me earlier says that he believes he's the best there is. Does the best commit suicide? I don't think so. Mohamad has a big ego. If that's true, would he take this mission if he didn't think there was a way to pull it off? No,'' Hyte said, answering himself. "If he gets away, he becomes a bigger force in the PLO, doesn't he?''

Arnel studied Hyte. He nodded.

"Mohamad isn't after martyrdom, he's after power,'' Hyte said.

"Even if that's so, what good does it do us?''

"We have to make him believe he's got a shot at pulling it off. But he can't think it's too easy.''

"You're playing with Prestone's life,'' the agent said.

"I don't know that I am. If Mohamad wanted Prestone dead, if the whole hijacking was just to kill Prestone, it would have been done out of the country. Mohamad isn't stupid. You made that clear enough. So why would he go to the hassle of sabotaging Prestone's plane when it would have been simpler to blow it out of the sky? No, Mohamad's after something else. It could be a part of his demand that the U.S. pursue an active dialogue with the PLO. Perhaps he's trying for a public statement by our country that we'll withdraw from any involvement with the peace talks, in exchange for Prestone's life.''

Arnel stared silently at him, his face devoid of expression.

But when he shrugged and started away, Hyte sensed he was on the right path.

He found newsman Dan Carson waiting for him in the ready room. Carson was a good-looking man. Six feet two, trim, with sharp eyes and straight brown hair. The reporter was a former NYPD detective turned television journalist. His specialty was crime reporting. Hyte, like most policemen, accepted Carson on the scene. He knew the reporter wouldn't do anything foolish for the sake of a story.

"What's up, Ray?" Carson asked.

"I need your help and cooperation."

"It's yours."

"Do you have a live feed set up or just tape?"

"The transmitting van is out front. Got here about five minutes ago. We can go either way."

Hyte didn't bother to ask how the van had gotten by the airport road blocks. He'd learned that TV people were better at those things than the CIA. "The terrorists have demanded that a camera be set up in the plane and a live feed run to the networks. I want to give it to them, up to a point. That point," he said, his finger indicating the media communications area in the far corner of the ready room.

"No problem," Carson said. "And if it becomes necessary to broadcast, we can use a time delay when appropriate."

"Do you have the equipment with you?"

"All that we'll need."

"I'll be going in with you," Hyte told him.

Carson's eyebrows flicked upward. "That could be risky. You don't know your way around the equipment."

"I'm a fast learner."

Carson smiled. "You haven't changed since you made sergeant. Okay, give me fifteen minutes to get it all worked out."

"You'll have to pool everything with the rest of the media or they'll be screaming for my scalp."

Carson smiled again. "That goes without saying. But I won't have to pool our follow-up interview, will I?"

Hyte didn't have to answer, it was an already accepted fact. "Set up your equipment," Hyte instructed.

While Carson, with his cameraman and his sound man, began to set up, the rest of Hyte's team arrived in the ready room. Cohen told him there had been no communications while he was gone.

Hyte gathered the men in a semicircle, and then outlined his talk with Arnel. "Because of the Prestone aspect of this situation, we'll have to break the rules we've been taught," he told them. "We will appear to give the terrorists what they want, but not too easily. If they don't have to fight for each concession, they'll know something's wrong."

He went to the mike. "Rashid Mohamad?"

Silence for a minute, then the almost too genteel, "Lieutenant Hyte?"

"The television crew is almost ready."

"There will be no crew. Only a camera and a microphone. It will be set up and left. We will guarantee the news people safe passage in and out. If the camera cannot be controlled from remote, then it shall be left on at all times. Is that understood?"

Hyte cursed under his breath. What the hell was Mohamad doing? "I understand. How many men will be permitted to come on board?"

"Two. The same restrictions. No clothing. Just underwear."

"We'll also be sending a field telephone. It will give us better communication."

"Don't you mean more private communication? No telephone." Mohamad paused, then, "Yes, perhaps a telephone would be helpful. I can talk to you and watch my hostages. Now, what of our brothers?"

"The helicopter is on its way to pick them up."

"Do not play games with us. The money?"

"Being counted."

"Very good. Our amnesty?"

"Working on it."

"You may send out the cameramen."

Hyte tensed. *Now!* It was the moment he had been waiting for. The first yes given by the hijacker. His hands curved around the edge of the desk in anticipation. "Not yet. We've been dealing in good faith. We want something in return."

Mohamad laughed. "You are in no position to ask for anything."

Hyte persisted, his voice level. "A show of good faith. Give us some hostages to prove to us that the television people will be given free passage."

Hyte closed his eyes. He heard the expectant breathing of his men behind him. The radio remained silent for several seconds, until: "Good faith? You sit there and judge us, do you? You look at this airplane and say to your-selves—'There is a mad animal inside that tube of metal who is trying to hurt us. A man who cares nothing for life.' "

"Oh shit," someone whispered behind Hyte. He couldn't identify the speaker.

"But you are wrong. Our very actions this night are be-cause we care for life. Our lives, our families' lives, and our people's lives. You sit in judgment of us from your self-righteous heights. Have you ever been thrown off your land? Have you ever been denied your home? Have Zionist killer squads murdered your families and deprived your children of their birthrights? No. So don't you presume to judge us until you have lived in the way we have been forced to—moving from country to country, living in filthy refugee camps. And don't think for a moment that we will stop until the Zionists who have stolen our lands and homes have been removed from Palestine. Good faith? What in Allah's name is that?"

Hyte stared at the plane, wishing he could see through the hull. He needed to watch the man's face as he spoke. Was the hijacker's rhetoric meant to throw him off? Hyte didn't believe a word of Mohamad's speech. True, there had been passion in the terrorist's voice, but the words had been too mechanical.

"PR," he mumbled. Mohamad had a mission. Part of his mission would be to make the world think that the Pal-estinians we persecuted and terrorized victims.

"It's decency we're talking about, Mohamad. Good faith is decency," Hyte said. "It's a willingness to show that you're capable of being more than those whom you seek to destroy."

"Very good," Mohamad said. "You are a worthy adversary. Very well. We will show the world that Palestinians have . . . 'good faith.' We will release *all* the people being held in the coach section."

Hyte sucked in a startled breath. Behind him, Junior Atkins said, "Wow." The release of the coach passengers was a good sign, but his relief at having won some hostages free was tempered by the ease of the victory.

Something's wrong, Hyte thought, nothing comes this easily. "I have a time schedule," Mohamad had said. Hyte wondered if the coach passengers would interfere with that. Yes, he told himself. That was one explanation for their release. The other was that they knew they had J. Milton Prestone.

"We'll have a bus for the passengers brought to the plane. It will be empty except for the driver and the two cameramen. The interior lights will be on," Hyte explained. "A debarking ramp will be attached and the workers will leave. You can open the door and watch them."

"So your snipers can pick us off?"

"No snipers. Good faith, Mohamad. Good faith," Hyte reminded him. That, and the fact that if a sniper were to shoot, every passenger would be at risk.

"Agreed," Mohamad said.

Hyte thought he heard a low chuckle. "Ten minutes," Hyte said and shut off the microphone.

While Jonah and Anita Graham sat in their first-class cabin under the watchful eyes of the terrorists, their daughter Emma paced the confines of the Trans Air VIP lounge. Her long, tapered legs moved her smoothly. Her shoulders, squared back, gave the impression of height. Her dark hair was stylishly short and businesslike. Her eyes, hard and direct when necessary, were those that romantics describe as liquid brown.

She had strong features. Her nose was a trifle crooked but suited her face. Her mouth was generous. Her teeth were that unusual shade of almost pure white that models dream of. Her chin was rounded—not sharply—accenting the high, well-defined cheekbones of her one-quarter Russian ancestry. In all, Emma Graham's twenty-eight-year-old face was handsome. Not model pretty, but lovely to look at just the same. Her body, sheathed in a mauve Chanel business suit, was slim and well proportioned.

She went to the window and looked down at the main waiting area. The terminal was mostly empty; Trans Air had shuttled to LaGuardia the passengers who had been waiting for flights when the airport was closed down. Behind her, thirty or so people milled about. For the most part, their faces reflected shock. Some looked angry, others lost or anxious, as they waited for some word about a relative or friend on board Flight 88.

The door to the lounge opened. Emma turned. The newcomer, a man, walked in with confidently powerful strides. Her breath escaped in a relieved sigh. He'd gotten her message.

"Jerome," she called.

Jerome Rosenthal, formerly a Manhattan district attorney and currently the mayor's assistant on Community Relations, turned to look for the woman who had called his name.

Emma went to him. They embraced as friends who have survived a love affair. He held her to him for a comforting minute.

She looked into his eyes. Her stare was direct. "What's happening?"

"The hostage negotiation team is talking with the hijackers. I haven't been to the control tower yet. The mayor asked me to speak with the people waiting here first."

"My parents," she whispered.

"They've got the negotiating team working on it," he repeated. "They're good."

66

"What's happening?" she asked. "Are they PLO?"

"That's the consensus."

Emma fixed her gaze on the toes of her beige pumps. The Grahams were Jewish.

"Try to relax," he said, wrapping his arm protectively about her shoulders.

Emma choked back a fear-induced giggle. Relax? But his voice did give her a modicum of comfort.

She looked up at him. "Can you take me to where they're negotiating? The control tower?"

"They won't let you in. I'm on my way there now, though, and I'll keep you posted."

"Thank you." Emma looked at her watch. It was ten past twelve, June twentieth. "Happy anniversary," she whispered to her parents.

Eight

A small dictating machine, camouflaged as a cigarette case, lay in the breast pocket of Jonah Graham's shirt. Strangely, he'd felt no fear since the initial rush of horror at the death of the flight engineer. He was calm now.

When the hijacking began, he had been dictating notes about his trip, using the prototype recorder. It was a voice-activated dictaphone recorder using a new type of micro-cassette. It weighed five ounces, with a special four-hour, self-reversing tape, and had a battery life of thirty hours. Its built-in microphone could pick up words at twenty feet.

The recording unit's secondary appeal was its disguise as a leather-covered case. The design was integral to its value. Executives could use it during meetings and no one would know they were being recorded.

Now the hijacking would be the recorder's biggest test. Jonah wondered, idly, if it would be of any help to the authorities.

"Emma will be worried," Anita said.

"I know. But she's strong."

"I'm afraid."

Jonah Graham drew her tighter. He had nothing to say to comfort her. He looked around the compartment. Senator Prestone was in the first row. His eyes were glazed with hatred, staring at the terrorist named Khamil.

The rest of the passengers were silent, too. Most just

stared vacantly. Across the aisle from Jonah was the young, good-looking woman and her older husband.

When Mohamad had taken their passports, he'd called out everyone's name in a loud voice. The couple's name was Mofferty. Jonah saw they were badly frightened.

Behind him were the two stewardesses. After the plane had landed, and everything had been secured, the hijackers had moved the bound women to the fourth row of seats and then released their hands. Across from them was the copilot. The plane's captain was sitting on the floor near the lavatories. Jonah admitted the man's calm. He did not miss the determination in Haller's eyes.

A movement in the front drew Graham's attention. Mohamad stepped out of the cockpit. His face showed nothing.

"Everything is going as we planned," the terrorist said. "I hope that in three hours you will all be released." There was a low click of the recorder when Mohamad stopped and another when he spoke again.

"In a few minutes, two men will come onto the plane. They will set up a TV camera and leave. I am sure that one, if not both, will be policemen. If any of you attempt to do anything, they will be killed, as will whoever moves."

Click went Jonah Graham's recorder. Click went Jonah Graham's mind as a brief glimmer of relief waxed. It waned with Mohamad's next words.

"All the coach-class passengers will be released. They are unnecessary and could create problems. You are sufficient. I will be going to the rear until the camera and men arrive. As I do, I will inspect each of your seatbelts. Keep your hands on the top of your heads. Make no move whatsoever."

"Mohamad," called William Haller. Mohamad turned to look at him. "Let the girl leave with the others."

Although Jonah could not see Mohamad's face, he heard the snarl in the man's voice. "You should have left her in the rear. She stays." And once again, click went Jonah Graham's recorder.

* * *

While the bus was being brought over to the control tower, Hyte briefed Jerome Rosenthal. Hyte liked Rosenthal. They had worked well together on several cases when Rosenthal had been an assistant D.A.

"Don't take any chances," Rosenthal told him. "You're more valuable here than you will be stuck in the plane."

"No chances, Jerry. But I have to see the situation inside. I need to gauge the hostages' conditions."

"Bullshit. The camera will do that for you."

Hyte smiled. His eyes reflected no mirth. "I have to look Mohamad in the eye. But he'll let us go. It's a part of his overall plan. This is a well-set up, well-rehearsed hijacking. We're dealing with pros. They're cool and calm and they know they have the initial advantage. We need to get some of our own leverage."

"If we can," the mayor's assistant said. "There's a couple on board. Jonah and Anita Graham. He's got gray hair, a mole on his cheek on line with his earlobe. Left cheek. Anita is gray, too, short hair, pretty. They're both in their early sixties. Let me know how they are."

"I will."

"What shall I tell the mayor?"

"We're doing the best we can."

"He already knows that. He wants more."

"Don't we all?" Hyte asked.

"At least the little girl will be released. That could have become as sticky as Prestone."

Hyte didn't let his surprise show. "There are no children listed on the passenger manifest."

"No one told you?" When Hyte shook his head, Rosenthal said, "There's a seven-year-old, traveling alone. Her parents are waiting in the VIP lounge."

Hyte drew in a deep breath. "You're sure she's in coach?"

Rosenthal nodded. "That's what her parents said."

"I'll watch out for her," Hyte promised.

"Ray, this is Billy Meadows, my cameraman. Follow his lead," Carson said. "He'll do all the work. Make sure the bus goes slowly. Billy will be feeding cable out the door."

"Okay, Dan, thanks," Hyte said, his mind already working on the next step. He lifted his walkie-talkie, thumbed the sending switch. "Sy?"

"Here."

"Call Mohamad. Tell him we're on our way." He started into the bus. The interior lights were on. The driver was Junior Atkins, the hostage team's sharpshooter. In the space between the driver's seat and the hull of the bus was a Parker-Hale M-82 rifle.

The walkie-talkie crackled. "No response," Cohen said just as the rear passenger door opened. A man stepped into the light. He held a pistol on another.

"They're ready," Hyte said, motioning the driver ahead.

Mohamad's refusal to reply to Cohen's call was just another of the terrorist's counter maneuvers, Hyte knew. Mohamad was creating varying scenarios in an attempt to confuse Hyte and his team. By keeping radio contact to a minimum he was impeding a negotiator's most important tool—the ability to talk to the hijacker. Obviously, Hyte decided, Mohamad had studied the same books as he. Yet, the knowledge that the terrorist was attempting to throw off the standard negotiating maneuvers was a factor that Hyte believed he might be able to use against Mohamad.

Junior Atkins drove cautiously toward the plane. Hyte knew that the hijacker expected Hyte, or someone like him. An irrational spark of admiration rose. He quenched it with a dose of reality. The man was good, but he was a killer. There could be no admiration.

Hyte thought about the little girl in the plane. A seven-year-old alone would be terrified. Then he thought about his daughter, Carrie, safe in bed.

When the bus stopped fifty feet short of the plane, Hyte turned to Atkins. "Your job is to cover the passengers. Nothing else. Understood?"

Atkins nodded. The lines at the corners of his eyes told of his tension.

Hyte and Billy Meadows stepped down from the bus. In full view of the hijacker who was standing on the upper step of the ramp, Hyte and the cameraman stripped.

71

Hyte wore blue briefs. The cameraman wore white. They appeared luminous against the cameraman's deep brown skin. Hyte refused to acknowledge his near nakedness. It was a vulnerability he was sure the hijackers were counting on. A man almost naked could be a man defenseless.

Hyte motioned to Meadows, who picked up the camera and pointed it toward the doorway. Hyte lifted the spools of cable and a large toolbox and started toward the plane. They moved to a position at the foot of the ramp.

The terrorist looked down at them. When he was satisfied, he motioned to the passenger beside him. The man started down the steps. Behind him the next hostage emerged, and then the next. They moved with jerky, hesitant steps.

While the cameraman filmed, Hyte studied each face. Fright was paramount; relief had not yet arrived. When the first passenger's foot reached the ground, he sighed.

"Move to the bus. Quickly!" Hyte ordered.

Behind him the next hostage followed more swiftly.

Hyte counted each coach passenger and crew member. Seventy-nine. The number was wrong. There were eighty passengers and five crew listed as part of the coach section. Were there more terrorists than they had thought, or more dead passengers? And the girl? Where was she? Hyte looked up. Only the gunman was in the opening. The last person off the ramp was almost abreast of him. It was a stewardess. Hyte stopped her.

"The little girl?" he asked.

Hyte watched the way her amber eyes darted fearfully back toward the plane. "She's in first class."

"The hijackers took her?"

The woman shook her head. "No, the captain put her there when he saw she was alone." She drew in a shallow breath. "He thought he was doing something nice."

"Are there any more?" Hyte asked.

She nodded. "One man was hurt," she whispered, then walked toward the bus. Hyte tapped Meadows on the shoulder and they started to the ramp.

"Wait!" the gunman commanded.

Hyte and Meadows froze. Three figures emerged from the doorway. Two men carried a third. He appeared semi-conscious.

It took two minutes to maneuver him down the stairs.

"Shot?" Hyte asked, concerned by the man's bloodied face.

The man on the left shook his head. "He tried to rush one of them. They hit him with a gun."

The speaker was a young man. A student, Hyte guessed, of Middle Eastern origin. "Get him to the bus."

Hyte recalculated. The three brought the total to eighty-two. The girl would have been the eighty-third. That placed two of the terrorists as coach passengers. There would be two more terrorists from first class. All told, fourteen hostages remained.

The gunman motioned for Hyte and Meadows to come up. Hyte held the cameraman back. He waited until the last three men were on the bus.

"Okay, Billy. Shut off the camera and let's keep it cool."

Meadows started up the steps. Hyte followed five feet behind with the cable in one hand and the toolbox in the other. Inside the toolbox was the portable field telephone. The gunman backed into the plane.

Hyte saw plastique spread around the door. An electronic detonator was set in the first beige oblong. He could feel the pulsing of his blood through the artery in his neck. Within the airplane, he heard a concert of sound: the low whoosh of the ventilation system, the hesitant whisper of Billy Meadows's breathing.

Two men stood on guard before him. One held an Uzi. The other, a bearded man, held a Mac-10. More squares of plastique were attached to two emergency window exits. Well planned, well prepared, Hyte told himself again.

The bearded man moved toward them. "Place your equipment on the floor and step back five feet. Keep your hands on the top of your heads. Do not move after that."

It was Mohamad's voice, but the timbre seemed different in person. Hyte stared at the terrorist, memorizing his face. The plane was stifling.

Mohamad bent over the mini-cam and inspected it carefully before going to the cable coils and separating them. Then he opened the toolbox.

Mohamad took out the field telephone, turned it over, and checked it carefully before putting it down. He took all of the tools out and inspected each one. Then he ran his fingers along the toolbox's interior. Satisfied, he stood and faced the two men.

"You may lower your hands. Bring the equipment forward. Suli," he called over Hyte's shoulder, "remain at the door. They will not try to shoot you."

Meadows picked up the camera. Hyte put everything back into the toolbox and followed Mohamad and Meadows forward, letting out cable as he moved. One of the gunmen followed.

Hyte's nerves hummed. He pictured the muzzle of the Uzi centered on his back. He knew how large an exit hole would be opened in his chest if the man fired.

He noted two more sets of plastique charges rigged in the midsection of the plane, and guessed that the cargo doors were wired as well.

Too damned thorough! Again came a reluctant spark of admiration. This time he accepted the feeling for what it was—admiration—not for the man, but the method.

He looked at the cameraman's back. Meadows was sweating as profusely as he. But Meadows moved steadily forward.

When they entered first class, the passengers turned almost in unison to look at them. Hyte took inventory: His calculations had been right. There were the nine first-class passengers plus the crew and the little girl. He recognized the Grahams from Rosenthal's description. He glanced at the little girl. She was staring vacantly, her mouth open and slack, showing all the signs of psychological shock.

Mohamad held his palm forward. "That will be far enough. Hook up the cameras so it will pick up everything in front of it."

"Where?" Meadows asked.

"Find a place," Mohamad snapped. "Do it quickly."

"Can we hang it from one of those?" Hyte asked Meadows, pointing to the overhead storage compartments.

Meadows studied it for a moment. "It'll work. But I need something to hang it with."

"A belt?" Hyte suggested.

"Two," Meadows replied.

Hyte looked at Mohamad.

"There are canvas straps in the galley," said one of the stewardesses. Hyte estimated her age to be in the late thirties. She was scared, but holding up well. Her training had been very good.

"Get it," Mohamad ordered her.

Hyte glanced at Mohamad, wondering if the terrorist was losing his calm. There were several valid reasons for his thought. Mohamad was facing new and unknown people. He had also given up a lot of hostages.

While they waited for the stewardess, Hyte bent over the toolbox.

"Don't," Mohamad ordered in a calm voice.

Hyte straightened. He looked at the terrorist leader. "The field phone?"

Mohamad stared at him for several seconds. His eyes seemed to bore into Hyte. "Pass it down."

Jonah Graham caught Hyte's eye. The older man's right hand tapped lightly on the cigarette case in his shirt pocket. It seemed to Hyte that Graham was trying to give him a message. Unable to decipher it, he handed Graham the phone just as the stewardess returned with two canvas straps.

"To use the phone—"

Mohamad cut Hyte off abruptly. "We use them all the time. We are neither stupid nor ill-equipped. Get on with your work."

Hyte looked up at Meadows. He had slipped the straps into the carrier. Hyte took a hole punch and two half-inch bolts from the toolbox and handed a wrench to the cameraman.

After a minute and a half's work, Meadows motioned with his head for Hyte to slip the camera into its new harness.

"You can let it go," Meadows said.

Hyte released his hold. The camera swiveled left, stopped, swiveled right—a dying horizontal pendulum swing. The front hung slightly lower than the back. Meadows moved around it. Then the cameraman levered himself up to look through the viewfinder.

"Hold the front up about a half inch," he told Hyte as he undid the bolt.

While Hyte cantilevered the camera, Meadows made another hole and drew the strap up. After he bolted it, he motioned for Hyte to release the camera.

"There is a microphone?" Mohamad asked.

"It's built into the unit."

"What else must you do?"

"Rig the wire and test the camera."

"Get it done," Mohamad ordered.

Hyte took a large roll of two-inch duct tape. He and Meadows began to tape the wire to the carpet, following the center of the aisle. As they worked their way to the rear, Hyte again studied the layout of the plane. He recounted the packets of plastique and noted the style of the detonators.

It wasn't going to be easy if they had to storm the plane.

At last they were at the rear door. They stood, their knees covered with dirt. "Let's check it out," Meadows said to Hyte.

They returned to first class. "I'm turning the camera on," Hyte told Mohamad. "We need verification that it's working."

Mohamad picked up the field phone and turned his back on Hyte. The terrorist spoke in a low voice. He turned back suddenly, staring at Hyte and the television technician.

"Who are you?" Mohamad said into the phone.

Hyte visualized Cohen talking in level tones, introducing himself. There would be no emotion from Cohen. No tension. He saw Mohamad relax slightly.

"Very well. Is there a picture?" Mohamad was silent for a moment. Then he hung up. "It is working."

Meadows sighed. He stepped back.

Hyte looked around again. His gaze paused briefly on Senator Prestone. The man didn't look good.

"You may go," Mohamad said. It wasn't a request. "And remember, we keep our promises. All of them."

Hyte motioned for Meadows to start out, but before Hyte could leave, Mohamad said, "Wait!"

Hyte stood absolutely still, his eyes locked on the terrorist.

"I want you," Mohamad said, his eyes narrowing on Hyte, "to tell Lieutenant Hyte that I gave him the coach passengers. That I am dealing in good faith, and I will accept nothing less! And, I anticipate that all of my requests will be met. Is that understood?"

"I'm just a tech," Hyte said, giving his voice a nervous edge. "Why don't you call him yourself?" Hyte pointed to the field phone.

Mohamad smiled. "The man I spoke with a moment ago said Hyte was . . . unavailable. If I must use an intermediary, it shall be you. However, I would wager that by the time you return to the control tower, Lieutenant Hyte will be there as well. Don't you agree?"

He knows! Stick to the rules, Hyte reminded himself. Act out Mohamad's game. To admit who he was would be to play into the man's hands. "I'll tell him. May we leave now?"

Mohamad lifted his machine pistol, pointed it at Hyte, and nodded.

Nine

"That was a little too close," Sy Cohen said. "I thought he was going to keep you on board."

Hyte waved off Cohen's words. "He just wanted me to know he wasn't fooled by my act. He didn't want a professional as a hostage. That would be a major risk on his part." Hyte looked around the ready room. The television equipment was set up on the far wall. A thirteen-inch RCA monitor sat on a table. A Sony one-inch reel-to-reel video tape machine was positioned next to the monitor; a separate audio control board was hooked up to the tape machine. A gaunt television technician hovered over the equipment. Hyte had decided to tape everything.

The camera that he and Billy Meadows had placed in the plane was the type of mini-cam used for undercover investigative coverage. It featured a wide angle lens and a highly sensitive miniature microphone that could pick up the sound of a pin hitting the floor. Its picture tube was designed for low-light situations.

A second monitor resided on Hyte's desk, giving him a complete view of the first-class cabin. A separate speaker was hooked up to the sound control board, its volume set high enough so that any sound inside the plane would be heard.

At present, Mohamad stood against the front bulkhead. A minute before, he had been pacing restlessly. Another terrorist stood off to the side. He was about three feet from

Captain Haller, who was sitting on the floor in front of the lavatories, hands tied behind him. The other two terrorists were not on camera. Hyte guessed they were in first class, but behind the mini-cam.

On Hyte's desk was a diagram of the interior of the plane. He'd penciled in the names and locations of the hostages by using the passenger manifest and visual identification.

Hyte looked at the third row. Jonah Graham was holding his wife's hand. Across the aisle were the Moffertys. Behind the Moffertys lay the unconscious form of the copilot. The stewardesses were exactly where Hyte had seen them last, behind the Grahams.

The little girl was still behind the stewardesses, huddled against the side of the plane, under a blanket.

Hyte had spoken with Captain Lacey of the counter-terrorist squad and had given him the locations of the hostages, explosives, and detonators.

Lacey had been worried about the plastique. "We'll have to have the door opened for us—from the inside," he'd said. "Or we'll have to blow a hole in the fuselage."

Hyte looked at his watch. There were two hours left.

"Why didn't they ask for a television set?" Dan Carson said. "Without a set, how can they know if we're complying with their demands?" Carson looked from Hyte to Cohen, and then to Arnel.

Sy Cohen shrugged. Arnel made no movement other than to raise his eyelids a fraction of an inch higher.

Hyte had been working himself through the same question, worrying at it with every spare second he had. Now he took the time to think about the hijackers' motives. Their main goal had to do with Prestone. Their other objectives were the five convicted terrorists and the money. He rubbed his eyelids. The stinging did not lessen. He was thinking in circles and knew it.

Something was wrong. What?

Out of the maelstrom of his thoughts, a vagueness solidified. One second he had nothing; the next, the answer was his. He lifted his head, opened his eyes. Oh, they were smart! They had asked for a live feed, but knew it would end up as a looped circuit. If they had a television set, the only picture they would see would be the one of what they were doing. They were self-contained. They had no contact with the outside world. Their demand for public acknowledgment meant nothing, for it would be all too easy to simulate a newscast for them. Even their demand for amnesty was only an expected gesture—it was an accepted part of a hijacking.

"We don't have to worry about the political demands, or about the amnesty. Mohamad's plan is all nerve and egotism. The reason he hijacked the plane to New York, instead of staying in the Middle East, is that he wants to get his allies out of our prison, take our money, and use Prestone to get us to withdraw from any involvement in the peace talks between the moderate faction of the PLO and Israel. To do all of that, he has to negotiate directly with us, not through a foreign government," Hyte said.

"Can you risk that?" Rosenthal asked.

Hyte nodded. "That's why they didn't ask for a television set. But they wanted the camera because they know that whatever happens will eventually get on the tube. Tomorrow, the next day, whenever. It's a big story—it's living history. The first time a hijacking has been seen from the inside. It'll get out. That's what they're counting on."

"Possibly," Arnel admitted. There was still no emotion on his face.

Harvey Bennet entered the ready room and went over to Hyte. "The press wants you to talk to them."

Hyte looked at Rosenthal. "You go."

"They've had enough of me. It's your turn, Ray."

Hyte glanced over his shoulder at the plane. He looked at the monitor. Nothing had changed. "Come with me anyway," he told Rosenthal. Both men went outside.

Only Emma Graham and three others remained in the VIP lounge. Two men and a woman. The rest had gone to the customs waiting area to greet their loved ones.

When the announcement came that the coach passengers

80

were being released, a couple standing next to her began crying. Earlier, she had heard them telling an airline official that their adopted daughter was on the flight. It was the first time she had left her country.

Emma stared at the television set and studied the man standing next to Jerome Rosenthal. He was about the same six-foot height as Jerome, and she guessed he was in his late thirties or early forties. He had a prominent cleft in the center of his chin. His face was angular and etched with strength. He looked capable, this Lieutenant Hyte. He had a good voice—rich. He spoke intelligently. It was obvious that he was well educated.

He gave Emma Graham a little more confidence. But she was still afraid for her parents. Turning, she went to the Trans Air ground attendant.

"How far is the control tower from here?"

He told her where it was. "They won't let you in."

"We'll see about that," she said.

Emma walked toward the door. Before she reached it, the couple who had been so relieved that their newly adopted daughter was being freed, returned. The woman's face was tear streaked. Her husband held her shoulders tightly. Following behind was an airline official who tried to calm them.

"She'll be all right. Really, she will," the man said.

The distraught father whirled on the speaker. "What the hell was she doing in first class! She was supposed to be in the coach section! We paid for a coach class ticket, not first class!"

The airline official shook his head. "I don't know."

Seeing the panic on their faces, Emma knew that she couldn't stay in the lounge any longer. She had to get into the control tower, to be near her parents.

Emma forced away her debilitating fears in an effort to think more clearly. There had to be a way! Then, she remembered.

In a Gucci card holder in her purse, pushed out of her mind by her worry for her parents, was an outdated identification card showing her to be a member of the mayor's staff. It had been true, once. Two years ago, she had been a co-chairperson of the Mayor's Coalition for Urban Business Revitalization. A fancy term for bringing businesses back to the slums. Emma was sure that the official-looking card would, at a quick glance and with the right phrasing from her, gain her admittance to the ready room. It had to!

"That's all I can say for now. But I'll reiterate that the situation is hopeful. Except for the one shooting, the hijackers have made no other threats."

"Lieutenant," shouted a reporter in the back of the crowd. "What about the girl? Why wasn't she released?"

Hyte cut him off. "No more questions for now. You will be kept abreast of the situation."

Hyte turned, taking Rosenthal with him. From the side of the pack of reporters, a woman broke free. "Jerome!" she called.

Rosenthal tensed. "How the hell . . ."

Hyte looked at the woman. She was tall, graceful, and attractive: Her proud bearing told Hyte that she was used to getting her own way. The determination in her brown eyes was accented by the precise cut of her clothing.

When Hyte and Rosenthal paused, the reporters surged forward like a defensive line on a quarterback blitz. Rosenthal reached out and propelled the woman ahead of them. Once inside the building, Rosenthal stopped.

"I asked you not to come here."

"I couldn't stay in the lounge," she said, her shoulders squared, eyes challenging Rosenthal and then Hyte.

Rosenthal exhaled sharply. "Ray, this is Emma Graham."

Hyte allowed none of his surprise to show. "Miss Graham," he said.

"How are my parents?" she asked.

"They seem to be doing all right."

"How can anyone be doing all right in that plane?"

"They have no choice."

"I want to see what's going on."

"Emma—"

Hyte cut Rosenthal off. "Miss Graham, I wish that was possible, but it isn't. We're crowded, and you would be a—"

"Distraction?" she challenged.

Studying her, he sensed deep-rooted strength. He liked what he saw. "No. You'd be an inhibition."

"An inhibition? You mean that you don't know any of the passengers personally, so you're emotionally removed from them if you have to take the sort of action that puts them in danger?"

Smart! "Yes."

"Jesus, Ray," Rosenthal said.

"It's all right, Jerome," Emma said. "I prefer the lieutenant's honesty to half-truths and reassurances."

Very smart.

"What are my parents' chances?"

"I won't guess." Hyte held his hands before him, palms up. "If everything continues the way it has—good."

"Is that a big 'if'?"

"Uncertainty is always a factor in hostage situations."

"Thank you, Lieutenant. I appreciate your frankness." Her eyes turned soft. Her tongue flicked out to moisten her lips.

Hyte was fascinated by the movement.

"Get them out, Lieutenant. Please," Emma Graham said.

"We're all doing our best," he told her as the security office door opened and Sy Cohen poked his head out.

"Ray, he wants you."

Hyte had no doubt about who the "he" was. He turned to Rosenthal. "Jerry, she can't go back out there alone. Have one of the uniformed men take her to the terminal."

"Is there someplace here where I can wait?" she asked. "I need to be near them, and I won't be a bother."

Hyte glanced at Rosenthal. The mayor's special assistant nodded once. "There's an employee lunchroom on the second floor," Hyte said. "Take her there." He turned to Emma. "The waiting won't be easy."

Hyte went to the door, stopped, and then glanced back at the handsome woman. "Miss Graham."

"Yes?"

"When I was in the plane, your father kept tapping his chest. Could it mean something? Was it some sort of signal or message?"

Her features reflected puzzlement. "Not that I know of."

"I just wanted to check. Thank you."

Inside the ready room, Hyte picked up the phone. "I'm here, Mohamad," he said into the mouthpiece of the field phone. He watched the hijacker on the monitor.

Mohamad's head snapped up. He stared at the camera. "Do you see me?"

"I see you." Hyte didn't like the hijacker's tone. "It is hot in this plane. We are beginning to wonder if you are playing games with us. Where is our money?"

"Being counted. Five million dollars takes time."

"Lying takes up time also. Are you lying to us, Lieutenant? I think you are."

"To what purpose? Your hostages are more valuable than the money."

Mohamad aimed his black machine pistol at the former senator. "He is. Yes. And this one, too," he added, pointing the weapon at the Portuguese financier. "Aren't you?"

Everyone in the command post watched the scene on the monitor. Cristobal Helenez held the hijacker's gaze. Slowly, he nodded.

Then the terrorist looked at the camera. "This night will be remembered for a long time, by your people and mine. The world will see that we are not afraid to do whatever is necessary in our battle to regain our homeland. Where are our brothers?"

The question, coming so suddenly on the heels of Mohamad's harangue, caught Hyte off guard. "On their way."

"They should have been here already."

"We discussed that. It takes time." Hyte looked at the wall clock. There was an hour and twenty minutes left. He found it hard to believe that only a few minutes had passed since he'd left to talk to the press.

84

"The trip takes two and a half hours including your extra unnecessary time. Do you think us fools? Where are they?"

Hyte turned to Cohen. "Give me an estimate."

Arnel spoke first, glancing at the notepad in his hand. "According to your time schedule, your mythical helicopter has just passed Tarrytown."

Hyte uncovered the mouthpiece. "The helicopter is approaching. It will be here in accordance with your time schedule."

"Our patience is running out," Mohamad hung up the field phone.

The sound of metal striking metal came through the TV camera's speaker not unlike a gunshot. Hyte turned to Atkins. "Tell Captain Lacey that he'll have to leave in fifty minutes, if not sooner."

Joseph Moran came in from the back door and went over to Hyte. "Lieutenant, the reporters want to interview the passengers."

Hyte didn't think it would matter. And it would take some of the pressure away from the command post. "I don't see a problem. Arnel?"

The FBI agent went to a phone. He dialed and spoke in a low voice. When he hung up, he nodded. "One news team. Pooled tape feed to the others. The interview is to be held in the customs area."

As Moran went outside to relay the information to Bennet and the reporters, Hyte stopped him. "What about the injured man?"

"He's okay, Lou. A mild concussion. The doctor patched him up and he's resting in one of the customs offices."

Hyte looked at the monitor. Mohamad was parading back and forth in front of the passengers. Hyte knew that Mohamad's movements were calculated to bring fear to the hostages. Every few moments Mohamad would stop, scan the hostages' faces, and then point the machine pistol at one of them.

Presently, Mohamad turned from the stewardess he was threatening, and went over to Michael Barnes. He aimed the pistol at the redheaded hostage.

Hyte studied the terrorist's moves. He felt that Mohamad would do whatever was necessary to pull off his mission. Hyte also believed that if Mohamad did not get what he wanted, the terrorist would kill the hostages. In fact, Hyte thought, if it came to killing them, part of the terrorist's plan would succeed. For with the deaths of the hostages, would come Senator Prestone's death. By killing Prestone, he would temporarily interrupt the peace talks, if not completely sabotage them.

But there was more involved in this situation than just the deaths of the hostages. What more, exactly?

He was certain there would be no extensions in this negotiation, and, therefore, no room for error. Everything would have to be timed down to the last possible second.

He felt something trying to rise into his consciousness. Intuitively, he knew it was an answer to the puzzle, a clue to what was really going to happen.

He pursued the evasive tendril of thought, but it remained elusive. He stopped himself before he became mired in frustration.

He watched the hostages, felt their fear.

It will come, he told himself. It has to!

Ten

Jerome Rosenthal left Emma Graham in a small lunchroom. An old black and white television was on a wire stand in one corner. There were three white Formica tables. Four chairs surrounded each. A variety of vending machines lined one wall.

She turned on the TV, seated herself at one of the tables, and watched the black and white pictures for half an hour. All the stations were covering the hijacking.

Interviews with the released hostages were aired. She listened intently for any mention of her parents. But the only reference to the remaining hostages was the speculation of the fate of the adopted seven-year-old girl.

Then another interview came on. The reporter was standing next to a young man of Middle Eastern origin, who introduced himself as Barum Kaliel.

Emma watched the interview carefully. It helped to keep her dark fears at bay.

"You did not see the crew member shot?" the reporter asked.

"No. We were all in the back."

Emma listened to the peculiar way in which the man emphasized certain words and softened others. His accent was Semitic.

"What about the man who attacked the hijacker?"

"He was a fool. He could have gotten us all killed. I tried to reason with the hijacker," Kaliel said. "I know their mentality, for I am from that part of the world. But he wouldn't listen to me."

"What did you say to him?" the reporter asked.

The camera went in for a closeup of the student's face. Emma saw that his skin wasn't as smooth as she'd first thought. His cheeks were pitted, his lips full.

"I told him that he had no quarrel with us. That we were like him. We understood his cause. His fight was against the governments and the capitalists who run those governments. He should release us. After all, he was holding the rich capitalists up front, wasn't he?"

"You cold-blooded bastard!" Emma said.

"The money's on the way. Fifteen minutes," Rosenthal said, hanging up a phone. "The major has spoken with General Emmett at Maguire Air Force Base. Two fully armed F-16s are on standby."

Hyte slammed the desk with an open hand. "It's all so fucking easy when it's done on the phone." He shook his head in an attempt to clear his rage. He had fourteen lives to save; the mayor was worrying about money. No, that wasn't accurate. The orders about the money came from the federal government. The mayor had no choice about that.

"You must get the passengers out before the plane takes off. When it's airborne, they'll intercept it. If the terrorists won't land, the jets will shoot it down," Arnel said.

Hyte pointed to the monitor with a finger that trembled with suppressed rage. "They'll never let all the passengers go. They'll let some out, but Prestone won't be among them. They know you won't shoot the plane down with him on board."

"Lieutenant," Rosenthal said formally, "if you can't get the hostages free by talking them out, the mayor will order an assault on the plane." The words rolled easily off the mayoral aide's tongue. He was presenting a fact. Everyone in the room knew it whether they liked it or not.

"Fuck you," Hyte said in an all too calm voice, "and fuck the mayor."

Mohamad's voice burst from the speakers. The field phone rang. "Where are our brothers?"

The anger of moments ago helped turn Hyte's mind cold and calm. He picked up the field phone. Easy, he cautioned himself before speaking. "They're almost here."

"We are tired of waiting. You are all liars. You are all taking orders from the Zionist pigs. But there is a price to pay. Tonight you will pay that price."

Hyte decided on a calm rejoinder. "Your people are on their way, as we promised, and—"

"No! I talk—you listen! The Palestinian people are strong. We have declared *Jihad* against the Jews who have stolen our land. We shall push them back to the sea. We will not stop until every last Jew has been eradicated from the face of the earth!"

Hyte refused to be baited by Mohamad's descent into political and religious irrationality. The man was a professional, not a fanatic, Hyte reminded himself. "The money will be here in fifteen minutes," he reiterated, his tone placid.

"Along with our brothers."

"As I told you, they're on the way."

The terrorist's features relaxed. A half smile formed. "Are they?"

"Yes, they—"

"Watch your television!" Mohamad ordered. "You are trying to stall!"

Hyte grinned. Mohamad was indeed an expert at mind games. His vacillation between rationality and rage was too well timed to be anything but planned.

"We're not stalling," Hyte protested. "It takes time. You gave us three hours. There's still a forty-three min—"

"Quiet! Watch!"

Hyte watched the monitor while Mohamad stepped up to Cristobal Helenez. Raising the black pistol, he aimed it at Helenez's head. The distance between the weapon and the man's forehead was six inches.

"This man," Mohamad proclaimed, "is guilty of crimes against the Palestinian people. He has given financial and economic aid to the Israelis. He has opened factories in Palestine where Israelis work while my people live in squalor and die of sickness in refugee camps."

He waved the gun. "But this man is devious. There are no records to show it is his corporations that fund these factories. His records do not reveal the loans made to the Israeli banks. They are camouflaged in paperwork. But they were not hidden well enough. We learned of it because we are everywhere! Everywhere, although you people choose to deny this.

"He is a rich man. Very rich. But he is also a Zionist minion. Just as you are, Hyte. Like you and your men and all the policemen who try to stop us." Again, the pistol waved. "He lied to us, just like you have been lying to us. The helicopter should have been here by now. For your deception, Lieutenant Hyte, I sentence him to death!"

"Mohamad!" Hyte shouted into the field phone, the desperation in his voice not feigned.

Mohamad lifted the field phone to his ear. "Isn't that right? Aren't you deceiving us?"

"They're almost here." Hyte felt Sy Cohen's hand on his shoulder, reminding him that he was not alone. Hyte nodded at his friend and took a deep breath.

"But they aren't here, are they?"

"Just a few more minutes and your people will be with you. Wait, Mohamad. We're doing what you've asked for. We told you how much time it would take. We haven't changed your schedule—we haven't asked for more time."

"Too late," Mohamad whispered. He dropped the phone. The sound echoed eerily through the audio speaker. Hyte clenched his hands into impotent fists as he watched the scene unfold.

Mohamad centered the pistol on the Portuguese financier's head. Helenez's wife screamed. The back of her hand covered her mouth.

Then Hyte saw a movement behind Mohamad. His breath caught. Haller had risen; the pilot's face was tense.

"No," Hyte whispered ineffectually, "it's a game. It's a—"

Haller lunged, his head lowered, his hands still tied behind him. Screams and cried sounded from the speaker.

From the captain's left, the second hijacker swung his Uzi. The stock caught the captain on the shoulder, knocking him off balance. He spun, missing Mohamad and falling into the aisle.

Mohamad recovered quickly. His machine pistol was now aimed at the pilot.

When the captain was hauled to his feet, Mohamad looked at the camera. He shook his head sadly, like a teacher who had caught a student in the middle of a prank.

A shiver rippled through Hyte. Mohamad's eyes were angry. Hyte wondered if the terrorist leader would keep to his plan, or if the captain's attack justified a change in strategy.

"That was very stupid," Mohamad said into the field phone. "Don't you agree that the captain was stupid, Hyte?"

"Don't," Hyte pleaded.

Mohamad raised the pistol. He aimed it at the captain's head. Hyte saw Mohamad's jaw tense.

"I'm not filming this!" Hyte said. A muscle ticked angrily just below the skin on his left cheek.

Mohamad kept the pistol at Haller's head while he faced the camera. "Yes, you will. You can't shut the camera off even if you wanted to—this is your opportunity to study us. To better prepare yourselves for the next time. But it won't work. We are unpredictable because we must be."

"Please," Hyte asked, his voice gentle. "Don't kill him. We can talk. Your men are on their way. The money is almost here."

"Lies."

Hyte's experience, and Mohamad's eyes, told him what the terrorist's next move would be. Haller's chances were bad, unless Hyte could distract the terrorist long enough to make Mohamad back down without appearing to give in.

Hyte moistened his dry lips. "Mohamad, if you kill him,

it will turn the people away from you. But it's not too late. You can talk to me, Mohamad, we can work something out. Isn't part of the reason for what's happening tonight to let the people of the world see your plight and sympathize with your desperation? If you kill again, you'll turn those people away from your cause."

Mohamad seemed to be listening. "Perhaps you are right," he said. "But perhaps you are wrong."

He pulled the trigger.

Eleven

Mohamad laughed into the camera. The sound grated on Hyte's ears. Behind him, William Haller stood, his face parchment white. A puckered bullet hole marred the wall an inch from his left ear.

"You have fifteen minutes to deliver our brothers and the money," Mohamad said. "In fifteen minutes and one second the captain will die. After that, there will be one dead passenger for each minute our brothers are kept from us. Believe my words, Lieutenant."

Hyte turned cold. The coldness carried through in his voice. "We're moving as fast as we can, but we need the time schedule you gave us in the beginning."

"I thought my example made it clear that there is no more time!"

Hyte stared at him, revolted by the scene he had witnessed. *Talk to him,* he told himself. *Do your fucking job!* "Mohamad?"

"Yes?" Mohamad said. His voice was soft and calm.

"Give me a moment to check on the copter's location."

"Take all the time you want. Or at least the next fourteen minutes."

Hyte held the mouthpiece to his side and called out to Atkins. "Get that copter up. Now!" He looked at Rosenthal.

Rosenthal picked up the phone. "Mr. Mayor . . ."

"The money's here!" Harvey Bennet cried as he burst

through the door. Two uniformed men followed. Each man held a suitcase.

Hyte had two almost instantaneous thoughts. The first was of Emma Graham in the lunchroom on the second floor. The second was of Lea D'Anjine, sitting almost catatonic in seat 5D.

Hyte saw Rosenthal hang up the phone and turn to him. "The mayor has authorized the use of the Counter-Terrorist Tactical Unit."

Hyte picked up the field phone. He didn't have to ask how long the copter would take to get to Kennedy; he knew. It took exactly twelve minutes, from takeoff to landing, which left him with time to reason the hostages free.

"Mohamad. The copter is thirteen minutes away. The money is here now. Shall we deliver it?"

"No. Bring it with our brothers."

Hyte felt relief. He'd gotten his door opener. "All right. But don't harm anyone, you'll be on your way home soon. We also have a fresh flight crew standing by. Shall we send them with your men?"

"Absolutely not."

Hyte shrugged. The flight crew was a way to get three more policemen on the plane. He hadn't really expected Mohamad to take him up on the offer.

Hyte watched Mohamad carefully. The terrorist turned to the passengers, but still held the field phone. "Your Lieutenant Hyte says our brothers are almost here. Somehow, I doubt him. But we shall see. If he is lying, it will be you who shall have to pay for his hoax. After all, he is safe from our bullets. He has you people as a shield for his deceptions.

"But," Mohamad said, his voice suddenly expansive, a trace of humor lacing his tone, "since the United States of America is a democracy, and since we of the PLO respect this . . ." Mohamad paused. He looked up at the camera for a moment. He smiled. His stare was meant for Hyte, and Hyte knew it.

"He's rambling," Sy Cohen said. "He's over the edge."

Hyte cut Cohen off with a wave of his hand. "No. This message is for me."

". . . since we respect this democracy, we will allow you to decide who shall die, one minute after the pilot, if Hyte and your great democratic country does not have our brothers here in"—he looked at his watch—"thirteen minutes and twenty seconds."

"Who will it be?" Mohamad asked.

Hyte wrenched himself from the madman's gaze. To watch any longer would strip away the calmness he needed to maintain. He turned to Cohen, Rosenthal, and Arnel. "I'll be making the money drop."

Arnel stepped away from the wall. "Don't forget the senator. Nothing is to happen to him."

Hyte ignored the FBI agent. "Sy, you're manning the phone. When the copter is over the airport, I'll bring the money to the plane. I'll use a baggage truck. I'll take a second field unit as well as my walkie-talkie. We'll land the copter where they can see it. Mohamad will accept my offer of personally bringing him the money. It's his wisest move."

"Contingencies?" Cohen asked.

Before Hyte could answer, Atkins went to the window. "I've got a clear line from here," he said.

"If it's necessary," Hyte said to the sharpshooter before speaking to Cohen. "We'll only have the one chance. I'll put a pistol inside the suitcase, under the money. When Lacey's boys board, I'll try to take out Mohamad before he hits too many of the hostages."

"If he'll let you in," Cohen said.

"He'll let me in. He wants me there," Hyte said, looking at the monitor. He was certain that former Senator J. Milton Prestone was Mohamad's escape route. Prestone wasn't the secondary fail-safe as Hyte had earlier told Jerome Rosenthal; he'd been the primary safety all along.

With that thought, the elusive ideas Hyte had been trying to bring out came together. Finally, he was able to envision Mohamad's plans. All of the terrorist's tirades and threats to the passengers had been made in a challenge to Hyte. It was an integral part of Mohamad's plan to have the hostage negotiator primed for the moment when the terrorist released the passengers—all except for Prestone. Mohamad

95

was counting on two things: Hyte's relief at getting the hostages free and his willingness to allow Mohamad and his people to leave, with Mohamad's assurance that Prestone would be released when they landed.

It made perfect sense. Every promise Mohamad had made so far, he'd kept. He'd released the coach passengers. He would release the first-class hostages, too, once his men were delivered to him. He had even spared the captain's life. But Mohamad would keep Prestone.

And, Hyte also realized, that by not killing Haller—by staging his theatrics—Mohamad had finally given him something important. Rashid Mohamad was keeping his word because the terrorist wanted it all. He wanted the money, his men, and he wanted to get away.

But Mohamad's plan would not work, because his men were still in the federal penitentiary. When he discovered that . . .

"Ray, I don't think you should go in there," Rosenthal said.

"I have to. It's the hostages' only chance."

In the first-class section of the plane, the passengers had long since ceased to notice the smell of fear, sweat, and death. Only the odor of cordite lingered in their awareness.

Jonah Graham had his arm around his wife, comforting her against the occasional tremors that shook her.

"Attention!" Mohamad barked. "You have all heard what I said. Now it is time to choose. Who will die after the captain, if your government fails you? Who? Will anyone volunteer?"

Jonah's recorder clicked off when the terrorist stopped talking. Irrationally, he was pleased that the device was holding up the way he had been promised it would.

Prestone stood. His arms hung before him, his wrists still taped together. "Me."

Mohamad laughed. "You are brave, but stupid. Perhaps that is why you stand now. Can you really be so simple as to not know that you must be the last to die? You are the reason this plane will not be stormed. Why else would we have sabotaged your private plane? Your presence was planned! Your government cannot take the chance of losing so vital a link between your government and the Israelis. Because of that, you will watch everyone else die before you. Sit down!''

"You're wrong. I'm not that important,'' Prestone said, his stare unwavering.

"It is easy for someone who knows his life is not yet over to be brave,'' Mohamad told the passengers. "He knows that we cannot kill him . . . yet.''

Prestone glared at him. Hatred poured from his eyes with such fury that even Mohamad turned away. He signaled the man with the Uzi, who stepped up to the bound senator and shoved him back into the seat.

Mohamad looked at the hostages. The only passenger he did not glare at was the child. "Is there no one else who will offer his life for the others?'' When no one did, he went back to Cristobal Helenez. "You?'' he asked the financier.

Helenez tried to speak. His lips moved soundlessly. He shook his head and closed his eyes.

"You?'' Mohamad asked, moving the pistol to Helenez's wife, shoving it into her breast. "N-n-no,'' she stammered, her voice shrill in the confines of the plane. "Please. No. Not me.''

Mohamad looked at the Portuguese financier. "You will withdraw all financing from the Israelis. You will close your factories. You will call in your loans.''

"I . . . I can't do that.''

"You will do that or I will kill you and then your wife.''

Helenez swallowed. "All right.''

"If you fail to keep your word,'' Mohamad warned, a smile breaking his lips, "you and your wife will die. Do not think that if I die tonight, your words will go unheard. It has been planned. You and your wife will be dead if your promise has not been fulfilled in thirty days.''

Mohamad straightened. He looked at the man sitting behind the Helenezes. "You?'' he asked Michael Barnes, the redheaded businessman sitting in the aisle seat.

The man shook his head quickly. "I don't want to die."

"Should it be someone else?" Mohamad asked.

The man bent his head. "Yes," he whispered, "someone else."

"See," Mohamad declared loudly. "We Palestinians know the workings of democracy. We value the freedom of choice we have been denied since 1948.

"You?" Mohamad asked as he moved across the aisle to silver-haired Sylvia Mossberg. Mohamad stared pointedly at the gold Star of David hanging from her neck.

"You," he said. "It will be you."

Sylvia tried to speak. She couldn't.

"Stand up!" Mohamad ordered. He grabbed her hair and yanked her to her feet. The woman screamed in pain. Mohamad jammed the pistol into her chest. "You?" he asked again, his face not two inches from hers.

Sylvia began to hyperventilate. "N-n-not me—"

"Yes," Mohamad whispered, cutting her off.

Mohamad jammed the pistol harder against her chest. She fainted.

Mohamad sneered at the unconscious woman. He looked around. There were four passengers and three crew members left. His eyes fell on Sonja Mofferty's face. He smiled again.

He looked at Jack Mofferty. "You?"

Mofferty clutched his wife's hand reflexively.

The pistol veered toward Sonja. Smiling, Mohamad reached out with his free hand and stroked one breast. His hand rose upward along her trembling body. It snaked along her neck, traced her mouth.

He turned to Jack Mofferty. "You have a beautiful wife. A desirable woman. Will you offer yourself to save her?"

Sonja saw her husband start to move. She knew he would do what the terrorist asked.

"No!" she cried.

"No?" Mohamad asked.

Sonja swallowed. She moistened her lips with her tongue. "You want me," she whispered. "Take me. Let us live."

Mohamad smiled again. "We value our women, for they

are the comfort and promise of paradise on this earth. But I have no need for a woman's comfort now. Yet . . .'' Mohamad paused. His mouth formed a half smile. He glanced toward the back of the cabin at the two men holding Uzis. He raised his eyebrows in question.

When he received the response he sought, he smiled and looked down at Sonja Mofferty. "I will accept your offer. But you must say the words."

Sonja Mofferty looked at him uncertainly. "What words?"

Mohamad pressed the barrel of the pistol to her cheekbone. "Will it be you?"

Unable to meet his eyes, Sonja Mofferty whispered, "Not me. Please, someone else, not me."

Twelve

Hyte prepared himself to go to the plane. A phone rang.

"Lieutenant," Moran called.

"What?"

Moran met Hyte's gaze. "Trouble with the copter."

Hyte grabbed the phone. "What the hell's going on?"

A harried sergeant explained that the helicopter's fuel line had become blocked during takeoff. They had stripped and cleaned it and would be ready to leave in half a minute.

Hyte checked his watch. Four minutes and thirty-four seconds had elapsed since Mohamad's newest deadline. "That's fucking great!"

"We're doing the best we can," the sergeant said.

Hyte slammed down the phone. He turned from the eyes that watched him. "The helicopter will be delayed five minutes."

No one said anything. They were all thinking the same thing. Five minutes could mean five deaths.

Hyte tried to figure out how he could stall Mohamad for another five minutes.

"The vest, Lou," Junior Atkins reminded him, holding up the bulletproof body armor.

"What's the point of the vest if he's going to make you strip?" Arnel asked.

"That was to make us feel exposed. That part of the game's over now. But if he makes me strip, so be it," Hyte said as Atkins helped him on with the equipment. When

100

Hyte had the vest fastened, he put his shirt over it, and then his jacket.

Then Junior Atkins had taped a Beretta 9-millimeter automatic to the bottom of one suitcase. It would be hidden by the money: two million five hundred thousand dollars in twenties, fifties, and hundreds.

Hyte hefted the suitcases. They weighed less than he had expected. He clipped the walkie-talkie to his belt.

"Oh shit," came Joseph Moran's low voice.

Hyte turned to the monitor and watched Sonja Mofferty being drawn to her feet. "What?" he asked Moran.

"She just traded her body for her and her husband's lives."

Hyte swallowed. No matter what the terrorist had promised, he would kill whomever he wanted, whenever he wanted.

"The commissioner," Moran called. The detective held out the phone.

Hyte stared at him, then took it. "Yes?"

"I heard about the helicopter, I'm sorry."

"Tell that to the victims' families," Hyte snapped.

"There's no need for that," the commissioner said in a low tone. "What's happening in the plane?"

Hyte didn't bother to hide his anger. "Rashid Mohamad is trying to get a volunteer to be the first passenger to die if we don't have the helicopter here by his deadline. Another terrorist is raping one of the women."

Silence. Then, "What are you going to do?"

"Whatever I can."

"The mayor is on his way to Kennedy—with McPheerson. Lieutenant, ah, don't forget about the senator."

Hyte handed the phone back to Atkins and looked at Sy Cohen. "It's going to be tricky," Hyte said. "If we call Mohamad now, he just might blow someone away before schedule. We'll wait until the last minute to tell him about the delay. While I'm gone, I want no contact with the plane. Once I'm in place, I'll see if I can get an extension. Listen in and follow up accordingly."

Hyte started out. Behind him, Atkins opened the window

101

and set up the sniper rifle. A scream of pain and terror exploded from the speaker. Everyone in the room turned to look at the monitor: The passengers, their expressions frozen, stared at the coach section, to where Sonja Mofferty and the terrorist had gone.

Outside, Hyte smelled exhausted fumes, oil, and salt air mixing together. Overhead, clouds were rolling in. Hyte tasted the edge of humidity. He thought about Carrie and wondered if he would see her in the morning. Then he wondered if his daughter would forgive him if he didn't come home.

He thought of Lea D'Anjine. For a few seconds he pictured not the seven-year-old, but his own daughter sitting on the plane. He sensed that if he were to die, the only way Carrie would ever forgive him, was if he managed to save the little girl. It was an irrational thought, yet it helped settle his nerves.

He went to the luggage scooter, which had been detached from its freight car. The cop standing next to it took the two bags of money from Hyte and set them in the back. Hyte placed a field phone on the floor of the scooter. He studied the gear shift and controls for a moment and then started the scooter.

"Good luck," the policeman said. Hyte saw relief in the cop's eyes. The policeman was glad he wasn't going out to the plane.

Hyte looked at his watch. Three minutes. His stomach tightened. He floored the accelerator. The drive took a minute.

He stopped the scooter twenty feet from the cockpit and picked up the walkie-talkie. "I'm going to try and reach him," he told Cohen. "What about the copter?"

"It's coming. They're pushing it as fast as they can. At least five minutes."

Hyte got out of the scooter. He unloaded the two suitcases and set them down a yard from the vehicle. He went back and lifted the field phone. The phone rang five times before it was answered.

"There's been a problem, Mohamad."

"Of course, Lieutenant. Problems come with lies."

Hyte didn't like the calmness in Mohamad's voice. "The copter developed engine trouble—a blocked fuel line. It took five minutes to clear. Your men are almost here."

"Almost here is not here. You have one minute left."

Hyte used the only thing that remained. "I have your money. Good faith, Mohamad. Just like when you gave us the coach passengers. Let *me* give you the money. It will prove I'm not lying."

"Fifty-seconds."

"Look out the goddamn window," Hyte shouted. "I'm here. Alone! I have the money. And I have myself, Mohamad. I'm offering myself to show my good faith. Give us the time we need. If I'm lying, you'll have me to do what you want with. Isn't that worth waiting an extra four minutes?"

There was a pause. "You have all the money?"

"Five million dollars."

"Bring it to the stairs. Walk up slowly. Place the bags at the top. Put your hands on your head and wait."

A glimmer of hope surfaced: He was being allowed in; and, they had not made him strip. Hyte replaced the receiver of the field phone. He didn't bother with the walkie-talkie. He knew Sy Cohen had heard everything.

Hyte picked up the suitcases and stared toward the portable ramp. He was sweating beneath the bulletproof vest.

At the top step, he put the suitcases down and settled his hands on his head.

The door opened. Two men armed with Uzis stared at him. One man inched into the doorway and motioned to Hyte to pick up the bags. Both stepped back to let him enter the plane. The second hijacker used the barrel of his Uzi to do a quick body-skimming frisk. He was not gentle.

It was hot inside. The air was putrescent, worse than when Hyte had been there almost two and a half hours before. The tip of an Uzi urged him forward. He went toward first class, one suitcase held behind him, one in front. The suitcases themselves had made him powerless to do anything.

Ninety seconds after hanging up the field phone, and for the second time that night, Raymond Hyte stepped into the first-class section of Flight 88.

"So nice for you to visit us, again. You really didn't think you fooled me earlier, did you Lieutenant Hyte?"

Hyte said nothing. All the hostages were staring at him. To Mohamad's left was Lea D'Anjine.

"Two minutes have passed since my deadline," Mohamad said. "Where is the helicopter?"

"Can I release the bags?" Hyte asked.

Mohamad nodded.

Hyte dropped the cases. "I am going to take my walkie-talkie from my belt," he explained to the terrorist. He lifted it to his mouth. "The copter?"

"Three minutes. Maybe two."

Mohamad backstepped until he was next to the unconscious Sylvia Mossberg. He pointed his pistol at her.

"Will anyone stand forward?" he asked.

"You said I would be first," William Haller said.

"I have changed my mind," Mohamad said, lowering the pistol to the woman's head.

"No!" Hyte shouted. "The helicopter is almost here!" He took a half step forward. He was caught from behind and held fast.

"You have no say here, Hyte. Look at him!" Mohamad said to the passengers. "He betrayed you, while I have kept my word. He let the time run out, not I. He is the one who has sentenced you to death!"

"Then take me!" Hyte said.

Mohamad's face contorted with rage. "You are the cause for their deaths, don't you understand? And now you will witness, in person, the result of your lies."

Mohamad put the pistol to the area behind Sylvia Mossberg's left ear. Hyte started to say something but was cut off by another.

"Stop it!" came an unexpected feminine voice. Everytone turned to stare at a standing Anita Graham. Her husband was pulling on her arm. She ignored him. "You have

104

nō right to do this!'' she said. Her voice was eerie in its calmness. "You aren't God. We've done nothing to you.''

"Yes, you have!'' Mohamad shouted, sweeping his arms to encompass all the passengers. "You have done so by your inaction! By turning your backs on what has happened to my people! By allowing the Israelis to steal our land and by letting their soldiers and tanks and planes kill our children!''

Mohamad stepped across the aisle and raised the machine pistol in Anita Graham's forehead. *"You* shall die for my people!''

"No!'' Hyte shouted. By his reckoning, there was only one minute left.

Jonah Graham rose swiftly to his feet and grabbed the pistol, moving the barrel to his own forehead. "Kill me,'' he said, "not her.''

Hyte, held fast in the two terrorists' grip, ticked off the seconds in his head.

Mohamad met Jonah Graham's gaze. "You are a brave man, perhaps the only brave man here. I sensed that when I first looked at you. Very well, release the gun.''

Jonah Graham released the gun. He drew in a deep breath. His last breath. He did not close his eyes. He would not look away from his murderer.

"Are you ready?'' Mohamad asked.

Jonah looked at Anita. "I love you,'' he said. He turned back to Mohamad, stared into the terrorist's eyes, and nodded.

In a smooth and instantaneous action, Mohamad swung the pistol from Jonah to Anita and fired.

"No!'' Jonah cried, clutching for his wife. He caught her before she fell and, ignoring the blood spurting from her head, pulled her desperately to him. Behind them, Lea D'Anjine screamed for the first time.

Five seconds later, the field phone rang.

Thirteen

Lea D'Anjine's scream ended abruptly. The little girl curled in upon herself, hiding her face from everyone. It was better that way, Hyte thought, looking at Mohamad and waiting for the terrorist to pick up the phone.

A moment later, Mohamad answered. "Yes?" He held the phone slightly away from his ear, so those nearby could hear.

"The helicopter is here." Hyte recognized the voice as Sy Cohen's.

"Send my men to me," Mohamad said.

"When you release the hostages."

Mohamad gazed stonily at Hyte. "I am told that our brothers are here at last. This fool who has taken your place thinks we are stupid enough to release our hostages. Tell him, Lieutenant."

Hyte unhooked his walkie-talkie. Although the camera's mike would pick up whatever he said, he wanted Mohamad to get used to his holding the radio. "Sy?"

"Here."

"Land the copter fifty yards from the plane. Have the five prisoners step outside."

"Are you sure?"

"Do it, Sy!" Hyte hooked the walkie-talkie onto his belt, knowing that the lives of the hostages depended on how well Captain Lacey and his counter-terrorist squad played the part of the released prisoners.

"Very good," Mohamad said. "Now, let us see if there is money in those suitcases or are they booby-trapped—will they explode when one of us opens them? Is there a gas canister? Open the suitcase, Lieutenant. If they don't kill you, empty them on the floor."

Hyte had expected to have to show the money, but not dump it. He prayed the pistol hadn't come loose.

A burst of Arabic came from the terrorist at the window. Mohamad nodded. "Our brothers are getting out of the helicopter. Open the cases, Lieutenant. Let us see if you have condemned yourself or someone else to death."

Hyte opened the first case and lifted the top. He gripped the inside edge and turned it over. Two and a half million dollars spilled out. Everyone's eyes went to it, passengers and hijackers alike.

Hyte opened the second case. He gripped the side and turned it over. As the money fell free, Hyte released the gun. He glanced at his guards. They were looking at the money.

Turning slowly, he tossed the empty suitcase away. He used the movement to slip the pistol into his jacket pocket.

"Satisfied?" he asked.

The terrorist grinned. "Satisfied?" We asked for five things. You have given us two. Money and a television camera."

"Your men are outside," Hyte stated. "See for yourself."

Mohamad didn't move. A thin smile tugged at the corners of his lips. He brought the field phone to his ear. "Send our brothers to the plane. No one is to come with them. No one!"

"We have acted in good faith. You have your money. Your men are here. Release the hostages and we will send your men to you," Sy Cohen said.

Mohamad stared at the camera. "You do not understand. We are not negotiating. We never have been. There are still thirteen people alive. There is also your Lieutenant Hyte. They will all die."

Mohamad pointed the pistol at Hyte. "Tell him to send in our brothers."

Unclipping his walkie-talkie, Hyte matched stares with Mohamad. "Send them." When he lowered the unit, he made a show of putting it on his belt.

"Perhaps you will live, Lieutenant, and the others as well. Kneel on the floor, exactly where you are," Mohamad said, then spoke rapidly in Arabic.

The two hijackers who had been guarding Hyte went to the rear door. "When our brothers are here, you will each be released," Mohamad told the passengers. "You will leave one at a time. The lieutenant and"—Mohamad flicked the pistol toward J. Milton Prestone—"him will be the last. Until then, if there is any movement, everyone dies! Khamil," he called to the remaining terrorist, "the detonator."

Using his left hand, Khamil picked up a black box with a small aluminum antenna. His thumb hovered over its switch.

Hyte's hand inched toward his pocket. When he'd knelt, he'd shifted his body to hide his right arm and hand. Slowly, his fingers went around the Beretta's grip.

In the rear of the plane, the two hijackers stood near the door.

Five men wearing dark clothing came toward the ramp at a run. The first reached the steps and lunged upward. He tripped, fell back, and cried out in pain.

Two of his companions bent over him for a moment, then lifted him. Two others were right behind them. As the ungainly trio led the way up the ramp, the two men who supported the third drew automatic pistols from the holsters on the injured man's back. One of the hijackers stepped into the opening of the doorway, his arm out.

The second hijacker shouted for him to stop. He was too late. The injured man lunged forward, tackling the first hijacker around the waist. They fell backward into the plane.

The next two men rushed the second hijacker while the

108

last two disarmed the hijacker on the floor. The second hijacker dodged back and raised his Uzi.

The first commando fired.

The hijacker was hit in the shoulder. He spun, his finger squeezing the Uzi's trigger.

The commandos hit the floor. They fired five more shots.

The terrorist's body was flung backward, the Uzi spitting. Bullets tore holes in the fuselage. The first hijacker screamed when one of the bullets struck him.

Twenty seconds after the first shot was fired, the plane was silent.

"Goddamn it!" cried Captain Lacey, pushing himself up from his position on the floor. "Move it!"

Hyte's muscles quivered with suppressed tension. His eyes shifted from Mohamad to the terrorist holding the detonator. In the man's right hand was a machine pistol.

Hyte had no choice. He had to take out the man with the detonator first. If he was lucky, he would get him while the commandos eliminated Mohamad. But Hyte accepted the fact that the chances were no longer good for him to come out of this alive—even with the protection of his body armor. Mohamad would not permit that—he would go for the head.

Slowly, knowing the commandos should be near the door, Hyte inched his weapon free. He held it against his hip. His breathing was shallow.

A sudden gunshot sounded from the rear compartment. Hyte didn't think. He moved instinctively, twisting toward Khamil.

In an instant of suspended time, the terrorist looked at the passageway and Hyte fired. The bullet hit Khamil just above the bridge of his nose, right between the eyes.

Blood sprayed from the back of Khamil's head. His thumb never touched the detonator button. As Khamil fell, Hyte shifted. His pistol was now leveled at Mohamad, wondering why Mohamad had not shot him when he had fired at Khamil and then saw his answer, clearly. Mohamad was pivoting toward Prestone, his pistol going to the senator's head.

Behind Hyte came the sound of running footsteps. "It's over, Mohamad!" he yelled.

The terrorist leader shook his head. Hyte saw the flickering of Mohamad's eyes.

In the split second that followed, three simultaneous actions occurred: Hyte pulled the trigger; Mohamad shouted, *"Ins'Allah,"* and fired the Mac-10; William Haller lunged from the wall, putting himself between Mohamad's pistol and the senator, taking the bullet meant for Prestone.

Hyte fired three times. His first shot killed Mohamad. The next two rounds tore through the terrorist's throat.

Mohamad spun like a marionette, his death spasm sending a spray of bullets ricocheting within the cabin. One of the rounds hit the camera, angled downward, and struck Hyte in the shoulder, a quarter of an inch outside the protection of his vest.

Hyte felt a flash of pain, not unlike a sharp slap, followed by a sudden numbness in his shoulder and arm. His eyes swept the cabin. J. Milton Prestone was still alive. The gunfire had pulled the seven-year-old out of her fetal ball.

Behind, the commandos burst into the cabin.

"All secured?" asked Captain Lacey.

"All dead," Hyte replied, unable to take his eyes from the still smiling face of Rashid Mohamad. He knew the rushing of his blood would soon slow and the trembling of his hands would stop. What would never cease would be his memories of this night.

"It's over, Ray. You did a hell of a job," he heard Captain Lacey say. Hyte looked to where William Haller lay in a pool of his own blood. Then he pointed to Jonah Graham, who still held his dead wife.

"No, I didn't," he said.

Fourteen

At three minutes before five, Richard Flaxman drew on his tan London Fog and picked up his gold-braided captain's hat. As he settled it on his sandy hair, two delicate porcelain hands wound around his waist, locking together across his flat stomach.

"I'll miss you," whispered Katherine Sircolli.

"Good," Flaxman said, grinning. He turned within her embrace to gaze down at her. "I'll be back tomorrow night by seven."

"You'd better be. I promised my father we'd have dinner together."

"Right," Flaxman said, his voice no longer casual. Katherine's father was Antonio Sircolli, also known as Tony the Fist, head of the Tiacona crime family.

"He's not what the papers say he is," Katherine said.

"Of course not."

"But then again, you're fucking his baby daughter."

Flaxman winced. "Don't even joke about it."

She slipped one hand from his back, stroked his cheek gently, and then trailed her fingertips lower. "Sure you have to leave so early?"

Flaxman felt himself stirring. He reached down and firmly removed her hand. "Tomorrow night," he said.

111

"Or else." Suddenly, her smile disappeared. "Be careful, please."

He picked up his flight bag and went to the door. "Me? I'm always careful."

Katherine smiled. "I do love you, Richard."

"I love you, too." He was surprised to realize he meant it.

By the time Flaxman reached the front door, the doorman had it open for him. "Have a nice flight, Captain Flaxman."

Flaxman stepped into the cool pre-dawn air, walked to his car, and put his flight bag in the trunk.

He heard a tapping sound, and watched an elderly man walk toward the corner, using a cane.

Flaxman got in his car and started the engine. He pulled out of the parking space and made a sharp U-turn. The old man with the cane started across the intersection. In the man's left hand was a shopping bag.

"Move it," Flaxman urged.

The old man stopped, turned, and looked into the windshield. In the wash of the car's headlights, his face was deeply creased. Flaxman wondered why the man was staring so angrily at him.

The old man's eyes widened suddenly. The cane fell from his hands. He clutched at his chest.

"Oh Jesus!" Flaxman said when the man fell in front of the car. He put on the emergency brake and got out. The old man was lying on his back, his left hand clutching at his chest, his right behind him.

Flaxman went to one knee. The old man opened his eyes and tried to raise his head. "Are you all right?" Flaxman asked.

"I . . ." The man's voice was too low for Flaxman to hear.

He leaned closer. The old man moved. His right hand came out from behind him. In it was a black, T-shaped object. For a fleeting second, Flaxman wondered what it could be.

Then Flaxman saw the gleaming thing that rested in the

112

center of the cross. He threw himself back, but he was too late. A low twang resounded in the quiet morning, followed by a thud as the stainless steel tip met the flesh of Flaxman's upper chest.

Flaxman jerked back. His hand went to the projectile protruding from his chest. He felt a burning sensation. His arms grew heavy. He tried to speak, but his tongue was numb. His vision blurred; his lungs refused to accept air.

"Now I'm all right," said the old man.

MARCH 26

At two-fifteen in the morning, a yellow checker cab crossed the Triborough Bridge. The driver's attention was divided between the road ahead and the passenger in the back seat.

He liked the way the blonde's head lolled on the seat, and the way the missing button on her blouse gave him a glimpse of her lace bra.

His passenger was an exhausted Elaine Samson. The past week had been a hard one, emotionally. Her ex-lover and fellow survivor of the hijacking of Flight 88 had been killed a week ago. At his funeral, her sense of loss had deepened, not because she was still in love with him, but because they had shared something that would always bond them together.

Why had he been killed? she asked herself again.

The police had no ideas. There was no motive. The detective who'd interviewed her was of the opinion that Flaxman was a victim of a random street crime.

The taxi reached the FDR Drive. Four minutes later, the driver exited the drive at Ninety-sixth Street, drove down York Avenue, and turned onto Eighty-second Street. Halfway down the block, the cab stopped. "Eighteen-fifty," he said, turning to look at her.

Elaine paid with a twenty, got out, and started up the steps of the brownstone. She ignored the driver's muttering about cheap women tippers.

From behind her came a shuffling sound. Elaine noticed

a woman bent with age, holding a large brown shopping bag.

Elaine shrugged, opened the door, and stepped into the small entryway. The sound followed.

"Excuse me, miss," the old woman called in a quavering voice.

"Yes?" Elaine asked, pausing.

The old woman said nothing; she climbed the steps until she was only two feet from Elaine. She smiled.

Elaine thought it was an odd-looking face—surreal and masklike. "Yes?"

"Inside! Now!" the old woman commanded.

Elaine became aware of two things: The old woman's voice had changed, and her gloved hand held a strange weapon.

"Move!"

Elaine Samson's eyes were fixed on the weapon. "Please," she said, "Please don't hurt me."

APRIL 2

The Atlantic Avenue section of Brooklyn, which once housed hundreds of thousands of Jews, was now a teeming confluence of misplaced Arabs: Palestinians, Libyans, Iraqis, and Syrians all lived within its confines.

And on this Friday night, Atlantic Avenue was filled with thousands of Arabs, many of whom were welcoming the end of the Moslem sabbath, which had passed with the sun.

Groups of men and women, mostly college students, sat in coffee houses, drinking the thick coffee of their homeland and discussing philosophies of insurrection.

At one small table, surrounded by eight students, Barum Kaliel held court. He was from Jordan and did not hide his leftist politics as he railed against the workings of the democratic country he studied in. His own country, and the Arab countries surrounding Jordan, were indeed in the thrall of the United States, he said, and as long as they stayed that way, Israel and the Zionists would always be able to keep them separated and weak. He espoused a doctrine of solidarity: He believed that by uniting all the Arab countries under a single socialist regime they would become one of the most powerful forces in the world.

One of the students, a Palestinian, laughed at him. "And how would you do that when a single country can't even run itself properly?"

"By *making* them run properly. Our history is long, and in it one can see that there has been no unity since the time of the Crusades."

"Since before that," said a twenty-eight-year-old graduate student, her black eyes good-naturedly mocking Kaliel.

"How would you go about unifying the Arab world?" asked a nineteen-year-old Palestinian boy.

"By creating a unilateral movement in each country with a core of believers who would grow within each government and regime. When the cores reach the inner heights of the governments, they would unite. At that point, each country would become a separate state, run as such, but under the authority of one central government."

"The United States of Arabia," said another student.

"The name is unimportant. Only the act is important."

"If enough optimists can be found. But Barum," said the female graduate student, "Muslims are not predisposed to optimism."

"But youth is. And that is where we must recruit from."

"We?" asked an Iranian student.

"We," Kaliel agreed, looking from face to face.

"It is late," the Iranian said, pushing his chair away from the table. "Goodnight."

Barum Kaliel stood. It was almost 2:00 A.M.

He said goodnight to the rest of the students and started toward his apartment building.

He walked along Atlantic Avenue for five blocks before turning onto a small side street. The lampposts glowed dully in the cool night. A swirling mist thickened the night.

His building was halfway down the street. He walked slowly, his mind whirling with the thoughts of revolution.

He saw a bent old man shuffling toward him.

Kaliel shook his head. He would never allow himself to

115

be beaten down like that poor fool. When he drew nearer to the old man, he saw that the man's eyes were turned to him.

"What are you looking at?" he asked.

The old man straightened, smiled. A mass of wrinkles spread across his face. His eyes glistened. "You!"

Barum Kaliel stared at the old man. He stepped back, but he was too late.

The old Arab pulled a weapon from beneath the folds of a ragged cloak.

Kaliel looked at the gleaming black cross. He sensed danger. "Who are you?" he asked, raising his hands.

The old man remained silent. He squeezed the trigger smoothly.

A stainless steel projectile was propelled forward.

Barum Kaliel screamed. The scream lasted only the time it took for the steel tip to pass through his left eye and lodge in his brain.

Fifteen

Raymond Hyte left the window and returned to his desk. The overcast afternoon, so typically March gray in April, offered little to dwell upon. His desk was littered with reports of the sex crime unit and the borough homicide squads: equally gray.

There had been eighty-two rapes in March: eleven by unknown assailants, sixty-nine by husbands and boyfriends, and two homosexual rapes.

The monthly homicide report showed nothing unusual either. Of the twenty-seven violent deaths in March—a rather low number—only three were unsolved. The other twenty-four were, in the parlance of the Department, grounders, crimes that needed no investigation. Twenty-four deaths and twenty-four perps. Eighteen of the homicides had been committed by husbands, wives, or lovers. Two men had been killed in a gang fight in Spanish Harlem; four had been shot by a drug distributor in Bed-Stuy who thought the men were robbing him. The distributor was out on bail.

The three unsolved cases were still open. They were mysteries, and Hyte thought that they would stay that way. That's what usually happened if the perpetrator wasn't caught in the first week.

He picked up his coffee. It was cold, but he drank it anyway. It was almost two. The daily computer report would be in soon.

Hyte exhaled slowly, thinking about the changes in his life these past nine months. After the hijacking of Flight 88, he had undergone surgery to remove bullet fragments from Mohamad's ricochet. There had been permanent damage to his left shoulder. He would have only eighty percent use of the arm. It was, the doctor had added, enough to qualify Hyte for a medical pension.

He'd thought about retirement. It hadn't been a pleasant notion. Two days later, Chief of Detectives Philip Mason, his mentor, had come to visit him. Mason had read the surgeon's official report.

"What are you going to do?" Mason asked.

"I don't know. Try to be a lawyer again?"

"You're a cop, not a lawyer."

"Not anymore. I'm not comfortable behind a desk."

"You could try it for a while. I want you on my staff. Remember that idea you came up with last year? The one about coordinating crime information between PDUs? Why not give it a shot? The worst that can happen is you add a little more time to your pension."

Hyte had agreed. And, during his metamorphosis from a lieutenant with the Criminal Investigation Resources Division Special Crimes Unit to a desk jock at headquarters, he'd come up with an idea that would help spot pattern criminals faster. With Jon Rosen, one of the Department's computer specialists, he had set up a special program in the main computer. Within two weeks, Hyte had found his first criminal. A pattern burglar-rapist.

The program allowed Hyte to come up with the thread that tied all the victims of the criminal together. He was then able to direct the detectives to the rapist. It took four months, but Hyte found the man, and the unit was able to capture him.

The only hitch in the program was that it correlated every type of crime. He'd asked Rosen if he could narrow its parameters. "It can do anything you want," the sergeant told him, "but each time you have a new set of parameters, another program has to be set up. That will slow things down. Leave it alone, Ray. Get a human brain to sift through the debris."

He did. That human brain was Patrolman Sally O'Rourke, his combination assistant, secretary, and road-block. Patrolman O'Rourke was in much the same situation as Hyte. She had come to him from the Eighty-first Precinct, where she had been hit by a truck driven by a man who disliked the fact that women were out on patrol and not in the kitchen.

O'Rourke had been given a choice not unlike Hyte's— disability retirement or a clerical spot at headquarters. O'Rourke, at twenty-seven, had opted for headquarters. Hyte was glad she had. She was invaluable.

"Back to work," he muttered, picking up the forty-eight on the top of his in basket. A forty-eight is Department code for official letterhead stationery. This particular one was from the first whip of the Twentieth Precinct. It was a follow-up to Hyte's memo about a rash of burglaries that had plagued Riverside Drive. Hyte's computer program had picked up a pattern. Hyte had sent it over to the Precinct Detective Unit.

The PDU caught the man five days later.

The intercom on Hyte's phone rang. It was Philip Mason. "Come upstairs, now."

"On my way," Hyte replied.

"I'll be with the chief," he told O'Rourke when he stepped into his outer office.

Two minutes later, Hyte entered the chief of detective's thirteenth-floor office. There was a woman with azure eyes seated on Mason's couch.

"Lieutenant Hyte," Philip Mason said, "may I introduce Deputy Commissioner McMahon, of Public Affairs."

Hyte went over to McMahon and shook her hand. She had a firm grip. Her skin was dry and cool. "Commissioner," he said guardedly.

"Lieutenant," she replied with a curt nod.

"Scotch?" Mason asked them both.

The offer of the drink was unusual; Mason knew he rarely drank at this hour. Hyte wondered what was behind it.

He went to a seat across from McMahon, while the chief poured the drinks. Mason's actions added to his sense of discomfort. The chief of detectives does not pour a drink for a lieutenant, not even for the man who had called him "Uncle Phil" for most of his life; usually, Mason would tell Hyte to make himself the drink. Mason was putting on an act for the deputy commissioner and Hyte took his cue.

He used the opportunity to study McMahon. According to Department rumor, she was barely thirty-six and much too inexperienced for her job. But, as he looked at her traditional Irish face, he got the feeling she was a lot tougher than anyone gave her credit for.

Mason handed out the drinks, still maintaining his silence.

McMahon raised her glass and sipped. When she lowered it, she looked at Hyte. "The commissioner wants you to know that he thinks you did a top-notch job with the West Side rapist."

"Thank you," Hyte said. His drink remained untouched. He disliked praise, especially when it came from the higher levels of the Department. He sensed there would be a kicker—there always was.

McMahon set the glass on the marble coffee table. "I'm a bit puzzled about your declining Joan Leighton's request for an interview on the evening news. Why was that?"

"I don't believe in giving other people ideas about how to commit crimes."

"Please, Lieutenant," McMahon said. "Discussing the method of apprehending a criminal can't be considered as giving guidelines to would-be rapists."

"More than you think. Besides," Hyte said, crossing his leg, "I don't like to be the focus of attention. There were a dozen men on that case. All of them were responsible for the capture of Dantan. I just gave them the means."

McMahon's face did not change; her tone did. "That's very noble of you. But there are certain people who seem to draw the focus of the press. You happen to be one of them." She paused to sip her drink. "The PC and the mayor feel that the Department has had too much bad press

120

lately. We think it would be in the Department's best interest for you to do this interview."

Hyte held McMahon's stare. "In other words, you're ordering me to do the interview."

"Let's say it's good advice for you to call Leighton today," McMahon said. She stood. "Nice meeting you, Lieutenant."

"Do it, Ray, it's the right move," Mason said when they were alone.

Hyte easily translated Mason's statement. If he wanted to be made—to be promoted to captain—he'd better do what he was told. That was the way things worked on the Job. You follow orders and you get someplace, as long as you have someone behind you, like the chief of detectives.

The phone rang. Mason went behind his desk to answer it. Hyte gazed at his mentor.

Phil Mason was fifty-nine. Hyte's father and Mason had grown up together in Brooklyn, and had joined the Department at the same time. They'd gone through the Academy together, had even been assigned to the same precinct.

Raymond Hyte, Sr., and Philip Mason had risen through the departmental ranks until the time had come for them to make their most important career decisions. Patrol or detective.

Raymond Hyte, Sr., had elected to stay with patrol—he had believed in the presence of the uniform. Philip Mason had gone for his detective's gold shield. Yet their careers continued to parallel each other's.

They made sergeant at the same time, and then lieutenant, and finally captain. Hyte's father had become a precinct captain; Hyte's godfather, Philip Mason, had become the captain of an elite unit that eventually became the foundation of the Organized Crime Control Bureau. Both men had wanted to become a chief. But a sniper's bullet had prevented Raymond Hyte, Sr., from reaching One Police Plaza.

Mason hung up the phone. "Ray?"

Hyte nodded. "All right, Phil, I'll call the TV station."

"Today."

"Today," Hyte agreed.

"Six o'clock," Hyte said and hung up.

He disliked the reporter. Joan Leighton would do anything for a story, and she didn't care whom she hurt when she went on the air. But because Phil Mason had asked, he would do the interview. Leighton had told him to be at the studio at six. The interview would be live.

There was a knock on his door. Sally O'Rourke stepped inside. "Lou, the computer picked up something."

She put several sheets of paper on his desk. "Two homicides, one in Queens, one in Brooklyn. Two weeks apart. Both killed by similar weapons, both killed on a Friday night-Saturday morning."

"What about the crime scene unit reports?"

"Nothing yet."

Hyte looked at the first sheet. It was a duplicate of the original sixty-one, the crime report filed by the first officer on the scene.

He read the victim's name: Richard Flaxman. The name had a familiar ring, but he couldn't quite place it. He noted that the victim had been killed sometime between 5:00 and 6:00 A.M. The murder weapon was a "small arrow."

"What the hell is a small arrow?" he asked O'Rourke.

She shrugged noncommittally.

Then Hyte looked at the victim's name again. He couldn't shake the feeling of familiarity it produced. He read further, and he remembered. His pulse sped up. Beads of sweat broke across his forehead. "No . . ."

"Lou?" O'Rourke asked.

Hyte didn't hear his assistant's word; it was Rashid Mohamad's taunting threats that echoed in his mind. He saw the face of the copilot of Flight 88. He smelled the stench of fear and blood inside the plane. His mind spun as the memory of the long ago night came forth.

Forcefully, Hyte wrenched himself from the past and carefully examined the report. There was nothing of any consequence in it, other than the strangeness of the projectile. He exhaled, calmed himself, and looked at the next report. The victim had been killed between 2:00 and 3:00 A.M., three nights ago—on Friday last. He had been killed by a projectile resembling an arrow. It was about six inches long.

He studied the second victim's name. Barum Kaliel. He did not recognize the name.

The third and fourth sheets were the coroner's reports as to the cause of death. In Flaxman's case, an artery was severed; the second victim had died when the arrow penetrated his brain.

Hyte forced himself to think about the crime, not the victim he knew. It wouldn't be the first time he'd known a homicide victim, he reminded himself.

He looked up at O'Rourke. "We've got two points of connection—a similar weapon and the same day of the week. It may be something. But I don't see any connection with the victims. We need more. Get the reports from the crime scene unit, the PDUs, and borough homicide. I want to know exactly who Barum Kaliel was."

O'Rourke started out, but Hyte stopped her. He had an uneasy feeling that he was seeing the beginning of a new pattern of death.

"Sally, after you call for the reports, do a PDU phone message—no teletype. Give the precinct dicks the M.O. and tell them I want to be notified immediately if there are any more victims that match."

O'Rourke nodded and left the office. Hyte looked down at his desk. Richard Flaxman's name leapt out at him from the top of the report. A sensation of déjà vu crept over him. He fought it. For months afterward, he had tried not to think about what had happened on Flight 88. He did not want to now.

He had a date at seven, but the TV interview changed that. Again, his mind wandered back to that long night.

Denying the memories, he picked up the phone and dialed. When his call was answered, he asked for Emma Graham.

Sixteen

He had gone to Anita Graham's funeral. It had been on the day after Hyte had received a phone call from his ex-wife, Susan, telling him that she was taking Carrie back to Boston and that Carrie would not be permitted to return to New York.

Her cutting words had caused him more pain than had Mohamad's bullet; she had used his love for Carrie to hurt him. Following the phone call, Hyte had left the hospital without the doctor's permission. He'd caught up with Susan and Carrie at the airport. There, silently daring Susan to try to stop him, he'd talked privately with his daughter, explaining what had happened without making any excuses. Then he'd promised Carrie that he would come to Boston to visit her whenever he could.

Instead of going back to the hospital, where he had been scheduled for surgery on Monday morning, he'd gone home and opened a fresh bottle of Scotch and watched the evening news rehash of the hijacking. He'd caught a reference to Anita Graham's funeral. It was scheduled for eleven the next day.

A picture of Emma Graham, as she'd looked during their brief meeting, had flashed in his mind. He had wondered if his ex-wife would have shown Emma's strength in a similar situation.

Hyte had decided to attend the funeral. It was the least he could do for the brave woman who had died. A little while later, he'd received a call from the police surgeon, demanding that he return to the hospital. Hyte had promised that he would go back, the following night.

"It's your shoulder," the doctor had told him before hanging up.

The waiting room of the Victorian funeral home had been empty. He'd taken a black satin yarmulke from the box by the door, put it on, and went into the temple. A young rabbi, standing at the raised pulpit, was conducting the service.

A simple pine casket, closed, rested on a blue-draped table. The rabbi's voice had a husky, plaintive quality. It was a fitting voice, Hyte decided, as he chose a seat that afforded him a view of everyone. His eyes roamed over the rows of heads.

There'd been at least a hundred people in attendance. Seated in the first row were Emma Graham and her father. On Emma Graham's left was Jerome Rosenthal, the mayoral aide.

Hyte sat back, his mind spinning with self-criticism. If he had moved faster, thought quicker, he might not be attending this funeral.

He had stopped the flow of thoughts, knowing that to dwell on failure would only lead to more failures, and looked at Emma Graham's profile. She'd sat proudly, her shoulders drawn back, her hair brushed neatly away from her face.

The prayer had ended. Emma rose and went to the pulpit. She looked outward for several seconds; Hyte thought she was trying to compose herself. Although he was fifty feet away, he was able to see her clearly. Her facial muscles were tense. Her cheeks were drawn. Dark circles shadowed her eyes.

She cleared her throat. "You all knew my mother." Her voice caught on the last word. "There is nothing I can say about her that you don't already know. She was a kind and gentle and loving woman, and a very special person."

Tears fell from Emma's eyes, but her voice grew stronger. "My mother lived a full life. She cared about people. All people. My mother will be missed by more than just myself and my father. She will be missed by her friends. And she leaves behind her something that will never be forgotten. A legacy of love and devotion.

"I . . ." Faltering, she turned to the casket. "Good-bye, Mother. I love you.'"

Hyte swallowed the lump in his throat. Emma Graham's simple and dignified eulogy had touched him. He felt her loss.

When Emma stepped down, everyone stood. They went to her and her father, surrounding them, extending love and condolences.

Hyte remained where he was, offering his own silent prayer.

When the crowd started out, Hyte was the first to reach the sidewalk. He slipped into his car, waited while the hearse and the limousine carrying the Grahams left for the cemetery, then joined the procession in the middle.

Twenty-five minutes later, he was standing at the gravesite beneath the strong June sun. Once again he lingered at the periphery of the crowd, unwilling to impinge on anyone's private grief.

He listened as the rabbi led them in the mourner's prayer in both Hebrew and English. When it ended, and Anita Graham's body was lowered into the ground, Emma stepped forward.

She took a shovel and dropped red earth onto her mother's coffin. Then she handed the shovel to her father.

Jonah Graham's gray hair was partly obscured by the black yarmulke. To Hyte, he appeared smaller and more frail than when he was on Flight 88.

He dug into the mound and raised the shovel, looking down at the pine box holding his wife. Suddenly, the shovel fell from Graham's hands. His face turned red. A gasp escaped his lips an instant before he collapsed. He landed half in the exposed grave.

Emma cried out and started toward Jonah. By the time

she reached her father's side and started to pull him back from the grave, Hyte was running through the stunned crowd of mourners.

He reached Emma and helped her pull Jonah back.

"Get an ambulance!" he ordered a local cop.

The left side of Jonah's face was slack. It was as if all the muscles had turned to rubber. Hyte had seen it before. He felt for a pulse and found it.

Hyte began mouth-to-mouth resuscitation, using two fingers of his right hand to keep Graham's tongue from rolling backward. He heard Emma ask what was wrong. He didn't answer. A few moments later, he felt Jonah respond.

When he raised his mouth from Jonah's, he saw that Rosenthal had moved Emma away. She was staring at her father. Her face was ashen.

Blood seeped from Hyte's bandaged shoulder and he knew he'd torn the wound open. "I think it's a stroke," he said as the wail of an ambulance siren reached them. Over Emma's shoulder, he saw a camera crew moving in. The local cop cut them off and motioned them back.

The volunteer ambulance arrived, driving as close to the gravesite as possible. Two paramedics raced to the fallen man. It took them only a few seconds to put an aspirator over Graham's mouth and nose.

They maneuvered Graham onto a gurney, strapped him securely down, and started back to the ambulance. Emma broke away from Rosenthal to follow the paramedics. Hyte walked behind her and waited until she climbed into the ambulance after her father. "Miss Graham," he began, wanting badly to offer her words of support. "I'm very sor—"

Emma cut him off, her voice bitter. "What have you to be sorry about? You haven't lost anything except for a little blood. I lost my mother, and now I'm losing my father! It will never be over, will it? *Will it?*"

The force of her emotions caused him more pain than he wanted to bear. His heart went out to her, he wanted to comfort her, and make her understand how he felt. But he had no answers for her. His guilt at what she had already

127

gone through, and would go through because of him, kept him silent.

Then the ambulance door closed.

Rosenthal turned to Hyte. "Ray, can you drive me to the hospital?"

Hyte looked down at his shoulder. The blood had soaked through his suit jacket. "I think you'd better drive," he'd said.

Rosenthal had called him on Monday night. He'd told Hyte that the doctors were optimistic about Jonah's recovery from the stroke. But the news didn't help to ease Hyte's troubled thoughts. He could still hear Emma Graham's angry words and accusations. During the remainder of his stay in the hospital, Emma was never far from his thoughts. His sense of responsibility for Anita Graham's death was compounded and made oppressive by Jonah Graham's stroke.

At the same time, he was experiencing a desire to see Emma and explain what had happened during the hijacking. He had never felt this need before. Always, in the past, he had been able to separate himself from the victims of crimes. He didn't try to analyze his reaction to the hijacking, he accepted it, just as he accepted the fact that he couldn't shake Emma Graham from his mind.

He had never met a woman who appeared to be so in control of herself as Emma Graham, and she fascinated him, Hyte finally admitted to himself. Not even her angry challenge at the cemetery diminished his view of her.

When he was released from the hospital, the Friday following Anita Graham's funeral, he went straight to the Westchester hospital where Jonah Graham was being treated.

Emma was in her father's hospital room, sitting next to him. Wires led from Graham's chest and head to the monitors on the walls. Oxygen tubes ran from his nose.

Hyte stood in the doorway for several minutes, watching her.

"Miss Graham," he said.

"Emma turned. Her eyes widened. She stood. "Lieutenant," she said. She looked at the sling supporting his left arm. "I want to thank you for helping my father at the funeral. And apologize for my behavior."

When Hyte waved her words away, her eyes became warmer. He relaxed. "Can we talk?"

She looked at him a moment longer, then nodded. He took her down to the cafeteria, where they got coffee and went to a corner table.

"Jerome called me at the beginning of the week. He told me the doctors said your father will recover," he said.

"If recover means he'll live, yes. But the stroke was worse than the doctors had originally thought. The damage to his brain was massive." She paused, her eyes fixed intently on his. "He'll never again walk, or talk, or smile. The doctors believe that he'll be aware of everything. They say his mind will be completely functional, but he won't be able to communicate. Goddamn those hijackers!"

Hyte started to reach across the table to take her hand. He stopped himself when he realized what he was doing. "I'm sorry, Miss Graham. I came here because I wanted to explain what happened during the hijacking."

Emma shook her head. "I'm sure you did your best. But it's hard to accept losing my mother, and now my father as well. And all because of a madman."

"I understand how you feel."

Emma's eyes flared with passion. "I lost the two people I loved most. You didn't lose anyone. So please don't tell me you understand."

Hyte met her enraged stare. "I'm telling you just that. You see, the hijacking cost me my daughter. And while it may not be permanent, it's still a hard loss." Without giving her a chance to say anything, he explained about his wife taking Carrie away, and why.

Emma picked up her coffee and sipped it. She gazed at him for several seconds. "I didn't . . . I was wrong," she said.

"What about your father," he asked. "What are your plans?"

Her expression turned defensive. "You sound like those doctors. Do you mean am I going to put him out to pasture? Send him to a facility? No! When he's released, I'm taking him home. I'll care for him."

Hyte nodded. Her answer didn't surprise him, it was a part of her character. He stood slowly, not wanting to leave her but knowing he couldn't stay. "If you need anything, please call me."

Emma smiled tentatively. It was the first time he had ever seen her smile. Hyte liked the effect it had on her face.

"Thank you," she said.

On the drive back to Manhattan, Hyte came to the only decision he could. He had to put Emma Graham out of his mind. His attraction to her was wrong. It had been born out of guilt, grief, and loss.

For weeks, Hyte had tried not to think of Emma too often. When he did, he would call the hospital and check on Jonah Graham's condition, which remained the same. Twice, he had the switchboard ring through to Jonah's room. Each time, Emma had answered the phone.

Then, on the Monday before he returned to work, Emma had called him and asked him to join her for dinner. He'd agreed immediately. He spent the rest of the day calling himself a fool.

After dinner, Hyte had dropped her off at her co-op on York Avenue. They stood outside. It was a warm night, cloudy. He gazed at Emma, wondering if his emotions were leading him astray. Strangely, he didn't care.

"I enjoyed this evening," Emma said.

"So did I. Are you free Saturday night?"

She glanced away. Then, hesitantly, she had said, "Yes, I am."

Hyte shook away his memories of the early months following the hijacking when he heard Emma's voice on the phone. Hyte smiled. He'd had no inkling when he'd asked her out for that second date, that he would still be dating her now, seven months later.

"There's a problem with tonight," he said and explained about the television interview.

"I don't mind waiting until you're finished. Or, if you'd like company, I'll go to the studio with you."

Hyte smiled. "I'll meet you there. At six."

"Wonderful," she said and hung up.

Hyte looked out his window. The past was still on his mind. So much bad had happened during the hijacking, that he found it hard to accept the good that had come of it: his ongoing and deepening relationship with Emma Graham.

Then he looked at the report of Flaxman's death, and remembered Emma's words from the funeral. *It will never be over, will it?*

Seventeen

Patrol car 15, attached to the Nineteenth Precinct, was parked on the corner of Eighty-sixth Street and York Avenue when a call from central came through. Patrolman Sean Reagan, a veteran of twenty-one years, responded.

Patrolman Raul Santiago, six months out of the Academy and riding shotgun, asked, "See the super about a bad smell? What the hell does that mean?"

Reagan gave him a sideways glance, shrugged, and opened the car door. "Be right back." When he returned, he was carrying three fat cigars.

The rookie was puzzled, Reagan didn't smoke.

When they arrived at the building, they found the super, a short and thin Hispanic, standing on the sidewalk with several tenants. "Which floor?" Reagan asked.

"Five D," the super said. "Name's Elaine Samson. Here's the key."

Reagan went back to the car. He took off his heavy blue coat and put it in the front seat. "Lock the car," he told Santiago. "Leave your coat behind. Stink clings."

Santiago followed the veteran's orders. Both cops went into the elevator. As it rose, Reagan lit a cigar. He offered Santiago one.

"They make me sick."

Reagan smiled.

They got out on the fifth floor. Santiago sniffed the air. "Nothing."

But as they approached apartment 5-D, a faint stench of decay began. Reagan puffed harder on the cigar. At the door, the veteran cop looked down. The edge of a doormat was wedged between the bottom of the door and the floor, sealing the space under the door. He took out a white linen handkerchief, inserted the key in the lock, and looked at Santiago. "Ready?"

"For what?"

Reagan turned the key. Placing the handkerchief over the doorknob, he pushed the door open.

The first rush of putrescent air hit them in a sickening wave. Santiago bit his lip.

Reagan chomped down on the cigar. A cloud of smoke clung to his face. "Inside," he said.

Santiago followed Reagan in. The rookie made it five feet before turning and racing back to the hallway, where he vomited. Reagan kept puffing on the cigar.

Reagan spotted the legs at the far end of the room. The feet were at a sixty degree angle, the toes of the shoes touching. Half the torso was in the living room. Behind him, Santiago came inside once again. "Wait here," Reagan ordered.

Reagan approached the body slowly, making sure he didn't step too close. His eyes searched the floor for signs of violence or weapons. The smell got past his cigar. His stomach convulsed. The body was bloated. Dark fluid seeped out from beneath it.

She had once been pretty. But now her face, twice its normal size, was grotesque. Her lips were distended and her eyes were open, the eyeballs swollen almost completely out of their sockets.

Reagan's gaze stopped at her left shoulder, and at the projectile lodged there. As soon as he saw it, he knew the first part of his job was over. This one would go to the dicks. He wasn't happy about it.

Very carefully, he backtracked to Santiago, motioning him out of the apartment.

Outside, Reagan closed the door, again using the handkerchief. "You okay, kid?"

Santiago nodded. "I never smelled anything like that."

"I've got to call the squad," Reagan said. "You wait up here for the dicks. Want a cigar?"

Santiago took the cigar, and let Reagan light it for him.

Downstairs, Reagan dialed the precinct and was put through to the detective unit. Sergeant Simon Cohen answered the call. Cohen was the One-Nine's second whip. He was the boss of the PDU's four to midnight shift.

"Sarge," Reagan said, "I think you got a mystery. . . ."

The overcast day had given way to a surprisingly clear evening by the time Hyte got out of the cab on the corner of Broadway and Sixty-first Street. Emma was waiting in front of the television studio. She wore a pale blue suit. Her short hair, brushed away from her face, accented her strong cheekbones.

Her presence helped ease some of the tension brought on by the discovery of Richard Flaxman's death. Hyte knew he would say nothing about the copilot.

She saw him and waved. Her head was cocked to one side, regarding him seriously. He thought of how nice it was, seeing her waiting for him.

When he reached her, she kissed him softly. He saw anxiety in her eyes. "Bad day?" she asked.

"There've been worse." He gave her a reassuring smile as they went into the main entrance.

On the fifth floor, a young blonde sat behind a low desk. Hyte went over to her and gave his name.

"Haveaseat," she said.

"Pleasant lady," Hyte murmured.

"Child," Emma corrected.

Hyte gave her an arch look, holding it until they both laughed. Less than a minute passed before the door behind the desk opened and a thin man came toward them. "Lieutenant Hyte?"

Hyte stood.

"I'm Bill Winston, Ms. Leighton's producer."

Hyte shook the man's hand and introduced Emma.

"If you'll come with me, we'll get you prepared." Winston turned to Emma with a plastic smile. "You can wait for him in the green room while he's on."

They trailed the producer down a long hallway to an open door. Inside were five barber-style chairs. A white Formica counter ran the length of two walls. The space between the ceiling and the counter was solid mirrors. Two women and one man lolled in a corner. All three turned when Hyte came in. Their eyes appraised him. The man started forward.

"Just his hair," the producer said.

One of the women detached herself from the group and came over to him. "Haveaseat," she said.

"I'll be right back," the producer said, and disappeared through another doorway.

Hyte let the hairdresser brush his hair. One of the men attached a small microphone to Hyte's tie and ran the wire inside his jacket. "They'll hook you up on the set," he said.

Emma readjusted the microphone so it sat smoother on his tie. She raised her hand to his face. Her fingernails traced the groove etched at the corner of his mouth. "Try to relax."

He kissed her finger tips, feeling a familiar rush of desire for her.

"Don't let her goad you," Emma said. "She has a reputation for being catty if she doesn't get the answers she wants."

"How do you know about her reputation?"

Emma smiled. "I know people in the business."

The producer returned. "Lieutenant, if you and Miss Graham will come this way. . . ."

They followed him into the hall, and then to another door that opened into a pale blue and empty room. A velvet modular couch dominated the far wall. Across from it was a large table complete with coffee urn, donuts, bagels, and soft drinks.

A monitor hung from a single pole, catty-cornered to the

135

seating area. "You'll be on in fifteen minutes. Someone will come for you."

When the producer left, Emma covered his hand. He leaned back, exhaled, and prepared himself for the inevitable.

Sy Cohen looked down at the body. The bloated, disfigured woman resembled a plastic blow-up doll more than a real body.

He looked for more wounds but could see none. There was only the small, strange-looking arrow jutting from her shoulder.

She was dressed in the remnants of a stewardess's uniform. The blouse and skirt had ripped as the body distended. Moving around the body, Cohen saw the gold wings of her name tag.

He read the name. Elaine Samson.

What the smell hadn't been able to do to him, the name did. Sy Cohen went to his knees and spewed up his dinner.

"We only have time for one more question, Lieutenant," Joan Leighton said. "Do you think Joseph Dantan will go to jail or plead insanity? I mean, wouldn't you call a man who raped forty-two women insane?"

"I'm not a psychiatrist, Miss Leighton. I won't hazard a guess. Dantan has not yet gone to trial, and I wouldn't want to infringe on his civil rights by answering that question."

"Then on a personal level, what do you think?"

"I think that Joseph Dantan should stand trial for the crimes he's suspected of committing. If found guilty, he should go to jail."

"For all the women in our audience, I would like to thank you for apprehending Joseph Dantan and for joining me here, tonight."

The instant the announcer took over, Hyte detached the microphone and stood. Joan Leighton favored him with a searching stare. "Maybe the next time I ask for an interview, you'll be a little more available."

"Don't count on it," he said as his beeper went off.

The second he entered the green room, he went to the phone and dialed central. "Lieutenant Hyte," he said.

"Identification please," the operator asked. "Color of the day and tax number."

"Silver," Hyte replied, and gave his tax identification number.

"Lou," the operator said, "we have a homicide at six twenty-two East Eighty-second Street. Sergeant Simon Cohen requests your presence."

"On my way," Hyte said. He turned to Emma.

"She was a real bitch, and it showed when she tried to play with you. But you more than held your own."

"Thanks," he said. "Emma, I've got—"

"I heard. What happened?"

"A homicide. It may be part of something . . . I don't know. I'll make it up to you."

Her eyes played across his face. "Don't worry," she said, smiling gently. "You go to work. . . . Call me later, or come by."

He cupped her chin and drew her mouth to his. He kissed her, brushing his lips lightly across hers. "I'll try," he said.

Eighteen

Hyte spotted Sy Cohen standing with Lieutenant Cal Severs of the Borough Homicide Squad. Both men were leaning against the medical examiner's car. He went over to the two cops and shook their hands. He noticed Cohen's face was grim, his coloring unusually pale. "What's up?"

Cohen ran his fingers through his gray hair. He didn't look directly at Hyte. "An old-timer was first on the scene. He did it all by the book. Nothing was touched. He didn't even open a window. When I got here and saw the M.O., I called you. Crime scene and Doc Lester are upstairs now."

"The victim?"

Cohen paused and moistened his lips. "You knew her, Ray. Elaine Samson from the 88 hijacking."

Hyte's bowels locked. A sense of disorientation washed over him. First Flaxman, and now the stewardess! What the hell was going on? He was surprised to find himself trembling. "Let's go upstairs."

Inside apartment 5-D, Sy Cohen and Cal Severs hung slightly back while Hyte approached the body.

The crime scene unit had finished dusting for prints and was in the process of measuring all the angles and distances from the body in relation to the walls and doors and windows so that their sketches would be accurate.

The assistant medical examiner, Dr. Harry Lester, was bent over the body, his face perplexed. Hyte stopped near the M.E. to look down at Elaine Samson. At first he didn't see the bloated features; he saw the young face of a woman terrorized by an insane fanatic. "Harry?"

The M.E. glanced up. " 'Lo, Ray."

"How long?"

"The condition of the body puts it somewhere between nine and twelve days. But no more than twelve days. The body's still too bloated. All the windows were closed. The weather's cool, so there are no flies and maggot castings."

He thought about the computer printout, and he knew the when. "Make it ten days, on a Friday night into Saturday morning. Cause?"

"The only thing I can find right now is the crossbow bolt in her shoulder," the M.E. said, pointing to the aluminum shaft. "It may be a quarrel, but I won't know until I take it out. But it didn't kill her, not where it is. Very little blood around the impact point. No, something else killed her. I'll know more when I do the autopsy."

A phrase from the computer report popped into Hyte's mind. Cause of death—a projectile resembling a short arrow. But it wasn't just a short arrow, it was a very specific arrow—a crossbow bolt. "When?"

"First thing in the A.M.," the M.E. said. "Ray, do you have another crazy?"

"I don't know. Maybe. She shouldn't have died."

He caught the flash of surprise that crossed Harry Lester's face. "You knew her?"

"I met her . . . once." Hyte took a breath of the foul air. Death was a smell you never got used to, but this time he wanted to remember it.

Signaling to Cohen and Severs, he started out of the apartment. "What do you have so far?" he asked Cohen when they were in the hall.

"A blank. No one here has seen her in the last two weeks. The super said she flew a lot."

"You call Trans Air?"

"Yes. Roberts caught the case. I'm supervising. He'll go to see personnel tomorrow. If homicide has no objections," he added, looking at Severs, "I'd like Roberts to stay on this one."

139

"We'll have to clear it with your boss," Severs told Cohen, "but it's okay if he wants to work *with* us."

"I want everything," Hyte said, ignoring the interdepartmental byplay. "I want the sixty-one report on my desk tomorrow and I want to see every piece of paperwork that's done on the case. I don't want a single word breathed to the press."

"Ray, what's going on?"

Hyte worried his lower lip before answering Cohen. "Elaine Samson is the second hostage from Flight 88 who's been killed," he said. "The copilot, Flaxman, was killed three weeks ago. The cause of death is listed as a short arrow."

Sy Cohen's already strained face seemed to age before Hyte's eyes. The sergeant blinked. "Why would anyone want to hurt them after what they've been through?"

The dark and choppy waters of the East River lapped at the cement embankment twenty feet below where Hyte sat. He'd been at Carl Schurz Park for over an hour, trying to sort out his thoughts. The chill breezes blowing off the water assured him of solitude.

Behind him and to his left, the lights of Gracie Mansion glowed. The mayor was having another reception. Hyte didn't dwell on that. He thought about Elaine Samson and Richard Flaxman.

What about the other victim? Barum Kaliel. He had been number two. What connection, if any, did he have with Samson and Flaxman?

And why were these people being killed? Revenge? By whom? Could others of Rashid Mohamad's terrorist group be trying to murder the former hostages to avenge the deaths of the hijackers?

He rejected the notion. If that were the case, there would have been propaganda statements as soon as Flaxman had been killed.

And why would someone use an archaic weapon when

140

there were so many alternatives available? Just where in hell does one get a crossbow? A museum?

The only thing Hyte was certain of was that someone had killed three people, two of whom had been hostages on Flight 88. Coincidence? He wondered if he would find a deeper connection between Samson and Flaxman.

He gave a mental shrug. All the speculation in the world was useless without facts. He would have to wait until tomorrow, when more reports came in.

He wished he had a cigarette. Then he wished the day could start over again. Then he laughed at himself. He could have stayed a lawyer, he could have stayed married to Susan and by now be on the board of directors of her father's bank. And if he had, he would be at home now, helping his daughter with her homework.

He could have done a lot of things, but he hadn't.

He thought about Emma. He wanted to see her. No, he corrected himself, he *needed* to see her, just as he'd needed to see her after the hijacking.

He stared out into the darkness. Was he in love with Emma, or was it something else? Maybe it was compulsion, a psychological need, to be in love with a woman who was the opposite of his ex-wife.

Laughing at himself, Hyte left the park. He walked to York. There, he looked up at the tall building on the corner of Eighty-seventh Street: forty-one stories of cooperative apartments that sold for a minimum of six hundred thousand dollars.

He followed the curved drive to the main entrance, where he asked for Emma Graham, gave his name, and waited for the doorman to call apartment 36-H.

He felt the familiar build-up of anticipation begin. He always felt it when he was going to see Emma. It was a good sensation.

The ride up took two minutes. But as he walked down the long hallway, Elaine Samson's bloated face appeared before him. He stopped halfway to Emma's door and pushed aside the image.

141

The door opened. Emma's brown eyes gazed at him in concern.

"Hi," she said. She kissed him lightly and handed him a Scotch.

He smiled. "I see you were prepared."

"Anxious, I guess," she said as they walked into her living room. The room never failed to amaze him. It was about twenty-two by thirty with surprisingly high ceilings for a modern building. The furniture was contemporary, with smooth flowing lines and sharp but uncomplicated angles. The color scheme was a melange of earth tones, from brown to pastel rust.

Set on its own wall, with a double spotlight shining down, was a Picasso. Jonah and Anita Graham had given it to Emma on her twenty-seventh birthday—the same day she had been promoted to vice president of Graham International.

"Are you okay?" Emma asked.

Hyte sat next to her. "I'm fine."

"Want to talk about it?"

He gazed at her. Yes, he wanted to talk about it, but he didn't want to bring the Job into their personal lives. He didn't want to dirty Emma's world with what he had seen tonight; even more, he didn't want to alarm her.

"The homicide was a woman who was murdered about ten days ago. She was killed in the same way as two other people."

She frowned. "Do you know who did it?"

He shook his head. "I have no idea. And I don't want to talk about it right now."

She reached up hesitantly. Her fingers grazed his cheek. "All right," she said. She lowered her hand but did not turn away from him. "Are you comfortable with me?"

"With you or with us?"

"Both. It's something we've never talked about."

He nodded thoughtfully. "Yes, I'm comfortable with you, and with us."

She sighed. It was a gentle whispering sound. "I'm not trying to press you about our relationship."

142

He caught her hand between both of his. "A cop's life isn't easy. The hours are long and the job interferes with relationships. I know that what I'm saying sounds like a worn-out cliché, and maybe it is. But it's also the way things are for me. Even when I'm off duty, I'm on. I want you to think hard about me, Emma, and about any future we might have together."

Her eyes locked on him. "I have, Ray. Believe me, I have."

The intensity of her words startled him. He searched her face, seeking for something but not sure of what. "I can't promise you a hell of a lot."

Her mouth grew taut. "I don't want promises. I don't believe in them. What I want is you."

Nineteen

"Thought you'd be here sooner," Harry Lester said, in his Bellevue Hospital office.

"What do you have so far?" Hyte asked.

"It wasn't a quarrel. It was a broadhead."

Hyte studied the projectile that had been removed from Elaine Samson's shoulder. The doctor had put it into a clear plastic bag. The innocuous looking bolt had a black plastic double-fletching, set at a hundred and eighty degree angle, rather than the triple-fletching of a standard type of arrow. The nock end was ungrooved. The shaft was gold anodized aluminum.

"What's the difference?"

"The quarrel derives its name from medieval times," Harry Lester explained. "A quarrel's tip is a quartered head—a narrow X—so it can penetrate armor. If it hit an unarmored man, it would go straight through. A broadhead is for hunting, it's meant to be stopped in flesh."

"Any prints on the bolt?"

"Clean as a baby's ass."

"Did it kill her?"

"No."

"What did?"

"I don't know yet. I'm ordering full drug and tox screens. I'm going to run some scrapings from the broadhead as well."

"Poison?"

144

"From what I've seen," he said, "her vital organs shut down. There are no visible signs of poison, but it's been a long time since she died. There are exotic nerve poisons that leave the body with the body fluids."

"So you can't tell me anything, then?"

"I can tell you a whole lot. She hadn't had sex before she died. She had a low grade vaginal infection from a recent abortion. Her nasal passages are lousy and she'd done coke sometime before death." Hyte detected apprehension in the M.E.'s eyes. "But the weapon bothers me. I've been a pathologist for twenty-six years. This is my first crossbow assault."

"Mine, too," Hyte said. "Harry, if you do find poison, and before you call in the chief M.E., check your counterparts in Queens and Brooklyn. Each one has a victim."

"I'll take the samples to toxicology myself. I'll call you later." The M.E. glanced at the bolt. "You do have another crazy, don't you?"

"Not a word, Harry. Not one fucking word to anyone."

Sally O'Rourke smiled at Hyte when he walked up to her desk. "I have the report on Kaliel, the copies of the PDU sixty-ones on both homicides, and the borough squad reports."

He motioned her into his private office, hung up his jacket, and sat at his desk. The handle of his service piece snagged on the seatback. He unholstered it from his hip and put it in the top drawer.

O'Rourke opened the thick manila file folder. "Barum Kaliel," she read, "was in New York on a student visa. He was from Jordan, here attending N.Y.U. Lou, he was a passenger on Flight 88."

"I don't remem—" Hyte cut himself off and turned away from O'Rourke, grappling with the staggering implications her words brought to mind.

It tied the three deaths to a common point: the hijacking. And for Hyte, it brought forth the knowledge that a part of that long ago night of torment and death was still not over.

145

"He was a coach class passenger?" he said at last.

"Yes. Immigration says there was no trouble with him at all."

Hyte wondered what the connections between the three could be. Had they been involved with Mohamad? He rejected the idea immediately. The copilot and stewardess had been too terrified during the hijacking to have been faking.

"What about Flaxman?"

"The building canvass turned up a girlfriend. She was in the apartment when he was killed. Her name is Katherine Sircolli."

Once again, he was caught short by the unexpected. Katherine Sircolli was the only child of Antonio—Tony the Fist—Sircolli. The years peeled away with the mention of Sircolli's name. Hyte had first met Katherine when she was six. She had been a cute child, with huge eyes and matchstick arms and legs.

He had been undercover for seven months, working for Phil Mason and the Organized Crime Control Bureau when he'd met Sircolli, the head of the Tiacona crime family.

It had been Hyte's job to infiltrate that family. It had taken him almost four years to work his way close to Tony the Fist.

"Go on," he said.

O'Rourke looked down at the report. "The last time she saw him was in his apartment, five minutes before he was killed. She said he told her to make sure the door was locked after he left. He was due back the next night. They were supposed to have dinner with her father. Flaxman had never met him."

"Who took the statement?"

"Queens Homicide."

"When we're finished, get me the dick who caught the case. What else?"

"Nothing. Homicide interviewed his friends and co-workers. Flaxman was liked. According to several stewardesses, he played around a lot."

"Is there an Elaine Samson listed?"

O'Rourke skimmed the witness interview reports. "Yes. She stated that they had dated at one time, but they didn't see each other anymore."

He snorted. Two of the three victims knew each other intimately. But where, exactly, did Kaliel fit in? Could Tony the Fist be involved?

Hyte dialed the CD.

"Is it important?" Philip Mason asked.

"Very."

"I've got fifteen minutes before a meeting with the PC."

"On my way." He hung up and looked at O'Rourke. "When I get back I want to speak with the detective who interviewed Katherine Sircolli. Make it ten o'clock."

"You fielded Leighton's interview nicely," Mason said.

"She's an egotistical twit."

"But a necessary one," Mason said. "What's so important this morning?"

Hyte took a sip of coffee. "I picked up a pattern yesterday. I think I confirmed it last night. I'm waiting for a toxicology report before I make a formal commitment. There have been three homicides in three weeks in three boroughs. The M.O. is the same, and the probability is high that the murder weapon is the same."

Mason's face was unreadable. "What else?"

"All three victims were on the Trans Air flight that was hijacked last June. Two were crew members, one a coach passenger." He explained about the three homicides and the connections between the victims. "Chief," he said formally, "I want permission to look into this."

"What do you make of it?"

Hyte didn't like the guarded tone in Mason's voice. "I'm not sure yet. It could be any of a number of things. Terrorists avenging the deaths of their brethren, a passenger who went over the edge, even some psycho who wasn't involved at all but decided he wanted a taste of what happened. Christ almighty, I don't think there's a person in

147

the country who hasn't seen one of the television specials on the hijacking.''

"Ray—"

"I'm all right," he said sharply. Then he sat back and made himself relax.

Mason continued to stare at him. "I'll bring it up at today's meeting.''

"Not yet. Let me dig a little deeper, get my facts straight. I need that toxicology report from Harry Lester. If it *is* poison, we'll also have to get corroboration from the other two M.E.'s."

"If these three homicides have a set M.O., can we afford to wait?''

"If the pattern we found is right, we've got four days. Let me do the follow-ups. I need to speak with the borough medical examiners, homicide, and the PDUs.''

"Then why are you here now?''

"Because I thought you should know. And, I want to get a head start on setting up a task force if we need it.''

"Who?''

"Sy Cohen and Jimmy Roberts from the One-Nine. Cal Severs from Manhattan Homicide.''

Mason shook his head. "O'Leary just put in his papers. Severs is next up for captain. I want him where he is.''

Hyte knew that the chief of detectives had to make his own department. Mason had inherited Captain O'Leary, who commanded the recently reestablished Manhattan Borough Homicide Squad. Now he wanted his own man there.

"Who else?'' Mason asked.

"I'll use O'Rourke. That should be enough for now.''

"Ray," Mason began, "ever since—"

Hyte cut his boss off. "This has nothing to do with the hijacking, at least my part in it. This isn't some fantasy I've come up with to salve my conscience.''

"You're sure of that?''

"I'm sure.''

The chief of detectives glanced at his desk clock. Hyte took the hint and stood. "Phil?''

"You have twenty-four hours to come up with something."

At five minutes to twelve, ten minutes after speaking with the assistant medical examiner, Hyte sat at the head of a long table in one of the seventh-floor conference rooms. Sy Cohen, Jimmy Roberts, Sally O'Rourke, and Cal Severs were with him. While Severs would not be a part of the investigation, Hyte had wanted him at this meeting.

"I've talked with the M.E. The Samson death will be ruled homicide by poisoning. The fucking arrow was loaded with a puffer fish poison. The M.E. says the poison paralyzes the nervous system in forty to sixty seconds." He gave them a moment to digest his words. "The poison is Oriental, and very hard to come by."

"That's just great," Severs said. "And those two other bolts are sitting with the property clerks. If they're from the same perp—"

"Sally, when this meeting's over, I want you to call the property clerks in Brooklyn and Queens and warn them about the bolts," Hyte said. "Have them sent to Bert Hanson at the toxicology lab. When Hanson's finished with them, I want to try for some sort of ballistics match."

"If the poison is the same, won't that do?" O'Rourke asked.

"I still want to know what kind of a weapon was used. I mean, did someone swipe a crossbow from a museum, or is it a modern version?"

When no one said anything, he looked at Cohen and Roberts. "You two come up with anything?"

Roberts spoke first, his voice low and steady. "I went over to Trans Air this morning. Elaine Samson was last seen on Friday night, March twenty-sixth. She'd been working a Dallas to New York flight. She'd stopped working overseas flights after she was involved in the 88 hijacking.

"The plane arrived on time—one-fifteen. She signed out at one thirty-five. That was the last anyone saw of her."

"Why wasn't there a check on her?"

"She was officially on a two-week vacation."

Hyte jotted down a note: *Could the killer be someone in the airlines?* "Anything else?"

"No one on my squad came up with anything in the neighborhood," Sy Cohen said.

"Cal?"

Severs shook his head. "Nothing on the license plates or the street canvass."

"All right, gentlemen, and lady," Hyte said. "I think there's a good possibility we have an honest-to-God pattern killer on our hands. What I don't know is if the killer has a scrambled brain or is out for revenge. What I do know is that someone has killed two crew members and one passenger from Flight 88, which was hijacked last June. And I have a feeling that this may only be the beginning."

"How do we find out?" Severs asked.

"By not having another killing on a Friday night," Hyte said. "But we've got a few things to do first." He looked at Sy Cohen and Jimmy Roberts. "Effective as of now, the two of you are on temporary assignment to the chief of detectives' staff. I'll clear it through your boss later. Sy, I want you to see if there's a deeper connection between Samson and Flaxman, and if Kaliel was somehow involved in it. But don't reinterview Katherine Sircolli. I'll handle that."

"Cal," he added, "I asked the chief for you. But he's got other plans that you'll be hearing about soon. You have anyone to recommend?"

"Tim Smith from the Queens squad, the one who caught the Flaxman case, is a good man if you can get him."

"Okay. Thank you for coming in." Hyte didn't ask Severs to keep things to himself. He knew he would.

When the lieutenant was gone, Hyte turned to the three remaining cops. "Sally, I want the passenger manifest from Flight 88, addresses of the passengers, current status, and a rap sheet check. Also, do a teletype to the FBI and Interpol on similar M.O.'s. Roberts, we need the whereabouts of all the victims for the forty-eight hours prior to their deaths. Maybe a check will show a connection between the three.

"And all of you, when you have a spare minute, try and

150

figure out a way to turn up a weapon. Who the hell sells crossbows—hunting and sporting goods stores?''

"I'll see what I can do," Cohen said, rising.

"One more thing." The three looked at him silently. "The chief has given me twenty-four hours to come up with something solid."

"That's magnanimous of him," Cohen said.

"Sally, call Dan Carson and ask him to send over an unedited tape of the 88 hijacking. I think we'll all need to look it over." He paused and smiled at them. "I want everyone back here at six to go over it all again."

"You want company when you go to Sircolli?" Cohen asked.

He gazed at the man who had been his first partner, the man who had taught him most of his street sense, and slowly shook his head. "I can handle it, Sy, thanks."

Hyte parked across the street from an impressive brick house on a well-to-do street in Whitestone, Queens. The three-story house, red brick with white framed windows, dominated the street. So did the two men standing idly on the front sidewalk.

The men were part of a revolving contingent of body-guards maintained by Tony the Fist Sircolli. Hyte knew one of the two from his undercover days. His name was Carl Betaglia. His street name was The Pin. At six-two, and weighing a bare hundred and sixty pounds, the hood had earned his nickname.

The second man was unfamiliar. He had a bullet head, no neck, and small dark eyes. Hyte decided the man's street name would probably be Attila.

He got out of the car. The man he didn't recognize turned away. Betaglia didn't.

"Where you going, pig?" Betaglia snapped.

"Don't push it, Carl," Hyte said in a low voice.

"You got a warrant or somethin'?"

Hyte wasn't worried about Betaglia or the other man,

151

they wouldn't do anything here. "Official business," he said.

"Don't," Betaglia warned, signaling his partner to block Hyte's way.

Hyte grinned at the two hoods. "I said I'm here on official Department business. Now, if you want to push me, I'll have both your asses hauled in for obstruction as well as weapons charges."

"We've got tickets for our pieces," Betaglia stated. *"O-fish-ell* tickets!"

"Not as official as mine," Hyte said, challenging Betaglia with a hard glare.

The hood broke eye contact. "Wait here."

While Hyte waited, Attila glared. When Betaglia returned, he told Hyte that Mr. Sircolli would see him. Then the skinny hood held his hand out, palm up. "The piece."

Drawing his revolver, Hyte opened the cylinder and emptied it into Betaglia's hand. Then he walked past Betaglia and up the steps.

He found Tony the Fist waiting for him. Antonio Sircolli's nickname came only in part by his reputation for ruthlessness. The other part was the size of his hands—slabs that could beat an opponent senseless. His face, though, was smooth and babylike. His eyes, blackish brown, were intelligent; although it was brute force that had won him his high position, it was his mind which had kept it.

"Long time," Sircolli said without offering his hand. "Never thought you'd have the balls to come here again."

"Some things can't be helped. I didn't think sending one of my men would be the right thing."

"You had me cold, back then. I trusted you, I believed you were who you said you were. And I never once made you for a cop."

"I know," Hyte said. When he'd been undercover for the OCCB, he'd played the part of the unhappy son of a dead cop to the hilt.

"Inside." Sircolli led Hyte into an ornate living room. Three of the four walls were sheathed in blue flocked wallpaper. Centered on the fourth was a huge marble fireplace. The furniture was Italian, imported from Rome.

"Drink?"

Hyte shook his head. "It's about the Flaxman murder," he said. Hyte didn't miss the flash of surprise in Sircolli's eyes.

"Katherine's made a statement already. Why is a lieutenant on the chief of detectives' staff interested in this? Or is it because she's my daughter and you and your boss have been after me for too many fucking years?"

Hyte ignored the question. "Tony, I want the truth. Did you have it in for Flaxman because he was having an affair with your daughter?"

Sircolli's laughter caught him unprepared. "I never met Flaxman. I checked him out real good, but I never met him. Katherine's got a mind of her own. And, she loved him. That's all that mattered."

Hyte believed him. "What have you come up with?"

Sircolli's eyes narrowed. "Nothing. Not a fucking thing. Who the hell kills a man with an arrow?"

Hyte didn't have an answer for the gangster, but Sircolli had answered one of his questions when he'd said "arrow" instead of bolt. "I need to speak with Katherine."

"About what?" came a woman's voice. Turning, Hyte saw the grown version of the child he had known. She was no longer the skinny kid of his memory; rather, her limbs had filled out nicely. Her eyes, large and gray, still dominated her face but no longer overpowered her other features.

"Hello, Katie," he said.

"Hello, Lieutenant Hyte."

"I have to ask you some questions about Richard Flaxman."

Katherine nodded. "Go ahead."

Hyte glanced at Sircolli. "Alone."

"Why?"

Hyte's eyes hardened. "Because I'm interviewing a witness."

Sircolli smiled. "I forgot how good an actor you are.

153

Don't push her. And Ray, if you need a hand on this, for anything, just say the word. It's real personal. . . ."

When Sircolli left, Hyte motioned Katherine to the couch, and sat next to her. "Tell me about Flaxman."

Her eyes took on a look of loss and pain. "There's not a lot to tell," she said. "I met him when I was on vacation. We hit it off. We became lovers. Then I fell in love with him."

"Was he in love with you?"

Katherine's eyes flooded with tears. "The night he . . . he was killed, was the first time he told me that he loved me. We'd been seeing each other for five months. He'd never said it before."

"Did he say anything to you about someone being after him?"

"No. And I think if there was someone, he would have told me."

"Flaxman had a reputation of being a ladies man."

She surprised him by smiling. "He had, Lieutenant. And I knew all about it. But something happened to him and he stopped playing."

"What happened?"

Her eyes narrowed. "Don't you know? You were there."

Hyte nodded. "I read your statement from the files. Is there anything else you can tell me? Anything you forgot about? Some small detail? An old conversation?"

She shook her head. "After the first cop spoke to me, I spent days thinking back, trying to remember something Richard might have said. But there was nothing. I only wish there had been."

"Thank you," Hyte said, standing.

"Lieutenant?"

He waited, gazing down at her.

"You find the bastard who killed my man."

For a fraction of a second, she reminded Hyte of her father. "I will," he said.

Twenty

At five minutes to five, Hyte entered the Blue Room, a neighborhood bar situated diagonally across from Bellevue, and ordered two Scotch and waters.

Harry Lester came through the front door and ambled over to the stool next to him. He drained half the waiting drink, sighing, "God, what a day. And yes, the other two bolts arrived. My friends in Queens and Brooklyn thank you for the warning."

Hyte studied the M.E. "Since you've become my specialist in medieval weapons, what about looking for a match? Is it possible?"

"The three bolts are from the same manufacturer. Whether or not they were fired from the same weapon, who knows?"

"Can we find out?"

"How? There are no barrel grooves, no powder, and no ballistics match points. The boys in the crime scene lab can look, but I wouldn't hold out much hope."

"Have you formed any opinions on the killer?"

"Using what for a basis? If it was a knife I'd be able to get a possible height and weight by the entry of the blade. But a crossbow? The only thing I can tell you is that the killer fired the bolt level with Samson's shoulder."

Hyte held his arm straight out. "You're saying that the killer's extended arm is the height of Samson's shoulder?

155

That would make the killer about the same height as Samson—about five-six or five-seven."

"It's possible, but don't take it as gospel. The killer could also have held the bow high if he's short, or low if he's tall."

"That's modern forensic pathology," Hyte murmured. "Accurate to a fault. So you have no ideas."

The M.E. shrugged. "Opinions, uneducated guesses."

"You've got an illiterate for a student. Go ahead."

"To begin with, a crossbow's bolt, unless it hits a main organ or artery, is not always fatal. And Ray, the killer knows that. The poison is there to insure death. If the tip of the bolt penetrates the outer layers of the skin, there's no chance for survival. A crossbow is a man's weapon. A regular bow and arrow could be a woman's weapon, but psychologically and historically, the crossbow has always been associated with a warrior, and a warrior is associated with a man."

"Then you think it's a man?" Hyte said.

"If I had to guess, I'd say yes. But that's all it is, a guess."

"What about the poison?"

"Just what I said. He didn't want to leave anything to chance."

"When will I get the complete tox results on the other bolts?"

"Tomorrow morning."

"Early," Hyte said. "I need to give the chief something by tomorrow."

"First thing in the morning."

"Thanks."

Hyte fell silent, thinking that almost twenty-four hours after the discovery of Elaine Samson's body, he had only three facts: She was on Flight 88 with Flaxman and Kaliel; she died by poison; and the odds, dictated by the killer's choice of weapon, favored the killer to be a man.

His job was now to connect the three assumed facts to one common killer. But he knew he didn't have a chance of stopping the next murder, if there was to be one.

* * *

The sight that greeted Hyte when he returned to his office stopped him dead in his tracks. Neatly lined up on his desk were two crossbows and a dozen bolts. He looked at O'Rourke. "Where?"

"Thomas Outfitters, off Centre Street."

He approached the weapons and array of crossbow bolts. "The gun shop?"

"It's a little fancier than a gun shop," O'Rourke said. "The hijacking tapes came. I set up the conference room with a television and tape deck."

"They sell these over the counter?"

"Uh-uh. The sale of crossbows is prohibited within the city limits."

"We're lucky no one's used them to chill anyone before. How did you get them?"

"Richard Thomas is a personal friend. He had these delivered from his Jersey store when I explained that you needed to see them."

Hyte picked up the crossbow and checked its balance and telescopic sight. He put the scope to his eye and aimed out the window. The cross hairs centered on the ramp of the Manhattan bridge. He followed a Volkswagen.

"According to the brochures, these weapons are more than just deadly. Their accuracy range is around fifteen to twenty yards. The 'scoped model is called a magnum. Effective range is about twenty-five yards. They're powerful, Lou. Real powerful."

"He showed you how they work?"

O'Rourke picked one up. Butting the back end of the weapon against her abdomen, she used both hands to draw the string.

"This one has forty-five pounds of draw weight tension on the prod—the bow. When it's first strung, the safety is automatically engaged."

She flicked the safety off and pulled the trigger. "It makes a silenced gun sound like a cannon. And they even have multi-shot revolving barrels and a foot stirrup and hand hook set up for easier and faster reloading."

Hyte took it from her and strung the crossbow. He chose a round head from the bolts on his desk.

"That's used for target practice."

He slid the bolt into its groove under the flat metal clip that held it immobile in the release seat above the trigger mechanism. He pointed the weapon at the stuffed chair against the wall, clicked the safety off, and fired.

He wasn't able to track the bolt. But he heard the low sound of its release, and the thunk it made when it struck the wood through three inches of cushion.

"Jesus," he whispered. It took him a quarter of a minute to work the bolt free.

"Richard called them toys," O'Rourke said.

"They're anything but. Did you hear from Cohen?"

"Cohen and Roberts should be here by six. Miss Graham called about four."

"Thanks." He hoped Emma would understand that until they found the killer, his time would no longer be his own.

The conference room table was cluttered with empty food cartons, paper plates, and dead beer bottles. Midnight was fifteen minutes away. Tuesday was almost over. Sy Cohen and Jimmy Roberts had left a half hour before. Hyte had chased a reluctant Sally O'Rourke out ten minutes later, after telling her that starting tomorrow, she was to go plainclothes.

It had been thirty hours since he'd gotten the phone call about Samson. He had another nine hours before his meeting with the chief of detectives.

He picked up the passenger manifest for Flight 88 and looked at the names of the first-class passengers.

Sylvia Mossberg lived in Englewood, New Jersey. Michael Barnes resided in Rockland County, just outside of Manhattan. Sonja and Jack Mofferty lived in Bay Shore, Long Island. Jonah Graham was in Westchester. The Helenezes' address of record was Portugal. J. Milton Prestone resided in Santa Fe, New Mexico.

Hyte scanned the coach passenger list. He crossed off Kaliel's name. That left eleven passengers living in the New York Metro area; among them was Lea D'Anjine, who lived in Manhattan with her adoptive parents. Her name was now Lea Desmond.

His eyes locked on the name. It had taken the little girl months to recover from the hijacking. He'd felt, perhaps irrationally, that he had an obligation to help her. Shortly after the hijacking, he had begun to visit Lea and her parents. Emma had gone with him, and had developed a strong tie with the girl. Hyte had often wondered if he was using Lea to replace the time he'd always spent with Carrie.

For Hyte, going to Boston once a month and staying at a hotel while Carrie slept at home was a far cry from her twice monthly visits to New York. The intimacy between them had lessened, and it hurt.

He stopped himself and studied the crew list. He crossed off Flaxman, Samson. The next name was Joan Bidding. She lived in Rego Park, in Queens. Of the five stewardesses, two lived in Manhattan.

Earlier, he'd divided the passenger list between Cohen, Roberts, and O'Rourke. They would check on the current whereabouts of each passenger.

He had also assigned O'Rourke the task of contacting the manufacturers of the various crossbows to get a distributor list as well as the current retail outlet list.

He wondered what else he could do. He glanced at the video tape cassettes of the hijacking. There were five of them. Each was an hour long. Two were edited down versions of the hijacking done as television specials. The last three were banded together and detailed every minute the camera had spent in first class.

He had shown the unedited version to the three cops, forcing himself to watch when Anita Graham was killed. It had taken almost an hour for him to lose the taste of bile from his mouth.

Then he looked back at the list. Flaxman and Samson

were beginning-to-end hostages. The Jordanian student had been released almost at the beginning.

He sensed that there was a purpose for their deaths, a purpose tied into the hijacking itself. But what?

"Goddamn it!" he shouted, his hand sending the legal pad skittering across the table.

Hyte unlocked his apartment door and went wearily inside. He turned on the stereo and poured two fingers of Martell's cognac into a snifter. An old Beach Boys song came on as he turned on the shower, using the hot water to help ease his tension.

Wrapped in a towel, he returned to the living room. He sat on the couch, cradling the cognac, and took a long swallow.

He thought about Emma.

She'd stopped by his office, earlier. She had wanted to see him tonight. He explained that they couldn't meet because he was working on the new case. She told him that she was going to San Francisco. A problem had developed with one of the new catalogue stores. Following that, she'd favored him with a long and searching gaze that he had not been able to fathom.

"When are you leaving?"

"Tomorrow night. I've got a seven o'clock flight."

"I'll take you to the airport."

"I was hoping for more, but I won't argue."

Hyte swirled the cognac. Emma was quite a woman. Susan had been quite a girl. Susan had been given everything by her father and expected her life to be well ordered. And it had been, until Hyte had broken her rules and forsaken her father's bank for the Department.

His hours had added to the wedge that had divided them. The other things came later: his unwillingness to talk about the Job, the secrecy of what he was doing. She complained that her life was becoming pointless. That there was a void that was never filled.

But Emma was vastly different. He was fascinated by her.

160

She was a strong woman who was capable of having a career and a relationship. She had no need to live life through another, but was able to share her life and accept his without trying to change what he was. And while he sometimes believed that he was trying to make up for what had happened to her mother and father, he had no doubts as to his feelings for her.

Hyte swirled the snifter and smiled. It was at times like tonight, he admitted, that his feelings for Emma bordered on compulsion.

He knew, too, that if he were to remarry, it would be to someone who could accept his work. If I get married, he told himself, it will be to an Emma Graham.

He laughed. The trouble was, he added to his silent dialogue, there was only one Emma Graham.

Hyte drained the cognac and stood. The doorbell chimed. Puzzled, he went to the door. "Yes?"

"Is that any way to greet me?" asked Emma.

Hyte stepped back to let her enter. She shed her coat in the living room and sat down. "I hope you don't mind," she said mischievously.

Recovering from the surprise of seeing her at his door, he smiled. "Not at all."

"It's funny," she said. "I keep thinking about going to San Francisco, and leaving you." She laughed lightly, a trace of self-embarrassment underlying the sound. "I tried to figure out a way to bring you with me."

"I wish I could go, but . . ."

". . . you have a case. I know. It's all right. I'm just in a mood."

"How about a drink?"

She shook her head, patting the cushion next to her. He joined her, slipping his arm around her shoulders. She leaned her head back.

"The manager of the store is having problems. But it shouldn't take too long. A few days at the most," she said. "It's not necessary for you to take me to the airport."

"I know."

"But I needed to be with you tonight."

They fell silent; the only sound came from the stereo. He drew her closer, kissing her forehead lightly. Her simple statement made him feel closer to her. Then Emma lifted her head and looked at him. "Have you made any progress on the new case?"

He studied her face. Her eyes were wide, the black pupils almost blending into the brown irises. He wondered how to tell her that someone was blowing away the survivors of Flight 88, and that her father might be a victim. He knew he'd have to, eventually. But not tonight. He didn't want to spoil the warmth of the moment.

"No. I've got nothing, yet."

Twenty-one

The room was shrouded in darkness. The only light, coming from three small floods set in a ceiling tract, was directed to one wall.

The sixteen-foot wall was a new addition, built seven months before. It was plywood, painted a flat white, and it covered the two windows behind it. A horizontal row of photographs was spread across the wall. The first three had crosses, made by a thick black marker, marring their glossy surfaces. The first picture was of Richard Flaxman. The second, Elaine Samson. The third, Barum Kaliel.

There was one chair in the room. A workbench was set against the wall opposite that with the photographs. On a third wall, a television rested on a stand.

The television was on, its picture fed by a VCR. The figures on the screen were the passengers on the hijacked Trans Air Flight 88.

The room's solitary occupant, sitting in the chair and holding a black crossbow, turned from the television and looked at the photo wall. The occupant of the room had taken a new name, Samael, God's Messenger of Death. It was the name of a little-known figure from Hebraic mythology. It would be Samael's divine mission to teach the lessons of life, one of which was the acceptance of death to those who thought they had outwitted it.

The crossbow was set. Seventy pounds of tension held the prod stiff. A hunting bolt rested in the triangular rapid fire barrel. Samael stroked the weapon, one finger caressing the anodized aluminum shaft. Samael raised the weapon toward the fourth photograph. Slowly, Samael drew the trigger back.

The sound of the bolt's release could not be heard above the sound of Rashid Mohamad's voice berating the passengers. In the semidarkness, nothing could be seen of the golden bolt's flight. But the thud of the broadhead into wood could be heard. The bolt's shaft vibrated. The arrowhead was buried two-thirds of the way into the wood.

Samael, God's Messenger of Death, teacher of acceptance, smiled. The hunting bolt had bisected the head of the next victim.

Twenty-two

At exactly 8:45 A.M., Hyte gave Mason his report. "The problem is that we don't have a single hint as to who the killer might be," he summarized.

"Have you given any further thought to the possibility that they're terrorist reprisals?"

"Yes. And it doesn't add up. Terrorists don't use crossbows; they use machine pistols and bombs."

"If not terrorists, then who?" Mason asked.

"I make it as one of three possibles—a passenger who's gone a little nuts, a psycho, or a relative of one of the original victims."

"All right," Mason said, nodding ponderously. "You have conditional authorization to extend the preliminary investigation."

"That's pretty damned noncommittal. Contingent upon what?"

"I have to bring this to the PC and chief of department. Ray, you're still a lieutenant. There are protocols to be followed."

Hyte sighed. The rules were simple. A task force must be headed by someone of the rank of captain or above. "I want this one," he said urgently. "It's important to me."

"That's horseshit and you know it."

"No," Hyte said stubbornly. "In the sixteen years I've spent on the Job, the favors I've asked of you haven't been that many or that big. I want this case and I don't care what you have to do to get it for me!"

"Ray, you're a desk cop. That hijacker made sure of that."

"No!" Hyte repeated. "When my father died, you had no business taking on his murderer yourself. But you did it because it was a personal obligation." He stopped speaking until he gained control over his emotions. "To a degree, this case is like that for me. I know things are a little sticky up high, but I have to have this case and I don't want it turned into a political issue. And I don't give a damn who heads the task force, so long as he doesn't interfere with me."

"Even a nominal head of a task force will want input if he's taking the responsibility."

"Then get me a temporary promotion to captain."

"I can't justify that in this instance," Mason said, meeting Hyte's eyes openly. Then, slowly, he nodded. "But I'll think of something. How many more people will you need?"

Hyte exhaled slowly. Without putting it into a direct command, Phil Mason had given him his task force. "One more for now. A clerical as well."

"Give me the names and I'll okay them."

"I'll also need to borrow half a dozen bodies for a day or two for interviews with the coach passengers and crew."

"I'll see what I can do," Mason said. "Maybe pull in a dozen off-duty uniforms for overtime. Get it done quicker that way." He paused. "I'll call a press conference for five."

"I'd like to keep this one close for a little longer."

"You'll handle this exactly the way I tell you, because if you don't, someone else will. Ever since Son of Sam, it's been departmental policy to inform the media of a serial criminal as soon as we have established a pattern. If you want this case, you'll play by my rules!"

Hyte knew he had no choice. "I'll play," he said reluctantly.

"Have a statement ready for the conference."

"Phil—"

"Just do it. And Ray, no matter what you think I owe you, you're going to owe me big on this one."

"Sure."

"Don't give me sure! Give me the autopsy reports, the sixty-ones, all the follow-ups, and a list of possible suspects. And I want it on my desk in an hour."

One hour later, Hyte sent the copies of all reports to the chief of detectives, along with a short, written update of his own. The suspect list was a Xerox copy of the passenger and crew manifest, with the names of the dead people crossed off.

Then he called the boss of Queens Homicide and asked him to put Tim Smith on loan to the CD's staff. Captain Kelsey was more than obliging. Hyte knew that it wasn't the polite request that had garnered him Smith; it was the fact that Kelsey did not want to have the chief told that he was not a team player.

He called O'Rourke into his office. She wore a three-piece suit: gray skirt, white blouse, and matching gray jacket. The shirt had a no-nonsense collar that showed off a slender neck.

"You look good in plainclothes."

"Thank you."

"Where are Cohen and Roberts?"

"Doing the passenger check," she said.

"What about you?"

"I found only three major manufacturers of the cross-bows. They also make the bolts. They're sending in distributor lists."

"Feds?"

"No response yet. Interpol wired that they have no M.O. that fits our killer. They did have two cases of death by crossbow, but both perpetrators were caught. One is dead, the other's serving life in a Greek prison."

"Tim Smith from the Queens squad will be in today. Make him feel welcomed."

"Sure. What happened with the chief?"

"We're covered. Call down for a clerical to fill in on your job. Written authorization will follow."

O'Rourke's smile illuminated the room. "Thanks, Lou."

He winked. "Where are you carrying?"

"Purse."

"Backup?"

O'Rourke stood, raised one leg, and put her flat-heeled shoe on the chair. She hitched her skirt up without embarrassment to reveal a lightweight .32 holstered to her thigh.

"Hope your boyfriend doesn't mind."

This time it was O'Rourke who winked.

When she left to make her calls, he looked at the list of names, and stopped at Joan Bidding.

He dialed her number. A woman with a Hispanic accent answered, "Beeding reseedence."

The maid informed Hyte that Mrs. "Beeding" was out, but would be back at noon. He left his name with the message that he would stop by then to see her.

He went back to the list, noting all the addresses of the passengers and crew who lived outside NYPD jurisdiction.

From his middle drawer, he took out the preprinted address book listing the various police departments in the surrounding counties.

He called O'Rourke on the intercom. "The clerical here yet?"

"Just now."

"Bring her in."

When O'Rourke came in, he saw that the "her" she had in tow, was a tall and slim black man in his early twenties. He wore a silver mezuzah on a thin silver chain. "Lieutenant Hyte, this is Randal Schwartz," O'Rourke said.

He blinked. "Schwartz?"

Schwartz smiled pleasantly. "It takes a little getting used to. My great-great-grandfather was a Falasha, an Ethiopian Jew who immigrated here. I guess, like most immigrants, he wanted to sound more American. Ankushabale isn't exactly a common American name."

"No it isn't," Hyte agreed, amused. "Randal, you are now on temporary assignment to the chief of detectives' staff.

Everything you see, do, and hear, will remain in confidence. Is that understood?''

''Absolutely.''

Hyte handed O'Rourke the list he'd written out. ''I want a call made to each of these jurisdictions, asking for cooperation. We want an eye kept on each of the former hostages, but don't spell it out all the way—no mention of the weapon. Show Randal how it's done and then get to work on your things.''

Sy Cohen entered. He stopped short when he saw Schwartz. ''Randy?''

''Hi, Sy,'' the clerk said, and followed O'Rourke out.

''You know him?'' Hyte asked.

''His father was on the Job. We were together in patrol cars before I made dick. The kid has a heart problem— nothing major, just enough to keep him a civilian. He's a good boy, though. His father retired after twenty. He was a standup cop. Had to put up with a lot of crap, being black and Jewish.''

''I'm sure,'' Hyte said as he picked up the intercom. He got Schwartz. ''Randal, I need a map of the five boroughs, and a chalkboard and stand. Sally will show you where they are.'' He looked at Cohen. ''From you, my friend, I need some input.''

Cohen shook his head. ''I don't know what to make of this one.''

Hyte laced his fingers behind his head and stared at the ceiling. ''Mason gave me the case because I pushed him. You and I were in this from the start, so don't tell me you don't know what to make of it.''

Cohen shrugged. ''It's just a feeling. . . . It has to be someone involved with either the pilot, the flight engineer, Anita Graham, or the Mofferty woman.''

Hyte leaned forward across his desk. ''That's how I read it.''

Cohen shifted. ''Are you going to check up on Emma?''

His friend's words startled him. Until that moment, he hadn't wanted to connect Emma to the case. ''No,'' he said. ''I'm too close to her. You handle Emma, very qui-

169

etly. Do a discreet check, including the past three Friday nights. We'll need a list of all the other relatives. Then we'll divide the workload between us.''

He checked the time. It was a quarter to eleven. He looked at the passenger list, noting the first name. ''Put Roberts and Tim Smith, when he gets here, on the rest of the first-class passengers. They can start with Michael Barnes. Have O'Rourke check the stewardesses from the flight, except for Joan Bidding—I'll do her.''

''Right away. Do you figure another attempt Friday night?''

''No reason not to,'' Hyte admitted. ''Which leaves us with forty-eight hours to come up with something.''

Sy's look said more than words as he left the office. Again, as one person went out, another came in.

''Lieutenant Hyte, I'm Tim Smith.''

Hyte found himself face to face with a wide-bodied black man. He went over to him and shook hands. ''I've heard good things abut you from Cal Severs. Do you know why you're here?''

''The captain said I was being put on temporary assignment to the CD. Something about the Flaxman case.''

''Close enough,'' Hyte said. ''Come with me, Sergeant Cohen will fill you in. You married?''

''Yes, sir.''

''Tell your wife you're going to be doing a lot of overtime.''

''She's used to it.''

Hyte looked at his watch again. He would need ten minutes to get his car. It would take another forty minutes to get to Rego Park through the noontime traffic. He'd have to leave by eleven.

''Let's get you started,'' he said, leading Smith through the outer office and down the hall to where Sy Cohen was working. He told Cohen he would need an up-to-the-minute report by four o'clock.

''We haven't gotten this investigation off the ground yet,'' Cohen said. ''What kind of up-to-the-minute report can I give you?''

170

Hyte thought about the press conference scheduled for later. "Anything that you think might be a possible lead," he said. He left then, his thoughts venturing along paths that he hoped might lead to a killer.

Deep inside him, a sense of excitement was brewing. He knew this was only the beginning, and that there would be long days of hard work ahead. But he was no longer sitting behind a desk, watching others solve his puzzles.

Hyte paused halfway to the elevator. His eyes went out of focus as he realized just how badly he wanted to catch this killer.

For atonement? he wondered.

He sighed. The underlying reasons didn't matter. It all came down to the same thing. He needed to catch the killer—for whomever the next victim might be, and for himself.

Twenty-three

At 62-30 Saunders Street, Hyte pressed the bell for apartment 3-C and waited.

"Yes?"

"Mrs. Bidding, it's Lieutenant Hyte. I called earlier."

The buzzer rang and Hyte opened the door. The lobby was well kempt, the linoleum floor polished. He waited only a minute for the elevator. When he reached the third floor, he stepped into a brightly lit hallway.

He knocked once on the door of apartment 3-C and took out his identification.

"Good afternoon Lieutenant," the stewardess said. "I must say it was a surprise when Maria told me you had called. But it gives me a chance to thank you for . . . for everything you did that night."

Hyte nodded and followed her into the living room, where she motioned him to a blue leather couch. "Coffee?"

"If it's no bother."

"I have a pot up. I'll be right back."

When she left, he looked around more closely. The couch was flanked by two barrel-style chairs covered in the same soft kidskin leather. A natural-wood coffee table was set in front of the couch. Across from him, an oak modular wall unit filled the solid wall. Pictures of Joan's children occupied almost every shelf.

The stewardess returned from the kitchen, placing a white plastic serving tray on the coffee table.

"Why are you here? Does it have something to do with the hijacking?"

Again, he saw the anxiety pulling at the skin around her eyes. "How well did you know Elaine Samson and Richard Flaxman?"

Joan Bidding picked up her cup. Her hand trembled. "I knew it," she whispered.

"Knew what?"

"You'd think that once the hijacking was over, life would get back to normal," she said. "But it doesn't, Lieutenant. We're all victims, and we're staying that way. Ever since that night my . . . my life hasn't been the same. I don't fly anymore. Did you know that?"

He shook his head.

"I asked to be transferred to ground staff. I'm a supervisor now."

"Mrs. Bidding—"

"Their deaths have something to do with the hijacking, don't they?" she whispered.

"That's what I'm trying to find out."

"They do," she stated unequivocally.

"Why do you say that?"

Bidding gripped her coffee cup. "When Flaxman was killed, it was called a case of random street violence. I tried to accept that, but when I heard about Elaine I knew something was wrong. They were killed by the same person, weren't they?"

"We don't know for sure."

"No? Then why are you here?"

"I'm trying to piece together what happened. A murder investigation is conducted with background checks on the victim's friends, family, co-workers."

"You're lying. You're here to see if I'm still alive."

He didn't bother to point out that if she were dead he would know about it. "Flaxman and Samson were lovers."

"Flaxman and a lot of stews were lovers at one time or another."

"Does that apply to Flaxman and yourself?"

Bidding stiffened. "Everyone thinks that a stewardess

173

hops in and out of men's beds as often as she flies. I'm a flight attendant. It's my profession, just as being a policeman is yours. And I believe in fidelity, if that means anything."

"It means a great deal." Hyte paused. "Was it over between Flaxman and Samson?"

"It ended shortly after the hijacking. As I said, nothing was the same afterward. Didn't it affect you at all? Or are police immune to that sort of thing?"

He met Joan's stare. Before he could reply, she spoke again. "No, you aren't immune. I can see it in your eyes."

"Then Samson and Flaxman were just co-workers?"

"They worked for the same company. Flaxman was promoted to pilot almost immediately after the hijacking. He flew international flights. Mostly Paris and London. But Elaine only flew stateside flights."

"Has anything unusual happened to you lately?"

Bidding laughed. "Everything is unusual lately. I had a solid marriage until nine months ago. Now I don't know if it's going to last another week. Do you know how hard it is to trust someone after you've lived through a night like I did?"

"I'm sorry, but I have to ask these questions."

She sighed. "What do you mean by unusual?"

"Has someone been following you? Have there been phone calls when you're home, the kind where there's no one on the other end?"

She shook her head. "We have an unlisted number. And I'm not aware of anyone following me. Lieutenant, what's going on?"

"We're not sure yet."

"I think I deserve the truth. You're here because you think that I'm either a likely victim, or . . . or the killer."

"Hardly," he snapped. "I'm here because you knew both Flaxman and Samson and you were on Flight 88. I'm here because I was on that plane, too. I thought it would be better for me to come than a stranger."

Joan Bidding nodded. "You're a good man, Lieutenant, but you aren't a good liar."

"That depends on who I'm lying to," he said, placing one of his cards on the coffee table. "If anything unusual happens, call."

She nodded. "I will. When you know more, will you tell me?"

Hyte stood. "There was another death. One of the coach passengers."

She blinked. Her teeth caught at her lower lip, worrying it.

"When you go out, don't go out alone. Try to avoid Friday nights if possible."

"I work nights one weekend a month as a supervisor."

"Have someone accompany you to and from work."

"Do you have any idea of who it might be? Any suspects?"

Hyte thought of the passenger manifest. "Too damned many."

Hyte returned to headquarters at three and went straight to his office. Randal Schwartz had set up the five-borough map and had put colored push pins at the locations of each killing.

A memo on his desk reminded him to be in Mason's office at a quarter to five. He called Emma and told her about the press conference, but promised her that he would meet her at the airport before flight time.

Then Hyte settled back and reread all the reports on the killings.

At a quarter to five, he went up to Mason's office. He found a Scotch and water waiting for him. He didn't like the omen. "Something wrong?"

"What could be wrong? I got you your task force."

"Who heads it?"

"I do," Mason said in a low voice.

Hyte halted the drink halfway to his mouth. He had found out what was wrong. The chief of detectives does not head a task force.

"Why?"

175

Mason drained his glass and set it down on the desk. "You asked me for a favor. It was the only way I could give it to you."

He went to the window and looked out. "McPheerson wanted his man, Inspector Conner, to take it. I told the commissioner that I wanted to handle it personally, since it was my department who came up with it. Rutledge saw it my way.

"But," Mason added, pointing a finger at Hyte, "you'd damned well better get something going on this, and fast. McPheerson is chief of department, and if push comes to shove, he'll pull the case from us."

"I intend to."

"Good. Now about these things," Mason waved his hand absently at the copies of the papers Hyte had sent up earlier. "They don't tell me a damned thing. I want to know more, and I want daily reports. I'll field the press when I can and keep you in the background."

"Thank you," Hyte said, wanting to say more but sensing it was inappropriate.

Mason poured himself another drink. "All right, here's the way it goes down. A telephone number, manned by two operators will go into operation tomorrow. The usual bullshit—anyone having information, et cetera. It will take the pressure off the precincts. And I've already sent out a call for off-duty volunteers. What else do you need?"

Hyte thought for a moment. "I'd like the various PDUs from the scenes to recanvass the neighborhoods. With the publicity, maybe a few memories will be jogged."

"I'll call the precinct commanders in the morning."

"I'd like to keep certain things out of the press conference. Such as the type of weapon and the fact that the three victims were on the hijacked plane."

Mason nodded. "The connection between the victims won't stay hidden for very long, not from the press in this city. But we've got the conference worked out already. And I've covered you with McMahon. After the conference, she'll field as much of the press as possible.

"That's big of her."

176

"The commissioner told her to give me her full cooperation. She'll open the conference, turn it over to me, and then I'll give you an intro. You've been good press and, according to McMahon, the public has confidence in you." He stood. "Let's go down."

They found Deputy Commissioner of Public Affairs, Alice McMahon, waiting for them in the small room adjacent to the press room.

"You handled Joan Leighton nicely, the other night," she told Hyte.

"Thank you. Commissioner, I have a six o'clock appointment. I'll have to leave as soon as possible."

"We're not enemies," she said suddenly. "As soon as you've done your part you're free. Just a few words of encouragement to the media, okay?"

She led the way into the press room. Hyte was the last to enter. He spotted Dan Carson off to the side. Joan Leighton was there as well, wearing her predatory smile.

"Ladies and gentlemen," called Alice McMahon. A dozen bright lights, like mini-suns, flooded the podium. "We have an announcement of the gravest importance. There will be no questions until we are finished.

"On Monday last, Lieutenant Raymond Hyte of the chief of detectives' staff uncovered what appears to be a series of homicides. To date, three people have been killed. The New York Police Department has evidence linking all three deaths to a single perpetrator."

Hyte approved of the tone McMahon set. Three minutes later she introduced Mason, who gave out the basic facts and issued the regular warnings concerning a serial murderer. "The man who first discovered the pattern of this particular killer is Lieutenant Raymond Hyte," he said, finishing. He motioned to Hyte.

Hyte stepped up to the microphones. "I don't have much to say, except that a task force is in full swing. A special phone line is being set up and will be in operation as of tomorrow morning for anyone who might have information concerning these killings."

"How can they have information if they don't know who

died, or where the crimes were committed?'' Joan Leighton asked.

''The homicides occurred in Queens, Brooklyn, and Manhattan.'' He looked at McMahon. ''Commissioner . . .''

Smoothly, McMahon took over. ''The number for the special line is 555–1000. And now, questions?''

Hyte slipped out the side door and started toward the elevators. Behind him, Dan Carson called his name. ''I can't talk about it now,'' Hyte said.

''Off the record.''

Hyte appraised the cop turned reporter. Carson's off the record would be just that. ''Go ahead.''

''Is this connected to last year's hijacking?''

''Why would you think so?''

''Your assistant called for the tapes of the hijacking.''

''It may have something to do with it. We're not sure yet.''

''Why is Mason heading this himself?''

''Why not?''

Carson smiled. ''Ray, I'm not just a reporter, I've been in your shoes. Don't try to flake me on this. You know as well as I do that the CD doesn't handle a task force.''

''He's doing me a personal favor.''

Carson whistled. ''And a big one it is. When you make the connection, I want to know about it.''

''You will.''

''I've got some backup footage of interviews with the passengers of 88. You want me to send it over?''

''I'd appreciate that,'' Hyte said. ''Now, you'd better get back to the press room.''

''I'll send the film over tomorrow,'' Carson promised.

At six-fifteen, LaGuardia was jammed. Flashing his shield at the Port Authority cop angling toward him, Hyte left his car parked in front of the United entrance. Inside, he checked for Flight 371. It was at gate 27, scheduled to leave on time.

He found Emma standing outside of the boarding area. She saw him and started forward. "I was afraid you'd get caught in traffic."

"We have a few minutes," he said, guiding her into the lounge. While Hyte ordered drinks at the bar, Emma went to a small corner table. He brought the drinks over, lifted his glass. "To a safe flight."

Emma touched her glass to his. "What was the press conference about?"

"The new case. It involves the murders I mentioned the other day. They're all connected."

Emma covered his hand. "You're talking about a serial murderer?"

"We're not sure. Emma, it may involve you."

"Me?" Her hand tightened suddenly around his. Her nails bit into his palm.

"Not you directly. But possibly your father. The three people who were killed were either crew or passengers from Flight 88."

She stiffened. "Can't there be some mistake?"

He wanted nothing more than to reassure her. "Everything points to the hijacking. All the victims were on the plane. The copilot, a stewardess, and one passenger have been killed."

She closed her eyes. "Goddamn it, it's not fair!"

"Emma, I want you to hire private security for your father."

Her eyes snapped open. "A bodyguard?"

"I think it would be wise until we find out who is doing this."

"Why would anyone want to harm him? He's already dead to the world."

"Sick people don't think the way you and I do."

The first boarding call came from the overhead speakers. "How can I hire someone when I'm in California?"

"I'll handle it."

"No. I'll stay."

"That won't do you any good. Get your business taken

179

care of. I'll make all the arrangements for your father. Please, trust me."

She leaned forward, squeezing his hand. "I do, Ray."

He smiled. "Okay, then let's get you aboard that plane. Call your father's house tomorrow morning. Tell the nurse that someone will be there around four; he'll have proper identification."

Emma frowned. "You're sure he'll be okay?"

"I'm sure," he said. "Come on."

When they reached the gate, he pulled her close. She seemed to flow against him. "Concentrate on business," he advised. "Everything will be all right here."

Her eyes searched his face. Unexpectedly, her tense features relaxed. She smiled. "I know it will." And then their mouths met.

Hyte broke off the kiss. "Go," he whispered.

Emma went to the boarding gate. He watched until she was gone, aware of the two things he had failed to tell her. The first was that she was being investigated. The second was that he loved her.

Twenty-four

"And now you know where I think this case began," Hyte said. It was ten o'clock. He and his team had been in the conference room since eight that morning. He'd played two of the tapes of the hijacking for the members of his task force who hadn't been involved last year. The three, Smith and Roberts and O'Rourke, had been silent throughout.

Coffee cups littered the conference table. Note pads were open before each cop. In the center of the table were the two pistol-grip crossbows Sally O'Rourke had provided.

"At present," Hyte continued, "the only common link between the three victims is that they were hostages on Flight 88. But unlike Flaxman and Samson, Barum Kaliel was released with the other coach-class passengers."

"We also have a damned good idea as to what the weapon is," Hyte added, pointing to the crossbows. "And we know they're illegal within city limits."

"Which means nothing," Tim Smith volunteered. "Anyone could get them—anywhere. How can we trace it?"

"We can't. We've asked distributors to supply us with a list of all stores they sell crossbows to in the Northeast. Then we'll contact the stores and ask for the names of all purchasers. Roberts," he said, turning to the detective first grade, "what did Michael Barnes have to say?"

"Not much. He was reluctant to talk. He said all he

wanted to do was forget the hijacking. When I told him about the victims, he said it had nothing to do with him."

"What do you think?"

"It shook him up," Roberts said. "But it was new news. It wasn't a put-on. I think he's straight." Roberts paused. "I don't know if it makes any difference, but he said something odd. 'I was a hostage once and I'll be damned if I'll be one again, especially to the thought that someone *might* want to kill me.' "

Hyte didn't think Barnes's words peculiar. He'd been there. "What about the last three Friday nights?"

"Says he was with his family. Want me to check with his wife?"

"Not yet. O'Rourke?"

"Neither of the two stews living in the city has noticed anyone following them. Nothing strange has happened to them. Both of them were on flights when Kaliel was killed."

"Sy?"

"I'm still running backgrounds on the dead hostages."

"Okay." He paused to look at everyone. "For the present, we're going to concentrate on the full-term hostages. I want to know everything about them, from their current whereabouts to where they were on the past three Friday nights."

"Why just the full-term people?" Roberts asked.

"A hunch," Hyte admitted. "They were there from beginning to end."

"What about Kaliel?" Roberts asked. "He was in coach."

"It's possible that he's tied into it in another way."

"Do we have anything on the killer?" Smith asked.

"Nothing. But, it's the M.E.'s unofficial opinion that the killer is a man. His guess is based on the weapon."

"Poison is a woman's way," Sally O'Rourke said. "It's not messy."

"And a man's way, too." Hyte shook his head. "Let's not get ahead of ourselves; speculating on the killer's sex won't do anything for this investigation."

"Tonight's Friday night," Cohen said. "What's the agenda?"

Hyte motioned to the blackboard. "Joan Bidding and the little girl, Lea Desmond, are the only full-term hostages who live in our jurisdiction. There'll be a blue and white sitting in front of their buildings all night."

"Do you really think someone could be sick enough to go after that little girl?" O'Rourke asked.

"I don't want to, Sally, but we can't take a chance with her life." Hyte paused, collecting his thoughts. "The coach passengers and crew—the short-term people, who live in the five boroughs—will have increased passbys of their residences by precinct squad cars. This will go from eight tonight until eight tomorrow morning.

"Notification to the authorities, where the rest of the coach passengers and crew live, has been taken care of. And a similar notification went out to Jersey, Rockland County, and Long Island—for the full-term people. But, that's all we can do at this time."

"He's taken out two full-term and one coach hostage. What if he goes after another coach passenger to even the number?" Roberts pressed.

"I don't think he will."

"Shouldn't we warn them to be on the safe side?" Sally O'Rourke asked.

"And tell them what? That there's a crazy out there with a crossbow and arrow who may have them on a hit list?" Hyte asked.

"Don't they have a right to know?"

Hyte didn't like the accusation he saw on Sally's face. "Yes, they have that right—but the timing is wrong. The way I see it, the killer doesn't know we've put it together already." Hyte pointed to the newspaper headlines. "And the press will emphasize that, since they don't know either."

"If I had been one of the passengers, I'd sure as hell like to know," Cohen said. "I'd want some protection."

"We can't assign cops to watch every passenger because

we *think* the killer's after them. We don't have any evidence, only conjecture.''

"We have to wait for another murder, don't we, in order to know whether you're right about who the victims are?'' O'Rourke asked.

Sally O'Rourke had finally voiced the subject that Hyte had been reluctant to broach. "I'm afraid so.'' Hyte waited a moment, and then said, "O'Rourke, Roberts, and Smith, you three are going out as a team. I want you to interview the first-class passengers living in the area—that's Sylvia Mossberg and the Moffertys. I want your individual impressions on these people. You can suggest they hire private security. Sy, it's time to talk to the volunteers.''

Downstairs, in a small meeting room set aside for them, a dozen off-duty cops waited. When Hyte and Cohen entered the room, all conversation died.

Hyte gave each of the cops a list of coach passengers to check. Each interview was to be fully detailed in writing. The subject's whereabouts on each of the Friday nights in question were to be logged.

Then Hyte and Cohen went into the office set up to handle the calls. Two women wearing telephone headsets sat at consoles. They nodded to him when he entered.

"Anything?'' Hyte asked.

"We just sent up the first list,'' replied a woman in her late forties. "They all seemed to be crank calls.''

He'd expected that. The women knew that if any caller sounded legitimate, they were to transfer the call to his office. But every call that came in would be recorded and listened to by the task force, no matter what the operators said or thought.

They returned to Hyte's office, where he called Steve MacLean, an old friend who had retired and opened up a private investigation agency. Hyte asked his friend to assign one of the agency's detectives to Jonah Graham's home in Westchester.

Hanging up, Hyte turned to Cohen. "Have you started checking on Emma?''

"Not yet.''

184

"Do it. This one goes by the numbers. Every piece of brass in the Department will be looking up our asses, waiting for us to fuck up. And I can't do that to Phil." A knock on the door interrupted them. "Come in."

Randal Schwartz entered with a package and a manila file folder. He handed Hyte the package. "This just arrived. Dan Carson sent it over. A tape of passenger interviews taken during the hijacking."

Hyte looked at the penciled note Carson had scribbled on the envelope: *You'll find the ninth interview interesting. Call me when you have a chance.*

Then Schwartz gave Hyte the file folder. "This just came up from Records. It's the check you requested on all the hostages."

"Thank you," Hyte said.

He opened the file as Schwartz left, read it quickly, and then looked at Cohen. "Only one positive. Jack Mofferty has a rap sheet. He was arrested for assault . . . twenty-five years ago. He waltzed—a suspended jail sentence and a five thousand dollar fine."

"It's a starting point," Cohen said.

"Maybe. Let's get some lunch before we look at Carson's tape."

An hour later, sitting in the conference room with Cohen, Hyte ran the tape. The ninth interview was the one with Barum Kaliel.

"You did not see the crew member shot?" the reporter asked.

"No. We were all in the back."

"What about the man who attacked the hijacker?"

"He was a fool. He could have gotten us all killed. I tried to reason with the hijacker. I know his mentality, for I am from that part of the world. But he wouldn't listen to me."

"What did you say to him?"

"I told him that he had no quarrel with us. That we were like him—that we understood his cause. His fight was against the governments, and the capitalists who run those governments. He should release us. After all, he was holding the rich people up front wasn't he?"

185

Hyte turned off the VCR. "He was a cold-blooded son of a bitch."

"Nasty," Cohen agreed.

A cog fell into place. Kaliel's death no longer seemed inconsistent. He was certain he could discount one of the theories about the killings. They weren't terrorist reprisals against the hostages.

"It's revenge, Sy. What that fool kid said to the terrorists, about letting the coach passengers free because the terrorists had the rich ones up front, put him on the same level as the terrorists. That's why he was killed. We never saw this interview. We were too busy that night."

"What he said could be taken a lot of ways."

"Not to someone unhinged by the hijacking. Listen to him! He even sounds like a junior grade terrorist." He rewound the tape and played the interview again. He looked at Cohen. "Terrorists wouldn't have touched him. Not after he played advocate to their cause."

"Who wouldn't have touched who?" asked Sally O'Rourke, leading Roberts and Smith into the conference room.

Hyte motioned to the chairs around the conference table and rewound the tape. "Watch."

When the interview ended, he looked at them. "First reaction?"

"Stupid!" Roberts declared.

"A schmuck," the black detective agreed.

"He killed himself," O'Rourke said.

Hyte allowed no sign of the pride he felt in O'Rourke to show. "Maybe. Okay, we concentrate on the full-term hostages. I'm going to ask for a plainclothes team to be put on Bidding and Desmond tonight, not just blue and whites. Now let's hear what you three came up with."

"Sylvia Mossberg is clean," Roberts said. "She lives in a senior citizen complex—all condos. It's self-contained, for the most part, and she only leaves to shop or go to temple."

"And," O'Rourke added, "her daughter and son-in-law usually take her shopping for food. After the hijacking, Mossberg's daughter wanted her to move in with them, but

Mrs. Mossberg refused. She says that it would mean leaving her friends and losing her independence."

"Friday nights?"

"Every Friday night, her neighbor, Ethel Greenblatt drives her to Sabbath services. We suggested that she not go to temple tonight."

"The Moffertys?"

"That one didn't go as smoothly," Roberts said. "Jack Mofferty is a very angry man. He wouldn't discuss anything about the hijacking."

Tim Smith nodded. "And when we brought up the three killings, reminding him that the dead people were hostages with him, he didn't so much as blink."

"What about his wife?" Hyte asked.

"Mofferty wouldn't let us talk to her. He told us to leave him and his wife alone," O'Rourke said. "And he refused to answer any questions about Friday nights."

"Without authority in Suffolk County," Roberts said, "we couldn't push him."

Hyte decided he would talk to the Moffertys himself. "So far Jack Mofferty is the only hostage with an arrest record. But it's nothing to get excited about." He paused, his thoughts shifting gears. "All right, if we picked up on a true pattern, the odds say the killer will hit again tonight. But for now, all we can do is hope that we have a long and boring night of phone duty. I'll be taking the eight-to-two phones. Who wants to join me? O'Rourke?"

She shook her head. "I'll take the second watch. It's payback time for the crossbows," O'Rourke laughed. "I traded a date for the weapons."

"That's one way of getting information," Hyte said with a smile. "Okay, Detective Smith, you're the one with a family, you take the first shift with me. Roberts, you and Sally work the second. Sy, you come in at eight tomorrow. Now," he added, returning to the table, "the early interview sheets are in, I want all of you to go over them tonight while you're waiting for the phone to ring."

* * *

Hyte sat at his desk. Smith sat on the chair across from him. They were going over the hotline reports for the day. A half hour earlier, he'd spoken with Carrie. His daughter told him that she had again asked her mother to allow her to start visiting him in New York. Susan had refused.

A radio was tuned to an all news station. The announcer gave the time, the weather, and then said, "The police have made no further comments concerning the three deaths attributed to the Friday Night Killer."

"That's just great." Hyte had been wondering what the press would call this one.

The phone rang. "I'll take it," Hyte told Smith when he realized it was his regular line and not the hotline.

"Hyte," he said.

"Hi, Lou," came Emma Graham's voice.

He exhaled. "Hi."

"Things weren't as bad here as I thought. I've got a few hours of work left, and I'm finished. I couldn't get a seat on the red-eye, so I've got to make a stopover in Chicago. Want to pick me up at LaGuardia?"

It took him only a second to realize why she'd changed her plans. "You don't have to rush back. Your father is being well protected."

He heard her laugh. "Men are supposed to have big egos. You're supposed to think that I'm rushing back because I miss you."

"Do you?" he asked.

"Too much. Ray—"

"Your father's all right," he said, cutting her off. "You can stay out there until you've got things under control."

"Actually, things are fine. The flight arrives in Chicago at six, and I'll make the seven o'clock Chicago to New York flight. I'll be at LaGuardia at ten—if my connecting flight is on time. Will you pick me up?"

"I'd rather be in San Francisco with you," he said.

"I'm glad you're not."

He frowned. Before he could speak, Emma continued. "I keep thinking about you. I'm looking forward to seeing your face."

The hotline began to ring. "I've got to go," he said. He hung up, started the tape, and answered the phone. Smith picked up the other receiver at the same time. "Lieutenant Hyte, may I help you?"

"Yeah! This is the Friday Night Killer, and I'm going to get them all!"

Smith jerked to attention, his eyes meeting Hyte's.

"Get who?"

"The whole fucking world! I'm going to blow everyone away with my three-fifty-seven magnum! They're all gonna make my day!"

"Really," Hyte said, his voice calm. "May I make a suggestion?"

"Sure."

"Start with yourself."

Twenty-five

The April night in New City, New York, was cool; the midnight sky was clear. The scent of early blossoming trees added a light and sweet fragrance.

Michael Barnes pulled his Volvo into the driveway of his Tudor-style home, and put the automatic gearshift into park. "What happened to the light?" he asked his wife.

"It must have blown," she said.

"Or the timer's gone out again. Send Elyse out."

"I don't mind driving her home," Francine Barnes said.

He winked. "While I'm taking her home, you can put on something sexy."

She unfastened her seatbelt and leaned toward him, sliding her hand along the inside of his thigh. "Don't take too long."

He covered her hand. "We can always put the seats down."

"Not in this neighborhood we can't," she admonished, pulling her hand free and opening the door. "I'll see you in a few minutes."

Three minutes later, fourteen-year-old Elyse Lomen hopped into the car, and Michael Barnes backed out of the drive.

Samael, God's Messenger, watching the scene between husband and wife, smiled. Yes, the driveway floodlight was out, but it had not blown out. A divine bolt had shattered it an hour before.

Samael peered at the bedroom window on the second floor, watching the elongated shadow of Francine Barnes as she undressed. The bathroom light came on. Samael waited patiently. It was important that the woman return to the bedroom.

Eventually, the bathroom light went off. In the bedroom, the elongated shadow bent over a table.

"Very good," Samael whispered.

Samael had spent a long time watching this house and its occupants. Samael knew exactly what would happen. In five minutes Michael Barnes would return.

Moving with stealth, God's Messenger of Death maneuvered to the vantage point that had been marked out weeks before.

At the prepared spot, Samael lifted the crossbow from the bag and drew the bowstring back, using a special foot attachment.

A wash of headlights turned the corner.

Samael stepped back into the bushes, blending with the darkness.

The car turned into the driveway. Michael Barnes's arm reached out. In his hand was the remote control that opened the garage door.

When the car was abreast of Samael, God's Messenger stepped from the bushes and released the safety. "Michael Barnes," Samael called.

Barnes stopped the car and stared at the old man who had appeared from nowhere. "Who—"

"It is your time," Samael said, bringing up the crossbow. "You have postponed your death for long enough."

Barnes's eyes widened. He thought of the detective who had come to see him. "Wait," he pleaded.

Samael smiled.

The bolt struck Barnes in the temple. The sound it made was louder than the crossbow's release. Barnes's head jerked back. His thumb ground down on the remote. The door began to open, a low humming in the quiet suburban night.

Samael opened the door and maneuvered Barnes into the passenger seat. Then God's Messenger of Death put the Volvo into reverse and slowly backed out of the driveway.

Twenty-six

The plane arrived a half hour late, but Emma looked fresh and wide awake. She carried a flight bag over her left shoulder, and walked quickly to Hyte.

He kissed her gently.

"We have to do this more often," she said lightly. Despite her cool tone, he saw that her eyes were bright and dancing with . . . excitement? Anticipation?

"Yes, we do," he said, surprising himself by the solemn tone of his statement.

Her face flushed with pleasure. "Been waiting long?"

"Not very." He started them back toward the terminal. "How was the trip?"

"I slept through most of it, except the layover in Chicago. The flight from there took off late. Something mechanical."

"Did you eat on the plane?"

Emma shook her head. "It throws me off more than jet lag. I like to wait until I get back."

"How does a nice lunch sound?"

"That depends on where."

"My place."

He liked the way her smile reached all the way to her eyes. "That sounds wonderful."

"Yeah," he agreed as they made their way toward the exit.

They were in the parking lot when Hyte's beeper went

off. Emma froze. Hyte spotted a pay phone. "I'll be right back."

He dropped the quarter in and dialed. Sally O'Rourke answered. "Lou, we have another one. Seventy-ninth Street boat basin."

"Who?"

"Don't know yet. Just got the call from central."

"I'm at LaGuardia. Figure twenty-five minutes."

He turned to Emma. She was staring at him, her eyes narrowed, lips taut. "It's not your father," he said. "But there was another killing."

The car was parked at the edge of the strip overlooking the boat docks. No other cars were nearby. The crime scene unit was in full swing: photographs taken, measurements called out. The Twentieth Precinct captain was present, standing off to one side and talking to a plainclothes detective.

Hyte started toward the car. The precinct captain broke off his conversation and walked over. "He was found around ten. As soon as the call came in, I had your office notified."

"Your people pick up anything?" Hyte asked.

"No. A man out walking his dog found him. He said he thought the way the man was sitting was strange. He rapped on the window. When the victim didn't respond, the dog-walker flagged a blue and white. I've got my men doing a sweep of the boat residences. If they come up with anything, I'll notify you."

"Thanks," Hyte said.

Sally O'Rourke and Sy Cohen joined Hyte.

"Michael Barnes," Cohen said. "Shot in the temple. Crossbow. The body's cold."

"What the hell was he doing here?" Hyte asked, bending to look at the body.

"He disappeared last night when he took the baby-sitter home."

Hyte frowned. "Did his wife report it?"

194

"She called the Clarkstown police. Thought he might have been in an accident."

"Accident? We notified their day watch commander about Barnes. Why the hell didn't they notify us when his wife called?"

"I checked with them a few minutes ago. They said it was an oversight. The day man forgot to put it on the night watch sheet."

"Great." Fighting off anger, he turned to the assistant medical examiner. "Harry?"

"Within the last twelve to sixteen hours—between midnight and four."

"Lou," O'Rourke said, pointing to the barricades.

He saw Deputy Commissioner McMahon step out of a limousine.

"I asked the Rockland County people to hold off notifying Barnes's family until I got back to them with a positive I.D.," Cohen said. "Thought you might want to speak to his wife."

Hyte nodded and turned to the crime scene technician. "Any prints?"

"Plenty," he said. "But a lot of blank spots, too. Whoever drove the car was wearing gloves."

Hyte had expected no less. "Same weapon?" he asked Harry Lester.

"Almost surely. But real close this time. Without opening him up, I'd say the bolt did a lobotomy. I'll know more when I have him on the table. There's a little blood on the outside of the driver's door. He was killed behind the steering wheel and moved to the passenger seat."

Hyte looked at the car. "It doesn't make any sense."

"What doesn't?" O'Rourke asked.

"He was killed near his home. Why the hell was he driven here?"

"You don't know that for sure," Harry Lester said.

"Yes I do," he stated flatly. "Sy, remember what Roberts said about Barnes?"

The detective sergeant nodded. "Barnes would never let himself be a hostage again."

195

"Exactly. If someone tried to make him drive somewhere, he would have fought—this time. Sy, stick with it. Brief the DC. Sally, you come with me. And Sy, call Rockland. Tell them I'm on my way, and that I'll handle next-of-kin notification."

He took a final look inside the car. On the driver's visor was a clip for a remote control garage opener. He searched the interior. It was not in the car.

They met the deputy commissioner halfway to the barrier. "Was it our killer?" she asked.

Hyte nodded. "Sergeant Cohen will fill you in, Commissioner. I've got to get to the man's widow before the press does. Do me a favor?"

"What?"

"The press hasn't made the connection between the victims yet. I'd like to keep it that way a little longer."

The houses on Barnes's street were all large, and each sat on at least an acre of land. The homes were expensive. A half a million dollars for each was Hyte's estimate.

He started the car forward. A local patrol car, with two men in it, was parked one house down and across the street from the Barnes's house. He parked behind the car and got out, O'Rourke following. When he reached the patrol car, he flashed his gold. "Hyte and O'Rourke."

The driver got out. "Bill Lennox. I'm supposed to go with you."

"No need," Hyte said. "There's nothing in your jurisdiction unless we prove he was murdered here."

"I was told—"

"Whatever," he said, starting along the driveway, O'Rourke at his side, the uniformed man five steps behind.

He studied every bush he passed. Small decorative stones covered the earth around the drive. The lawn was carefully tended, the landscaping meticulous. The driveway ended at the garage's double doors. One door was open, the garage bay empty. Hyte followed the fieldstone walk to the front door and mentally prepared himself for the next part of his job.

The local cop stepped ahead of Hyte and pressed the doorbell.

A woman with dark circles under her eyes opened the door. "Yes?" she asked through the screen.

Hyte showed his identification. "Mrs. Barnes, I'm Lieutenant Raymond Hyte. It's about your husband."

Francine Barnes choked back a sob. She opened the door and motioned them in. Then she looked at Hyte. "I remember you," she half whispered, "from when my husband . . . the hijacking."

"This is Officer O'Rourke. Mrs. Barnes, I'm very sorry to inform you that your husband died last night. He was murdered."

Francine Barnes stared at him. Then she turned away. Her back shook, her head was bowed. He nodded to O'Rourke, who stepped forward, put her arm around the woman, and started her toward the kitchen.

Hyte watched them, feeling detached yet responsible. Michael Barnes might be alive today if he'd lived in the city, where Hyte could have protected him.

O'Rourke seated Francine Barnes at a butcher-block table. She placed her hand over the woman's, gently. "The children?"

"At a friend's," Mrs. Barnes said. Her voice was hollow. "I sent them there this morning. I've had the strangest feeling ever since Michael didn't come back last night. And this morning . . . I didn't want them here if . . . Oh, God, this can't be happening. How can I tell them? They'll never understand."

Hyte went into the kitchen. The local cop hung back. Francine Barnes looked up at Hyte. "Why?"

Hyte saw, as he had too often in the past, that the reality of her loss had not yet set in. Francine Barnes was in light shock, able to function behind a veil of disbelief.

"Didn't he tell you that I had sent one of my men to see him on Thursday?"

She looked at him without comprehension.

"Mrs. Barnes, we believe three other people have been murdered by the same man. All three were on the flight your husband was on, the one that was hijacked. The detective who saw your husband told him about the killings."

"He never said anything," she said in a hollow voice. "I thought all of that was over."

Sally O'Rourke went to the sink, filled a glass with water, and brought it to the woman. When Francine Barnes took the glass, her hand was trembling. "Michael was a good man. He . . . What am I going to do now?" she asked Sally. "Oh God, the children."

"Help us find out who killed your husband," O'Rourke said. "Tell us what happened last night. Everything, every last detail, no matter how inconsequential it might seem. Start from the minute your husband came home."

Francine Barnes looked from Sally O'Rourke to Hyte. "I . . . there was nothing unusual. Everything was fine."

O'Rourke put her arm around the woman again and held her. "Is there someone we should call? A friend, a relative?"

She wiped away tears. "My sister lives in Pomona—it's only a few miles away."

Hyte got her name and address and turned to the local cop. "Can you get her for us?"

"Sure," the cop said, leaving.

"Mrs. Barnes. Where did you go last night?" Sally asked.

"To the movies. Michael . . ." She paused. Her eyes became distant. "Michael loved movies. We went to the movies every Friday night. He has a collection of movies, almost a thousand," she whispered. "But he says that it's not the same—watching a movie on television. You need a big screen to feel the movie." She stopped again as more tears came.

"Did anything unusual happen there?" Hyte asked.

"Nothing. We went out for coffee and then came home. Michael took the baby-sitter home, he . . . he told me to p-p-put on something sexy and he'd be right back. B-b-but I never saw him again."

"Everything was in order when you got home?"

"The light blew out, but that happens all the time."

"What light?"

"The driveway light."

"Did you turn it on when you left?"

"It's on a timer. It goes on by seven."

"Mrs. Barnes, I know this is very difficult, and I wish I didn't have to ask it, but please, think back. Was there anything else?"

She closed her eyes for a moment. "Yes, there was something else. But I don't know if it's important. This morning, the garage door was open. It happens sometimes. Michael says it has something to do with infra-red codes."

"Could your husband have opened it before he took the baby-sitter home?"

She shook her head. "He never opens the garage unless he's pulling in."

"May I look around?" She nodded. Hyte turned to Sally. "Stay here until her sister comes. Mrs. Barnes, I'm very sorry for what happened. Very sorry."

In the garage, he gazed at the painted cement floor. There was nothing on it at all. The garage was as clean as the kitchen had been.

Metal shelves lined the walls. On the far side, behind a small station wagon, was a peg board filled with tools. He went back outside and looked up at the floodlight. The bulb was shattered.

He bent down over the bushes directly under the light, pushing aside the dense branches. Sunlight reflected from a piece of metal.

He caught the object with a handkerchief and drew it out. A crossbow bolt! This one was different, though. It was a target bolt, not a broadhead.

He doubted that there was poison on it but handled it carefully nonetheless. As he walked down the driveway, he looked down, his eyes crisscrossing the drive. To his left, he saw a square object lying on the rocks. He went over to it. The remote. It was shattered. He guessed the car might have driven over it. Hyte scooped up the broken device and put it in his right jacket pocket. Maybe the crime scene boys could find something on it.

The police car pulled into the driveway. Before it came to a stop, a woman jumped out and ran to the front door.

Mrs. Barnes's sister. Even she could not ease the grief, Hyte reflected. Only time could do that.

In a convenience store, Hyte bought a box of large baggies and put the bolt in one bag, the remote in another.

When they were on the road again, he explained to O'Rourke where he found each item. "It was well planned," he said. "Whoever is killing these people is watching his victims. He knew exactly what Michael Barnes did on a Friday night—every Friday night. He was waiting for him."

"In the garage?"

"The remote device was too far away. Our killer was hiding in the bushes."

"Barnes was shot as he drove into the driveway?"

"No. He'd stopped."

"He knew the killer?"

"Or the killer startled him enough to make him stop. Whatever happened, Barnes did the wrong thing."

"And you were right," O'Rourke said. "The victims are the full-term hostages."

Twenty-seven

"I'm sorry about today," Hyte said to Emma. "I'd have much rather been with you."

"It's all right, really. It gave me a chance to drive up and see my father." She paused. "Want to tell me about it?"

"No," he said. "I don't want to talk about it."

Emma poured drinks, returned to the couch, and handed him his. "Not this time, Ray. I know you want to keep your job separate from your private life. But it won't work with me. I'll live with a lot of things, but I won't accept being shut out."

Reflected on her features was the core of inner strength that had drawn him to her from the very beginning. Now, sitting in his living room, he knew that he would either have to accept what she had just said, or he would lose her.

"It's not as easy as it seems."

"It's not as difficult either," she said. "It's called trust. Trust that what you tell me won't turn me away from you. That's it, isn't it? You keep the . . . the 'job' from us so that I won't be soiled? But what you do is part of you. If you live two lives—one with me, and the other with your job—then you can never give all of yourself to either of them. I'm not asking for the gory details, I just want to help share some of your burdens."

He experienced a new sensation. It was as if he'd become two people: one who watched life, another who acted. He wondered why it was so hard to talk about his work. His reticence had destroyed his marriage and to a degree, had cost him his daughter. Looking at Emma, he realized it wasn't the Job itself that stopped him, it was the fear of contaminating her with the dirt that was part of his work.

"I love you, Emma," he said suddenly. He saw her eyes widen in surprise. But before she could speak, he sketched out the case.

He did not detail the clinical aspects of the victims' deaths, the type of weapon, or the poison. Sixteen years of police work, combined with the possibility that Emma's father was a potential victim, stopped him from spelling everything out.

Emma looked at him keenly. "Why do you think it's revenge and not a terrorist retaliation?"

He took her hand in his, and repeated what he'd told Mason when he'd asked for the task force. "It's the only thing that makes sense."

"Why so long after the hijacking?"

"Planning takes time. And the killer is an expert at planning. He—"

"How do you know it's a he?" she asked.

"That's the consensus. For instance, he must have been watching Barnes for weeks, maybe months. He knew every move that Barnes made on a Friday night. And Barnes helped him by never varying from his routine. As for Flaxman and Samson, it would be easy to find out what flights they were on. The Arab boy was predictable, too. He always hung out at the same place on Friday nights."

"Can't you protect the rest of the passengers?"

"Only those living in the city. But we can't do anything for those who live outside our jurisdiction, other than to notify the local authorities—which we've done for the first-class hostages. Our only other option is to speak with the passengers and advise them to hire bodyguards."

"Like you did for me."

He nodded.

"You say Michael Barnes was killed at home. Why was the body brought to the city?"

"I don't know."

"Do you have any suspects?"

"Everyone who was on that plane, and all the victims' relatives."

Emma moistened her lips with her tongue. "I'm a relative. Am I a suspect?"

"Barnes wasn't killed with a guided missile," he stated dryly. "Which is what you'd need to kill someone when you're three thousand miles away."

"I don't sell missiles. Just executive toys. But I'm still a relative of a victim. I . . . I have to assume I'm being investigated."

"Sy is doing a check on you."

Her eyes went distant. A funny, crooked smile lifted the corners of her mouth. "Yes, that's logical. Like you. What are you going to do now?"

He was relieved she'd taken it in stride. "Look for clues. Maybe find a witness. Go over everything, and then do it again and again. If we're lucky, we'll find the killer."

"Is luck what it takes?"

"To a degree, but it's usually the kind of luck we make for ourselves. I just wish that there was more. Something to tell us a little about the killer."

Emma cocked her head to the side. "Like what?"

"Anything! We have very little to go on. There are no witnesses, no notes. There's usually notes in a serial case. Pleas from the killer to stop him, threats from the killer, stating that he's invincible. But this one gives us nothing. He's good, he's smooth, and he's so damned careful."

"But you must have something."

Hyte shrugged. "If you want to call a guess something, then yes. It's my guess that there are nine victims left."

"Nine? How do you—"

"Enough," he said abruptly. "Let's talk about something nice."

"Such as?" she asked, leaning toward him.

"You. Us."

Emma smiled. "Did you really mean what you said before?"

"That I love you? Yes."

"Who would have ever thought I'd fall in love with a cop?" she asked.

"Not me." He drew her closer. "It won't be easy."

Emma reached up and stroked his cheek. Her eyes roamed his face. "I'm not looking for easy; I'm looking for real."

Hyte woke up at seven. Next to him, Emma slept soundly. He watched the even rise and fall of her breasts.

With elation, he realized that although he had never really believed Emma was a suspect, there had been that faint possibility.

But the logistics proved the impossibility. Harry Lester believed Barnes was killed sometime between midnight and four. According to his wife's story, Barnes drove the baby-sitter home at a quarter after twelve. He should have returned home around twelve-thirty.

If he was killed in his driveway, and driven to the city immediately, it would have taken the killer forty minutes, which brought the time to a 1:15 A.M.

Emma couldn't be the killer, not if she'd been on the 12:30 A.M. flight to Chicago.

Her arrival in New York, on the 7:00 A.M. flight from Chicago, confirmed her inability to have been in New City. When he'd checked with the airport to make sure Emma's flight was on time, he'd gotten a recording that had given all flight times from Chicago to LaGuardia, and vice versa: every hour on the hour, starting at 7:00 A.M., and ending at 9:00 P.M. There were no flights between the time of Michael Barnes's death and seven in the morning. Emma could not have left New York at the same time she'd left Chicago.

She had called from the coast, Friday night. That call put her there at eleven, Eastern time. Nothing short of a time machine could have allowed her to kill Michael Barnes.

He slipped from the bed. He showered, made a pot of coffee and then got the Sunday *Times* from the hallway.

One look at a headline describing the death of the fourth

victim was enough to sour his morning. He threw the paper aside and dialed Phil Mason's home number.

"Where the hell were you yesterday? I expected a call," Mason said.

"I had nothing to tell you yesterday. Today I do."

"Give me a couple of hours to get myself together. I'll meet you at the office at noon."

Feeling better, Hyte poured two cups of coffee and brought them into the bedroom. He had a few hours before he had to leave, and he intended to make the most of them.

Hyte arrived at One Police Plaza at a quarter to twelve to find Randal Schwartz at the desk.

"What are you doing here?"

"They had no one for the hotline. I volunteered. The calls are being rerouted up here so I can catch up on my paperwork."

"Where are Roberts and Smith?"

"In the conference room."

Hyte walked to the conference room. "Anything?" he asked.

"One of the uniforms from the Two-Zero found a woman who remembers seeing the car drive up and the driver get out," Roberts said. "She was sitting on the deck of her houseboat. She thought it was strange that the man went to another car and drove away."

"She was positive it was a man?" Hyte asked.

"I spoke to her this morning," Smith cut in. "She believed it was a man."

"Time?"

"Somewhere between one and one-thirty."

"What about crime scene, they come up with anything?"

"Nothing we didn't have yesterday."

"What about the coach passenger interviews?"

Roberts pointed to the stack of reports. "So far nothing. The eighteen people living in the area have been interviewed; twenty-three out-of-state passengers have also been called. Everyone has an alibi for the last three Friday nights.

The off-duty boys have already confirmed at least half the alibis.''

"I'll be up with the chief if you need me," Hyte said. The witness's description was worthless. All she could have seen was a shadow in the streetlights.

"Damn it!" he snapped, feeling helpless. He had nothing. No, he had something—he had the names of the next victims.

"Coffee?" Mason asked when Hyte entered.

"Something stronger."

Mason set out two glasses and a bottle of Pinch. He poured three fingers into each glass.

"I spent most of last night on the phone with the PC and the mayor," Mason said. "They're foaming at the mouth. Ray, I need something."

"Give them this," Hyte replied, handing Mason the list of the living full-term hostages. "Among those nine names is the next victim."

"You know that for sure?"

"I feel it."

"Don't shit around with me. I can't give the PC a hunch."

"It's not a hunch anymore. It's coming together like a crossword puzzle."

"Then fill in the blanks for me."

Slowly, patiently, Hyte gave Mason all the details he had, including his theory about Kaliel's death. The only thing he didn't tell Mason about was where Barnes had died. He wanted the crime scene report on the bolt and remote control device first.

"Nothing you have is concrete," Mason said. "It could still be anyone, including terrorists, coach passengers, or just a fucking psycho."

"No!" Hyte snapped. "This is revenge. A psychopath doesn't spend weeks or months following his victims. This is different. There's a plan, a method, and a purpose. But we've got an edge. We know when the next attempt will be, and we know on whom."

"According to you, there are nine possible victims."

"Exactly. We need to cover them all."

"We can't. Except for Joan Bidding and Lea Desmond, we have no jurisdiction. We'll have to ask the local authorities to watch the others."

"Fuck jurisdiction!"

Phil Mason stayed calm in the face of Hyte's anger. "We can't send cops to watch someone outside our jurisdiction. You know that."

"We'll notify the locals that we're there. They'll go along with it, if the request comes from the chief of detectives, NYPD."

"I'll call them, but the victims have to be notified and given the choice. There's to be no covert surveillance—I won't break the law to catch a criminal."

"Why don't we just call the news media and tell them what we have? That would make things a lot simpler. The victims will be on the lookout, and the killer will know everything that we do. He'll draw back until things quiet down. Then, when everyone forgets about him, he'll start again. No Phil," Hyte said angrily, "it's got to be covert."

"Ray, you're an attorney as well as a cop. You know damned well that asking me to put these people under surveillance is a violation of their civil rights. This department can't be involved in a civil rights action. And that's exactly where your idea will get us."

"If we don't violate their civil rights, we may be condemning them to death."

"You'll have to find another way. But I'll talk to the commissioner about it. Keep yourself available tomorrow. Anything else?"

Hyte pointed to the list. "Right now I'm going to see Jack Mofferty."

In his office, Hyte wrote down three names and handed Schwartz the piece of paper. "See if you can find their current whereabouts and get me the phone numbers." The three names were Estella and Cristobal Helenez, and J. Milton Prestone.

Then he picked up the file on Jack Mofferty. Under it was Hyte's monthly calendar. On the upcoming weekend, he was scheduled to go to Boston to visit his daughter.

For the first time since his ex-wife had stopped Carrie from coming to New York, Hyte was going to have to cancel his visit to his daughter. "Damn it," he said, picking up the phone.

The Mofferty home was set far back from the road. An old stone wall surrounded it. Hyte could see the three-story stone colonial through the tall oaks and maples lining the circular drive.

Hyte went up the five wide stone steps and rang the bell at the side of the double-hung mahogany doors. The door was opened by a butler.

"Yes?"

Hyte produced his I.D. "Lieutenant Raymond Hyte to see Mr. and Mrs. Mofferty. My office called earlier."

"I've been instructed to tell you that your presence here is unwanted, Lieutenant."

"You tell Mr. Mofferty that if he won't see me now, I'll have a warrant issued for his arrest and extradition proceedings begun with the Suffolk County police. You can tell him that the charge will be four counts of suspicion of murder."

He watched the servant's face pale. "Excuse me a moment," the man said, closing the door.

Hyte looked at the front lawn. The smell of grass cuttings was fresh, the precise and even lines of the recent mowing still visible.

The door opened.

Smiling to himself, Hyte followed the butler into the house. He was led through the entrance hallway, lined by frosted glass French doors, and brought to a room at the end of the hallway. The servant opened the doors with a flourish. "Mr. Mofferty will be with you shortly."

Hyte stepped inside. The book-lined walls, the leather

couch and wing chairs, and the large stone fireplace were ample evidence of the room's intent.

He went to a bookcase and studied the titles. The books were leather bound and gilt imprinted. He took down *War and Peace*. The spine was stiff, the pages crackled when he opened the book. The library, he realized, like the house, was a showpiece.

Was Sonja Mofferty a showpiece as well? he wondered.

"What do you want, Lieutenant?" came a coarse voice edged with a slight Brooklyn accent.

Hyte turned to face Jack Mofferty. In the ten months since the hijacking, Mofferty had lost twenty pounds and a quarter of his hair. He had heavy dark bags under his eyes; his skin was sallow and drawn.

"What the hell is this bullshit about a murder charge?" Mofferty challenged.

Hyte slid the book back into its space. "You've heard about the Friday night killings?"

"It's impossible not to."

"You're making yourself a suspect."

"I'm *what?*"

"Why did you refuse to speak with the detectives who came to see you?"

"Because I had no reason to speak to them! I don't see anyone I don't know personally. No one!"

"Are you aware that the four dead people were on the plane with you that night?"

"Very aware, Lieutenant."

"Where were you on Friday night?"

"None of your business!"

Hyte kept his voice low, sympathetic. "I know what you've been through. I was there."

"Not the way I was."

"No, not that way. But what I told your man wasn't an idle threat. If you won't cooperate with me, I'll have no other choice but to ask for a subpoena."

"You can't seriously believe I killed those people?"

"You're giving me no choice! Goddamn it, Mofferty, I've

209

got a killer to stop. And you're the only passenger on that plane with an arrest record."

"That's twenty-five-year-old garbage! I got in a fight with someone who made a pass at my first wife. The only reason I was convicted was because he had a friend in court."

"That doesn't matter. I still have to find a killer. Where were you on Friday night?"

"We were seeing our psychiatrist. We go there three times a week," said Sonja Mofferty from behind him.

Caught off guard, Hyte turned in the direction of her voice. While Jack Mofferty was showing signs of stress and deterioration, Sonja Mofferty was calm. She carried her model's beauty like a shield. It was only when she came closer, and Hyte could see her eyes, that he was able to discern the changes.

"Go upstairs, Sonja," Mofferty said.

Sonja Mofferty glared at her husband.

Hyte's eyes flicked between them, waiting.

"No," Sonja said. Her voice was firm. "Are you forgetting that it was the lieutenant who saved our lives?"

"For whatever it's worth," Mofferty said. "We see Dr. Franklin Masters three nights a week. We have since the hijacking."

"Where is his office?"

"New York City. But we see him at his home, out here," Sonja said.

"What time are your sessions over?"

"Usually at nine, sometimes later."

"And afterwards?"

"We come home. Dr. Masters's house is nearby. We don't go out very often," Sonja Mofferty said. "We live a secluded life. However, this past Friday night we had house guests. My brother and his wife."

"They're here for the weekend?"

"No. They left yesterday morning."

"And where does your brother live?"

"In Bethesda, Maryland. Why?"

"I'll need to speak with him to confirm what you've said."

"This is ridiculous!" Mofferty said.

Hyte turned on him. "You tell Michael Barnes how ridiculous this is! Do you remember him? The redheaded man on the plane. He was killed Friday night, the day after a detective told him to be on his guard."

"Lieutenant, I've just dialed my brother's number," Sonja said, handing him the phone. "His name is Robert Cole."

When Sonja's brother came on the line, Hyte introduced himself and asked about Friday night.

Hyte hung up. "Are you satisfied?" Jack Mofferty asked.

Hyte wished he could see into the man's mind. "For now, pending corroboration by your psychiatrist." He paused. "Where were you on the three Friday nights previous to Michael Barnes's death?"

"Right here," Sonja said quickly. "We're always here. We don't go out."

"You had no company? No one saw either of you?"

"If you're looking for an alibi, you can speak with our butler and housekeeper. Both work Friday nights."

"That's exactly what I'm looking for," Hyte said.

"I'll get them for you," Sonja offered.

Hyte stopped her. "What time do they usually go to bed?"

"Unless we're entertaining, they finish their day at ten and go to their quarters."

"Don't bother disturbing them," Hyte said, certain that the servants would verify the Moffertys being at home. At least up until they'd gone to bed. "If it becomes necessary, I'll be back to speak with them."

Jack Mofferty's expression didn't change. Sonja stepped closer to Hyte. "Thank you, Lieutenant. Let me show you out."

He followed her to the front door, where she turned to face him. "Lieutenant," she began hesitantly, "my husband is . . . he has been suffering a great deal since the hijacking. Please forgive his manners."

"What about yourself?"

She smiled sadly. "I was a model. I guess I got used to

211

being used. And it's long over with. At least I thought it was over with."

Hyte watched her for several seconds, wondering if she was as good an actress as she had been a model. "So did I," he said, and stepped outside. He paused at his car, looking back to where Sonja Mofferty stood.

He noted how expressionless her face was. He remembered the point in the hijacking, when Sonja had offered Mohamad her body in exchange for her husband's life. The woman who now stood by the front door seemed a different Sonja Mofferty from the one who had been on Flight 88.

He thought about the scene he'd witnessed in the library—the open hostility between Sonja and Jack. Then Hyte thought about Sally O'Rourke's hunch.

Poison was a woman's weapon.

Twenty-eight

Hyte stayed in his office on Monday. His team was sequestered in the conference room, reexamining the coach passenger interviews.

At ten, he called Prestone in Santa Fe, New Mexico. "Senator," he said. "I'm sorry to bother you."

"This is about the killings, isn't it?"

"Yes, it is. Senator, although all the victims lived in the New York area, I feel you should be on guard—"

"Lieutenant, I'd prefer to have this conversation in person. I'll be in New York on Thursday."

"I don't think coming to New York would be wise at this time," Hyte said.

"Most especially at this time. If someone is murdering my fellow passengers, I'm not going to sit in an office two thousand miles away and do nothing. I'll see you Thursday, Lieutenant," Prestone said, hanging up before Hyte could speak.

"Shit," Hyte snapped at the phone. A second later his intercom lit up. "Yes?"

"Upstairs. Now," ordered Phil Mason.

Alice McMahon was in Mason's office. Hyte chose the seat next to her. "We've spent the past hour with the commissioner," Mason said. "He's very distressed about the Barnes murder. When I brought up your requests, he vetoed them all. You'll have to notify the passengers, Ray, spell it out for them. I've already ordered protective surveillance for all the passengers within our jurisdiction."

"And if one of them is the killer?"

"That's the chance we have to take. The commissioner wants a full public disclosure."

Hyte's stomach soured. "Jesus Christ, Phil, that'll make it three times as hard."

"Lieutenant," McMahon said, her voice softer than usual, "I happen to agree with you in this instance, but the public has a right to know, and the press is asking some pointed questions."

"They always do."

"Yes," McMahon agreed. "And we need to work out something. The boat basin was considered a safe area."

"He wasn't killed there," Hyte said.

"I didn't know that," the chief of detectives said, frowning. "Where was he killed?"

"In his driveway. I have the bolt that was used to knock out the garage light."

"You're sure?" Mason asked.

"As sure as I can be."

"Then why didn't you tell me?"

"I wanted the evidence at our lab, not with the New City police," Hyte said. He turned to McMahon. "There's no way that the locals could keep something this big from the press. And we'd lose the only things we have to weed out phonies—the murder weapon and the poison."

"If Barnes was killed at home, why did the killer bring him here?" Mason asked. "That was a stupid risk."

"Calculated, not stupid. And it was a message. But I haven't been able to decipher it."

"We still need to figure out what we're going to tell the press," Mason reminded them.

"Only what we have to," McMahon said. "We'll announce the connection between the victims. The public will be less afraid if they know the killer is only going after certain people. It is all we have, isn't it, Lieutenant?"

He met her look openly. "Nothing else is being held back."

When McMahon left, Mason glared at Hyte. "Don't pull that crap again."

"I wasn't pulling anything. I was waiting for the forensic report. It came in five minutes before you called. They confirmed the bolt as being from the same manufacturer."

"And what are you looking for now?"

"Anything," Hyte said. "Anything at all."

"Let's hear what we've got so far," Hyte said to his team. "Sy?"

"The Moffertys' relatives check out clean. The pilot, Haller, was an only child. He had a wife and son. The son is attending medical school in England. Haller's widow is living in Upper Saddle River, New Jersey. I spoke with her, she's clean."

"What about the flight engineer?"

"Another only child. He had three children, one three-year-old and twins who are five. His widow and children live in Los Angeles. LAPD confirmed her whereabouts on the night of the Kaliel death."

"Which leaves us with who?"

"Jonah and Emma Graham," Cohen said. "I checked with Jonah Graham's doctor. Graham is paralyzed from the neck down. He can't speak, either."

"And Emma Graham was in California Friday night," Hyte said.

Cohen nodded. "Which I confirmed."

Hyte ignored Sally O'Rourke's sharp breath of surprise. "And?"

"The airline's records show that Emma took Flight 172 from California to Chicago, where she made a connecting flight. She arrived in New York Saturday morning. La-Guardia."

"Where I picked her up, at ten-thirty," Hyte said. "Thank you, Sy. Anyone else have something to add?"

"What about that little girl's parents?" O'Rourke asked. "She was a full-term hostage also."

"By mistake," Hyte said. But he hadn't considered Lea's adoptive parents as suspects. He wondered if his lack of suspicion was because of the friendship that had developed between the Desmonds, himself, and Emma, following the hijacking. "Sy?"

Cohen nodded. "Just like you said. Everyone connected with the full-term hostages is being investigated. But so far, nothing's in on the Desmonds."

Randal Schwartz entered, carrying a large manila envelope. "This just came in," Schwartz said. "The label is typed and there's no return address—just the initials FNK."

"FNK? Friday Night Killer?" Hyte looked at the envelope. "Crime boys!" he ordered.

"I'm doing it," Cohen said, the phone already at his ear.

"How was it delivered?" Hyte asked Schwartz.

"The duty officer said a messenger just walked up and dropped it on his desk."

"Get that cop, now!"

O'Rourke left.

"Did you handle it much?" he asked Schwartz.

"Just by the corner."

Hyte looked up. Everyone was standing around him, staring at the envelope. He knew they all held the same thought. They might have finally gotten a break.

The crime scene man arrived at the same time as O'Rourke and the lobby cop.

Using long tweezers, the man moved the envelope to the center of the desk and powdered it. When the fine powder filmed evenly, he brushed it lightly, looking for prints. There were two full sets. The forensic specialist lifted the prints and turned the envelope over. He repeated the process and lifted another set of partials along with a double print from the upper corner.

Hyte turned to the uniformed man. His nameplate said LANETT. "Did you handle it, Lanett?"

He nodded. "I didn't—"

"No one's criticizing you. What did the delivery man look like?"

"Old. Sort of stooped over. Smiled a lot. And he carried the envelope in an old shopping bag."

"Shall I open it, Lou?" asked the technician.

"Carefully."

The technician placed a flashlight behind the envelope and turned it on. "Something in it, but no wires." He opened it with a razor blade, and used a thin probe to recheck for wires. There were none. He then upended it.

A crossbow bolt fell on the desk. A single sheet of paper followed. "Use the tweezers then bag it. Get it over to toxicology after you dust the letter," Hyte said.

The technician went over the note for prints. "It's clean," he pronounced.

"Take Lanett with you," Hyte said, pointing to the lobby cop, "I think you'll find the prints on the envelope are his. The ones on the corner are Schwartz's. I'll send the note down for a typewriter comparison."

"Forget it, Lou, it's not a typewriter, it's a dot matrix computer printer. They're next to impossible to trace."

Hyte stared at the note, sure of its authenticity. The crossbow bolt was confirmation. Had it only been two nights ago, Hyte wondered, that he'd told Emma there had been no messages from the killer?

Lieutenant Hyte: Know you that I am Samael, God's Messenger of Death, sent to collect those who think they have outwitted death. I cannot be stopped. I will have my due. When the last eight have been collected my work will be done.

Eight! The number flashed like neon in his mind. He looked at the chalk board, and at the names of the nine full-term hostages who were still alive.

"Randal," Hyte said, "get me the chief."

In the restaurant on the corner of Fifth Avenue and Eighth Street, Hyte spotted Professor Walter Alinski immediately.

His former clinical psychology teacher had changed. He looked older, his face wizened. The long shock of white hair was combed neatly back, the ends curling upward over his collar. Streaks of scalp could be clearly seen. His face was thin, the skin drawn tightly over sharp, Slavic cheeks. But his eyes were steady. Although Alinski had retired from N.Y.U., he was still a clinical psychologist of considerable repute.

They shook hands and sat down. The waitress appeared. Alinski ordered a deviled egg sandwich and iced tea. Hyte ordered roast beef and a Tsingtao beer.

"How can you drink that Communist swill?" Alinski asked, smiling.

"It tastes good. How have you been?"

"I manage."

He knew Alinski well enough to accept that if Alinski wanted to say more, he would. "Doctor—"

"You want a profile, yes? Tell me about your new killer."

Hyte told him everything he had. He finished just as the waitress arrived with their food.

Alinski ignored his sandwich. "You say you believe it's revenge," Alinski said, "which would rule out the traditional psychopath. And you have evidence that it's a man, yes?"

"Not physical evidence. But the assistant medical examiner feels that the weapon is masculine."

"I don't think you should lock yourself into gender. But a crossbow is definitely a male weapon. Unless of course the user is a woman with male-dominant homosexual tendencies."

"It's also among the most silent weapons I've seen."

"Ah," Alinski breathed. "So you have yet another objective in the use of the crossbow—silence. Man or woman, silence is inherent in the design. So we know it is not a killing for expediency. Are you positive that each murder was planned?"

"Meticulously," Hyte replied. "And the killer's careful to the point of perfection. We haven't found a single thing that points toward an identity."

Alinski nodded. "From everything you've said, a paranoid schizophrenic seems a likely possibility. A hostage who might suffer from delusions that the others are after him for some reason known only to himself."

"But definitely not a sociopath?"

"The note confirms that the killer has a purpose and specific victims. That excludes the apparent randomness of a sociopath."

"Which means that without any clue to his identity, there are eight weeks of hell left."

"Or that the killer is deceiving you, as paranoid schizophrenics often do, and the note is misleading in some way."

Hyte shook his head. "Is there another possibility? I don't think we're dealing with a schizoid—the pattern doesn't fit."

"I see," Alinski said. "If you rule out psychopaths, and schizophrenics, who by definition are paranoid, what you have left is a classic paranoid. Raymond, do you remember your Freud?" Hyte nodded. "Good, because his theory of repressed homosexuality is the basis of paranoia."

"But repressed homosexual or not, why would a paranoid kill people?"

"He's killing because he has a grudge against the people who survived. The character disorder of the killer is most likely long-standing but dormant. In most probability, it was set off during the hijacking by one of the killings.

"You must understand, Raymond, that a true paranoiac is among the hardest of all character disorders to diagnose. I cannot stress this too strongly. Although the paranoiac's basic premise may be faulty—in this case the other people surviving a disaster while the one the paranoiac cared for died, or was injured—everything that follows, the assumptions and thoughts based on the initial erroneous premise, will be faultless and make complete sense. And not only to the paranoiac, but to others as well."

Hyte shook his head. "All the relatives have been checked out. They are all accounted for on the nights of the deaths."

"Don't be so certain. The principal reason classic paranoia is so hard to detect is because the paranoiac is intact outside his delusional structure. The paranoiac will present a perfect picture of lucidity. He will function in all social situations, as well as in business. If he is intelligent, he will have planned for many contingencies, including having what, on the surface, seems to be a foolproof method of averting any and all suspicion from himself.

"Raymond, you cannot spot a paranoiac from a conversation, from a business deal, or even from the most intimate of relationships. You may be able to detect something out of the ordinary—a hint given by an expression, or a strangely turned phrase—but only if you know the person very well. And in order to uncover a paranoiac, you must first learn what the basic misconception was—the very source that produced the delusion."

"Which is nearly impossible, if I've followed your line of reasoning," Hyte said. "So, if you're right, and we're dealing with a paranoiac, what you've said boils down to one simple thing. Someone is lying—either one of the passengers, or one of the relatives."

"Yes," Alinski agreed. "And there's one other thing you should keep in mind. You can't separate a paranoiac's delusion from reality. There will be no reasoning with your killer if you are able to confront him." Alinski picked up his sandwich, took a bite, and chewed it slowly. His eyes looked troubled. "Raymond, classic paranoia is untreatable."

Twenty-nine

"We have four days to come up with something," Hyte said, addressing his small task force. "Sometime after ten o'clock on Friday night, our man will strike again."

He tapped the chalk board. "We have to go with the assumption that there are eight victims left."

He paused to scan their faces. "You've all heard what I learned from Dr. Alinski. If our killer is a paranoiac, he'll be very hard to spot. Ideally, our best shot would be to start at the night of the hijacking and check out what every passenger and relative has done since then. But that's a realistic impossibility. So, we start with the first killing and work forward.

"I want to know everything that each of the victims did the night they were killed. I want a record of every step they took, every person they spoke to, and every place they might have gone. I want the neighborhood people interviewed again. But I want it from a new perspective.

"Roberts, you take the Flaxman murder. Smith, you take Kaliel. And Sally, you get Samson. Sy, do the relatives once more, and also check to see if any of them have been seeing a shrink since the hijacking, or before. And, staring tomorrow, each of you will take inside duty shifts. I think we're going to get a whole bunch of crazies turning themselves in. One of us will have to weed them out if they get past the precincts.

"I've put Schwartz on the name the killer gave us. He's

calling seminaries to get a make on Samael." Hyte covered the chalk board. "All right, people, let's go to work."

Sy Cohen lingered until the other three were gone. "You didn't mention surveillance on the out-of-jurisdiction people. Why?"

"The PC wouldn't go for it."

"That leaves our man free to do whatever he wants."

"Maybe, maybe not," Hyte said without elaborating.

Hyte remained in his office during the press conference, preferring to sit out what he knew would become a circus the moment the commissioner told the reporters about the note.

As usual, he found himself staring at the chalk board. One column listed the nine people from first class who were still alive. The second column was comprised of the four victims, in the order of their death. The third column listed close relatives of the original victims, a fourth contained the names of four people: the three who'd been killed by the terrorists on Flight 88, and Sonja Mofferty, who'd been raped.

Eight of the nine people were marked for death. Was one of the nine Samael? He felt disgust rising. A moment later there was a knock on his door. "Yes?"

Dan Carson came in. "You wanted to see me?"

He had called Carson shortly after talking with Sy Cohen about the out-of-jurisdiction people. "The press conference over already?"

"It was more like a zoo."

"I bet. Dan, I need a favor. What I'm about to tell you is confidential and completely off the record. If a single word gets on the air, it will cause considerable harm to the investigation. Is that understood?"

"You have my word."

"As you know, the killer told us that there are eight more people slated to die. What you don't know is that it isn't just any eight passengers from Flight 88, it's eight specific people."

Carson blinked. "The press is about to swarm over all the passengers and scare them even more than they are. Is that what you want? Is that why what you've told me was withheld at the conference?"

"Yes, I want them scared because we can only protect the people who live in our jurisdiction. And what I've told you is guesswork. The press conference was accurate, as far as the note goes, but if the killer had given us a name-by-name list, I would have withheld it. I want all the passengers, not just the ones who are targeted, to be on their guard. It may save lives. We don't know if the killer is telling us the truth." Hyte thought about his talk with Phil Mason. "That's why I need you to go on the air and call for protection for all the passengers of the hijacking, no matter where they live."

"What good will it do?"

"It may help ease the passengers' fears. And it will also tell the killer that we don't believe him. Maybe he'll get careless."

"You can't really think that an outraged cry for protection will trick the killer into making a mistake."

"It's worth a chance. But more important, I need surveillance on the passengers out of our jurisdiction. And protection is another form of surveillance, isn't it?"

Hyte fought through a crush of reporters to get to his office on Tuesday morning, where he found memos from Phil Mason, the crime scene unit, and three precincts who were holding confessed Samaels.

He asked Cohen to check on the Samaels, and Schwartz to set up an appointment with the Moffertys' psychiatrist. Then he called the crime scene lab and was told that the bolt Samael had sent them had been coated with the same poison that had killed the other victims.

As soon as Hyte hung up, Schwartz popped his head into the office. "Dr. Masters says that ten-thirty is his only free time today. Shall I tell him you'll be there?"

"Ten-thirty it is. Any word on the name?"

Schwartz shook his head. "All I've been able to learn so far is that Samael is not a name from the New Testament."

Hyte spent the next half hour going over reports. At ten, he left headquarters and drove to Franklin Master's expensively furnished Park Avenue office.

"I really don't understand why you wanted to see me, Lieutenant," the psychiatrist said. "I can't discuss my patients' cases with you."

"Dr. Masters, I wouldn't be here now if it wasn't necessary. Both Jack and Sonja Mofferty were hostages on a hijacked plane—"

"Really, Lieutenant, why do you think they're seeing me?"

"And," Hyte continued, "they are involved in what the papers are calling the Friday night killings."

"As victims, yes. A psychotic has targeted the passengers from that plane, and the Moffertys are well aware of that."

"They're also suspects," Hyte said. "And you're their alibi."

"A good one, too. Neither of them could possibly be the killer."

"What makes you think it's a psychotic?"

"It's a wastebasket term I use when I don't have enough information. Psychotic or sociopath—all the signs are there."

"Such as?"

"The delusion. You received a letter, did you not? Something with a biblical name. Delusional."

Hyte let Masters's comment slide by. "Of all the passengers, the only people we know for certain to have sustained a long-term relationship with an analyst are the Moffertys. The only hostage to have a criminal record is Jack Mofferty."

"That old arrest is meaningless. Neither Sonja nor Jack are capable of committing these crimes."

"I don't see it that way. Jack Mofferty's got hate built up inside him from what happened. Why couldn't he be my killer?"

"Lieutenant, please," Dr. Masters said. "As Jack Mofferty's psychiatrist—"

Hyte leaned forward. "Look at it from my point of view. If you can't give me something concrete, I'm going to arrest him on suspicion. He'll stay in jail until another murder is committed, or you and a lawyer get him out for a complete psychiatric evaluation overseen by the courts."

"You don't have that kind of authority," Masters said, "and if you push me, I'll go right to your chief."

Hyte reached across Masters's desk and picked up the phone. "555-1200, extension 801. Ask for Chief of Detectives Philip Mason."

"You're bluffing."

"Which will be something you'll find out when I announce to the press that we are seeking extradition on Jack Mofferty from Suffolk County."

"I believe you're bluffing," Masters said again, "but I can't have Jack Mofferty held up to public ridicule. To disprove your suspicions, his problem would have to be made public. If that happens, it will set back whatever progress we've made in his therapy."

"Then talk to me."

"I can't, even if I wanted to. All I can say is that if you arrest Jack Mofferty, you will be arresting the wrong man and at the same time do irreparable harm to him."

"No, Masters, you'll be doing the harm, because you could have stopped it. Doctor, for God's sake help your patients!"

Masters stood. "Excuse me a moment." He left his office, returning several minutes later.

"I spoke with the Moffertys," the psychiatrist said. "I explained the situation as you outlined it to me. I also gave them my opinion that to withhold the information of their treatment would be detrimental to their overall therapy. I was given permission to discuss certain aspects with you. However, anything I am about to say will and must remain off the record. If this goes to court, I will invoke medical privilege. Is that understood?"

"Of course."

"Just remember that I'm doing this strictly with my patients' well-being in mind. Ask your questions."

"Did the hijacking bring out any manifestations of paranoia?"

"Not in the traditional sense. You see, for a man of my patient's background, a man who grew up in a strongly male-dominated household, and one who went on to become a self-made millionaire, having his wife save his life by allowing herself to be brutalized is a devastating, ego-shattering experience. Yes, there's paranoia, but its manifestation is that Jack Mofferty cannot deal with other people any longer. He believes everyone thinks he allowed his wife to be raped so that he could live. What happened during the hijacking emasculated Jack Mofferty."

"He's impotent?" Masters nodded. Hyte leaned back. "Which would bring out latent homosexuality because of his shame. Why wouldn't he want to silence the people who saw what happened?"

The doctor laughed. "Don't quote Freud to me. Try Marshal McLuhan. If the hijacking hadn't been video-taped, your theory might—just might—hold water. But realistically, I don't think anyone is capable of killing the entire world. Everyone who has a television has seen tapes of the hijacking. That, Lieutenant, is what makes Jack's treatment so damned hard! He believes everyone he meets, everyone he sees, is accusing him of using his wife to keep himself alive."

"And Sonja?"

Masters smiled. "She's definitely not your killer. The hijacking brought out a character trait Sonja never knew she possessed—self-sacrifice for the benefit of another. For ten years, she was a highly paid model who was pampered and taken care of and given everything she ever wanted.

"The hijacking changed all of that. At first, it took several months to get over her initial feelings that it had been her life-style that had condemned her to be victimized. But she now realizes that what she did, she did out of love for her husband."

"Which means that she forgives everyone involved?"

"No, Lieutenant, she simply feels she did what was necessary to keep herself and her husband alive. Nothing more, nothing less. It was a horrifying experience, but one which has helped her grow emotionally. Until the hijacking, she was immature. Now she's coming to terms with herself. Which is to say, Sonja Mofferty is growing up."

"When I visited them, there seemed to be a fair amount of stress between them. It wasn't what I'd call an example of a loving relationship. In fact, neither of them seem to fit the picture you're drawing for me."

"Every relationship has its times of stress. This happens to be such a time for Sonja and Jack. I'm sure that once they've worked their problems out, they'll be as loving as they once were."

On the trip back to headquarters, Hyte thought about the doctor's diagnoses and protestations on behalf of the Moffertys. Nothing the psychiatrist had said was enough to make him believe that Jack or Sonja was incapable of committing murder.

He was just passing the Pan Am building when he heard his number called from the radio. He picked up the microphone and replied. A moment later he was patched through to his office.

"Lieutenant," said Randal Schwartz, "I just got a make on the name."

Hyte pulled to the curb. "Go on."

"The name Samael is Semitic. It's from Hebraic mythology."

Thirty

Hyte woke, and tried to push aside the dream. It was a familiar dream: the hijacking. The killing of helpless people.

He wondered what Samael's mind was like. Did the killer have tortured dreams? Did he wake in the middle of the night, sweating? Hyte hoped so. He wanted to feel some sort of mental affinity with the killer.

Samael was secure in the knowledge that he could outwit Hyte. That was the note's purpose. Was it also the reason he'd brought Michael Barnes into the city?

Hyte glanced at Emma. His restlessness hadn't woken her. Moving carefully, he left the bed and went into the living room, where he looked down at the two books on the coffee table. One was a psychology text; he had thoroughly studied the section on classic paranoia. The second was one Schwartz's father had loaned Hyte. It was a compilation of rabbinic literature and Hebrew mythology.

Samael, according to the writings, was God's Messenger of Death—not an angel of death, but a messenger sent to find those people who had somehow outwitted death.

The name gave Hyte reassurance. It was verification that he was right about the victims. They were the full-term hostages who had not died—they had outwitted death.

Nor did he necessarily believe that because the name came from Jewish folklore that the killer was Jewish. There had been three Jewish passengers on board Flight 88: Anita and

Jonah Graham, and Sylvia Mossberg. Anita was dead, Jonah was as good as dead, and Sylvia had been cleared.

But the killer was smart, and devious, Hyte reminded himself. Using a Hebraic legend could be a method of sending Hyte to chase a dead end. The more he thought about it, the more convinced he became that all the name signified was the killer's intent.

He thought about possible suspects. The overtime men had completed their detailed checks of the coach passengers. Each had been cleared of suspicion. So had all the relatives of the murdered hostages.

There was one tenuous lead. It had come from Jim Roberts, after he'd re-interviewed the doorman of Flaxman's building. The doorman had described an elderly pedestrian who, wearing a hat and a trench coat, using a cane, and carrying a shopping bag, had walked past the building moments before Flaxman was murdered.

Roberts had tied the doorman's description to the one the woman at the Seventy-ninth Street boat basin had given the police the day after Michael Barnes was killed.

Sally O'Rourke, after learning that Elaine Samson had taken a taxi on the night of her murder, was on the trail of the driver.

And, of all the passengers from Flight 88, only the whereabouts of the Helenezes were unknown. Nothing Hyte had been able to do, or any pressure he had exerted, had been able to pry their location from corporate headquarters. Cristobal Helenez had left instructions that no one was to be told where he and his wife were. Hyte didn't like dealing with wealthy people. They believed their money could buy them anything, including safety and protection. Sometimes it did, but often it was never quite enough.

"You have no choice!" Phil Mason thundered.

"How in the hell can you even consider doing it?" Hyte asked.

"Damn it, Ray, you sit in your office and ponder the nuances of this case. You check and recheck all your facts,

229

and you can do it without anyone staring over your shoulder because I'm running interference for you. I'm the one who everyone is focused on. The press is on me all day long. And to make it worse, I've got McPheerson parting the hairs on my ass, looking for a way in."

"It stinks."

"So does the Jersey Turnpike! Look, you got your protection, and surveillance, for the coach passengers. And don't for a moment think I don't know that you and Carson hatched out that little bit of media coercion together."

"Phil—"

"Chief, to you right now. The PC personally called every outside jurisdiction to reinforce my request for their cooperation in watching the passengers on Friday night. So when Rutledge asked for our cooperation with the senator, I told him we'd take care of it. And, since Prestone has offered to act as bait, we're going to use him."

"It won't work," Hyte said. "Samael is a strategist. He's already chosen the order of his victims. He's staked them out, watched their every move. He won't go after Prestone until he's ready."

"What are you—God? You know what this maniac will do and when? Come on, Ray, we're throwing out the bait. How many psychos can refuse bait? It's worked before. It'll work again."

"We're not dealing with a psycho!" Hyte said.

"Regardless, you will be seeing Prestone at 1:00 P.M. Keep in mind that all the passengers are being protected. If Samael doesn't take the bait, he still won't be able to get at the others."

Hyte left Mason's office and went to the conference room. "We've been given a new plan," he told the team. "Senator Prestone is now a member of our task force. But before we get into that, has anyone come up with anything new?"

"Yes," Sally O'Rourke said, "I went to see the cab driver who took Elaine Samson home. His name is Herman Oberman. And he remembered her because she gave him a buck and a half tip on an eighteen-fifty fare. He said most stewardesses tipped better.

"I asked him if he saw anything unusual that night. He said he was doing up his trip sheet before he left and saw an old woman go into the building. She had a scarf on her head, wore an old trench coat, and carried a large shopping bag."

"That's a pretty concise memory."

"I thought so, too. When I asked him how he could remember her so clearly, he said it was unusual to see a bad lady in that neighborhood, and more so for one to talk to the woman instead of just talking to herself."

"The bag lady talked to Samson?"

"That's what the man said. Went inside with her, too."

"Lou," Roberts said, his voice tense, excited. "Except for sex, that could be the same description as the man seen before the Flaxman hit and after the Barnes one. Old, overcoat, something on the head, and the shopping bag. That's important, isn't it, the shopping bag?"

Hyte grunted. "Oh yes. It's where he kept the crossbow."

"Our man disguised himself as a woman on the Samson killing?" Smith said.

"Or vice versa—or, they're all disguises. But it tells us that we have to keep a lookout for anyone with a shopping bag in the vicinity of a possible victim."

"All right," Hyte said, "we're starting to get somewhere. I just wish to hell I knew where. Sy, any luck with the Helenezes?"

"I'm waiting to hear from Immigration," Cohen said.

Because Helenez's company had refused to tell the task force if Helenez was in the States, an immigration check was the only way to find out if they were. "Use whatever pressure you have to, but find them."

"I will. By the way," Cohen added, "the Desmonds are clean. Confirmation just came in on Harold Desmond's statement. They were in Hawaii from March twenty-fifth through April fourth. With Lea."

* * *

At one o'clock, Hyte stepped into the understated reception area of the Lentronics corporation, on East Fifty-seventh Street. Two conservatively dressed men came to attention.

He categorized them immediately. Both had the clean-cut looks and dress of high-level federal agents. Their faces were ordinary, their eyes intelligent. They wore custom-tailored suits that gave no sign of the weapons Hyte knew they carried.

"Lieutenant Hyte," said the man on the left, "I'm Rawling, this is Collins. We're with the NSA."

After shaking hands, Rawling took him into a large, wood-paneled office. Behind a mahogany desk, J. Milton Prestone presided.

"Thank you, Rawling," Prestone said as he came around the desk to shake hands with Hyte. "I'm sorry we're meeting again under these circumstances."

"Why are we meeting?"

"Drink?" Prestone asked. Hyte shook his head. Both men sat down.

"Lieutenant, I'm aware that you've seen fit to check up on my whereabouts for the past month. Why?"

"Because every first-class passenger is a suspect in this case."

"As I thought. And the results of your queries have absolved me from suspicion, have they not?"

Hyte nodded. "Why are you here, Senator? Why are you involving yourself?"

Prestone moistened his lips; Hyte caught the nervous tick of the senator's left eye. "Because what's happening is my fault. If I hadn't been on that plane, no one would have died. And the pilot would not have been killed trying to save my life."

"You had no control over any of that. Your plane was sabotaged."

"Nonetheless, it was my presence that endangered the others. Three people died because of who I am. And now four more people have died as well."

"Which has nothing to do with you. Senator, all you've

accomplished by coming here is to put yourself in danger and give me more problems.''

"I came here to help you, just as you helped me on that plane, just as the pilot helped me to stay alive. We both know that what's happening now is linked to the hijacking. I want to put an end to it; if I have to offer myself as a victim to achieve that goal, then that's what I'll do.''

"It won't work," Hyte said, knowing his argument with Prestone was as hopeless as it had been with Mason.

"It's worth a try. Besides, I'm well protected. You met my bodyguards. And I didn't hire them, Lieutenant, that's not my style. After the hijacking, the President assigned them to me.''

"Good. Maybe they'll save your life. But it would be smarter and safer for you to leave New York.''

"I intend to make my presence very well known over the next few days. I have meetings to attend, and several fund raisers as well.''

"These fund raisers, were they scheduled a while ago?''

"No. I invited myself to them the other day. And I've also invited myself to be a guest on several news shows between now and tomorrow night. I intend to show the public that I'm not afraid to move freely about.''

Why was Hyte the only one who saw the senselessness of Prestone's plan? As he'd told Mason, Samael was a strategist. The Friday Night Killer would not go after someone spontaneously. Yet, Hyte knew he couldn't make Prestone believe him. "You realize you're making yourself a target for anyone with a grudge against you, not just our man?''

"That's one of the chances I have to take." Prestone stood. "How do you intend to cover me?" Gone was his easygoing manner. In its place, Hyte faced the famous man who had controlled the Senate Arms Appropriation Committee for two decades.

"I'll send you the route you'll take to and from the fund raisers. You'll go to a lounge of our choosing for your nightcap. You won't see us, Senator. But we'll be there. And you will leave your two bodyguards behind.''

Prestone smiled at Hyte. "Good.''

"Don't carry that pistol tomorrow."

Prestone's eye flickered. "I didn't think it showed."

"Senator, you've stepped into the middle of a murder investigation, pulled myself and my team off stride. We now have to stop what we're doing in order to baby-sit you. So you either leave your weapon in the apartment, or stay there yourself. I won't have someone injured because you want to play cowboy. Is that understood?"

Prestone smiled. "You should have been in politics."

"That's what my father always said. Good day, Senator."

When Hyte returned to the office, he called in his team for another meeting. He told them that Sy Cohen and Sally O'Rourke would be on duty Friday night, and that Smith and Roberts would be off.

The two detectives protested immediately.

"As you know," Hyte said, looking at Smith and Roberts, "it's against Department regulations for an NYPD officer to work out of jurisdiction without the knowledge, consent, and cooperation of said outside authority. But if the two of you are off duty, no one can stop you from driving out to Long Island and looking at real estate, say in Bay Shore? I understand there's a lovely estate that may come on the market. It's presently owned by a Jack Mofferty. Am I making myself clear?"

"Perfectly," Smith said.

"Isn't Suffolk providing protection?" Roberts asked.

"They are. You're not looking to protect anyone; you're there to see if Jack Mofferty skips protection."

The two detectives glanced at each other. "You think it's him?" Roberts asked.

"You two just make sure you know where he is every minute of Friday night. I mean that literally. Sally, you're going to be a third set of eyes on Joan Bidding. She'll be the only victim in the city."

Hyte spent the remainder of Thursday and all of Friday setting up the logistics of the Prestone stakeout. With Sy

Cohen, he mapped the route, and worked out stations for the cops who would be watching.

At four o'clock, the long overdue phone call from Immigration came in. Cohen took the call in Hyte's office. When he hung up, he said, "You aren't going to like this."

"On this case, what makes that an oddity?" Hyte said.

Cohen laughed. "You were right about Immigration. Cristobal and Estella Helenez entered the United States three months ago through the Juarez-El Paso border. According to Immigration, they have not left."

He stared at Cohen. "Juarez? Why the hell would they come in that way?"

"To keep a low profile, I'd imagine."

Hyte nodded. "Where are they now?"

"All Immigration says is that the Helenezes have an open visa, which means they could be anywhere."

"That's just fucking great!"

At five, Hyte sent Cohen over to the senator's apartment with body armor and the command that the senator was to wear it.

He called in Schwartz, who had volunteered to stay at the office on phone duty and to coordinate communications between Hyte, the men in Long Island, and Sally O'Rourke in Queens.

Then he got himself ready to face the forty cops who were waiting for him downstairs. He needed them to believe that their killer might strike Prestone tonight, and knew that his voice and manner could not show his own feelings that they were wasting time, money, and manpower on the wrong victim.

Thirty-one

"Lieutenant?"

"Go ahead, Schwartz," Hyte said, speaking into a hand-held radio from his position outside the Waldorf-Astoria.

"Smith and Roberts report that the subjects have not left the house since returning from Masters's. O'Rourke says there's no action in Forest Hills. And, Emma Graham called."

"Thank you Schwartz," Hyte said, lowering the radio.

"Heads up," came a different voice. Hyte turned to watch J. Milton Prestone exit the Waldorf-Astoria. When he reached the sidewalk, he paused to speak with several reporters before starting to walk uptown. With Prestone's first step, phase two of the night's operation went into effect. The former senator was on his way to a cocktail lounge off Fifty-fifth Street. He would stay there for one or two drinks, and then proceed to the company-owned Fifty-seventh Street apartment.

"Here we go," Cohen said.

Hyte spoke into his radio, alerting the forty cops hidden along the route. It was 11:48 P.M.

At 11:50, a figure wearing a long, shapeless overcoat slipped from the cover of a phone booth and sidled into the service alley of Crown Towers, a sixty-story building that

236

was a mix of offices and apartments on Fifty-seventh Street between Fifth Avenue and the Avenue of the Americas.

At midnight, a cab stopped outside the alleyway. The rear door opened and a woman wearing a light cape left the cab and started into the alley.

Samael blended into the shadows.

As the woman walked past, Samael's right arm whipped out, jerking her backward. Samael's left hand rose, holding a glistening steel needle. The hand fell swiftly, the needle passing through the cape and sleeve of the woman's blouse, biting deep into the flesh of her upper arm.

Theresa Lopinta struggled, but her effort was in vain. Less than a minute after the needle had stuck, the woman was unconscious.

Samael dragged the body behind two garbage dumpsters at the rear of the alley, and took Lopinta's cape and purse. Samael opened the purse and extracted a set of keys. Each one was marked. The third key opened the employee entrance.

Samael put on the woman's cape and looked down at her. Theresa Lopinta's face was in profile, a brown mole was centered on her left cheek.

Samael put on and adjusted a brimmed floral hat. Using Theresa Lopinta's keys, the Messenger entered the staff entrance of the building, paused to wave up at the surveillance camera, and turned slightly so the brown mole centered on Samael's left cheek could be seen.

The makeup and mole the Messenger had applied, the wig, and the floral hat, were exact duplicates of Theresa Lopinta's.

A buzzer sounded and the elevator door opened. Samael pressed the button marked PENTHOUSE.

"He's getting another drink," came the crackling report from the radio's speaker.

"He's getting himself looped," Hyte said, angry because he was letting Prestone's antics get under his skin.

"Two drinks isn't looped," Cohen said.

"Damn it, Sy, we're wasting our time," Hyte said, wanting to make Sy understand his frustration. "Samael's out there somewhere, and he's either killed or is getting ready to kill. I feel it. He's got his victim staked out. He's going to try again tonight."

"All the possible victims are covered," Cohen said. "Relax."

Samael the maid moved toward the penthouse. The door lock was electronic—a miniature computer-controlled access.

Once again, Samael dipped into the maid's purse and withdrew a plastic card key. Its surface was coded. Skintight white cotton gloves pushed the key into the slot. When a barely audible click sounded, Samael pushed the door inward.

Darkness greeted the Messenger. Bending, Samael lifted the black crossbow from the shopping bag and stepped into the apartment.

Samael paused. He listened for sound. From Samael's left came electrically amplified voices. Samael went right, toward the master bedroom. At the door, Samael peered inside.

The room was immense. Thick white carpeting covered the floor. Hand screened wallpaper decorated the walls. The bed was centered in the room below a skylight surrounded by mirrors. It held a single sleeping occupant.

Satisfied, Samael backed away and went in the direction of the voices. At the open door, Samael saw that the room's only light came from a large back projection television.

Samael stepped inside. The television screen was filled with naked bodies performing a choreographed orgy. Samael searched the room. Seated in a leather wingback chair was Cristobal Helenez.

Samael lifted the crossbow. It was cocked. The Messenger's bolt was in place. Without haste, Samael stepped between the television and the Portuguese financier.

238

"Theresa! What are you—" He stopped in mid-sentence.

"Quiet," Samael ordered. "You know who I am."

Cristobal Helenez's eyes widened. He held his hands before him, palms forward in supplication. "Please," he cried. "I'm withdrawing my interests from Israel. But it takes time. Please, leave me alone."

"Do you still think you can continue to outwit your death? No! It is your time."

The twang of the string's release went unheard against the rising cries of the orgy's participants. A flashing pain sliced through Helenez's chest.

Samael cocked the crossbow, turned the revolving magazine to bring a fresh bolt into place, and went to the master bedroom.

God's Messenger of Death walked to the bed and tapped Estella Helenez's shoulder, pressing the crossbow to her left breast.

Estella opened her eyes. "Cristobal?" she asked.

"No," Samael whispered. "Good-bye."

Hyte got the call at 5:18 A.M. He was sitting in his car. Sy Cohen was next to him. They were parked in front of Prestone's building, where they'd been since one o'clock, keeping an eye on the street and on anyone who went into the building. Prestone, Hyte was sure, had been sleeping for at least three hours.

Fifty-seventh Street, between Third and Lexington, was deserted. Hyte turned to Cohen, about to say something, when he heard his name come over the radio. His stomach twisted. He was asked to call Central from a land line. The request could only mean one thing—a homicide. In a highly publicized murder investigation, a homicide was never broadcast in the clear.

"I'll be right back," he told Cohen, going into the building to use the house phone. Two minutes later he was back in the car.

"The Helenezes have an apartment four blocks west

239

of here. They're dead." He slammed his fist on the steering wheel. "Everyone's got the fucking answer, don't they? No one will listen! Everyone has to do it his way!"

Thirty-two

"I know you're all tired after last night, so let's get the reports finished and then you can go home," Hyte said. "Roberts, you're first."

Jimmy Roberts looked at his partner for a moment. "We arrived in Bay Shore at seven. The Moffertys were having dinner. At eight, they drove to Dr. Franklin Masters's home. They stayed until ten and then returned home. Mrs. Mofferty read in the library. Mr. Mofferty watched television in his bedroom. Sonja Mofferty went to bed at one, Jack Mofferty went to bed at two-thirty."

"How do you know what time they went to bed?" Sally O'Rourke asked.

Smith coughed. "We spent most of the night looking in the windows."

"The Suffolk police didn't object?"

"They didn't know. They had one car parked on the street. Anyone could have gotten to the house, including our killer."

"Sally," Hyte said, "you're next."

O'Rourke opened her notebook. "Joan Bidding and her husband and two children left their apartment at 6:18 P.M. They went to the Hong Chow restaurant on Queens Boulevard for dinner. They returned home at 7:49 and did not leave again. Detective Richard Flannery watched the rear entrance of the building, Detective Arnold Seissman watched the front."

He turned to the chalk board and circled Joan Bidding's and Sonja and Jack Mofferty's names. "They are now low priority," he said, somewhat disappointed that his prime candidate seemed clean. "From this point on we concentrate on eliminating suspects. One of them is our killer."

"How did Samael know where the Helenezes were when we couldn't find out?" O'Rourke asked.

Hyte shook his head. "I'd give up a promotion for that answer." He looked at Randal Schwartz. "Let's hear your report."

Schwartz studied his clipboard. "The Jersey police said that Sylvia Mossberg stayed in her apartment after she returned from synagogue. I checked in with the Graham house every hour. Detective Grishold told me that Emma Graham arrived in Westchester at 7:00 P.M. Jonah Graham went to sleep around 8:00. Miss Graham was in the first-floor office and worked until 2:00 A.M. She went to bed shortly after checking in on her father. She also called you at 11:40 last night. The police officers from the One-Nine precinct assigned to watch the Desmonds reported that the Desmonds did not leave the building."

"Which leaves us with nothing. There are six passengers and one crew member left alive, each of whom has an alibi."

"Then it has to be someone else," Roberts said. "A relative?"

Hyte grimaced. "Or it's one of the people we watched last night, one who's clever enough to make us think they were at home. In that case, the only definites we have are Prestone and Graham."

"We're going around in circles," Cohen said.

Hyte rubbed his eyes. "We've all been up for at least twenty-four hours. I want you to go home and get some sleep. Tomorrow . . . Sunday, go back over the Helenez apartment. Treat the murders as a fresh homicide case and follow all the steps. Now, get out of here."

When he was alone, Hyte called Harry Lester and set up a meeting. Fifteen minutes later, he was sitting across from the assistant medical examiner, drinking coffee.

"You turn up anything new?"

"No," the M.E. said. "The bolts are from the same manufacturer. I'm sure it's the same poison."

Hyte nodded but remained silent.

"What's going to happen now?" the pathologist asked.

"We'll find out soon enough. But Phil's in trouble. McPheerson's been waiting for this, he's going to pounce like a hyena."

"Let Mason worry about himself. You concentrate on catching this guy. That's why Mason's out on a limb, so you can work freely. You figure out why Barnes was brought into the city?"

"I assume it's because Samael wants each death to happen, or to appear to have happened, in New York."

"Because the hijacking was here?"

"I don't know," Hyte admitted. "Harry, can a stroke be faked?"

The M.E. shook his head. "This is the age of the CAT scan."

"What about a recovery?"

"That would depend on the severity of the stroke. Why?"

"Just chasing shadows."

"You left the Helenez apartment pretty fast this morning. All you did was take the maid's story. You find something you aren't talking about?"

"Find what, Harry? Our man is slicker than anyone wants to admit. He knew exactly where the maid was last night. His makeup, duplicating the maid's face, was good enough to fool the guard in the surveillance room. Why else would he have let Samael into the elevator? Our man's no slouch. And Samael seems to have access to whatever he wants, from world-class poison and weapons to heavy sedatives."

"What are you going to do?" the M.E. asked.

"Go home and get some sleep."

His phone machine was blinking with its customary urgency. The first message was from Emma, asking him to call her at her father's house, then Phil Mason's deep voice told him to call. There was a second call from Emma.

The intercom buzzed. He picked it up. "Yes?"

Phil Mason said, "It's me."

Hyte pushed the buzzer for the lobby door, opened his apartment door, and returned to the living room. He poured two glasses of Scotch. When Mason walked in, he handed the chief one.

Mason went to look out the window. When he turned back, Hyte saw defiance in the set of his jaw.

"I just left the commissioner. He's retrenching, covering himself and fighting the political pressures from the Helenez killing. Ray, we've been shut down."

Hyte's throat constricted. "He can't do that."

"He can and did. The Prestone trap was a mistake. You were right and I was wrong. I'm getting too old for this crap anyway."

Hyte's hand tightened on the glass. "What are you going to do?"

"Wait a few weeks and then turn in my papers. Arlene's been after me to retire. She wants to travel."

"Phil—"

"Let it go. The PC gave McPheerson the nod to set up a new task force. Conner will be in charge. I've already turned my paperwork over to him. You're to give him whatever you have and go back to your liaison work. I'll arrange for a good assignment for you before I go."

"I can't walk out in the middle of this."

"I'm sorry, Ray, truly sorry, but I won't be able to keep you on it. Neither of us has a choice."

Hyte found it impossible to accept the way Mason was giving in. It wasn't like him. Phil Mason had been a fighter all his life.

Mason drained his glass and turned to leave. "Monday morning you hand over what you have to McPheerson's people."

Hyte knew why Phil Mason was a cop. Underneath all the cynicism and thanklessness of the Job, the idealism that had brought Mason into the Department was still there.

He paced the living room, his anger growing. Samael was doing more than just killing people, he was destroying careers. For the first time since he'd uncovered the pattern, he found himself hating Samael as he had never before hated another human being.

The phone rang. Startled from his thoughts, he picked it up and spoke sharply.

"Ray, what's wrong?" Emma asked. "I've been calling since . . . are you all right?"

"I'm fine."

"I heard about the Helenezes. Are you working today?"

"No," he said, not wanting to elaborate.

"Why don't you come out here and pick me up. We can go someplace quiet for the night. I'll have you back tomorrow afternoon, if you want."

"I won't be very good company."

"Maybe I can help you."

He thought about the soft fragrance that clung to her skin. And then he remembered Mason. "I don't have to be back until Monday. But I have to do something first. I'll be there in a couple of hours."

When the elevator door opened, Rawling and Collins snapped upright.

"What brings you here, Lieutenant?" Rawling asked.

"I want to see him."

"The senator is resting. He can't be disturbed."

"Disturb him!"

"I'm sorry, we have instructions to—"

"Do it," Hyte said, "or I'll do it myself."

Rawling glared at him. But before he had a chance to speak, J. Milton Prestone walked in.

"What took you so long, Lieutenant?" Prestone asked. His eyes were shadowed, his face was strained.

"Sir," Rawling began, but Prestone brushed him aside.

"Come with me, Lieutenant."

Once in the senator's office, Prestone turned to Hyte. "Are you here for the 'I told you so' speech?"

"I'm here to tell you that all you've succeeded in accomplishing was to interfere with my investigation and end the career of a cop who's spent his life working for the people of this city."

"What are you talking about?" Prestone asked.

"Haven't you been listening to the news?"

"Of course I have. And I feel terrible about the Helenezes."

"I'm not talking about the Helenezes, I'm talking about Philip Mason. I believe the Helenezes would be alive right now if they'd let us know where they were. But they didn't because they were afraid. Instead, they tried to hide from the killer. That was their biggest mistake."

"What has that to do with Mason?"

"Commissioner Rutledge has taken the task force from him and recommended he retire."

"Because of last night?"

"You got it."

Prestone frowned. "It wasn't his fault."

"No, it wasn't. But Senator, you know politics—scapegoats are crucial. And at the highest levels of the Department, it's all politics. The chief took a chance with you, against my advice. He lost. Now the city is going to lose a good man."

"I really am sorry."

Hyte gauged the senator's tone and expression. "Then would you do me a favor?"

"If I can."

"Go back to New Mexico. Get yourself out of New York so that the task force can have one less victim to concentrate on."

"You mean so you can have one less."

"No, sir. As I said, a new task force is being formed. I work for Phil Mason, not Chief McPheerson."

Prestone pursed his lips. "I didn't come to New York unprepared. And I damned well checked out your background myself. You're fully qualified to handle this investigation—more so perhaps than anyone else. You've proven yourself capable several times in the past, and you have an advantage in this instance. You know everyone involved.''

"Which means nothing to McPheerson, and less to the commissioner. Rutledge needs results; the chief of department wants glory and his own man sitting in the chief of detectives' office.''

"What do you want, Lieutenant?''

Hyte looked at Prestone for a moment before turning away. "I want the son of a bitch who's doing this.''

"You aren't dropping the case, are you?''

Hyte said nothing.

"Did you ever watch the tapes of the hijacking?'' Prestone asked.

Hyte's laugh was bitter. "Didn't we all? Senator, will you leave the city before next Friday?''

Prestone nodded. "I will. After I take care of some business.''

"Thank you.''

"And I'm very sorry about last night.''

Hyte paused, his anger waning. "What you tried to do was a brave thing. And I'm sorry it worked out the way it did.''

"If you had the chance to keep working on this case, would you?''

"I won't work under McPheerson. Good-bye, Senator.''

"You haven't answered my question.''

"Didn't I?''

Hyte pulled to a stop in the driveway of Jonah Graham's home. The house, a two-story, twenty-five-year-old brick and clapboard colonial, had a sprawling first floor that included a two-room office complex that Emma had used to run Graham International during the weeks following Jonah's stroke. She used it still whenever she visited her father.

Hyte rang the bell. Less than a minute later Emma was in his arms. "I've been so worried about you after hearing the commissioner's announcement,'' she said.

"I'm fine," he told her.

"Let me get my things and we can go."

"How's your father?"

"Why don't you go up and say hello? He's on the bedroom balcony with Fiona. I'll wait for you in the office."

"Does he know about the killings?"

"I think he does. He watches television. But he can't talk, Ray, he can't communicate."

"I'll be down in a few minutes," Hyte said and went upstairs to the master bedroom.

When he'd first visited Jonah, Emma had told him that she'd tried to retain the room's original atmosphere. She'd kept the oak furniture that had been her parents'. The bed was the same one that Jonah and Anita had shared for the last fifteen years of their marriage. But the medical equipment, oxygen tent framework, and vital sign monitors marred the memory Emma had tried to preserve.

Hyte was saddened by the sight as he walked across the room to the white French doors, and stepped onto the balcony.

Jonah Graham was in a wheelchair. His nurse was off to the side, doing needlework. Graham's face was a shadow of its former handsomeness. His cheeks were sunken, his skin pale. Yet, when his blue eyes fixed on him, Hyte sensed recognition.

"Hello, Jonah. Emma says that you know about what's happening. I'm sure you also know that the man who's been here on Friday nights is here to protect you, should this person decide he wants to come after you. But somehow I don't think he will. I don't know why Jonah, it's just a feeling.

"Damn it, Jonah," Hyte added harshly, "who would want to hurt these people?"

"Sir," the nurse called.

"Sorry," he said without taking his eyes from Jonah. "But you'll be safe, I promise you that."

As he spoke, Jonah's eyes seemed to take on expression. Hyte thought he was imagining it, but feeling Jonah's deep-set blue eyes bore into him, he knew Jonah was trying to say something.

"What?" he whispered. "What?"

The right side of Graham's mouth twisted. Hyte bent closer, but there was no sound. Jonah's eyes were pleading. And then Hyte understood. It was something he would want himself if he was in the older man's position. Jonah Graham *wanted* to be a victim. He wanted an end to his torment.

Thirty-three

A light film of perspiration coated Hyte's body. Emma lay in the crook of his arm, her left breast pressed to his side.

They had arrived in Connecticut at six and went to Emma's small chalet, which was set on a hilltop overlooking Green Lake.

They'd eaten a dinner of fresh mountain trout, sautéd green beans, and a salad. Afterwards, sitting on the deck, they had watched the sun set beyond the lake.

Then they'd made love. Again, he realized how special Emma was. Not once since leaving Westchester had Emma mentioned the case. She had the rare ability to sense his moods and act upon them.

But now, with his physical desires satiated and his mind once again seeking answers, the Friday Night Killer returned to taunt him.

He kissed Emma's forehead. "What?" she whispered sleepily.

"Nothing," he replied as he left the bed. "Get some sleep."

Dressing, he left the bedroom and went outside. It was cool. The sky was clear. He stared at the patterns of the stars.

"Want to talk it out?" Emma asked. He smiled. He hadn't heard her come out on the deck.

"There's not much to say." She wore a deep red velour

robe and leaned against the railing. Moonlight reflected from the translucent skin of her neck.

"Yes, there is." She paused. "You're not going to let it go are you?"

"I don't have any choice."

"Everyone has a choice. But I think I know you—at least certain aspects. You didn't leave your father-in-law's bank because all you wanted in life was to be a cop. You left because your spirit would have died there. There was no challenge, and you thrive on challenge."

She came over to him, and he caught her hand and kissed the center of her palm.

"You remind me of the sea otters off the California coast."

"I'm like a sea otter?" he asked, amused.

Emma nodded. "Yes. You have an inherent tenaciousness once you've set your mind to a task. Who the hell could have spent five years working undercover, having his life divided into two separate entities? Not very many people, I can tell you that."

"Which means what?"

"The sea otter spends every minute of his life finding food. His metabolism is so speeded up that if he doesn't eat all the time, he'll freeze to death. Solving mysteries is your food. That's why you aren't going to walk away from this case."

"I've been ordered off it."

She shrugged. "So what? It's your case, Ray. You know it and I know it. Nothing they can say or do will matter, will it?"

"You sound as though you want me to stay on it," he said. He saw a sudden tightening at the corners of her mouth.

"Why do you say that?"

"Because it's what I'm hearing."

"I'm only trying to get you to tell me the truth. You can tell everyone else what they want to hear, but you'll tell me the truth."

He drew her close to him. "The truth," he agreed. "I'm not walking away from this."

Emma's eyes sparkled in the moonlight. "Just be careful."

Hyte was in his office by seven on Monday morning. When he looked at his calendar, he realized that his daughter's birthday was two weeks away. He made a note to pick up a present for Carrie.

He spent the next half hour putting the case reports into a large cardboard box and sealing it with tape. As he began a second box, his intercom line buzzed.

"Upstairs, Ray," Philip Mason commanded.

Hyte found Mason sitting behind his desk, his chin pedestaled on thick, steepled fingers.

"Sit," Mason said.

Hyte settled himself on the leather couch across from the chief. "Where the hell were you yesterday?" Mason asked.

"That's none of your business."

Mason dropped his hands to the desktop. "It is my business when I've spent the last twenty hours trying to reach you."

Hyte tensed. Something had occurred that he had not foreseen. "I've been in Connecticut, with Emma. What happened?"

"At eight o'clock yesterday morning, I received a call from the PC, inviting me to breakfast at Gracie Mansion. It seems that pressure has been brought on the mayor. What kind or from who, I can't begin to imagine, but whatever the reason, the mayor wanted to know the justification for my being taken off the investigation. It seems that the mayor feels I was not lax in the Helenez murders; he now believes their deaths could not have been stopped. He outwardly agreed with the commissioner's decision to shift the focus of the task force to McPheerson. But he personally instructed the commissioner that I was to be absolved of any blame for my failure to prevent the killings. Furthermore, His Honor has decided, because of the ramifications of this case, that he wants a small and independent task force formed. This task force will report directly to him, through me as liaison, and will conduct an independent investigation. You are to head the task force."

"He wants me to stay on the case?" Hyte asked, exaltation rising. Then reality set in. "No, it can't be done. My people and McPheerson's will be stepping all over each other."

"No, you won't. McPheerson believes that terrorists are behind the killings, which means the task forces will be operating in different directions. You'll be put on special assignment to the mayor's staff. You'll work out of your office, but you'll also retain your position under me. And, you're to stay clear of Chief McPheerson."

"What did McPheerson have to say about it?"

"He wasn't there. It was myself, the PC, the mayor, and his number one boy, Rosenthal. McPheerson and his task force are only being told that you've been assigned to special duty work with the mayor's staff. Do your job, and do it very quietly. With luck you'll find Samael before McPheerson."

"What about my team?" Hyte asked.

"McPheerson has requested Smith and Roberts to be transferred to his task force. In the interest of cooperation, you'll have to do without them."

"No problem," Hyte said. "I can manage with Cohen and O'Rourke. Who brought the pressure, Phil?"

Mason shrugged. "I don't know. But when I find out, I'm damned well going to thank him."

Hyte's team was waiting in his office. Their faces were solemn, their eyes expressive. "We all know what's happened, so let's not waste any time commiserating. Smith, Roberts, I want to thank you both for the work you've put into this case."

"Does that mean we're going back to our units?" Roberts asked.

"No. You've both been reassigned to McPheerson's new

task force. You are to report immediately." He smiled. "I wouldn't mind being kept abreast of any developments, as long as it doesn't get you in trouble."

"I've been in trouble all my life," Smith said. "What the hell's a little more?"

When the two detectives were gone, Hyte sat on the edge of his desk. Sy Cohen was staring intently at him, his face expressionless. Sally O'Rourke was angry.

"I guess that means I go back to the desk," she said.

"If you want to. Or, we can let Schwartz stay where he is."

He watched O'Rourke's puzzled expression deepen. "I don't understand," she finally said.

"You, Sy, and I are still on the case. Covertly," he cautioned. "No one is to know."

"How . . . I mean who . . . ?"

He ignored her question. "There are four of us, including Schwartz. Sy, you spell it out for him, okay?"

"He'll keep it quiet," Cohen promised.

"I want you to follow up any leads you have. I also want to do the weapons check again. Maybe something new has come up." He grinned. "Check in with me every two hours. If I'm out, leave your number with Schwartz. And there's one other thing. The poison used on the bolts came from the Orient. Let's see if any of our suspects have been there."

"Any ideas about how Samael knew where the Helenezes were?" Cohen asked.

"None. It's almost as if he's got a pipeline to each victim. And to us as well."

When Hyte was alone again, he called Jerome Rosenthal at City Hall. "Who put in the word, Jerry?"

"Who said it had to be anyone? Perhaps the mayor knows how good Mason is."

"The mayor doesn't interfere in departmental politics without a good reason."

"Ray, let's just say the pressure was substantial. How's Emma?"

"Fine," he said in a calmer voice.

"She's a good lady. You're a lucky man."

254

"I know. Jerry, don't try to sidetrack me."

"You know who it was. You set it up yourself, if I read the situation right. Good-bye, Ray, have a good day." He hung up.

Hyte stared at the phone for several seconds. The other line began blinking. A moment later his intercom buzzed. "Senator Prestone," Schwartz announced.

Hyte lifted the receiver. "Senator?"

"I just wanted you to know that I'm leaving tonight. I have one more meeting this afternoon and I'll be out of your hair."

"I appreciate it."

"I'm sure you do. And, Lieutenant, I'm fully aware of what I caused. I hope the situation has been rectified by now."

"Then it was you."

"You made me feel like an old incompetent fool, putting my nose where it doesn't belong. Not many people are capable of that. So, yes, I spoke with the mayor. But you'd damned well better catch that murdering bastard."

"I'll bo my best, Senator. Thank you."

As he hung up, the phone blinked again. Schwartz stepped inside.

"Lieutenant, you have a strange call."

He wondered why Schwartz hadn't used the intercom. "And?"

"Deputy Inspector Conner is outside. He wants to speak with you. I didn't want him to know about the call. The caller says it's about the killings."

"Was it transferred from the hotline?"

"No, it's direct. We haven't gotten any calls since the task force was switched. The guy sounds like he's speaking through water."

Hyte lifted the phone. He motioned for Schwartz to stay. "Lieutenant Hyte."

Schwartz was almost right. The voice did sound as though it was coming through water. Only it wasn't. It was a synthesizer, the kind used to alter a voice.

"So you're giving up on me, are you?"

255

"Giving up on who?" Hyte asked.

"You know who I am. Or shall I send you another bolt? Did you like that one, Lieutenant? No one touched the tip, did they?"

Every nerve in Hyte's body came alive; his mind leapt outward. He wished he could order a trace but knew the uselessness of it.

"Why are you calling me? You know I'm not involved anymore."

"Of course you are. You have been since last July. Why else would—" Samael stopped. "Nice try, Lieutenant. Actually, I'm calling for advice."

"You want advice?" Hyte asked.

Samael laughed. "No, I want to give you advice. Stop looking for me. It's pointless and we both know it. No one will find me. And when I've collected those who are destined for me, I will be gone."

"How many more are you going to . . . collect?"

"There are six more. Six who thought they succeeded in outwitting death."

"Why don't you come in and talk to me? We can—"

"Don't insult me. This is not a hostage negotiation. The next time we speak, it will all be over."

"Wait!" Hyte said. His answer was the dial tone.

"Was it him?" Schwartz asked.

"Yes, goddamn him!"

"Lieutenant, I have it on tape. The tech set up a phone tap machine for the hotline."

Hyte smiled. "Good!"

"What about Deputy Inspector Conner?" Schwartz asked.

"Send him in," he said, thinking that he had finally found a handle. The call had given it to him. Samael was challenging him openly. Samael wanted— No, Hyte realized, Samael *needed* him on the case. All he had to do now was figure out a way to use that knowledge.

Thirty-four

Hyte's excitement remained high through the day. He left messages for O'Rourke and Cohen to meet him at his apartment, then called Professor Alinski and asked him to join them.

At five, with everyone assembled in his living room, he played the tape of Samael's phone call. When it ended, he asked Alinski for his impression.

"I couldn't tell if it was a man or woman, but I believe my initial diagnosis was accurate. It is a paranoiac. He is challenging you, Raymond. In his delusional state, he believes himself invincible—I would imagine it's because he believes in the absolute rightness of his mission. And, Raymond, you know him."

Hyte was caught short by Alinski's statement. "I know him? In the philosophical sense?"

Alinski ran a hand through his sparse white hair. "In the physical sense. Why else would he disguise his voice?"

"One of the passengers I talked to," Hyte thought out loud.

"Perhaps," Alinski agreed. "But without doubt, it is someone involved with the hijacking. His reference to the hostage negotiation is indicative of that."

"He also wants me to feel helpless."

"Is he succeeding?"

"Too much so. But I'm starting to understand him."

"Because he wants you to."

"Are you telling me that he wants to be caught?"

257

"No. If that were the case, he would have left more of a trail at the murder scenes. No, I believe it's because you were at the hijacking. He wants you to be involved with the killings. Perhaps he has marked you as a victim as well, but I think that unlikely. Rather, he's trying to show you he's as capable as you in managing events. He may even be emulating you. After all, you killed two hijackers. Perhaps to Samael's way of thinking, you 'collected' two people who thought they could outwit death. He's trying to prove that you're not the only one who can mete out punishment."

Hyte considered this. "Do you know Franklin Masters?"

Alinski nodded. "Good man. A shade ostentatious for my taste, but solid in his field."

"If Masters is certain that Mofferty cannot be paranoiac, would you accept his diagnosis?"

"Absolutely. He's good enough to pick up the original delusion. And now, Raymond, I must leave. It was nice meeting you both," he said to O'Rourke and Cohen.

Hyte escorted the psychologist out and returned to the living room. "You two were quiet enough. What do you make of the tape?"

Cohen shrugged. "Alinski said it. It was a challenge. Samael wants you coming after him. And I don't like that."

"Sally?"

O'Rourke took a deep breath. "I think it was a woman. The inflection—"

"The synthesizer."

"Call it a hunch."

"Who?" he asked.

"It could be anyone," O'Rourke began. "Haller's wife saw him killed. Sonja Mofferty was brutalized. If that had been me—" she bit off whatever she was going to say. "There's also the flight engineer's widow—"

"Who lives in California," Cohen cut in. "You might as well put the Desmond girl into that category. Or Emma Graham. Her mother was killed."

"We're going around in circles again," Hyte said. "Let's try to straighten up. What did you two get accomplished today?"

"I spoke with my contact at the phone company," Cohen said in his usual calm manner. "She's going to do a computer run on the numbers I gave her. We'll have a full listing of all calls made since the hijacking, but it'll take some time without the proper authorizations."

"That's not going to be a small list. And it's going to be tedious as hell. What's happening with the Oriental connection?"

O'Rourke fidgeted on the couch. "Since we can't be open about what we're doing, and I couldn't walk into the Immigration and Naturalization Service and ask for a trace, I asked Jon Rosen for a favor. I said it was for you." Hyte nodded but said nothing. "He knew about your being pulled from the investigation. I asked him if he could somehow get into the INS computer and see if he could match one of the names with their exit and entry records. He said he'd try."

Hyte knew that the man who had helped him set up the program that had found the match on the first two Samael murders would do more than just try. "You gave him the full list?"

"Every first-class passenger, each crew member, all the relatives of the dead victims, and all coach passengers."

"What about the weapons?"

Again it was O'Rourke who spoke. "All the lists from the distributors were taken by McPheerson's people before I could copy them. Sorry, Lou."

"What now?" Cohen asked.

"We wait for the phone records and the INS check."

The lobby intercom sounded. Hyte rose and went to answer it. "Yes?"

"It's me," said Emma Graham.

He buzzed her in, opened the door, and went back to the living room. "We'd better get going," Cohen said.

Hyte motioned him to stay seated. "Let's see what's on the news." He picked up the remote and flicked on the television set. Every night, at exactly 6:15 P.M., Joan Leighton did an update on the Friday Night Killer.

Emma stepped into the living room and took off her coat. Hyte went to her and kissed her lightly. "Hello, Sy, Sally," she said with a smile that disappeared when she heard the anchorman announce Joan Leighton.

"You're not going to watch that bitch?" she asked in surprise.

O'Rourke laughed. Hyte said nothing as the blonde reporter's face filled the screen.

"As most of you are aware, the task force investigating the Friday Night Killer has been reorganized. And in this reporter's opinion, it was done none too soon. The ineptness of the handling of the case by Chief of Detectives Philip Mason, and his top aide, Lieutenant Raymond Hyte, had become all too apparent on last Friday night when Cristobal and Estella Helenez were murdered in their home, only a few blocks from where the police were guarding former Senator J. Milton Prestone.

"However, the focus of the task force is changing, with Chief William McPheerson assuming overall command. High on the chief's priority list are terrorist organizations. Earlier today, Chief McPheerson and his top aide, Deputy Inspector John Conner, gave this reporter an exclusive interview. For the first time, the actual murder weapon has been revealed."

The camera zoomed in on the crossbow. Behind Hyte, Emma gasped. "What's wrong?" Hyte asked.

Her mouth was taut. "Dear God, why didn't you tell me what he was using to kill them?"

Hyte remained silent, waiting for Emma to explain.

"Ray, until seven months ago, the Graham International catalogue sold those crossbows."

"You said until seven months ago?"

"We've been selling them for years. I've always considered them toys, like most of the things we sell. But when we started getting strong letters from gun control advocates I discontinued them."

"Did you sell all the extras as well? The target and broadhead bolts?" Cohen asked.

Emma shook her head. "We offered only target bolts and the telescopic sight."

"Did you return all the stock to the manufacturer?" O'Rourke asked.

"The catalogue business is different from retail. And the Graham buying method is even more refined than most catalogue companies," Emma explained. "We have to keep a certain amount of stock, even when an item is discontinued, to service customers. Because we make a lot of low price deals, many items can't be returned. When we have an overstock, we usually look for an outlet where we can dump it."

"What did you do with the crossbows and equipment you didn't keep?" Hyte asked.

"I'd have to go over the records and check with the warehouse."

"Every sale you make is recorded, isn't it? There are no cash sales, are there?"

"Not in the mail order division, but we've been opening stores. Still, we take names and addresses. Anyone who buys from our stores goes onto the mailing list."

Hyte started to pace. "Oh, it fits so well."

"What fits?" O'Rourke asked.

"Think about it! Samael is obsessed with vengeance. But it's not an outright eye for an eye and to hell with everything else retribution. Samael is devious, and everything he does has a purpose! He does the unexpected, uses things we would never consider. He wants what he deems his justice, which he extracts systematically. But we always seem to overlook the obliqueness of his ways. Ten to one, Samael bought his crossbow from the Graham catalogue. He's using a weapon that one of his victims unwittingly supplied him with."

"But the bolts?"

"Hunting bolts are available outside the city. And it makes a distorted kind of sense. Emma, everything at Graham is computerized, isn't it?"

"Yes."

"Could you find every customer who bought a crossbow?"

"Through the catalogue division, yes. But we'll have to go back to when we first started selling the bows."

"No, you can begin with the date of the hijacking."

Hyte saw understanding grow in her eyes. "I'll get it started tomorrow morning," she said.

"I'd like to send Sy and Sally to your warehouse. I'd also like to check the inventory records against on-hand supply."

"There isn't much inventory."

"That doesn't matter," he told her as the phone rang.

The call was for Emma. She spoke briefly, then lowered the receiver. "Can I take it in the bedroom?"

Hyte took the phone from her and, when she picked up the bedroom extension, he heard her say, "Mr. Tanaka, this is a surprise," he hung up.

"The modern executive," Hyte explained to the two questioning faces. "Uses call forwarding."

Sy turned to stare at the bedroom door, his expression distant. "What is it, Sy?" Hyte asked.

"I'm not sure. Probably nothing," he said. "Ray, do you really think we'll find something on the mailing list?"

"It makes sense," Hyte said. "I want the two of you working together on this."

"What about the phone number check?"

"Give it to Schwartz." He paused. "We don't have much time to find our man, and, because we're working covert, we have no manpower except ourselves. We'll use my apartment for our base, and we'll meet here every evening. So," he added pointedly, "until tomorrow . . ."

Fifteen minutes later, Emma emerged from the bedroom. "They're gone?"

"They'll be by to see you in the morning. Hungry?"

"Upset. It hurts to think that I might have supplied the killer with his weapon."

"Don't worry about that. He would have gotten it somewhere else. If he did buy it from Graham, it's because of twisted logic. There's nothing you could have done about it. Let's get something to eat."

"A quick bite. That was Ahiro Tanaka of Mitsakashi. I have a meeting with him tomorrow afternoon, to make some last minute changes in our contract. I'm afraid I'll be working late."

He squeezed her hand. "No problem."

"Thank you," she said.

"No. Thank *you.* You may have given us a real lead."

Her voice surprised him with its fervor. "I hope so," she said.

Hyte woke early on Tuesday morning. He let his mind wander. He had learned more yesterday than he had since the Samson death. He wanted to learn more today.

He showered, dressed and, at ten past seven, poured his first cup of coffee and turned on the radio.

"This just in. A private jet carrying former United States Senator J. Milton Prestone has crashed. FAA spokesman Mark Kamen has confirmed that the plane exploded while en route to New Mexico. Lentronics officials have verified that J. Milton Prestone, CEO of Lentronics, and two associates were the only passengers on the plane. There were no survivors."

Hyte's stomach churned. "A splinter faction of the PLO has sent a message to the FBI claiming responsibility for the senator's death," the newscaster continued. "This is the same group of terrorists reputed to have been behind the hijacking of a plane Senator Prestone had been a passenger on last year. The FBI has not yet released the details of the message."

Hyte shut off the radio. His emotions were in flux. For all of Prestone's egocentricities and orneriness, Hyte held a grudging admiration for the man. Abruptly, he promised himself that Prestone's last act—his intervention to keep Hyte on the investigation—would not be forgotten.

The two passengers with Prestone would have to be the two NSA agents. Although he had not been fond of them, Hyte felt a loss, as he did whenever a fellow law officer died.

Samael? he wondered. Had the Friday Night Killer reached out into the sky to kill Prestone? No, it wasn't Samael's way.

He inhaled deeply, shook his head. Suddenly, he wanted

to hear his daughter's voice. He needed to hear the sound of innocence to help steady his own world.

He dialed the number in Boston. His ex-wife answered the phone. "Hello, Susan," he said.

"What is it, Ray?" she said, her voice cool and curt.

Tension knotted the muscles in his neck. Bad idea, he told himself. "I thought I'd catch Carrie before she left for school."

"She's not here. She spent the night with a friend."

He felt his sense of loss deepen, and had to work to keep his voice casual. "I see. Well, I just wanted to say hello."

"She'll be disappointed to have missed your call. And she was *very* disappointed when you canceled your weekend," Susan said, accusingly.

"How the hell do you think I feel?" he said, hanging up. He felt foolish for having called without thinking it out, and angry that his ex-wife was taking every opportunity to find fault with him.

Damn it, this has to stop! Susan wasn't just hurting him with her accusations and reactions, she was hurting Carrie as well. He knew he would have to find a way to change her feelings before she did more damage to Carrie. As soon as I catch Samael, he promised himself.

"Why did they go public with the weapon?" Hyte asked Mason, after bringing him up to date. "And all this terrorist crap as well." He jabbed his index finger toward the newspapers across Mason's desk.

"McPheerson had to give them something after taking over the task force. The media's been on his back. But there was no mention of the poison.

"Samael isn't a terrorist. At least not the kind McPheerson and Conner are thinking of." Hyte shook his head. "What about the cooperation from Jersey and Long Island?"

"Nothing's changed that I'm aware of. Do you really think this guy bought the crossbow from Graham?"

"It fits the pattern," Hyte said. "At least we'll get a partial list of East Coast weapon owners."

"Get it to me. I'll make sure that McPheerson gets it and has his people check it out. We'll get the results of the check, but he won't know it came from us. I'll make sure of that."

"Or from Emma."

"No problem. Shame about Prestone. I liked the man."

"It was Prestone who put the pressure on the mayor," Hyte said, watching Mason's face carefully.

"You went to him, didn't you?"

"Can I requisition overtime for Randy Schwartz? He's the clerical filling in for O'Rourke. I'm using him at home in the evenings," he said, pointedly ignoring Mason's question.

"Send it to me. And thank you, Ray."

Hyte leaned against the fender of his car. He was parked a dozen feet from the Desmonds' West Side apartment house. He had arrived ten minutes before and asked the doorman to ring the Desmond apartment. He was told that Mrs. Desmond was picking her daughter up from school but would return shortly.

Following the tragedy of the hijacking, and during his own convalescence, Hyte had paid a visit to the Desmonds, to see how the little girl was doing. He had liked Harold and Theresa Desmond immediately, and later he and Emma had visited the girl together. But he hadn't seen Lea, or her adoptive parents, in almost six weeks.

Now Hyte spotted Theresa and Lea Desmond turn the corner of Eighty-sixth Street.

Lea had changed since she had arrived in America. Without the equatorial sun, her skin had lightened to a tawny hue. Her long dark hair hung freely down her back. Her clothing—green plaid skirt, white blouse, dark shoes—was parochial school standard.

Lea saw him and waved. But Theresa Desmond's smile faltered. "Hi," Lea said when she reached him. "Is Emma with you?"

"No, she's working," he said. "Can we talk for a minute?" he asked Theresa.

She nodded. Hyte knelt next to Lea. "Will you wait for your mother in the lobby?"

Lea glanced at her mother. "I'll be just a moment," Theresa said.

Hyte watched Lea until she was inside, and then turned to Theresa. "She seems to be doing well. It's as if the hijacking never happened."

"It happened and she still has nightmares to prove it. But she's getting better. Are you here because of that killer?"

"What do you do on Friday nights?"

"I certainly don't go around killing people!"

He smiled apologetically. "No. I don't think you do. That's not what I meant."

"Is this killer really after all the passengers?"

"Just certain ones."

"Like Lea?"

He didn't like the panic he heard edging into her voice. "I have no hard proof, but I don't believe Lea is in danger," he said calmly.

"We usually go out for dinner on Friday nights, and then for a walk. Sometimes we go to a show, sometimes we visit friends."

"Is it the same restaurant each Friday?"

She laughed. "In New York? Really, Ray."

"Until we catch this killer, please stay home on Friday nights. And tell Harold that there'll be someone watching the building on Fridays."

"But you said . . ."

"It's just a precaution."

"All right. We'll stay home on Friday nights. When are you and Emma coming over for dinner?"

"Soon," he promised before leaving. "Soon."

Hyte let himself into his apartment at four, just as the phone rang. He didn't want to speak to anyone. On the second ring, the answering machine cut in and made its announcement. When the beep sounded, he heard Emma's voice. "Ray, I'll be tied up all evening with Tanaka. Call me at home later if you get a chance. Oh, my computer people say they'll have the list ready tomorrow. I miss you."

A moment later the machine clicked off.

O'Rourke and Cohen arrived at five-thirty. They handed him the inventory sheets and a crossbow and set of target bolts they'd borrowed from Emma's warehouse.

Randy Schwartz arrive at exactly six, carrying the chalk board. He handed Cohen a manila envelope. "This came in this afternoon."

Cohen opened it and withdrew two computer printouts, which he passed to Hyte. "The Barnes and Mossberg phone calls for the last six months," he said as he read the note. "The rest should get to me this week."

Hyte looked at the papers, put them back in the envelope, and handed it to Schwartz.

"What am I supposed to be looking for?" Schwartz asked.

"A match of some sort," Cohen said. "A call from one victim to another on a Friday night as well as any calls to the Orient."

Hyte took a sip of his drink. "Did anything else come across my desk after I left?" he asked.

"No," Schwartz said, "but I had to bring that last box of reports up to Deputy Inspector Conner's office. When I was there, I heard him talking on the phone. He said he was certain that the terrorist group who blew up Senator Prestone's plane is also responsible for killing the passengers from Flight 88. He said they had narrowed their search to three terrorist factions, and the task force was going to concentrate on them."

Hyte felt a sense of dread. If McPheerson and Conner were really that single-minded about the direction of their investigation, it would give the killer even more freedom.

Hyte knew he couldn't let that happen.

Thirty-five

Hyte walked toward Sylvia Mossberg's apartment in the Palisades Seniors Village of Englewood, New Jersey. Maples were coming into bloom. Waist-high evergreen bushes lined the walkways. Hyte saw all the landscaping as possible hiding places for the killer. He had no doubt that Samael could easily get past the two small security posts that screened visitors.

He pressed the button for Sylvia Mossberg's apartment. "Lieutenant Hyte, Mrs. Mossberg."

The buzzer sounded and he went through the door. There were four doors on the first floor. The left front door opened. "Good morning, Lieutenant," Sylvia Mossberg said.

The last time he had seen Sylvia Mossberg was when she'd been taken off the plane, wrapped in a blanket and sobbing uncontrollably. The woman before him now bore no resemblance to that terrified passenger. She wore a simple blue-flowered house dress. Her silver and white hair was cut short. Her eyes were tranquil. "Please, come in."

It was a one-bedroom apartment with a combination living room-dining room that overlooked the front walkway. The living room was decorated simply, with an expensive floral settee and two ladderback chairs with cushions on the same floral-patterned material.

"I prepared coffee after you called," she said, motioning him into the dining area.

He sat at an oak table where the elderly woman poured coffee into blue and white cups.

"Mrs. Mossberg, I know you're aware of what's been happening," Hyte said.

"More than aware, Lieutenant. If you're here to tell me to be careful, don't bother. I don't leave my apartment on Friday nights, except to go to temple."

"The detectives I sent here told me you agreed not to go out at all on Friday nights."

"No, I told them that I understood their concern and would act accordingly."

"You don't seem very worried."

"After living a nice safe life for seventy years, I learned what the word 'terrified' truly meant. When that plane was . . ." She faltered, and then pressed on. "When it was hijacked, I was never so afraid of anything, nor was I ever as ashamed of myself as I was for the way I acted."

"It was a normal reaction," Hyte said. He didn't bother to tell her how many cops had had similar responses when faced with death.

"It was the reaction of a frightened old woman. But I'm not a frightened old woman any longer. And I'm not afraid of this Friday Night Killer. If it's my time, so be it."

"Has anything unusual happened since the hijacking?"

"The detectives you sent asked me that question. And the answer is still the same. No."

"Have you had any contact with the other passengers?"

Sylvia Mossberg's eyes became moist. "I went to see Mr. Graham when he was in the hospital. And I went to his home a few months ago to visit him. I felt so guilty after seeing the tapes of the hijacking. I . . . His wife died because of my fear."

"Anita Graham died because four madmen took over that plane," he corrected her. "Mrs. Mossberg, have you ever been to the Orient?"

She smiled. "With Jake, in 1969. It was lovely. My husband was a clothing manufacturer. He had several factories in Hong Kong that produced his lines."

"Your son-in-law runs the company now, doesn't he?"

"Yes. He met my daughter when he came to work for us."

"Do you still have the factories?"

"No. Jake got rid of them in the mid-seventies and transferred the manufacturing to Mexico. He said it was an easier place to keep an eye on things."

"I see." He stood. "Mrs. Mossberg, please be careful. Don't let anyone in from sundown Friday night until after nine on Saturday morning."

"Who would I let in?" she asked.

Hyte showed the Trans Air security guard his shield and asked to see Joan Bidding.

She was on a break in the recreation room, working out on a Nautilus machine. There were only two other people in the room, both men. When Bidding saw him she left the machine and wiped her hands and face with a towel.

She wore a leotard exercise suit. Her stomach was almost concave.

"You do this a lot?" he asked, guiding her toward a private corner.

"Every day. I have been ever since they installed the equipment. It helps me to keep in shape."

"How are you holding up?"

"As well as can be expected."

"Has anything new happened? Phone calls? Things like that?"

The stewardess shook her head. "The only thing that's happened is that my husband has found someone else and asked me for a divorce."

Hyte looked away from her. "I'm sorry."

"I was expecting it. I haven't been the best wife since . . ."

"Why haven't you tried counseling?"

"I did. Trans Air has several psychologists available. They encourage all employees to see them."

"It did no good?"

"I suppose it helped to ease some of the blame I'd put

270

on myself about the hijacking, but Ron wouldn't go with me for marriage counseling. He doesn't believe in airing his dirty laundry in public.''

''A shrink is hardly public.''

''Not to Ron. Lieutenant, why are you here? I was under the impression you'd been taken off the investigation.''

''You could call it a personality quirk. I feel an obligation to make sure everyone is all right.''

Bidding smiled. ''It's a nice quirk. You said to make sure I didn't go out alone on Friday nights. I'm working a week from this Friday. Whom shall I tell?''

''Ask to be taken off of Friday nights until this is over.''

He saw her shoulders rise defensively. ''Lieutenant, I have two constants left in my life. My job and my children. I need them both. As a supervisor, I must set an example to the people who work under me. One of those examples is to be where I'm assigned, when I'm assigned.''

''I would consider the circumstances warrant a change. I think they'll understand.''

''No. It shows fear, which is the one thing I can't allow in my position.''

''I can't stop you from going to work. I'll let the proper people know. But when you go to work, make sure you're very visible.''

''I will, Lieutenant. Thank you.''

''Joan,'' he said, pausing at the door, ''did you fly any of the Orient routes after the hijacking?''

She wiped perspiration from her face. ''I stopped flying completely after the hijacking. But I was on the Far East run—Japan and Hong Kong—for two years before switching to the Middle East. Why?''

''Just curious.''

When Hyte returned to his apartment, O'Rourke and Cohen were already on the couch.

''I put coffee up,'' O'Rourke said.

Cohen handed him a thin bundle of computer printouts.

"Emma came through and you were right," he said. "Look at the fifth page."

Hyte flipped through the pages until he spotted a name circled in red:

NAME: SAMAEL, M. D. P.O. Box 3214,
             Central Valley, New York
ORDER NO.:   1127866549 Product No.:BCBSA
             1099
DATE: 8/12
PAID BY: M.O. # 13178556-96100066
             Commercial Valley Bank
AMOUNT: $179.00

Being right did not make him feel any better. He felt slow, as if he were playing catch-up with Samael. "A blind drop?"

He saw the answer on Cohen's face. "As soon as we found the name, we went to Central Valley—it's just off exit fifteen on the thruway. The box was rented at the beginning of August last by an M. D. Samael. No one had any recollection of the person. The box rental was paid for six months. It's now being rented to John Maddox, a local resident.

"We then went to the bank from which the money order was drawn. No one knows of an M. D. Samael, from the branch manager to each and every teller. A zero, Ray, another dead end."

"Not quite, I'm getting to know our killer now," Hyte said.

A knock sounded at the door. Randal Schwartz came into the living room. He was carrying the phone company envelope.

"Did you find anything?" Hyte asked.

"Mossberg makes one long distance phone call every Friday night between six and seven. I checked the number. It's her daughter's. Michael Barnes made a lot of long distance calls, but very few on Friday nights. None of the calls matched the numbers of the victims."

"Thank you." Hyte motioned toward the chalk board. "If we've interpreted Samael's note correctly, five of the six remaining hostages are scheduled to die," Hyte said. "Is the sixth Samael, or was the note meant to mislead us? To find out, we have to eliminate as many suspects as possible. Sy, you rechecked the relatives and did backgrounds on the rest. Who will you clear?"

"All of them. None of them."

"Sally?"

"I agree with Sy. They're all clean, and they're all suspects."

"Not quite," Hyte said. "I can eliminate a few. I saw Sylvia Mossberg today. She isn't capable of killing anyone. Not because of age, physical size, or stamina, but because she has no motive. As far as Jonah Graham, I don't consider him a suspect. The same goes for the Desmonds. I also talked with Joan Bidding today. She seems clean, but there's a hitch . . . she *did* fly to the Orient."

"Then she could have access to the poison," Cohen said.

"But that was prior to the hijacking," Hyte said. "Still, her life's been pretty loused up. She's losing her husband and she doesn't fly anymore. She's admitted to seeing a shrink." He paused. "And given the potential for personal disaster, she's still going to work on her next Friday night shift."

"A woman as the killer?" O'Rourke asked, a hint of satisfaction in her voice.

"Of the six people left alive, three are women. Allowing that neither Sylvia Mossberg, Jonah Graham, or Lea Desmond are Samael, that leaves us with Sonja Mofferty, Joan Bidding, and Jack Mofferty." He paused, turned to the blackboard. "Of the relatives, the only one we have who isn't cleared, is Joan Bidding's husband. Until we have more to go on, we'll have to consider those four to be our best suspects. But when we get the INS information, we may be able to narrow it down further."

"How do we play it?" Cohen asked. "We can't put a plant on each one, not with only three of us."

"I don't know yet. But we've got two and a half days to

work it out. In the meantime, Sy, I want you to find out about Ronald Bidding's new girlfriend. See if either Ron or Joan Bidding is coning us. Sally, you speak with the Trans Air shrink who Bidding saw. You don't have to pry, just find out if the man thinks she's capable of murder. Personally, I'm going to visit the Moffertys and see if I can rattle their cage.''

Emma arrived late that night. When she entered the apartment, he took her in his arms and kissed her deeply. ''That was nice,'' she said. ''Are you all right?''

''Finc. Just a little tired.''

''Are you making progress?''

''Some,'' he said. ''Drink?''

She nodded, and he made her a Scotch and water. ''Thank you for your help,'' he said.

''What help? I feel more responsible than helpful. Ray, Samael was on the list.''

''Yes,'' he said, cupping her chin and turning her face to his. ''And the list helped. It showed me more of how Samael's mind works.''

''How *does* it work?'' she asked.

''Linearly,'' he said as he watched a thin blue vein pulsing beneath the translucent skin of Emma's neck.

''I thought you said he was devious?''

''No doubt about that. But the pattern is linear. A straight line defined by whatever propels the delusion. The first step was the choice of weapon. A gun is too loud for stealth. But an arrow, or in this case a crossbow bolt, is silent. And the poison—''

''Poison? You never mentioned poison before.''

''Sorry,'' he said. ''It's hard to let go of old habits.''

''I'm sorry, too,'' Emma said. ''I wish you could trust me.''

Her words, spoken so low, hit him hard. He reached out, took her resisting hand. ''It's not easy to break a routine that's been part of my life for sixteen years. I have to learn

274

to trust myself enough to talk to you. And you have to give me time to do it."

He felt the tension ebb. "You're right," she said. "And I'm sorry. You're trying and I'm pushing. Let's just forget it."

"No," he said, suddenly determined to see this through. "The poison was to make sure of death if the bolt was not fatal itself. From the very beginning—from the conception of revenge—our killer followed a precise plan, the goal of which was and is the deaths of all the first-class passengers and crew who had not died during the hijacking. Samael spent months watching each of the survivors, tracking them, putting their habits to his own use.

"When Samael felt he knew all he needed about *all* of his intended victims, he began to kill. His biggest advantage is that only he knows the order in which he's decided to kill each victim, and I'm playing catch-up."

"But you know who the victims will be. Doesn't that give you an advantage as well?"

"I wish it did. But only Joan Bidding and Lea Desmond are in our jurisdiction. We can't protect the others."

Emma studied him. "What about the name? Doesn't that help somehow—give you a lead?"

"I have my doubts about that. I think the killer is using the name as a smokescreen. Too many psychopaths use biblical type names to hide behind. Psychotic delusions and revelations are well documented. Samael isn't a psychopath, not in the sense we're used to. Yet . . ." His voice trailed off as he felt the familiar prickling of an embryonic thought.

"Ray?"

It took him several seconds to react. "Sorry."

"What is it?" she asked.

"I don't know. I just can't seem to get a grip on it."

"Stop trying so hard. Ease up and it'll come. And I just might have a way to help you relax."

Emma unzipped her dress, stepped out of it, and held her hands toward him. "Let's go inside."

Afterwards, Emma lay in the crook of Hyte's arm, her

275

left hand playing absently with the hair on his chest. "We're good together, aren't we?"

He turned slightly. "We are." He smiled. "Emma, I love you. And I'd like to know how you feel about marriage to a cop. . . ."

"Yes."

"Yes what?"

"Yes, I think that marrying one cop in particular has future possibilities."

His muscles all seemed to knot at once.

"But they're *future* possibilities," she repeated. "You said it before. We both need time to learn about ourselves and each other."

"There's no rush," he said. "What about children? Have you thought about that?"

To his surprise, her face went rigid. "Oh no, not me," she declared. "Someone else can have that dubious honor. I'd never want another human being to go through what I have with my mother, my father . . ." Emma stared at him without blinking. "Think about what Carrie must have felt, must still be feeling, because she was told she couldn't visit you anymore. So no, not me! Besides, I'm an executive, not the motherly type at all."

He felt the blood drain from his face.

"Ray?"

He didn't answer her, he couldn't yet. He was in labor. The embryo of his earlier thought was breaking through, its birth helped along by her words.

He turned and kissed her. "Thank you," he said. "Thank you."

Thirty-six

Hyte looked out the window of Mason's office. "You'll have to bear with me on this," he told Mason and launched into the theory that Emma's words had evoked. "The five remaining victims do not include Jonah Graham and the little girl, Lea Desmond. I've watched the tapes over and over. Everyone except Graham and Prestone said 'Not me—someone else.'

"Lea Desmond never uttered a word. While it's true that she was a hostage, she wasn't supposed to have been one. She was in first class because of a whim on the pilot's part."

"Was Prestone a victim?"

"Absolutely! He was the reason for the 88 hijacking."

"You're saying that it was Samael who killed him? You think McPheerson's right about that?"

"No! Samael hadn't yet scheduled Prestone's death. I think it was terrorists who killed Prestone. It isn't Samael's way. Samael's not just killing, he's collecting the souls he believes outwitted death the first time. And those 'souls' are the full-term hostages who survived the hijacking."

Mason waved his hand in the air. "You've confused me. If Graham isn't a victim, and the girl isn't either, and if my math is right, that leaves four surviving hostages, not five."

"I know. That's where I'm stuck," Hyte admitted. "Did Samael pick the number eight because there were nine victims left at that point? Is there really one more victim or is it a con about who and how many victims there really are? According to the note, there were eight people to be collected. If Jonah Graham and Lea Desmond aren't on the hit list, that means—''

"What that means," Mason interrupted, "is that everything you've told me is speculation—you have no certainties.''

"Watch the fucking tapes again and tell me it's guesswork!''

"If we were handling the task force, you'd be roasted for this theory and you know it.''

"Phil, I told you my theory because I need help. I want to plant at least three people on each hostage. We can't afford to miss anything. Samael's good, possibly the best the Department has ever come up against, and he kills on Fridays.''

"No extra men. You knew the ground rules when you accepted this assignment. Either go it alone—the way the mayor set it up—or walk away from it. And I'm not supposed to be involved in it at all. I'm just the middle man. Jesus, Ray, you're conducting a covert investigation in direct opposition to the chief of department's task force.'' Mason paused. "You're the best deductive logistician I've ever known. Use that ability now, because it's all the help you can expect on this case.''

Hyte stood abruptly. "I'll keep you informed of events.''

"Just a second. There's something you should know. Information about the poison will be leaked to the press later today.

"What is it this time, Lieutenant?'' Jack Mofferty said.

"Just some clarification.''

"I thought you'd been pulled off the task force.''

"That's correct.''

"Then why are you bothering us again? Don't you think we've been through enough already?''

Mofferty's words shattered Hyte's calmness. "You're alive, aren't you? That's more than six other hostages can

278

say. Or is it that you're glad they're dead so there are six less people who saw what happened to you?''

"Goddamn you!" Mofferty roared, his face turning scarlet. "What right do you have to accuse me?''

"I'm not accusing you of anything. You're doing it all by yourself! Have you ever watched the tapes of the hijacking?''

"Never!''

"Then do it. Live it again and look at everyone. They acted no different from you! And then maybe you can understand what happened to you and to your wife. Good God, what the hell kind of a shrink is Masters if he won't confront you with the cause of your problem?''

"Dr. Masters has tried, Lieutenant. Jack won't watch them,'' Sonja Mofferty said, coming into the library through the outside doors.

"Then maybe it's time he did,'' Hyte said, again caught off guard by the woman's beauty.

"Look, Hyte, you got no business here,'' Mofferty said. "You're harassing us, and I won't have it. I want you out!''

"In a moment,'' Hyte said calmly. "For your own safety, I would recommend that you don't leave this house from sundown on Friday night, until at least 9:00 A.M on Saturday morning.''

"We always go to Dr. Masters's house on Friday nights.''

"I'm asking you to break that pattern until we catch the killer. I'm sure Dr. Masters will reschedule the appointment for you.''

"I'll discuss it with him,'' Sonja Mofferty said for both of them. "Is there anything else?''

"Have either of you been to the Orient since the hijacking?''

He watched Sonja's eyes dart between him and her husband. "Jack won't travel anymore. We don't go anywhere.''

"I see,'' Hyte said. Her answer felt wrong. He turned to Jack Mofferty. "Do you have many business dealings or clients in the Orient?''

"No.''

279

"Do you import cars from there?"

Mofferty sneered. "Hardly. I sell Rolls, Mercedes, and Bentleys—not Datsuns and Toyotas. Now, I think we've answered enough questions. Good day, Lieutenant!"

"I'll show you out," Sonja said, motioning Hyte toward the hallway.

Hyte hesitated. "One more question."

Mofferty stiffened. "Get a warrant. Arrest me, and then ask all the question you want. Now get out of my house!"

Hyte shrugged, and followed Sonja Mofferty out of the library. "Is it important, about having been to the Orient?" Sonja said at the doorway.

"It may be."

She moistened her lips. "I . . . I wouldn't want Jack to know."

"Know what?" he asked, his eyes probing hard.

"About three months after the hijacking, I was offered a modeling job. High fashion accessories. The client wanted only me. And . . . I agreed. At that point, I didn't know if I would have a marriage left. I needed some sort of security. The offer was substantial. When I discussed it with Franklin—Dr. Masters—he felt it would be good for me to travel. Get back on the horse I fell from, he said."

"How could you keep that from your husband?"

"I told him I needed some time away. That I was going to a health spa Dr. Masters recommended. At that point, Jack hardly ever talked to me."

"Where was this modeling assignment?"

"Hong Kong."

"Who was the client?"

"I don't know. The job was for an advertising agency. It's not that unusual."

"Which agency?" Hyte asked.

Sonja sighed. "It was seven months ago. I don't remember the name. But my modeling agency should have the records of the job."

"What magazines did the photographs appear in?"

"They were never used. The advertising people changed

their mind about the campaign.'' She shrugged. ''It happens.''

''When was this, exactly?''

''Last September, around the middle of the month. Please, Lieutenant, you won't say anything about it?''

''I can't promise you that, but I hope it won't prove necessary,'' was all he would say.

In his office, Hyte called Franklin Masters. ''I'm sorry to bother you, Doctor,'' Hyte said. ''But I want to know about Sonja Mofferty's trip to Hong Kong.''

''I thought it would be a good idea for her to go,'' Masters said without hesitation, ''but not for the reason she thought. She's past her prime as a high fashion model and I'd hoped that a trip in the company of younger women on the rise would show her that. I think it worked. When her photographs went unused, she took it well.''

''I see. Wasn't it unusual for Sonja to be offered this job, if she was, as you said, past her prime?''

''I don't think the job was on par with her previous work.''

''I see. Thank you for your time, Doctor.''

Hyte spent the rest of the day catching up on his precinct liaison paperwork and then, with Schwartz, went home to meet with O'Rourke and Cohen.

Cohen was the first to report.

''Ronald Bidding isn't lying to us,'' Cohen said. ''I spoke with several of Bidding's fellow employees. They were understandably upset that someone was investigating their friend and refused to answer any but the most general questions.

''But when I met with Bidding, he answered all my questions. He confirmed his wife's story, said that he had asked her for a divorce. His girlfriend's name is Sharon Henderson. He's been seeing her for the last six months and plans to marry her. She's a statistical analyst in Bidding's department.

"I then interviewed Sharon Henderson. She backed Bidding up completely. She's also four months pregnant."

Hyte didn't react to Cohen's last words, except to erase Ronald Bidding's name from the list of suspects. "Sally?"

"I spoke with the Trans Air psychologist, a Dr. Schmidt—Ph.D. He confirmed that Joan Bidding had seen him for several months after the hijacking. He does not believe her capable of taking another person's life—his words. When I asked about signs of paranoia, he said, and again I quote, 'If someone had held a gun to your head for three hours, wouldn't you be a little paranoid?' He said that Joan's main problem is two-fold. She has to learn to trust people again, and she must exorcise the idea that it was wrong to have shown her fear to the hijackers."

"Which doesn't get her off the hook. Randy, what have you turned up with the phone number check?"

"The only familiar number dialed on a Friday night was from Jonah Graham's phone in Westchester. It was a call to your office extension made on April ninth at 11:40 P.M."

"Yes. Emma called me the night of the Helenez killings. You gave me the message," he reminded Schwartz. "So the phone check is a dead end."

"We may still have a shot with the INS records," O'Rourke said.

"With them or without them, we have something else." He told them his hunch about Jonah Graham, and the possibility that Samael was deceiving them about the number of victims.

"No!" Sally O'Rourke cut in.

He lifted his hands in a palms up gesture. "Your floor."

"Samael hasn't followed any pattern common to a psychopath—which everyone agrees he's not. He's contacted us only twice. Once by letter, once by phone. The note said that when the last eight were collected—*the last eight*, not passengers, not hostages, just the last eight—he would be gone. I have no reason to think there will be any less than eight.

"The Helenez killings brought the total down to six; Prestone's death leaves five. According to your theory, Lea

Desmond was never an intended victim. And I agree with you about that. But, you've also excluded Jonah Graham. It's that part of your theory with which I disagree. You're excluding Graham because he didn't say, 'Not me—someone else.' But a paranoid might reason differently. Samael could think that Graham also outwitted death by saying, 'Kill me—not my wife.' Therefore, there are five victims left, and the original hit list is accurate.''

Hyte thought over her idea. ''We can theorize about every nuance of every word, but what we can't afford to do is take a chance with any of the possible victims. And that includes Jonah Graham as well as Lea Desmond.''

''Which means?'' Sy Cohen asked.

''We have to keep every possible suspect and victim covered. But we don't have to worry about Jonah Graham. He has a bodyguard. We also have plausible suspects in Sonja Mofferty and Joan Bidding. Mrs. Mofferty was in Hong Kong last September and Bidding spent two years working the Far East. She could have arranged to get the poison sent to her or brought in by one of her stewardesses. Both women's personal lives are a mess. Add a heavy dollop of paranoia, and either woman could have been turned into our killer.''

Hyte looked at the faces regarding him with unasked questions. ''Sally, you're going to be Joan Bidding's shadow. Sy, you'll be the same for the Moffertys. I want to know every move they make, every person they speak to, and every place they go.''

Hyte weighed his next words carefully. ''In two days, Samael will try to kill again. We have forty-eight hours left to save someone's life.

By late Thursday afternoon, Hyte still had the same two suspects: Joan Bidding and Sonja Mofferty. But he wasn't happy with either of them. The way suspicion seemed to settle on the two women was too convenient. It was almost as if events had been manufactured to point toward them.

Hyte let the thought grow, but could find no answering

283

response. He dropped that line of reasoning when he and Schwartz left his office at five-thirty and took a cab to his apartment. Neither Cohen nor O'Rourke had shown up yet. His answering machine contained only one message. It was from Emma.

When he called her back, she told him that she was going to Westchester in the morning and would work there all day. "I can't sit around the office or apartment knowing that someone might kill my father," she explained.

He agreed it would be for the best.

O'Rourke showed up a half hour later, reporting nothing more than that Joan Bidding went to work, stayed there, and went home. Cohen arrived fifteen minutes after O'Rourke and said the Moffertys had stayed at home all day.

When he was alone, Hyte made himself dinner. Afterward, he returned to his contemplation of the chalk board. At eleven, he turned off all the lights in the apartment, flicked on the stereo, and let his mind roam.

He fell asleep on the couch, listening to the Del Vikings. He dreamed about Samael singing "Come Go With Me" as the shadowed figure shot flaming bolts into a group of airline passengers.

But it wasn't the dream that awakened him at six-thirty; it was the radio announcer's excited voice.

"This just in from police headquarters. Chief William McPheerson has announced that following a midnight raid of a suspected terrorist support group, the Friday Night Killer has been apprehended. The alleged killer of six has been tentatively identified as Lester Smith-Henning, of London, England.

"Deputy Chief Inspector John Conner, second in command of the task force, said that a check is being made with English authorities to confirm the identity of Smith-Henning. Further updates as they come in."

"Who in the hell is Lester Smith-Henning?" Hyte asked aloud.

Thirty-seven

Hyte pushed through the crowd of reporters at headquarters and went up to his office. Schwartz was there, waiting for him.

"The chief wants you to call him ASAP."

He dialed Mason's number. There was no answer. "What have you heard?" he asked Schwartz.

"When I came in, everyone was in the coffee room talking about it. The word is that it's a terrorist who was avenging the other terrorists' deaths."

"Horse shit!" Hyte snapped just as Phil Mason came in.

Schwartz withdrew. "McPheerson pulled it off," Mason said.

"Who is this Smith-Henning?"

"That's not his name. It's Saad Mohamad, and he's the half brother of Rashid Mohamad."

Hyte stared at Mason, working it out. "That explains the raid of the terrorist group. But it doesn't fit. Why would he kill and not publicize what he's doing?"

"Give it up!" Mason snarled. "We lost, McPheerson and Conner won. Three undercover cops from the subversive activities squad overheard the suspect call himself Allah's messenger of death."

"He's not Samael!" Hyte shouted, his fist exploding on the desk.

"He said he was the messenger of death, sent to avenge

285

his brother's betrayal. There's also firm evidence linking him with the Prestone bombing."

"I want to see him."

"Ray," Mason said, shaking his head.

"Where are they holding him?"

"In a security room. Don't butt heads with McPheerson, no matter what you think, unless you want to spend the rest of your time working Bed-Stuy."

"I don't give a fuck where he sends me as long as I get to speak to this man. I'll know if he's Samael after that."

"You're obsessed, Ray."

"Did McPheerson find the crossbow and the poison?" Hyte asked. "Of course not," he said when Mason didn't reply. "And they won't be found either. Phil, we're running a parallel investigation, authorized by the mayor and approved by the PC. We have an obligation to speak to the prisoner. And if he's not Samael, we've still got a case."

"Ray, it's over."

"Not yet! Not until I talk to him," Hyte said. Then he smiled. "Coming?"

They found McPheerson sitting on the corner of a desk in Internal Affairs, holding court. Hyte let Mason take the lead.

"Chief McPheerson," Mason said formally, "we would like to speak with the suspect."

McPheerson looked at him suspiciously. "Why is that, Chief Mason?"

"There are questions that concern a parallel investigation involving terrorist groups. And, as that case is being coordinated by Lieutenant Hyte, I require his assistance."

"Really?" McPheerson asked, turning to look at Hyte. "Why is it that I'm unaware of this, ah, parallel investigation?"

Mason kept his face expressionless. "You are. It's the covert operation being run by my department, investigating the suspected kill-for-hire hit men that you approved the budget on. There have been eyes-only follow-ups."

"Bullshit, Mason," McPheerson barked. He turned to

Hyte. "You don't think he's the killer, do you, Lieutenant?"

"I didn't say that."

"You didn't have to. I don't like you, Hyte, and I don't like the way you work."

Hyte fought the dark rage McPheerson's words set off. McPheerson's gaze went to Mason. "And as far as you're concerned, I won't have you usurping my authority."

"I have no intention of usurping anything. As I said, I would like to see your *suspect,* who may be involved in another investigation, and I require Lieutenant Hyte's assistance."

"All the evidence indicates our suspect is the killer," McPheerson said. "All of it!"

"No one's arguing. We just want to speak to him. Bill, I don't want to make an issue out of this. The lieutenant has some questions that need to be answered. Come with us if you want."

"Go ahead," McPheerson said suddenly, jerking his thumb to the door behind him.

Hyte went past the chief of department and entered the first of the two rooms. Mason followed quickly. Inside, Deputy Inspector John Conner was just hanging up the phone. "What is it with you, Hyte?" Conner asked. "I thought you were smarter than this."

"The prisoner?" Hyte said.

Conner led them into the high security room next door. It was green and plain and windowless. The suspect was cuffed to a metal chair set against the far wall. He had dark skin and black pinpoints for eyes. His cheeks were sunken and pockmarked. Hyte thought he hadn't reached his twenty-first birthday yet. However, he was able to see the resemblance between the prisoner and Rashid Mohamad in the nose and mouth.

"What's his real name?"

"He says it's Saad Aboul ben Mohamad," Conner said. "The passport he was carrying is in the name of Lester Smith-Henning. We're waiting for word from Interpol."

"Was it a decent forgery?"

"Average."

Hyte went over to the prisoner. "I understand that you claim to be Samael."

He felt the hatred pouring from Saad Mohamad's eyes as if it were something physical. "I am the messenger of Allah, sent to avenge my people." Hyte was surprised by the man's thick Semitic accent. He'd expected the same upper-class English that Rashid Mohamad had spoken.

"Do you know who I am?" Hyte asked.

"My enemy! The enemy of my people."

"Why is that?"

"Because you are the police—the tool of the Zionists."

"That's all I am to you?"

Mohamad sneered. "That's enough."

"You are Rashid Mohamad's brother?"

The dark-skinned man preened. "His half brother. We share the same father. Rashid Mohamad was a great man."

"Until he was killed."

"He was made a martyr when the Zionist puppets murdered him."

"Did you kill the six former hostages from Flight 88?"

"I am the Messenger of Death!"

"Then I'll ask you again—do you know who I am?"

"You are a pig!"

"No," Hyte said, his blood pumping fast, "not just any pig. I'm the pig who shot your brother."

Rewarded by Mohamad's stunned look, Hyte turned and walked out of the room.

"Well?" McPheerson asked. "Are you satisfied?"

"Do you consider this a good collar? Are you going to go with this guy?"

"That's right," McPheerson said.

"You're shutting down the task force? Pulling the protection from the hostages?"

"Just as soon as the details are cleared up."

Hyte's hands shook with fury. "Chief, I think that would be a mistake."

"Wasn't the reason you were relieved of your duties on

288

the task force, Lieutenant, because your way of thinking didn't produce results?''

The vitriolic words turned Hyte's anger cold. ''Congratulations, Chief,'' he snapped and walked into the elevator. Mason followed, the doors closing behind them.

''Phil, someone is going to die tonight,'' Hyte said.

''McPheerson's evidence is solid. He has a statement from a reliable witness to the planting of the bomb aboard Prestone's private jet by Saad Mohamad. McPheerson also has Mohamad's taped confession, admitting to the bombing of Prestone's plane as well as calling himself the messenger of death. He claims it was done to avenge his brother's death. And McPheerson's certain he'll get a confession on the six killings.''

''That kid didn't know me.''

''So?''

The elevator stopped. They went to Hyte's office. ''If Saad Mohamad was the Friday Night Killer, he would know me. I was on that plane that night. I killed that man's brother.''

''Which means nothing.''

''Then try this out—he speaks with a thick accent. Samael is American.''

''How do you know that?''

Hyte smiled coldly. ''I spoke to him.'' From his desk drawer, he took out a tape recorder. In it was the tape Schwartz had made. He turned it on.

''You know that's our man,'' Hyte said when the tape was finished. ''And even though the voice was disguised, there was no accent. It wasn't Saad Mohamad!''

Mason moistened his lips. ''Oh shit, Ray. Why didn't you give this to me when you first got it?''

''I was too damned busy. Besides, I've had it analyzed. There's nothing. According to the lab, the synthesized voice was computer generated, not just electronically distorted. Very sophisticated equipment. There's no way to get an accurate voice match. We're conducting a covert investigation. If I turned it over to McPheerson now, he sure as hell won't accept it as valid. And there's no way to prove when that call came in." Hyte put his hand on Mason's arm. "Talk to the PC," he pleaded. "Explain what we have. Make him ask the mayor to keep the task force going."

"I don't know if I've got the weight to do that."

"Fuck the politics. This killer is going to hit, tonight!"

"Then stop him. And, I'll have to take that tape."

Hyte was back in his apartment by nine. He called Emma immediately, to tell her that McPheerson had the wrong man, and to make sure she did not cancel the bodyguard for her father. She took the news pragmatically.

When Cohen and O'Rourke arrived, he explained what had happened.

"How can he shut down the investigation?" O'Rourke asked.

"Because he's the chief of department."

"But he's wrong!"

"And only we know it. I asked Mason to speak to the commissioner, but he doesn't hold out much hope. All we can do now is wait and see what Schwartz digs up."

"If they're pulling the teams," Cohen said, "we're helpless. There are three of us and five potential victims. Even though Jonah Graham is being protected, we're going to end up playing Russian roulette with one of the other four."

Schwartz arrived, his expression confirming what they all feared. "All jurisdictions are pulling protective surveillance. The Bidding plant and the Desmond plant were canceled as well."

Hyte watched O'Rourke and Cohen's disbelief. "To compound things," he told them, "I'm in violation of departmental policy. I never reported the phone call from Samael or gave McPheerson's task force the tape. I think it's time for you two to pull back. Take the weekend off and report back to work on Monday."

"Have we been taken off the covert investigation?" Cohen asked.

"That isn't the point. McPheerson is going to be on my ass. I don't want you two getting in trouble because of me."

"Sorry," Sy Cohen said, "but I'm not walking away from this. I was with you when it started last year, I'm here to stay."

Hyte had expected no less from the man who had been his first partner, but still he felt relieved. He looked at O'Rourke. "I have no right to ask you to stick your neck out any further."

"I'm with you on this, Lou. All I ever wanted to be was a cop, and I put up with a lot of bullshit to become one. I sure as hell didn't take the job to sit at a desk."

He gazed at her, feeling the empathy her little speech stirred within him. "We have five people to cover, and there are only three of us. Thankfully, two of them live together. But we're still one short. So, we have to try and outguess Samael by figuring out who the next victim will most likely be."

"Joan Bidding or Sylvia Mossberg," O'Rourke said. "They're the most vulnerable."

Hyte nodded. "If Joan Bidding isn't Samael. Which brings up the secondary aspect of the victim surveillance. We're also watching them to make sure that one of them isn't the killer. Sy, I want you on Joan Bidding. Sally, I want you to watch the Desmonds."

O'Rourke's face showed disappointment. "Why? I thought we agreed that the little girl wasn't a victim."

"And I don't think she is, but I can't leave her unprotected."

"What about Mossberg and the Moffertys?" O'Rourke asked. "I think I should be on one of them instead of Lea Desmond."

"I don't," Hyte said. "I'll be covering the Moffertys, because if something does happen, my rank will help in a jurisdictional dispute. But at least that would be in-state; as far as Sylvia Mossberg is concerned, we'd be operating in New Jersey, way out of our legal jurisdiction. If any of us are caught near her, we'd be yanked from the case. We'll have to go outside the Department for Sylvia Mossberg."

"Private heat?" Cohen asked.

"In a way." He took an address book from the dining room bureau drawer, found the number he wanted, and dialed.

"Mr. Sircolli, please," he said to the woman who answered.

"Who's calling?"

"Lieutenant Raymond Hyte."

"Lieutenant? This is Katherine."

"Hello, Katherine, is your father home?"

"I'll see if he'll talk to you."

"It's about your financé's murder."

"Yes. You caught the man. Thank you, Lieutenant. Hold on."

A few moments later, Anthony Sircolli's voice boomed out of the receiver. "What now?"

"I need a favor," Hyte said.

Sircolli laughed. "You want the guy iced before trial?"

"Is this a clean line?"

"The line's clean. It's swept every hour."

"It's not him, Tony. McPheerson's been scagged. I need two very cool heads."

"For?"

"I want someone watched, very discreetly. One of the possible victims."

"I'm listening."

Hyte explained. He knew that Sircolli was too smart to accept anything less than the truth. When he finished, Sircolli agreed without hesitation.

"But, Ray, if my people get this scumbag, he's mine. He pays for what he did to my daughter."

"No, Tony. If they get him, they hold him for me. I need him alive."

When he hung up and turned around, he couldn't help but laugh at the expression on Cohen's face.

"You're nuts, Ray. You're as crazy as everyone thinks you are."

"I guess so. Randy, what about Immigration and Naturalization?"

"Sergeant Rosen wanted to know if you still wanted the INS search seeing that McPheerson caught the killer. I told him yes."

"Good." He swallowed. "It's Friday evening. Let's make it the last Friday we have to worry about. Randy, you're our coordinator again. But this time you work here. Everyone is to call in at half-hour intervals."

He went into his bedroom and called Emma in Westchester. "Did you drive out?" he asked.

"No. I used the limo. Ray, if they've got the wrong person, why won't they listen to you?"

"Because they think they're right and I'm wrong."

Emma hesitated. "And you're going to try and prove it tonight, aren't you? You're going after the killer."

"I don't have any choice. The three of us are the only ones who have a chance to stop Samael."

"You could wait until Samael makes a fool out of Mc-Pheerson."

"You don't believe I could do that, do you?"

"No, that's not the way you're made," Emma said. "Can I help somehow?"

"Possibly. Is the Jag in the garage?"

"Yes. Did your car break down?"

"No. I'll be in Long Island and I'll need a phone."

"A . . . oh, I understand. I'll call the garage."

"Thank you. And Emma, please don't worry."

"I won't," she said, though he knew by the tension in her voice that she would be waiting anxiously for his call.

Hyte reached Bay Shore just as the sun set. Instead of going to the Moffertys', he drove to Franklin Masters's house.

As Hyte expected, Jack Mofferty's Rolls-Royce was parked in Masters's drive. He circled the block, looking for any out-of-place vehicles. Then he parked across from Masters's house. He needed to make sure that Sonja and Jack left the doctor's and returned home, together.

If only one of them was at Masters's he would have Samael.

But if neither of them was the killer, Hyte thought, and if Samael followed his pattern, the Moffertys were in the greatest danger between the doctor's house and their own. Samael liked ambushes.

He picked up the cellular phone. A few seconds later Randal Schwartz answered. "I'm in position," Hyte said.

"Yes, sir. Sergeant Cohen called in a little while ago. Joan Bidding hasn't left home. Sally says the Desmonds are in their apartment."

"Thank you, Randy. If anything comes up, call me immediately."

Hyte hung up and leaned back.

Would Samael come after the Moffertys tonight?

At nine-thirty, the front door of Franklin Masters's house opened. Hyte watched Jack and Sonja Mofferty say goodbye to Masters and go to their car.

Thirty-eight

At nine-fifteen, the parking lot of Temple Beth Israel was only a third full. From the synagogue's open door, the sound of prayers reached the street.

In the synagogue's parking lot, the Messenger of Death opened the rear door of Ethel Greenblatt's car and slipped inside.

Samael's timing was again perfect, and the Messenger of Death was keenly aware of that perfection. Samael had waited patiently outside Sylvia Mossberg's apartment complex to see if any police were protecting the woman. The Messenger of Death had seen two men, driving a black car, follow Sylvia Mossberg.

The black car had New York license plates. Samael guessed the men were either private detectives or New York policemen.

They were good, and they were careful. If Samael hadn't known where Mossberg was going, and waited an additional minute before starting for the temple, the Messenger would have missed the men.

The black car was now parked across the street from the temple. The driver had found a spot where the street lamps did not reach, which made it difficult to see inside the car's tinted windows. Their position also gave the men a clear view of the temple entrance and the parking lot.

They are good, Samael thought, but I am better. The men had not reacted to the ancient crone who had hobbled past them. Nor had they shown any alarm when Samael, in the guise of an old woman, had dropped a cane. How could they know that when Samael stood again, a four-inch piece of wood with three large nails lay on a spot their front tire would pass over.

The sounds coming from the temple changed. A few minutes later Samael heard the echoes of feet coming down the marble steps. Car engines came to life. Voices bid each other a good *shabbas*.

Ethel Greenblatt and Sylvia Mossberg reached the car. Greenblatt unlocked the door for her friend and, after Sylvia was seated, sat down behind the steering wheel and started the motor.

Samael caressed the crossbow. The safety was off.

The driver started out of the parking space.

Samael raised up, the crossbow moving swiftly to the back of the driver's head. "Stop."

The driver stopped.

"Do not be afraid," Samael said. "You will not be harmed." The Messenger of Death looked at Sylvia Mossberg. "Do nothing and she will live."

Sylvia stared into the masklike old face. She closed her eyes for a moment against the pounding of her heart. "I understand. Please don't hurt her."

"Drive. Make a right turn. Go slowly." Samael dropped low, using the space between the bucket seats to hold the crossbow against the driver's side.

Ethel Greenblatt, her knuckles white on the wheel, did what she was commanded.

"Turn left at the corner, as if you are going home," Samael said. "Drive slowly."

The driver followed instructions. When Greenblatt slowed for the turn, Samael levered up just enough to peer out the rear window. The black car had pulled to the curb beneath a street lamp. Both men were out of the car, looking at the left front tire. The driver angrily slammed his palm on the fender. The second man began to run after Ethel Greenblatt's car.

Samael faced front. "Turn left again at the next block.

Go three more blocks and then turn right. You will take the George Washington Bridge to the Harlem River Drive. If you say anything to the toll collector, you will never see your children again.''

It took Sircolli's men fourteen minutes to change the tire and drive to Sylvia Mossberg's apartment. Both men were tight-lipped and anxious. They knew there would be hell to pay if they lost the woman.

They parked their car on the street and slipped unseen onto the grounds. One man walked past Mossberg's window while the second jimmied the front door of a car, which was parked in front of Sylvia Mossberg's apartment.

The living room light was on. the bluish flickering of a television could be seen through the drawn curtains.

When both men were seated in the car, the first man said, ''I told you she'd be home.''

A half hour later, the television's flickering ended and the living room light went off. A moment later the bedroom light came on. The men breathed a little easier with the knowledge that Sylvia Mossberg was indeed home, and they wouldn't have to face Tony the Fist's rage.

The car containing Samael, Sylvia Mossberg, and Ethel Greenblatt was parked beneath the Manhattan Bridge.

''Tie her hands behind her,'' Samael told Sylvia, handing her a roll of two-inch adhesive tape.

Mossberg taped her friend's wrists, and then looked back at Samael. ''Her mouth, too.''

Sylvia's fingers trembled as she tore off a small piece of tape and started to put it over Ethel's mouth. ''No,'' Samael said. ''Use a larger piece. Make it secure.''

When the tape was in place, Samael looked at Sylvia. ''Don't move. If you do, I'll kill her.'' When Sylvia Mossberg nodded, Samael got out the rear door.

''Out,'' Samael told Ethel Greenblatt.

The driver squirmed out of the car. Samael guided her to the back door. "Lay face down on the back seat."

When Ethel was lying on the rear seat, Samael took a syringe out of the raincoat's pocket. "You will not die," the Messenger said before injecting her. Soon, the woman was asleep.

Samael slid behind the steering wheel, turned, and pointed the crossbow at Sylvia Mossberg. "It is time."

Sylvia Mossberg stared at Samael. Suddenly, her eyes filled with recognition. "Oh my God, I know you!" Sylvia shook her head. "Why? After what happened to— Oh my God!"

"It doesn't matter now."

Sylvia stared at Samael, seeing behind the heavy layers of makeup. "It does matter. Please, turn yourself in. They'll understand. You'll get help."

"No, damn you!" Samael shouted. "You won't outwit death this time. Your fear won't save you tonight."

"I'm not afraid," Sylvia whispered.

Samael released the bolt. It struck the woman in the chest, penetrating her coat, biting deeply into her left breast. "No, you're not afraid now," Samael said. The Messenger of Death started the car and pulled out from beneath the dark cavern created by the overhead highway.

Samael's work was not yet finished for this night.

The Messenger stopped the car half a block from a private parking area, and waited patiently for the right opportunity to present itself.

Twenty minutes later, that opportunity came. The uniformed policeman on duty was called away by another officer. Samael drove into the parking area unobserved, parked the car in a reserved space, and left only seconds before the policeman returned.

Behind Samael, the lights coming from the windows of One Police Plaza reflected off the roof of Ethel Greenblatt's car.

298

Thirty-nine

Hyte stretched his legs to ease the cramps of having sat for too long. It was ten after six. The eastern sky was light, the west still a pale gray. The night had taken even longer to pass than he had expected.

The only things that had broken the lonely monotony of the vigil had been his contacts with Schwartz and two calls from Emma. Her first had been a little after eleven, the second at four that morning. She said she'd been unable to sleep. They'd talked for ten minutes.

Hyte debated on whether to take another close look at the house. He decided against it. It was getting light.

The car phone rang suddenly. "Yes?"

"Lieutenant, you were right," said Randal Schwartz.

Coldness spread through his intestines. "About what?"

"They found Sylvia Mossberg a half hour ago. She was killed with a bolt."

Bile rose in Hyte's throat. Not only had he guessed wrong, he had been outmaneuvered. "Where?"

"In a car parked at headquarters."

Hyte's mind raced. "Randy, as soon as Sy and Sally call in, tell them to meet me at headquarters."

Slamming the phone down, his thoughts flared angrily. Sylvia Mossberg had died because McPheerson and Conner's actions had put him in an impossible situation.

He'd had to weigh the risks to the various victims. It had been his concern for all the full-term hostages, combined with the possible jurisdictional entanglements, that had prompted him to have O'Rourke watch the Desmond apartment. Instead, he should have followed his intuition that Lea Desmond was not one of Samael's victims. Sylvia Mossberg was dead because of that decision.

How had Samael gotten past Sircolli's men to take Mossberg?

"Damn it!" he shouted. It should have been either himself or O'Rourke who covered Mossberg. Sylvia Mossberg might be alive if he hadn't forgotten the simplest rule of this case—that there were no rules.

But there were certainties, he knew now. Samael was playing a game of wits. The Friday Night Killer was challenging him, much in the way that Rashid Mohamad had during the hijack negotiations. Samael wanted Hyte on the case for reasons only the killer knew. That was the message Samael was giving him, by leaving Sylvia Mossberg's body at headquarters.

And you know him, Professor Alinski had told him after listening to the audio tape of Samael's phone call.

"Who are you?" Hyte asked aloud.

He clenched his teeth against the rage that was gripping him, refusing to give in to blind hatred. I'm better than that, he told himself. I have to be.

He started the car. By the time he reached the Southern State Parkway, Sy Cohen called.

"Randy told me what happened. Ray, Joan Bidding never left her place."

"You're positive?"

"I spent the night by the elevator. She never left."

"Meet me in my office," Hyte said.

Forty minutes later, he pulled into his parking space at headquarters. There wasn't a single member of the press present. Hyte attributed that to McPheerson's power.

He spotted the PC talking with McPheerson. Inspector Conner was with them. Phil Mason stood slightly behind them, head to head with Harry Lester. The crime scene people were all over the car. An older woman sat on a portable gurney. Two paramedics were checking her over.

As Hyte approached, Mason broke away from the pathologist and McPheerson. Their eyes met and held. Just as the chief of department whispered something to Conner, Mason grabbed his arm.

"Be cool, Ray. Don't blow it now. Just turn around and walk away. I'll be with you in a little while."

"He blew it, Phil, not me." He went to where Sylvia Mossberg lay.

The crime scene man was in the process of zipping up the body bag when Hyte motioned for him to wait. He looked down at Sylvia, then felt a tap on his shoulder. "What are you doing here?" Deputy Inspector Conner asked.

He turned. "How are you going to explain this to the press?"

"Don't make a scene, Hyte. Leave before you get yourself in any deeper."

The weeks of frustration struck him hard. Samael's success and his failures added fuel to his anger. "Are you going to put the task force back together?"

"For what?" Conner said. "We know who the killers are. It's just a matter of time before we catch all of them."

Hyte watched the body bag containing Sylvia Mossberg being taken away. Then he spun on Conner. *"Them?* There isn't any *them,* you stupid prick!"

He took a step forward, his fists clenched.

Mason quickly stepped between them. "You're off duty, Lieutenant. Go home."

From over Mason's shoulder, Hyte saw Chief McPheerson and Commissioner Rutledge watching them. Then McPheerson called out to Conner. Hyte fought to control his temper.

"We'll discuss this insubordination later," Conner said.

"Don't say anything else," Mason warned, placing a hand on Hyte's shoulder.

Hyte nodded. Then he saw Sy Cohen come out of the side entrance, and went to meet him. "Get O'Rourke and Schwartz and come to my place," he told him.

Mason arrived at the apartment an hour later. Hyte was only surprised that it had taken his godfather that long to get there.

"I want to speak to you privately," Mason said, looking at Cohen, O'Rourke, and Schwartz.

Hyte took Mason into his bedroom. "Why'd you stop me, Phil?"

"What the hell did you expect me to do? Let you hit a superior officer? Suspension would be the least that would happen."

"Who gives a shit. McPheerson and Conner killed Mossberg."

"Samael killed Mossberg!"

"Really?" Hyte asked. "And here I thought Samael was in jail? So, apparently, did you. If you didn't, you would have done something with that tape."

"I did," Mason told him. "I played it for the PC."

Hyte whistled appreciatively. "Why wasn't McPheerson told?"

"The commissioner reminded me that no one other than you and I has any firsthand knowledge that the mayor authorized a parallel covert investigation."

"Which means what?"

"Come on, Ray, everything was verbal. The man responsible for forcing the mayor and the PC into keeping you on the case is dead. If it were to become known that the mayor, with the consent of the police commissioner, had authorized a covert operation that went against the chief of department's own task force, the political ramifications would be enormous. No matter what happens, that information can never be made public."

"I don't believe it."

"You don't believe what?"

"That in order to save the mayor and the Department from a little embarrassment, you're willing to let more people die."

"You know me better than that! And no, I don't want

anyone else killed. But the Department can't afford an internal battle. And that's what you would have unleashed if you'd hit Conner."

Hyte didn't want to accept Mason's words, but there was no choice. "I can't figure out—not after this morning—how McPheerson and Conner can stay on the investigation."

"Because McPheerson covered himself. He claims it was a copycat killing, done by one of the terrorists in Mohamad's little band, to take suspicion away from Saad Mohamad."

"Bullshit. They could have smoked anyone. They wouldn't have gone to all the trouble of going after Sylvia Mossberg."

"Maybe not, but McPheerson's made a convincing case for himself. Last night Saad Mohamad said he was Samael and declared that *all* the passengers of Flight 88 are marked for death by his organization."

"All? Well, you also seem to have *all* the answers, so tell me, what do I do now?" Hyte asked.

"You do what you always do. Solve the puzzle. Catch Samael."

Hyte exhaled. "Catch Samael? I guess that means the throwaway cop and his invisible task force are still on the case. Why?"

Mason smiled. "Because I reminded the PC that if McPheerson wins, he loses. And, I won't let you be hung out to dry. So, cut the shit, we have a few problems." Mason hesitated, collecting his thoughts. "The first problem is that McPheerson and Conner want your ass and your shield for the way you mouthed off to Conner today. Second, with Rashid Mohamad's brother accepting the blame for the deaths, the press and public believe McPheerson. Public fear of terrorism is strong and it gives McPheerson the edge. He's had experts testifying that very little can be done to stop a determined terrorist attack."

"If it was a terrorist, he'd be right. But all he's doing is covering himself for when the next victim is killed. And once Samael's finished with the last victim, he's going to disappear."

"Exactly!" Mason said, cutting him off. "That leaves four victims—four more weeks to catch him or lose him forever. McPheerson's playing up the terrorists because he's counting on only four more deaths, and on using Saad Mohamad as his scapegoat. And Saad Mohamad is helping him. He's a stupid little ass who sees himself becoming as great a hero as his brother. He did blow up Prestone's plane—the Feds' proof is irrefutable. He isn't Samael, and I know it as well as you. But unless it can be proven, Saad Mohamad is going to stand trial for all the murders, and the real Samael is going to walk free."

"You haven't quite thought it through," Hyte said. "If Samael is put down during an attempt on a victim, we'll have to prove two things—first, that Samael was not a part of Saad Mohamad's group, and second, that the Mossberg killing was done by Samael, that it's not a copycat murder. We'd have to have absolute evidence of both."

"Then that's what will have to be done."

"I can't make any promises."

"I know you'll do the best you can. And, Ray," he added, "I have to ask you for a personal favor. Godfather to godson if it has to be that way."

Hyte avoided his eyes. "What?"

"I want you to run the investigation from a distance. I've already told you that McPheerson and Conner want to nail you. After this morning, there's a damned good chance they'll be able to. McPheerson told me he's going to file formal charges. So as of right now, you're on vacation. Don't show up at headquarters! Use O'Rourke and Cohen as your legs. It's important that you find the killer. And you don't have a lot of time to do it."

"You're pretty damned sure of me."

"I'm sure of what I taught you, and what your father taught you. Find him. Bring him in."

"Bring him in? Right," Hyte said, slowly drawing out the word.

He walked Mason to the front door. "There's one other thing, Phil. You're wrong about the time. We don't have four weeks, we only have three. The Moffertys will be killed together . . . unless of course Jack or Sonja is Samael."

With Mason gone, Hyte poured himself a drink and then explained the salient points of his talk with Mason to his three-member team.

The phone rang. It was Tony Sircolli. "What happened?" Hyte asked.

"My boys got taken," Sircolli said. Without making any excuses, he related the sequence of events outside the synagogue. "The Mossberg woman was out of their sight for the fourteen minutes it took them to change the tire and get back to the apartment complex."

"Long enough. Why didn't you call me?"

"Because the scam was beautiful. Lights on timers kept going on and off. When the living room light went out, the bedroom light came on. An hour later the living room light went on again. A half hour after that, around midnight, all the lights went out. They thought she was asleep for the night.

"They only put it together after they heard the newscast about the killing. They told me that when they were at the synagogue, an old woman dropped her cane near the front of the car. They didn't pay much attention to it then, but . . . she was carrying a shopping bag. And she was real old, they said."

"That was our man," Hyte said.

"Yeah," Sircolli agreed. "My boys took a little look-see in the apartment. They found light timers hooked up all over the place. Said they looked brand new. Ray, I'm sorry about this. I wanted him as much as you."

"I know, Tony. Thank you," Hyte said.

He hung up, a sense of loss and despair rising. He didn't like it at all. Then he picked up the phone again and dialed Emma. She answered on the second ring. He told her that he would be by to pick her up.

In Connecticut, Emma dropped him off at the country house before going into town for food. Hyte remained outside, concentrating on the beauty of the green mountains and the blue lake.

When Emma returned, it was almost seven. They ate a light dinner and walked down to the lake where they sat silently for a moment, hand in hand.

Then he told Emma the events of the day.

Her mouth thinned into an angry pale line. "You mean to say that McPheerson will stay on the case even though you have proof that he's wrong?" She shook her head. "But they took you off the case because of the Helenez deaths didn't they? How can they let *him* stay on?"

"The Department is a world unto itself—a state within a state. McPheerson is the head boy right now. And he has even bigger aspirations."

"You think he wants to be the mayor?"

"That's been the word around the Job for a few years. But it's more than that. A covert operation is being run behind McPheerson's back. That makes for big internal problems. The PC and the mayor need someone to take the heat if McPheerson or Conner learn what's been going on."

"And you're that someone?"

"I could be if I tell what I know without being able to produce the killer."

"But it's wrong." She paused to look at the lake. The water was still. Moonlight reflected across its surface in sharp, precise lines. "Are you going to do something about it? I mean, you're not going to let the killer get away, are you?"

He stared at the sky. "No, I won't let Samael get away."

Forty

Early Monday morning, Hyte put a pot of coffee on the dining room table, and scrutinized his three-member team.

"Randy, did you stop by headquarters and pick up the INS report?"

"I have it," Cohen said. "The Immigration computer came up with nineteen names matching the passenger and crew. Three of the stewardesses from coach class have worked Far East flights. Sixteen passengers have been to the Orient at least once since the hijacking."

"How many first class?"

"Two. Sonja Mofferty and Emma Graham."

"Emma?" he said, exhaling. "No, we know where she was at every killing." He took the sheet from Cohen, found Emma's name, and looked at the date. December third.

"Of course," he murmured. "I've been so wrapped up in this, I forgot. I took Emma to the airport myself. It was the first overseas trip she had made since the hijacking. Almost sixty percent of Graham International's goods come from the Far East. Jonah Graham used to go on several buying trips a year. Emma does all the buying now."

"Which puts us back to the beginning again," Sally O'Rourke said.

"Not really. According to Samael's note, we have four victims left. If we're right about Jonah and Lea not being targeted, then we know who three of them are—Joan Bid-

307

ding and Sonja and Jack Mofferty. Now we have to figure out who the fourth will be."

"Maybe there'll be another call," Cohen said.

Hyte frowned. "I don't think so. When Samael left Sylvia Mossberg at headquarters, it wasn't just a message to McPheerson and Conner telling them that they had the wrong man, it was also Samael's way of letting me know that nothing I can do will stop him. I think Samael believed that McPheerson would be kicked off the case just like I was."

"But it didn't work."

"Which is good for us. Maybe now Samael will think we're not playing his game and make a mistake."

"Until then, what do we do?" Sally asked.

"Think, wait, and do a lot of legwork." Hyte paused. "Sally, I want you and Sy to check with Sonja Mofferty's modeling agency."

O'Rourke scowled. "You said neither of them left their house Friday night."

"I said I didn't see Jack or Sonja leave. Don't forget Sylvia Mossberg was being watched, even as Samael took her out. Maybe one of the Moffertys snuck by me. Or Joan Bidding got past Sy. The way this case is going, anything's possible. Besides, if Sonja is telling the truth, I want to know who sent her to Hong Kong, and why."

Through the long hours of Tuesday, Wednesday, and Thursday, Hyte paced the confines of his apartment, an unwilling victim of police department mentality.

Sy Cohen and Sally O'Rourke did all the legwork, returning at the end of each day to give him their reports. Randal Schwartz had checked out the coach passengers and stewardesses who had visited the Orient and had cleared each of them.

Hyte's biggest concern was still Sonja Mofferty and the mysterious client who had hired her. At the modeling agency, Cohen and O'Rourke learned that her assignment had come through Dunsten and Thurmond Advertising.

Cohen had reported: "When the woman in charge of bookings there said, 'We have no record of who the client is,' I showed my tin and told her that I was going to run her in for obstruction of justice in a homicide investigation."

"And?" Hyte had asked, amused.

"She told me I could do whatever I wanted to, but they have no record of who the client was, only the advertising agency that contracted with them."

Then Hyte had assigned Cohen to watch Joan Bidding, and O'Rourke to keep surveillance on the Moffertys.

Hyte went to the chalk board. Tacked on the wall next to it was a large blank sheet of poster paper.

He wrote the date of the hijacking at the top of the poster. Under that, the date of Richard Flaxman's death.

In the next column, he wrote the date of every death, and then wrote three more Friday dates, the first of which was April thirtieth, tomorrow night.

Stepping back, he studied the list. Was there something significant there? If there was, he couldn't see it.

The phone rang. Schwartz answered it.

"Miss Graham," the black man called.

Hyte went into the bedroom, closing the door behind him. "Hi," he said when he picked up the phone.

"How are you holding up?"

"I've been better. How's Denver?" Emma had left Tuesday night. Graham International was opening its fifth retail store on Monday next. Emma's presence was needed for the opening ceremonies.

"Hectic but under control. Everything's behind schedule. Half the inventory is somewhere between New Jersey and Hawaii. I've done one newspaper interview, and all they talked abut was the killings in New York. I feel so damned guilty, being here. Should I come home Friday and fly back Saturday?"

"It's not necessary. Your father's well protected. Just concentrate on the store and make it a good opening. I'll see you Tuesday."

309

"I miss you. A lot. And I've been thinking abut what you said the other night. About getting married."

"And?" he asked.

Her throaty laugh was amplified by the phone. "You know the answer is yes. But only after this is all over with. When my father is . . . you know."

Hyte exhaled. "Safe. I know. I love you, Emma, and I miss you, too."

He went back to the living room. "Randy, see if you can get me Franklin Masters."

A moment later Schwartz said, "He's on the phone."

Hyte picked up the extension. "Dr. Masters, sorry to bother you."

"I've been expecting your call. Jack told me what happened last Thursday. Why are you harassing him?"

"I'm not harassing anyone. I'm trying to stop a killer. Doctor, would you please ask Sonja to call me? I need to know who the Hong Kong modeling was contracted by."

"I'll ask her."

"Soon," Hyte said sharply. "And Doctor, I think it's advisable that the Moffertys break their Friday night pattern of seeing you. At least until this is over."

"I agree, completely. In fact, after the last killing, I told the Moffertys that I would come to see them on Friday nights. Does that meet with your approval?"

Hyte detected no sarcasm in Masters's voice. "Thank you."

"I'll ask Sonja to call you."

A few minutes later, Cohen and O'Rourke came in. They gave the same report as yesterday's. The Moffertys had stayed home all day, and Joan Bidding returned home from work at four.

"What's this?" O'Rourke asked, looking at the poster board.

"Important dates. But nothing rings a bell."

"Why are there only three dates instead of four?" Cohen asked, pointing to the dates without names.

"The Helenezes were taken out together. I think that's the plan for the Moffertys."

"Joan Bidding is next," O'Rourke said.

Hyte looked at her. "Why?"

"The pattern. She's going to work tomorrow night. If Samael's homework is as thorough as we think she provides the only opportunity."

"Maybe. But Samael does the unexpected. Look at Mossberg. We all believed she'd be safe until after ten o'clock. Samael took her early, made everyone believe she was safe at home, and then waited until later to kill her. No, we can't make any definitive statements. Both Bidding and the Moffertys have to be watched."

"I think Samael's a woman," O'Rourke said. "Flaxman was killed nine months to the day of the hijacking. That number is significant to a woman. It takes nine months to give birth. Samael was conceived on June nineteenth and born on March nineteenth."

Once again, Hyte was surprised by the way her mind worked. "Maybe you're right."

The phone rang. "Mason's on his way over," Schwartz said.

Mason arrived at the apartment twenty minutes later, tired and harried.

"I feel like I'm in a war," he said. "This has been the worst week of the year. I've got every fucking precinct and borough squad working overtime."

"It's springtime, Chief," Sy said. "The scuzz like to work warm weather. They can run faster."

"Isn't that the truth," Mason said.

"Did you get tomorrow night's schedule?" Hyte asked.

"McPheerson isn't taking any chances. He's covering everyone. Three teams will be watching each of the remaining passengers who live in our jurisdiction. That's the Bidding woman, eleven coach passengers, one of the stewardesses from coach, and the Desmond girl.

"The Suffolk police are putting two dicks on the Mofferty house from 8:00 P.M. until 8:00 A.M.—shift change at 1:00 A.M. Westchester has been asked to do the same for Jonah Graham."

"He's got private help inside."

311

"I also spoke with the PC."

The hackles on Hyte's neck rose. "About?"

"Everything. This situation isn't his fault and you know it. He's given the okay for you to put someone on Bidding and the Moffertys. We'll clear it with the Islip PD—they cover Bay Shore. We both believe that if McPheerson's people get Samael, he won't make it to a cell, much less an indictment. The PC wants them watched. And I want *your* word that you won't move out of this apartment." He looked at his godson intently. "If any of McPheerson's people see you, the whole thing goes down the tube. You'll be put on suspension. And you'll never get a chance to find the real Samael. So you stay home."

Hyte knew he had no choice. When he spoke, it was as if a hook was being ripped through his intestines. "You have my word."

"Thank you. And now I have to go back to the office and figure out a way to reorganize the precincts. McPheerson has requisitioned thirty dicks to work tomorrow night."

As soon as the chief was gone, Sally O'Rourke spoke. "We're pulling guard duty? We're supposed to make sure that our killer makes it back to a holding cell?"

Hyte spoke in a monotone. "That's what the man said."

"And you're going to do it?"

"Sally, you've been working for me long enough to know that I do what I believe is necessary. And right now we've caught a nasty case with political overtones. There are careers at stake as well as lives. But there's something even more basic involved. It's who we are and what we represent."

He paused when he saw the doubt in her eyes. "The reason I'm going to stay home tomorrow night, when all I want is to put an end to Samael, so he can never hurt anyone else, is because I have to get Samael the right way. No games. No politics. Mason is right. If I don't stay home tomorrow night, and I'm seen near any of the victims, it will give McPheerson and Conner the opportunity to suspend me. If that happens, Samael may just win. Mc-

Pheerson sure as hell won't be able to stop him, even if he really wanted to.''

Hyte woke with a start. He looked at the clock: 6:55 A.M. It was Friday again. The seventh Friday since Richard Flaxman had died in Forest Hills.

He called Phil Mason at nine and requested two portable cellular phones and the locations of McPheerson's surveillance teams.

Sonja Mofferty called at 10:15. ''Dr. Masters gave me your message,'' she said.

''Have you been able to remember the company you did the modeling session for?''

''Yes. I went through my files. I found several of the proofsheet photographs from that session. The company was the International Accessories Corporation Limited.''

''Do you have an address?''

''Three-oh twenty-seven Victoria Boulevard, Hong Kong.''

The answer threw him. ''It's a Chinese company?''

''The people I dealt with were British. Does it matter?''

''I don't know,'' Hyte said, changing the subject. ''I understand Dr. Masters is coming to your home on Friday nights.''

''Yes, he felt it would be best.''

''Mrs. Mofferty, it'll be over soon.''

She laughed bitterly. ''One way or another, right, Lieutenant?''

''I don't understand.''

''Of course you do. The first time you spoke with Dr. Masters, you were trying to learn why Jack and I were seeing him. Franklin told me why it was necessary to explain my therapy; it was because you thought I was killing all these people. That's why you keep asking me these questions. Isn't it ironic that the only thing that can prove I'm not the killer is if that monster gets me? Is that what you're waiting to see, Lieutenant?''

''Mrs. Mofferty—''

313

Sonja Mofferty hung up.

He needed some air, and left the apartment, walking until he reached the East River, where he leaned on the cement abutment and looked down at the fast moving water.

The sky was overcast. Gray clouds outlined the buildings across the river. The water was dark.

He stayed for a half hour, thinking about Sonja Mofferty. His instincts told him she was not Samael, but the only thing he could trust were his eyes. When he saw Samael, he would know him—or her.

Everything about the murders was wrong. Samael's ability to locate the Helenezes when he himself hadn't been able to was part of what was wrong. And, he sensed that Sonja's modeling job had been a set-up to cast suspicion on her.

When he returned to his apartment, Hyte handed Schwartz the name of the company Sonja Mofferty had given him. "Give them a call and get everything they have on this place."

Fifteen minutes later Schwartz hung up the phone. "They no longer handle that account. And the account executive who did won't be in until Monday. The woman I spoke to said that they need verification that I'm from the police before they'll give us any information. I told them to expect someone from the chief of detectives' office on Monday morning and suggested that she have all pertinent information ready. She said there would be no problem as long as whoever came had proper identification."

"Good, Randy, very good. I'll have Sy go over there Monday."

"Do you think Sonja Mofferty is Samael?" Schwartz asked.

Hyte looked at Schwartz. "I don't know."

Two and a half hours after O'Rourke and Cohen arrived at the apartment, Deputy Inspector Douglas Mannering, of the CD's staff, showed up with the two cellular phones and a small manila envelope.

314

"The Chief asked me to remind you about your promise," the deputy inspector said.

"I haven't forgotten," Hyte said.

"He also wants you to know that he's been able to temporarily quash Conner's request for disciplinary suspension. But it's not over yet."

Hyte nodded. "Where will Mason be tonight?"

"Headquarters, with all the other brass."

"Thank you, Inspector."

"Good luck, Ray."

When the inspector left, the team gathered around the table. "I want check-ins every half hour," he told Cohen and O'Rourke. "Sally, I want you on the Moffertys."

He held up a hand to stop her protest. "It's the location that dictates the assignment. In a crisis situation, there's more of a chance that one of the security people working at Kennedy will recognize Sy. He was trained at the airport for terrorist situations. And Sally, Sy knows his way around the terminals, you don't."

O'Rourke nodded.

"Now, let's see what McPheerson's got in mind." Opening the envelope, he withdrew two sheets of paper. "Two men at the front and rear of Bidding's building. One man on the roof, another on the roof across the street. He's got the building sewn up tight." He paused, troubled by an omission in the surveillance schedule. "That's stupid."

"What?" Cohen asked.

"They're not covering Bidding while she's at work." He rubbed his eyes, wondering if McPheerson's people had read his report that Bidding worked one Friday night a month. "Sally, get moving. I want you at the Moffertys by seven-thirty."

She hung back. "I don't like this Bidding thing. Maybe I should go with Sy."

"We need a backup for the Moffertys. Who the hell knows what McPheerson told the Suffolk people. He might have given them his shoot-first-and-worry-about-things-later terrorist line. I need you there."

She picked up the phone and left. "How do I play it?" Sy Cohen asked.

"Bidding goes on at eight. That means she'll probably leave her place by seven or a quarter after. She drives. You tail her and then find the best place to work her from. And remember that Samael took out Mossberg between the synagogue and home. I'll call Mason and advise him of the situation. Stick close to Bidding without being seen."

Cohen picked up the portable phone. "I'll call as soon as she leaves for work."

When Hyte and Schwartz were alone, Hyte made himself a light Scotch. His stomach was knotted and his mind was dark. He felt totally, utterly helpless. His only positive thought was that Sy Cohen was one of the best.

He called Mason and told him about McPheerson's screw-up. "McPheerson talked to her husband," Mason said. "He agreed to make sure she stayed home."

"Phil, if you were Joan Bidding, and your husband knocked up another woman and then told you he was divorcing you, would you listen to him?"

Silence followed. Then, "I'll call Queens Homicide and have two men sent over to back up Cohen."

Forty-one

A pilot wearing the deep blue uniform of Trans Air airlines and carrying a bulky leather bag entered the employee section at ten-fifteen. Directly to the front was the men's room. To the left was a hallway opening into a waiting area. The pilot saw Sy Cohen sitting on a bench.

The pilot went to the men's room, walked to the mirror, and smiled. Samael's makeup did not crack.

The Messenger of Death went into a toilet stall and locked the door. Sitting on the closed toilet seat, Samael opened the leather bag and withdrew a pair of white cotton gloves. When they were on, the Messenger of Death removed the black bow of vengeance.

Next came a suede-wrapped bundle. Samael untied its binding, revealing three cork-tipped bolts.

Removing the corks, Samael placed each bolt into the revolving magazine, cocked the string, checked the safety, and put the crossbow back in the bag. The grip almost touched the handles.

Samael unlocked the stall door and went into the hallway. Stopping at the intersection, Samael looked toward the lounge area. Sy Cohen was still there. The Messenger of Death would have to wait. But not for too long. That would not be good. It was eleven o'clock.

Cohen went to the phone. When he hung up, Samael watched him peer into Joan Bidding's office, nod to himself when he saw the two young stewardesses with Bidding, and then walk toward Samael the pilot. Nodding politely when the policeman walked past, Samael tracked him until he entered the men's room and closed the door.

Joan Bidding's phone rang. She held up her hand to interrupt the stewardess she was talking to, "Night Supervisor."

"Joan Bidding, please."

"This is she," Bidding said.

"Mrs. Bidding, this is Officer Schwartz of Lieutenant Hyte's staff."

"Yes, Officer Schwartz? Is there something wrong?"

"Please don't be alarmed, Mrs. Bidding. But the Friday Night Killer has been captured while attempting to break into your apartment."

"Oh, my God!" she cried. "My children? Are they all right?"

"Yes, but they're badly shaken up. They witnessed a death. Can you come home immediately?"

"Right now!" she cried. Grabbing her purse, Joan Bidding ran out of her office.

Behind her, when she reached the first of the two exists, was a pilot carrying a battered leather bag.

In the underground parking lot, Bidding ran to her car. When she reached it, and put the key into the door lock, she felt something pressed to her head.

"Don't move," came a hoarse voice.

Joan Bidding began to tremble. She bit down on her lower lip. A flash of pain proceeded the taste of blood. She stopped trembling.

"Turn around," said the oddly inflected voice.

Bidding did. She found herself face to face with the pilot who had come into the lot with her. "What—"

"Be quiet. I have come to collect you. You have outwitted death for long enough. It is your time, Joan Bidding."

Joan Bidding's eyes widened. The killer's voice was no longer that of the pilot.

She tried to move back, but her car blocked her way.

Samael lifted the crossbow and pointed it at Bidding's face.

Bidding saw her death in the pilot's eyes. She lunged forward at the same instant Samael pulled the trigger. The bolt missed.

Five rows behind her, a car window shattered.

Bidding swung her hand at the pilot. It slipped along Samael's made-up cheek.

Samael fell back.

Joan Bidding ran toward the exit ramp.

Samael revolved the magazine, cocked the bow, and sighted the cross hairs on the running woman's back. Slowly, Samael pulled the trigger.

The surprised grunt from Joan Bidding, when the bolt struck her lower back, was loud, but not as loud as the sound her body made when it hit the floor.

And then Samael heard running feet.

"No," the Messenger of Death whispered before fading into the shadows. Samael waited quietly, breathing calmly while Sy Cohen ran toward Joan Bidding's car.

He stopped at the bumper of the Sentra, and began to turn in a slow three-sixty. When he stopped midway, Samael knew he'd spotted the motionless shape lying face down on the cement.

Samael waited as Cohen took a step forward, stopped, listened, took another step, and a third. Just as his left shoe touched the ground, Samael started back.

The leather of Samael's shoe struck a discarded soda can. Samael saw Cohen freeze, spin, and start in the direction of the sound, his pistol pointed forward.

Samael ran behind a car. "Stop! Police!" Cohen called an instant before he fired the gun at the moving shadow.

The sound of the ricochet was loud, the shot just missing Samael's left leg. Samael ducked behind a cement column and recocked the crossbow as Cohen approached.

"Don't move," Samael heard Cohen say. Quietly, the Messenger of Death faded further into the shadows, all the while keeping the crossbow aimed at the cop.

Cohen followed, his revolver tracking the Messenger. "Stop!"

Samael accepted the impossibility of escape. Cohen was too good. The Messenger of Death side-stepped into the light, and stopped.

"Put it down. Slowly," Cohen ordered.

The crossbow didn't move.

Cohen advanced, his revolver held steady at Samael's head.

Samael saw Cohen squinting past the crossbow's barrel, sure the policeman had not recognized the true face of the Messenger.

Samael waited. The right moment would come soon.

"Lower your weapon," Sy ordered.

"You know I can't do that. There are still three more to be collected."

It happened quickly—the recognition of who the Messenger was had come to Cohen when Samael had spoken—and, using the split second of hesitation brought on by Cohen's incredulity, Samael fired.

The bolt struck Cohen in the abdomen.

"Goddamn you!" Cohen screamed, firing.

The explosions were deafening. Two bullets struck the Messenger's chest. Cohen staggered back, his head shaking as he fought to pull out the bolt. On Sy Cohen's face was the understanding of why the Messenger was still alive, and the hatred Cohen bore for Samael.

Then Simon Cohen's body stiffened, his breathing stopped. He fell. Samael bent over him. "I am so very sorry," the Messenger of Death whispered.

From behind, Samael heard a woman scream.

Samael went to Bidding's car and started the engine as running feet echoed through the garage. A second later, the car charged out of the parking lot.

Forty-two

Sy Cohen's eyes were closed. His features were peaceful. His head rested on a blue velvet pillow. The upper part of his body was framed by blue satin. The lower portion was hidden by half of the pine coffin's cover. Hyte stood at his side, unashamed of the tears streaking his cheeks.

He had arrived at the East Side Synagogue at nine-thirty, so he could have a private moment to say good-bye to his friend before the ceremonies that marked an inspector's funeral began.

Turning from the casket, Hyte discovered he was not alone. Sy's wife, Sarah, had been sitting in the first pew. He sat down and took her hand.

Sarah tried to speak, but failed. He drew her against him, and waited. "Sy loved you, Ray," she'd said a few moments later. "He was always so proud of the way you played the game. He . . ." She paused, closed her eyes, and took several deep breaths. "He told me a long time ago, that one day you'd make chief."

"Where are the kids?" Cohen's three children were no longer kids. The oldest, Michael, was twenty-two, the youngest, Carolyn, was sixteen. But to Sy, and to Hyte, they had always been "the kids."

"In the rabbi's study. They're waiting for me."

"Do you want me to stay with you?"

She shook her head quickly. "Michael says it's important that you be a pallbearer. Sy . . . Sy would want that."

When Sarah left, Hyte remained seated, his freshly pressed uniform stiff from disuse. The collar of the jacket rubbed fretfully on his neck. But the chafing of the wool was nothing compared to the pain of losing his friend.

He should have been at the airport with Sy. He should never have given Mason his word.

Hyte temporarily set his anger aside as the synagogue began to fill with people. A moment later, a uniformed man sat next to him. He glanced sideways. It was Phil Mason.

"The commissioner has rejected the departmental charges brought by McPheerson and Conner. He has also authorized me to conduct a special investigation into Cohen's murder. That investigation will take over from and supersede the covert operation. I brought the full crime scene report and all the statements."

Hyte's eyes narrowed. "It's thirty-six goddamned hours too late to care about McPheerson's charges . . . or about your authorization. My friend is dead because I did what you asked."

"You're walking away from it? Is that what you're saying?"

Hyte didn't look at Mason. "I'll see you in hell before I quit."

Several hours after the funeral, Hyte sat on his couch, his uniform jacket off, his shirt open at the collar.

When the burial services had been concluded, Mason had come over to him. "It's up to you now. You can go after Samael legally, or you can do it out of anger." Then Mason had thrust a large envelope into his hands.

Now, Sally O'Rourke was at the dining room table reading the contents of that envelope. They were the crime scene, task force, and PDU reports of Sy Cohen's murder.

The Sunday *Times* lay on the coffee table; the Friday Night Killer was still in the headlines.

Emma sat next to Hyte. Her features were drawn, the dark half moons beneath her eyes turned their deep brown almost black. Hyte saw how badly Sy Cohen's death had affected her. She'd flown home from Denver, after the death of Joan Bidding and Sy Cohen were reported by the media. She had a reservation to return to Denver later that day.

Emma hadn't attended the funeral. Hyte understood why. It would be too much a reminder of her mother's death.

"What now?" she asked.

He shrugged, a gesture of weariness. "Find Samael. Stop him."

On the ride home from the cemetery, Hyte's anger had subsided enough for him to see past his own irrationality. Then, for a fleeting moment, he'd found himself glimpsing into Samael's mind. He'd understood the depth of Samael's need for vengeance.

It had been a sobering insight. It also made him realize that he had to take Samael legally.

Sally came into the living room carrying the crime reports. "I don't understand how Samael got through security."

"The pilot's uniform. How many people take a close look at an ID photo hanging on a uniform jacket? And the pilot who Samael waylaid never knew what hit him. He'd just come off a long flight. He was tired. He went into a bathroom stall, dropped his pants, and got zapped with a trank."

"Heavy dose," O'Rourke agreed. "He was out for six hours." She flipped the pages of the report. "Ballistics is certain that the three rounds they found were Sy's. Forensic says body armor flattened two of them. And from close range. Sy hit Samael point-blank. That confirms the witness's report of seeing Sy and Samael standing close together."

Hyte nodded. "Now we know that our killer doesn't take any chances. He wears a bulletproof vest. But why did Sy go for the body? He was too experienced a cop for that. He should have gone for the head."

"Maybe he wanted to take Samael alive?" O'Rourke said.

Hyte shook his head, thinking about the witness's report. The woman had said that she'd thought that Sy and his killer were talking. A moment later Sy had staggered back and fired. "He was taken by surprise," Hyte said. "Jesus Christ! Sy recognized Samael, and it must have been a hell of a shock. For just a second, Sy had to have been too surprised to react. Samael shot him then. That's why Sy fired point-blank in the chest. He had to be faster than the poison."

"But how could he tell through the makeup?" O'Rourke said.

"It was smeared. Bidding and Samael must have struggled. Sy might have recognized him, or if they were speaking—"

"He recognized the voice," O'Rourke finished. "Do you think they'll be able to get a trace on the makeup from Bidding's hand?"

"Unlikely."

"What about the car? Maybe some prints will turn up."

"*If* we can find the car," he said. "That's the only thing strange. Where the hell is the car?"

"Why is it strange?" Emma asked.

"Every time Samael has killed, the victim and the victim's car have been left. The Barnes killing was a message to me. The Mossberg death was an attempt to get McPheerson booted from the case. Samael had a reason for taking the car."

"Did you try the long-term parking lots at the airports?" Emma asked.

"Yes, it was done that night," O'Rourke said.

"Everywhere, or just at Kennedy?" Emma asked.

Hyte smiled at Emma. O'Rourke went to the phone.

A few minutes later, O'Rourke said, "They sent out the plate number to all borough parking facilities. Nothing's been called in. I also called the Queens Borough Homicide Squad and asked the duty man to recheck the parking lots, especially the long-term ones. He said he'd call back as soon as he finished." She paused, looked at the sixty-one report from the Queens Homicide dicks. "It says the two stewardesses with Bidding when she got the call that sent her running claim that she called the man on the phone Officer Schwartz. Why did Samael use Schwartz's name?"

Hyte stared past O'Rourke to the chalk board. The first of the final three blank spaces had been filled in. "It was another message. Samael knows all of us."

"Which confirms your hunch about Sy being taken by surprise."

Hyte took Emma's hand and held it firmly in the silence. Her skin was cool, her hand unresponsive. Ten minutes later, the phone rang.

"Lou, this is Stetman in Queens. I just got a confirmation on the vehicle. Your hunch was right. It's in a long-term parking lot."

"Damn it!" Hyte shouted. "How the hell did they miss it?"

"They didn't miss it. The car was brought into the lot Saturday afternoon, after they'd done the license plate check."

"Call crime scene to Kennedy. But I don't want a finger put on that car until I get there. Is that understood?"

"Lou, it ain't at Kennedy. That's why it wasn't found. When I called, they said it wasn't on their sheet. So I decided to check around."

"Where is it?"

"LaGuardia."

When Hyte and O'Rourke reached the parking lot, Stetman was waiting with the crime scene technicians. At Hyte's signal, the two crime scene men went to work.

It was in the trunk of Joan Bidding's car that Hyte found what he was looking for.

Pinned by a bolt that had been jammed into the carpet was a note. Behind it was the discarded pilot's uniform, discolored by smeared gobs of theatrical makeup.

He bent to read the note, which he guessed had been written with a makeup pencil:

I do not want to hurt the innocent. When the last is collected I will be gone. I can not be stopped as you now know. Please Lieutenant Hyte, do not let anyone

325

else get hurt. Please, do not send any more people to their deaths. There are three more to be collected. You must not let anyone else die before their time. You are responsible for their lives.

"Jesus," O'Rourke whispered. "I think it's an apology for Sy."

At nine-fifteen on Monday morning, Hyte and O'Rourke stepped into Dunsten and Thurmond's reception area. "Lieutenant Raymond Hyte to see Mr. Theodore Bromberg," Hyte said to the receptionist, flashing his shield.

"Do you have an appointment?" the receptionist asked, ignoring the badge.

The rage he had been working to contain since Sy Cohen's death, surged upward. He put his tin to within an inch of her nose. "Sweetheart," he said in a tight voice, "call Bromberg and tell him we're out here, now!"

She made the call. "Mr. Bromberg's secretary will be right out," she told him.

Almost immediately, a middle-aged woman came through the door on the far side of the reception area. Hyte and O'Rourke introduced themselves. "Mr. Bromberg is in his office now. Come with me please."

Theodore Bromberg was anything but what Hyte expected in an advertising executive. He wore a plain blue suit and had a half inch of gray fringe around his ears. The rest of his head was as slick as a bowling ball. He had small blue eyes, a proud nose, and the air of an efficient executive.

"Would you please clarify what this is about?" Bromberg asked.

"The Friday Night Killer investigation."

"What does International Accessories have to do with that?"

"That's what we're here to find out about. Mr. Bromberg, I need to know why Sonja Mofferty was hired to do a layout that was never used."

"Yes, Miss Franzman gave me that message earlier this

326

morning," Bromberg said. "When did she do this modeling?"

"September of last year."

Bromberg nodded. "Andy Spivak was handling the account then. He moved out to the coast last December, just before International pulled the account. I'm afraid that you're wasting your time, Lieutenant, I can't help you at all."

"Perhaps you can. I need to know about International Accessories of Hong Kong."

Bromberg knew little. The company manufactured a full line of contemporary fashion accessories, from costume jewelry to eyeglasses. The advertising the agency had done for them was not geared to the general public; rather, International Accessories sold to the trade. It was a company that put other company's names on their products.

Hyte asked for some samples of the advertising work Bromberg's agency had done for International Accessories.

"I have nothing available," Bromberg said. "It wasn't a big account, nothing that would warrant being used in our client book. I can dig up samples from the files, but it will take a few days. Where shall I send them?"

Hyte handed him his card. "As soon as possible, please." He started out, stopped, and looked back at Bromberg. "Do you know if there's any significance in the agency's losing the account and the account executive leaving?"

"Not that I'm aware of, but it's possible."

Hyte glanced around his office. It felt good to be back. Schwartz had brought the supplies from the apartment, including the chalk board, poster board, and video tapes.

Hyte looked down at the copy of the note Samael had left in the trunk of Bidding's car. As O'Rourke had said, the note was an apology for Sy's death. It confirmed that Samael wanted to kill the passengers who had pleaded for life at another's expense. Samael was letting him know that Sy Cohen's death was Hyte's fault.

His office door opened and O'Rourke whisked in, her

face and voice etched with annoyance. "The crime lab just finished with the contents of Bidding's car. They came up empty."

"We knew they would."

She looked at the note. "What is it, Lou? Something's been bothering you ever since you found it. What did you read into it?"

"The identity of the last victim," he said.

O'Rourke spun to look at the board. "Who?"

"Read the note again," he said. He waited until she finished.

"I don't understand," O'Rourke admitted.

"Samael is collecting the people who outwitted death during the hijacking, right?" O'Rourke nodded. "To a troubled mind, those people would be responsible for someone else being chosen to die."

"Possibly."

"Responsible, Sally."

O'Rourke stared at him, and then at the note. "It can't be."

"It is. On Friday night, Samael is going to take out the Moffertys. And then Samael is coming after me."

O'Rourke shook her head. "But you saved the hostages' lives!"

"Not all of them. Rashid Mohamad told me I was responsible for the deaths of those who died during the hijacking. It was something he said over and over throughout the negotiations. There was one specific time when I was on the plane, delivering the money, when Mohamad pointed to me and said, 'Look at the man who has sentenced you to your deaths!' I'm the last victim, Sally."

"What do we do?"

He smiled coldly. "There are two possibilities. Find out Samael's identity before Friday night, or reverse Samael's hit list and make me the next victim."

"How?"

"By putting me between Samael and the Moffertys."

"It's that simple?"

"It's that basic."

Forty-three

Hyte poured himself a Scotch and sat back in the couch. It was the end of the fourth unproductive day in a row. He had expected to find nothing, and his expectations had been fulfilled.

May seventh would be the last Friday. He took this for fact. He believed Samael did the same. He was certain that it had been Samael's intention, all along, to kill him and the Moffertys on the same night.

Hyte knew Samael's mind now. From the very beginning, Samael had marked him as the last victim. There was only one item remaining to be discovered: finding out who had made the decision to have Sonja Mofferty model for International Accessories. He had Schwartz checking with the Hong Kong company, but so far there had been no results.

He was positive that Samael was behind Sonja Mofferty's job in Hong Kong. It was a part of the scheme Samael had created to frustrate him. By using an Oriental poison, Samael had known that Hyte would check on anyone with Oriental connections. Sonja Mofferty's modeling job made her a prime suspect.

But tomorrow night would bring him all the answers.

He had laid the groundwork. Yesterday he had arranged to have information leaked to McPheerson that Hyte had proof Samael would strike Jonah Graham next.

Then he had asked Mason to contact Suffolk County and

329

have them pull their people off the Moffertys. He didn't want any interference. Tomorrow he would learn if Mason had been able to get the surveillance removed.

He had no doubts that tomorrow night would be his night. His and Samael's.

It was just after midnight. Friday had arrived, and with it, Emma.

"I can't believe the plane was delayed for two hours because of a spring snowstorm," she explained, kissing him and setting her overnight case down in the hall.

"Drink?"

"Bath first," she replied. "Then a brandy."

"Done."

When she left, he poured two Martells, sat on the couch, propping his feet on the coffee table, and fell asleep.

Later, he heard her call his name. She was standing on the other side of the coffee table, wearing a white negligee.

"Brandy's poured," he said.

Emma sat next to him. "It seems so long since we've been alone."

"Too long," he agreed.

"Will it be over soon?" she asked.

"Tonight."

Emma's eyes widened. "Tonight? Now?"

He smiled. "It's almost one o'clock. It's Friday, Emma. Tonight."

She shivered. He drew her close.

"My father—" she began.

"Your father is the safest man in the world. He'll have at least three dozen policemen guarding him."

"Why?" she asked. "Is he in danger?"

"No. I made McPheerson think that Samael is gong after your father. Only he's not. He never was. Samael's going after the Moffertys."

"I don't understand."

"You will, tomorrow, when it's over. And it will be, Emma, I promise you. I want you to stay with your father.

330

He may not be able to speak, but he can see. And there will be a lot of activity around him."

Emma nodded. "What's going to happen?"

"What I said would happen. It's going to end tonight."

Emma wrapped her arms about herself. "I feel cold, Raymond. Cold and scared."

Hyte woke at 6:00 A.M., calm and ready for the day. Emma was still asleep. He slipped from the bed without disturbing her, and went to shower.

Fifteen minutes later, he emerged from the bathroom. Emma was sitting up in bed, her back propped against the teak headboard.

"Good morning," he said.

She stared at the light coming in through the window. "I wish it had never come."

"It had to, Emma."

He saw her throat working. "I can wish, can't I?"

He sat next to her and stroked her cheek. "Life will get back to normal soon, I promise."

She laughed hoarsely. "I don't know what normal is anymore. I haven't since the hijacking."

"It will be over tonight."

She nodded and pressed his hand. He bent forward and kissed her. It was a soft kiss, a gentle kiss. When he drew back, he saw the tears in her eyes.

"I have to get dressed."

She released his hand. "Ray, use my car tonight. I . . . I need to be able to know that I can call you. I won't," she added quickly. "I just need to know I can."

He arrived at his office at seven-thirty. Sally O'Rourke was asleep on the couch; Randy Schwartz sat in Hyte's desk, his head cradled on his arms.

Hyte cleared his throat. Schwartz's head snapped up. O'Rourke struggled to a sitting position. "What the hell's going on?"

"We were working," O'Rourke said. "It got too late to go home."

"What were you working on?"

"The passenger manifests from last Friday night."

"I thought we agreed that it would be a waste of time."

"No, sir," O'Rourke said, "you said you thought it would be a waste of time. You didn't tell us not to work on it."

"It isn't important. But what is, is that you two go home and get some rest. I want both of you here by two. Sally, you and I are going to Bay Shore then. And leave those manifests here. Now, get out!"

He went upstairs for his meeting with Mason. The chief of detectives was at his desk. He pointed to the low cocktail table by the couch. "I brought you coffee. Black."

Hyte took a sip. "Did you make those arrangements I asked for, with the Suffolk people?"

"You'll coordinate everything with Captain Neil Tanner, of the Islip PD. He's agreed to keep his people out of the immediate area until you ask for them." Mason paused. "Ray, what if you're wrong?"

"I've got a fifty-fifty shot at it. It has to be one or the other. We're covered at Graham's. Roberts and Smith are part of the stakeout. If Samael shows up there, they'll know what to do. McPheerson won't get away with anything."

"But you're a little more than just certain that our man won't show up there, aren't you?"

Hyte nodded.

"I still don't like your going it alone," Mason said.

"I won't be. I'll have backup."

"A lady desk cop isn't my idea of backup."

"O'Rourke's a good cop. And she's not a desk cop. When this is over, I want her to get gold and a good assignment."

"We'll talk about it then."

Hyte cradled the coffee cup between his palms. "I want it done regardless of the outcome of this case."

"And now I'll tell you what I want," the chief of detectives said. "I want Samael alive. I want him to stand trial.

332

And I want to rub McPheerson's face in the bullshit he's created so he won't do it again."

"Samael wears body armor," Hyte said to O'Rourke and Schwartz the minute they'd returned to headquarters. "And so will we."

He opened his middle drawer and withdrew a shoulder rig which he handed to Sally O'Rourke. "You ever use one of these?"

O'Rourke drew the black 9-millimeter Beretta from its holster. "Just on the range."

"Don't tense with it. If you find yourself facing Samael, dump the entire magazine. If the body armor can withstand the bullets, three or four hits will knock him off his feet."

O'Rourke popped the magazine. It was full. "All right."

"Sally," he said in a low voice, "nobody knows for sure if a vest will stop a bolt."

"You're positive about tonight, aren't you?" she asked.

"It'll come down in Long Island. That's the way Samael set it up from the beginning. Randy, I have Emma's car. You still have that number in case you need me?"

Schwartz nodded.

"Then I guess this is it. Randy, except for Mason, you don't know where I am. But after six, if McPheerson's people hassle you, tell them that I'm already in Westchester. That should make them worry a little."

They walked slowly to the elevator. He pushed the call button, then turned to see Schwartz running toward him.

"This just came," Schwartz said. "It's the information from the advertising agency."

"Thanks," Hyte said, taking the envelope.

Schwartz stared at him. "It may be important. Aren't you going to open it?"

"Later," Hyte said, signaling O'Rourke to let the door close.

Forty-four

Hyte pulled the white Jag into the Moffertys' curving drive and stopped by the steps leading up to the double mahogany doors. O'Rourke was at his side when he rang the familiar doorbell.

Sonja Mofferty opened the door herself. "What now, Lieutenant?"

"Talk," he said, stepping inside before she could protest. He nodded toward O'Rourke. "This is Officer Sally O'Rourke. We need to see you and your husband."

"Lieutenant—"

"It's your turn tonight, Sonja," he said, cutting her off. "Are you ready to die?"

Her pupils dilated. "Damn you!" she whispered hoarsely. "First you act like I'm the killer, then you come into my home and tell me I'm going to be killed. Why can't you just leave us alone?"

"Because I don't want you to die," he said. "Please take me to your husband and let me explain."

"Jack won't listen," she said. But to Hyte's relief, she led him and O'Rourke to the back patio.

They found Mofferty sitting at a gray slate table. The umbrella was open, shading him from the afternoon sun. He was on the phone, his back to them.

They waited quietly until he hung up. "Jack," Sonja called.

Mofferty turned. When he saw Hyte, his expression darkened. "What the hell do you want now? You already cost me my help! After last Friday night, our servants walked out."

"You'll find others. If you live through tonight."

"What's that supposed to mean?"

"Just what it sounds like. I believe that the Friday Night Killer means to kill you and Sonja tonight."

"Maybe he'd be doing me a favor," Mofferty said.

Hyte took a step forward. "Look, you selfish son of a bitch. You can wallow in your self-disgust all you want. But nine people have been killed by this lunatic, including my friend! I don't really give a damn how fucked up your head is. But I do care about stopping the person whose only goal in life is to put six-inch poisoned arrows into you and your wife!

"Now, Officer O'Rourke is going to stay with you in the house. You and your wife will listen to everything she says. Everything!"

"Who the hell do you think you are? What gives you the right to come into my house and dictate to me?"

"Samael does. The Friday Night Killer is coming for you, and I'm the only thing between you and hell." He looked at Sonja, intuitively counting on her help. "Do you have any objections to our being here?"

"No," she said.

"This is my house!" Mofferty roared.

Sonja whirled on her husband. "And it's my life! They're staying. If you don't like it, go someplace else. What can I do to help?" she asked Hyte.

"You have two choices. Either go to a friend's house—"

Sonja shook her head, her eyes turning hard. "The second choice, Lieutenant?"

"Stay here. If the phone rings, answer it so that the killer knows you're here."

"Which would you advise?"

"I can't advise you."

"Because you want us to stay, yes?"

Hyte said nothing. He waited.

"We'll stay, Lieutenant."

* * *

The body armor was tight around the chest. The white cotton gloves were as close fitting as a second skin. Samael wore no makeup tonight, only a floppy rain hat, which, when tilted forward, hid the Messenger of Death's features.

Samael stood. It was time to leave. In the leather bag, the crossbow was set in the right position. The three poison-tipped bolts were ready.

Rashid Mohamad's voice rose from the television speaker. Samael watched the terrorist toying with Sonja Mofferty. The Messenger listened intently as the model bartered for her life.

Then Samael turned to the wall of photographs and looked at the picture of Sonja and Jack Mofferty. A target bolt had been shot into Sonja Mofferty's face. Next to that picture was Raymond Hyte's.

"Yes, Lieutenant, it ends tonight," Samael promised.

At six, Hyte was sitting in the passenger seat of Emma's Jaguar, which Sonja Mofferty had earlier put in the garage. He wore body armor, and carried a duplicate of Sally O'Rourke's Beretta.

Alone, finally, tension ebbed and flowed through him. He tilted the seat slightly back. He didn't want to be seen, yet he needed to see.

From the corner of his eye, he saw the white envelope on the back seat. He'd forgotten about it on the drive out. He had been too involved in detailing tonight's work to O'Rourke.

When Hyte picked up the envelope, he saw something hanging from it. He turned the large envelope over and found a smaller envelope stuck to the back flap.

He separated the smaller one from the larger, realizing that it must have been on Schwartz's desk, beneath the advertising agency mailer.

He read the handwritten address and his stomach twisted. It was addressed to Sergeant Simon Cohen, in care of the

Nineteenth Precinct. It had been postmarked the previous Friday.

There was a notation in red ink to forward the letter to Cohen at HQ, via interdepartmental mail. The letter should have gotten to the One-Nine on Monday. Hyte wondered why it had taken four days to reach his office.

He opened the envelope and withdrew a single sheet of paper.

Dear Sy:

About that trace you requested. I'm sorry, but unless you can give me the originating telephone number, I can't verify the forwarding. And even if we did have the originating number, the only possible way to check is to compare the forwarded number's calling time with the originating call. Also, the termination time of both phone calls would be almost identical.

I'm sorry I couldn't be of more help, but without the numbers the calls originated from, it is impossible.

Give me a call, you owe me dinner. Kiss Sarah and the kids.

Lill

The letter brought back the pain. What had Sy been looking for? Why hadn't he mentioned anything about it? He put the letter next to the thermos, and opened the advertising agency's envelope.

There was no letter, just brochures and photographs. The first one was a layout of seven watches. Two were black diving watches, the others were brightly colored accessory watches. Beneath the pictures, large letters proclaimed that *Your company can proudly display their name on the faces of any of the above watches.*

He looked through several more of the brochures. They told him nothing. He settled back to wait, knowing that time would reveal his enemy. His fingers drummed a tattoo on the car door's armrest. He looked down and saw the white edge of a magazine sticking out from the map pocket on the door.

Hyte took it out. It was the new summer Graham International catalogue.

The cover showed a handsome couple holding each other in a loving way inside a hot tub. He wondered who would buy a hot tub from a catalogue. Then he wondered how much it would cost.

He flipped the catalogue open, turning each page quickly, looking for the hot tub. He found it halfway through. It was thirty-seven hundred dollars—without installation.

Hyte whistled, turned the page, and saw a picture of a familiar looking leather-covered cigarette case.

Above the case, the bold print said: *You don't have to rely on just your memory when it comes to big business deals. Use Graham International's voice activated mini-dictaphone.*

In the fading light, Hyte stared at the disguised dictaphone. He read the fine print about its four-hour recording capability, as well as several other features. He closed his eyes and thought back to the hijacking. Jonah Graham had been tapping his shirt pocket. In the pocket was a cigarette case. He remembered Emma telling him that Jonah Graham had never smoked a cigarette in his life.

Hyte knew now, ten months too late, what Jonah Graham had been trying to tell him. Jonah had recorded the hijacking, from its inception. And he'd missed it!

He felt the familiar sensation of having something lodged in his subconscious but just out of reach. He glanced at the dashboard. It was 6:55 P.M. No more introspection, he told himself. Just Samael.

Hyte poured a cup of coffee from the thermos. He drank slowly, enjoying its warmth.

He picked up another International Accessory brochure. This one showed a black tank watch with Roman numerals. It wasn't a Cartier but it looked like one. In fact, it looked just like the watch that he had given Susan for their first anniversary.

Hyte turned the brochure over and froze.

He had not looked at the back the first time. On it was a list of International Accessories' clients. He brought the brochure closer, squinting in the low light, and read down the list. He stopped at the fifth name, unable to accept what the evidence was telling him. It was too sickening. He made himself think back to the Barnes killing. He went over the times in his head.

He thought about the night of the Helenez killings, and everything fell into place.

Walter Alinski had been right when he'd brought up Freud and paranoia. To Freud, the roots of all paranoia are in latent homosexuality.

Harry Lester was right, too. The weapon was a man's weapon, a warrior's weapon. His mind rebelled at the truth that had finally broken through.

A sharp pain lanced through his intestines. Hyte opened the door and threw up. Painful contractions squeezed through his stomach.

He held on to the side of the car, his muscles straining. Then the car phone rang. But before he could answer it, the ring stopped.

When the cramping eased, Hyte poured a half cup of coffee and rinsed his mouth out.

The radio burst into life. "Lou! Goddamn it, Ray, where are you?"

He wiped the back of his mouth and picked up the radio. "Here. Use the phone."

A minute later it rang. "JesusGodAlmighty," O'Rourke said, "Schwartz tried to call you. He made Samael from the airline passenger lists of last Saturday night."

"I know who it is, Sally."

"Are you sure?"

He couldn't get rid of the sour taste of bile. "Too fucking sure. I just put it together. Keep a close watch in there," he ordered and hung up.

How would I try to take me out? he asked himself.

He went over all the killings again, refusing to give in to the sick churning of his stomach. Barnes was taken in his driveway; the Helenezes within the security of their burglar-proof apartment; Samael got Sylvia Mossberg outside the synagogue; and Joan Bidding was killed in the Trans Air parking lot.

While he worked out the methods Samael could use to infiltrate the Mofferty house, twilight came. The trees turned gray, the house dulled. A row of low voltage lights lining the driveway came on, as did the wrought iron lamps at each side of the main door.

He picked up the radio. He wasn't worried about the sound any longer. He knew how Samael would do it. "O'Rourke. Find out what time Masters is supposed to arrive."

"Between seven-thirty and eight," she said a moment later.

"I want the Moffertys in their bedroom and the door locked. As soon as I hang up, I'm calling the locals. Wait for them. I want this house sealed with cops."

"What's—"

"Samael's going to come in Masters's place. That's the plan. And we've got less than a quarter of an hour."

Hyte flipped the frequency switch on the radio and called Captain Tanner who, with his men, was waiting for Hyte's signal.

"Captain, I think I know how it's coming down. I'm going to try to intercept our killer. But I'll need you and your men at the Mofferty house as backup. Inside and out. The Moffertys will be in their bedroom. And Captain, make your men aware that the killer uses a crossbow and poison. And no sirens, please."

"Lieutenant, are you sure he's coming?"

"Dead sure," he said, and shut the radio off.

Then he called O'Rourke. "Tell the Moffertys that the locals are on their way. Sally, wait here for them." He turned the radio off, got into the driver's seat, and started the engine.

Hyte pulled out of the garage and saw O'Rourke race down the steps and cut in front of the car. He stopped. O'Rourke opened the door and hopped in.

"I told you to wait."

"You're not going alone. Not now."

He turned to her, his mind numb and cold. "Get the hell out of this car! Wait here for the locals, and brief them. If

340

Samael gets by me, you have to direct the locals. Now get out!''

"Lou—"

"Damn it, Sally, get out!"

Hyte hit the accelerator the instant she closed the door. Two blocks from the Mofferty house, four speeding patrol cars passed him, headed in the direction of the Moffertys.

When he reached the cul-de-sac where Masters lived, he slowed, shut off his lights, and came to a stop two houses away. He drew the Beretta and checked the clip.

He looked at the pistol, remembering what Professor Alinski had told him, when Alinski had first brought up the possibility that Samael was a paranoiac. *Classic paranoia is untreatable.*

"Maybe," he said aloud, cocking the automatic.

Hyte walked slowly to Masters's house. He stopped at the edge of the circular driveway. Masters's blue Mercedes was parked by the front door.

The sky was banded in darkening shades. Twilight was ready to give way to the night. But it was still too light to walk in openly.

Bending low, Hyte inched toward the car.

He was ten feet away when the front door opened.

A figure wearing a floppy hat and trench coat came out of the house. He saw a bulky object in Samael's right hand. Self-loathing made his pulse erratic. He fought the emotion, beating it back until he could breathe normally.

When Samael reached the car, Hyte stepped from concealment. The sound of his shoes on the asphalt announced his presence.

Samael spun and, dropping the leather bag, raised the crossbow.

"No more, Emma. It's over," Hyte said.

Forty-five

"No more, Emma, it's over," Hyte repeated.

Emma Graham smiled coldly. "Not yet."

"No more collections. No more deaths. Put the crossbow down. I'll make sure you get the best help possible."

"I *have* the best help possible." She brushed her gloved fingertips across the crossbow's scope. "My little messengers of death. When did you finally understand? You didn't know last night." She paused, smiling sadly. "I'm glad you didn't."

He wanted to pull back on the trigger, but even with the proof of the warped actions of the woman he loved, he couldn't. The cop within had to have the answers. "Why, Emma?"

She stiffened. "They thought they had outwitted death. They believed they'd traded their lives for my mother's. You know they all had to die—just as the Moffertys must die. And then you. You're to be last. You can't outwit death anymore."

"You won't get them unless you take me out first. And that isn't the way you planned it."

"Plans can change." Her voice was calm and serene.

"The Moffertys have a dozen cops with them now. And Sally O'Rourke. You won't kill the others to get the Moffertys."

Her mouth tightened. "If I have to, I will."

"No, Emma, it's over," Hyte said for the third time. He

looked into the eyes of the woman he'd thought he knew, and saw a stranger. Then he felt a coldness spread through his mind, damping his emotions.

He fired.

The bullet caught her in the chest. She staggered, her face contorted with madness.

He fired again, and again, until the magazine was empty. With each strike, she was knocked backward. He fired nine times at her protected chest. And, on the ninth, Samael went down.

Hoping that the force of the bullets against the vest had stunned her, he discarded the Beretta and drew his service piece.

But before he could take a step toward her, Emma got to her knees, raised the crossbow, and squeezed the trigger.

He saw the bolt leave the crossbow, knew it would hit him, but could not get out of its way. It struck him in the midsection. He stumbled under the impact, but remained on his feet. Staring down, Hyte saw the missile sticking out from his stomach. Blood pounded against his temples as he yanked the bolt from the vest.

The vest had held. His breath hissed out. He looked up and found Emma standing a dozen feet away. The crossbow was cocked again, and aimed at him.

"Even if you kill me, you won't get away."

"It doesn't matter, Raymond, because you'll be dead."

The last dregs of twilight illuminated her pale and drawn face. Suddenly, he saw her eyes go flat. Now! He threw himself sideways at the same instant he heard the low twang of the crossbow's string. He hit the ground hard, rolled once, and fired blindly. When he gained his feet, Emma was gone.

"Why do you fight it, Ray?" she asked, springing out from behind the Mercedes, the crossbow tracking toward him. Another flathead bolt was in place.

He fired. The first shot hit her chest, knocking her back. She didn't shoot at him.

He fired again. She lurched. "Damn you!" she screamed, pulling the crossbow's trigger.

Hyte dropped even as she moved, firing twice before he hit the ground. The first shot struck the side of her head. The second went wild.

Emma Graham spun in a circle before she fell.

Hyte looked behind him. The bolt was quivering in a tree, heart high. He went to Emma. She was on her back. Blood seeped from her head. But, somehow, Emma lived.

She stared up at him, her eyes glazed. He wondered if she knew who he was as he calmly and coldly centered the Beretta on her forehead just above her brown eyes.

He thought of Sy Cohen, and of the other eight people her tormented mind had sentenced to death.

He thought of Lea Desmond, and of his daughter, Carrie.

He remembered J. Milton Prestone's words: *Find Samael. Stop that murdering bastard.*

He thought of himself and of what he was about to do.

He put on the safety and holstered the piece.

It was over.

The sun had crested the skyline. Heat shimmered from the tops of the buildings across the East River. Hyte turned to look at the people in Mason's office. Mason was behind his desk. Schwartz, Roberts, and Smith were sitting together on the couch. Sally O'Rourke and Deputy Police Commissioner Alice McMahon sat on chairs borrowed from Mason's outer office.

The hectic aftermath of Emma's attempt to kill the Moffertys was behind all of them. Franklin Masters had been found in his house, alive but unconscious. The Islip police had cordoned off the block so that no one was able to get in. An ambulance had taken Emma to the hospital.

After the preliminaries were over and Captain Tanner had, with the permission of the Islip police chief, turned the case back over to him, Hyte had gone to the hospital.

There, the doctor attending Emma had told him the chances were seventy-thirty that Emma wouldn't make it through the night.

But she had made it through the night, and he had the feeling that Emma would survive to live out her life in an institution, condemned to replaying her delusion for whatever time remained to her.

Classic paranoia is untreatable, Alinski had said.

Hyte shook away his thoughts. The press conference was scheduled to begin in fifteen minutes. But before he could face the reporters, and their inevitable questions, he wanted to explain everything to the people who had worked so closely with him.

He still felt numb, and was glad. He wanted to keep on feeling numb until it was all over, and he could take some time off. He had mourning to do, for Sy Cohen, and for Emma Graham.

"Ray?" Mason said.

Hyte looked at Mason, and nodded. "My mistake was at the very beginning, because I accepted a false premise caused by the weapon," he began, his voice low but even. "Harry Lester, and everyone else, said the crossbow is a man's weapon. And it is.

"Then Walter Alinski set it in my mind that our killer was a paranoiac. He suggested latent homosexuality as the underlying factor. Again I locked my thinking into picturing Samael as a man. It was seeing her mother shot to death that activated Emma's paranoia.

"As the Graham's only child, Emma chose to emulate her father. Which, I'm sure, was because of her latent homosexuality. A homosexual tends to love the same sexed parent. It's usually a homosexual's first and most important love. And, by Emma's emulating her successful father, she was proving she was her father's equal and could provide all her mother would ever need."

"But she wasn't a lesbian," O'Rourke said.

"*Latent* homosexual. Watching her mother's murder was the catalyst that brought everything together. The latent homosexuality had already manifested itself in paranoia—a subconscious fear of being a homosexual. And when the most important love object in her life had been taken from her, the paranoia manifested itself by twisting reality.

345

"Instead of understanding what had happened, Emma began to believe that her mother died because the other people had outwitted death—she thinks her mother died in the other people's place. Emma's delusion was reinforced every time she watched the tapes, until it turned into an obsession for vengeance. And there was more that fed the paranoia. Her father had a small tape machine that had been on since the start of the hijacking—"

"That's it! That's why he kept tapping on his pocket. He had a recorder in it, right?"

He glanced at O'Rourke, surprised she'd picked up on that from watching the tape. "Yes," Hyte said. "She was the only person, other than the hostages, who heard everything that was said throughout the entire hijacking, and not just from when the camera was set up in the plane.

"Then her masculine role model, the man she had emulated all her life, the man from whom she had learned to be strong, had a stroke and became as helpless as a baby. Emma's mind broke—her paranoia took control and she began to plan her revenge.

"In her delusional misconception, she believed that her mother died because the others said, 'Not me, someone else.' What Emma couldn't accept, would never accept, is that her mother wasn't killed for that reason; Anita Graham died because she was a brave woman. But from the basis of that single misconception, Emma incorporated everything else into it until it was all completely logical and acceptable—to her."

"But the weapon is masculine. Why did she choose the crossbow?" Schwartz asked, a frown pulling down the corners of his mouth.

"Because she'd put herself in the male role. Her mother represented femininity, Emma masculinity. She was an executive—what are today's executives if they aren't the warrior class of a thousand years ago? Emma chose a warrior's weapon, one that held meaning. She was using the weapons of her life, the very things that had given her wealth and power."

346

"I know how she got to Kennedy last Friday," O'Rourke said.

Hyte looked at her. "So do I. She flew into Kennedy earlier, tranked the pilot and, after she killed Bidding and Sy, drove to LaGuardia. She probably parked the car on a nearby street, or in a motel parking lot. She changed in the car and took the last flight back to Denver. When she came back for Sy's funeral, she moved the car to the long-term lot."

"She flew under the name M. D. Samael. How did you know?"

"She did it with the Barnes killing," Hyte said, surprised at how calm his voice sounded. "It was good, too. All the times were so absolute. Barnes died between twelve-fifteen and twelve-thirty. The drive to the city was another forty-five minutes. No way for someone to get to the airport and fly to California in time to make the flight she was booked on."

"But she was on that plane! You picked her up at the airport," O'Rourke stated adamantly.

"And she called you from California that night. I was in the office with you," Tim Smith said, speaking for the first time.

"The plane stopped over in Chicago. That's where she got on, not California. She flew from New York to Chicago, and picked up the flight there. It wouldn't be much of a trick to find someone to use her first-class ticket, and her name."

"But how did she get to Chicago?" Roberts asked.

"If you were rich, wouldn't you rent a private jet? It was most likely one of the executive air charter services at Teterboro, in Jersey, or at the Westchester airport. We'll find out in the follow-up. The flight would have been logged in at O'Hare. We can trace it back, or just call the services here.

"And the phone call," he went on, looking at Smith, "was done on her car phone, which sounds similar to that peculiar overlap of talk you get with a satellite call from the coast."

347

"God, the planning . . ." Mason said with a shake of his head.

"It's all part of a paranoiac's pattern. Everything is worked out to the most minute detail. And I'll give you odds that Cristobal Helenez, or his wife, had purchased something from the Graham International catalogue."

"Which is why she knew where he was, and we didn't. But what about you? How did she . . . I mean—" O'Rourke stopped herself.

"It's all right, Sally," Hyte said, easing her embarrassment. "You want to know how I ended up playing into her hands?" He met her gaze openly. "That was the easiest part, for her. I was attracted to her right from the start. And she knew it.

"I think the paranoia came on relatively fast—within a week or two of the hijacking. Then, once she'd decided on who would die, the method of reaching them followed. That first week, she was angry with me—blaming me for what happened to her mother. But within a month of the hijacking, we had our first date. She called me for it."

"What I still don't understand, is why she made you the last victim when she could have taken you out at any time," Mason said.

"I was last for several reasons. Emma held me responsible for her mother's death, as responsible as Mohamad, but she also wanted to use me to make sure she could complete her plan of revenge. And that plan was one from which she never deviated, until tonight. I was scheduled to die last, and she was going to make it happen that way. But when I intercepted her at Masters's house, she had no choice but to change it. I think she knew it would come down to that, because she knew I'd be waiting for her. I told her so last night."

"But the private heat said she was in Westchester all night during the Helenez killings," Schwartz said. "And I spoke to her also. The phone company call logs verified it. How could she get around that?"

Hyte explained about Sy's letter. "Emma snuck out. Then she used the call forwarding. She called her number

348

in Westchester, probably from a pay phone in the city. Her own phone was preprogrammed to forward the call to my office. The second part of the call, from Westchester to my office, registered on her phone. I think Sy began to suspect her that night at my apartment when she got the phone call from the Japanese businessman. Do you remember that?'' he asked O'Rourke.

When she nodded, Hyte said, ''Even though Sy started to suspect Emma then, finding out that he was right was a hard enough shock to slow him down at the airport.''

Hyte's gaze swept across the expectant faces. ''And I contributed to his death, because I missed all the little signs. Her expressions at certain times when we spoke. Her questions were always so carefully worded, so damned precise. Christ, I was her step-by-step investigation manual. Every time I got stuck, I told her what was wrong with the way Samael was doing things. And like magic, within a day or two, I'd have a new lead to follow.

''Samael's first note came a day after I'd told Emma that I was puzzled as to why we hadn't heard from the killer, as we usually do in cases like this. After the Mossberg killing, Emma was furious that McPheerson wasn't being pulled off the case. She pressed me that whole weekend to find out if I was going to stick with it, regardless of the Department. Samael's phone call came the next day. It was Emma's insurance, a teaser to keep me in action.''

Hyte exhaled. ''Alinski warned me that I probably wouldn't be able to spot a paranoiac,'' he said, and fell silent.

''I'm still having trouble with the idea of you as a victim,'' O'Rourke said. ''I can't accept the idea that she wanted to kill you because Rashid Mohamad said you were responsible.''

''It wasn't what Mohamad had said that had set Emma on me. She'd heard me say something that had condemned me, in her eyes. She must have heard me say it a thousand times. It was at the end, when Captain Lacey and the antiterrorist squad came into first class.''

O'Rourke shook her head. ''I've watched those tapes until I was sick to my stomach. I can repeat everything verbatim.''

''It was at the end, after one of the bullets from the assault team cut the audio cable. The last few feet of video were without sound, but Emma had Jonah Graham's audio tape. When Lacey got there, I had just smoked the two terrorists. He said, 'It's all over, Ray. You did a hell of a job.' I looked at the dead pilot and then pointed to Anita Graham and said, 'No, I didn't.' That was the reason why I was to be a victim.''

Alice McMahon looked at her watch, and then stood. ''Lieutenant, it's time. We have to go downstairs.''

Hyte drew in a slow breath. ''I know.''

''You asked me for a favor once. Now it's my turn.''

He stared at the deputy commissioner, trying to read her face. ''If I can.''

She handed him a sheet of paper. There were twenty neatly written lines on it. ''Just read the statement I prepared. Nothing more, nothing less. Then let me handle the media people. We don't have to delve into your personal life.''

''They'll find out about it eventually.''

''But not today, Lieutenant,'' she said with finality, and started toward the door. Everyone except Mason stood.

''Give me a minute,'' Mason said.

Alone, Mason walked over to his godson and put his hands on Hyte's shoulders. ''I'm very proud of you, Ray.''

Hyte swallowed. The numbness was fading and he didn't trust his voice.

Mason released his shoulders. ''I won't pretend to know what you're feeling, but I have a good idea of what this has cost you.''

''I've got a few weeks of vacation coming.''

''Take all the time you need,'' Mason said. ''You can start right after the press conference. I'll have O'Rourke and Schwartz handle the clean-up details.''

''All right,'' Hyte said, ''except for one. I want to see Jonah Graham.''

350

Mason pursed his lips. "Is that wise? He's already had one stroke. This may kill him."

"He deserves to know what happened to Emma, and from me, not from the media."

Mason nodded. "I want you to know that when you come back, there will be a promotion."

Hyte gazed at Mason for several seconds. His thoughts were rife with disjointed images of Emma lying on the ground, staring sightlessly at him; of Carrie, crying as she had boarded the plane to leave New York on the day after the hijacking; and of his ex-wife telling him he loved being a cop more than being a husband and a father.

"I don't know if I'll be back."

PINNACLE BRINGS YOU THE FINEST IN FICTION

THE HAND OF LAZARUS   (17-100-2, $4.50)
by Warren Murphy & Molly Cochran
The IRA's most bloodthirsty and elusive murderer has chosen the small Irish village of Ardath as the site for a supreme act of terror destined to rock the world: the brutal assassination of the Pope! From the bestselling authors of GRANDMASTER!

LAST JUDGMENT   (17-114-2, $4.50)
by Richard Hugo
Only former S.A.S. agent James Ross can prevent a centuries-old vision of the Apocalypse from becoming reality . . . as the malevolent instrument of Adolf Hitler's ultimate revenge falls into the hands of the most fiendish assassin on Earth!
"RIVETING...A VERY FINE BOOK"
—*NEW YORK TIMES*

TRUK LAGOON   (17-121-5, $3.95)
Mitchell Sam Rossi
Two bizarre destinies inseparably linked over forty years unleash a savage storm of violence on a tropic island paradise—as the most incredible covert operation in military history is about to be uncovered at the bottom of TRUK LAGOON!

THE LINZ TESTAMENT   (17-117-6, $4.50)
Lewis Perdue
An ex-cop's search for his missing wife traps him a terrifying secret war, as the deadliest organizations on Earth battle for possession of an ancient relic that could shatter the foundations of Western religion: the Shroud of Veronica, irrefutable evidence of a second Messiah!

Available wherever paperbacks are sold, or order direct from the Publisher. Send cover price plus 50¢ per copy for mailing and handling to Pinnacle Books, Dept. 17-178, 475 Park Avenue South, New York, N.Y. 10016. Residents of New York, New Jersey and Pennsylvania must include sales tax. DO NOT SEND CASH.